W9-DBC-374

NIGHT AND FEAR

Edited with an Introduction by
FRANCIS M. NEVINS

A CENTENARY COLLECTION OF STORIES BY

CORNELL WOOLRICH

An Otto Penzler Book

CARROLL & GRAF PUBLISHERS
NEW YORK

NIGHT AND FEAR

An Otto Penzler Book
Carroll & Graf Publishers
An Imprint of Avalon Publishing Group Inc.
245 West 17th Street
New York, NY 10011

First Carroll & Graf edition 2004

Library of Congress Cataloging-in-Publication Data is available.

ISBN: 0-7867-1291-0

Printed in the United States of America
Interior design by Jennifer Steffey
Distributed by Publishers Group West

CONTENTS

INTRODUCTION

FRANCIS M. NEVINS

O f all the authors whose forte was turning our spines to columns of ice, the supreme master of the art, the Hitchcock of the written word, was Cornell Woolrich. His centenary will be celebrated around the time this collection is published. Whatever honors he receives on that occasion will have been richly deserved, but if he were alive and well he wouldn't have enjoyed a moment of the event and probably wouldn't have shown up for it.

His full name was Cornell George Hopley-Woolrich. His mother, born Claire Attalie Tarler, was the daughter of George Tarler, a Russian Jewish emigre who had made his fortune in the import trade with Mexico and Central America. His father, Genaro Hopley-Woolrich, was of Canadian and Mexican descent, an adventurous macho who was both attractive and susceptible to women. Genaro's half-nephew Carlos Burlingham, who as a teen-ager in the early 1940s lived with him for a year, describes him as "a very good-looking man with deep blue eyes. . . . But you would never see him to smile. He always had a very narrow smile." Around 1901 or 1902, while in the U.S. and working on the construction of New York City's infant subway system, Genaro met Claire Tarler and soon married her. Their only child was born on December 4, 1903. In 1907 they left New York with three-year-old Cornell to resettle in Mexico but the marriage did not long survive the move. Claire returned to the Tarler household on West 113th Street near Morning-side Park and the child stayed with Genaro below the border. His schooling was punctuated by holidays whenever another revolutionary leader captured the town where they lived, and as a hobby he collected the spent rifle cartridges that littered the streets beneath his windows.

When he was eight Grandfather Tarler took him to Mexico City's Palace of Fine Arts to see a traveling French company perform Puccini's then new opera *Madama Butterfly*, an experience that gave the boy a sudden sharp insight into color and drama and his first sense of tragedy. Three years later, on a night when he looked up at the low-hanging stars from the valley of Anahuac, he understood that someday like Cio-Cio-San he too would have to die. From that moment he was haunted by a sense of doom. "I had that trapped feeling," he wrote, "like some sort of a poor insect that you've put inside a downturned glass, and it tries to climb up the sides, and it can't, and it can't, and it can't."

During his adolescence he returned to New York City and lived with his grandfather and aunt and mother in George Tarler's house on 113th Street. In 1921 he enrolled in Columbia College, a short walk from home, choosing journalism as his major but dreaming of a more romantic occupation, like being an author or a professional dancer. In his junior year, while immobilized with either an infected foot or a bad case of jaundice (his own accounts of the incident are at odds), he began the first draft of a novel. When it sold a few months later, he quit Columbia to pursue the dream of bright lights.

The main influence on Woolrich's early work was F. Scott Fitzgerald, the literary idol of the twenties, and his first novel, *Cover Charge* (1926), chronicles the lives and loves of the Jazz Age's gilded youth, child-people flitting from thrill to thrill, conversing in a mannered slang which reads today like a foreign language. But several motifs from his earlier and later life and his later suspense fiction can be detected in this rather amateurish debut. The fascination with dance halls and movie palaces. The use of popular song lyrics to convey mood. Touches of vibrantly colorful description. A long interlude in Mexico City complete with performance of *Madama Butterfly.* Romance between Alan Walker, the ballroom-dancer protagonist, and two women each of whom is old enough to be his mother. An extravaganza of coincidence to keep the story moving. And a despairing climax with Alan alone in a cheap hotel room, his legs all but useless after an auto smashup, abandoned by the women he at various times loved, contemplating suicide. "I hate this world. Everything comes into it so clean and goes out so dirty."

Woolrich's second novel was *Children of the Ritz* (1927), a frothy concoction about a spoiled heiress who impulsively marries her chauffeur. The book won first prize of $10,000 in a contest cosponsored by *College Humor* magazine, which serialized it, and First National Pictures, which filmed the story in 1929. Woolrich was invited to Hollywood to help with the adaptation and stayed on as a staff writer, although he never received screen credit for whatever contributions he made. One of First National's dialogue and title writers at this time was named William Irish.

With novels, movie chores and an occasional article or story for magazines like *College Humor, College Life, McClure's* and *Smart Set,* Woolrich must have been a busy young man indeed. By the time of his gritty and cynical third book, *Times Square* (1929), he had begun to develop the headlong storytelling drive and the concern with the torments and the maniacal power of love which were to mark his later suspense fiction. The first half of his semi-autobiographical novel *A Young Man's Heart* (1930) is set in Mexico around 1910 and the viewpoint is that of a young boy during and after the collapse of his parents' marriage.

In December 1930, while still working in Hollywood, Woolrich suddenly married 20-year-old Gloria Blackton, a daughter of pioneer movie producer J. Stuart Blackton, who had founded Vitagraph Studios in 1897. The marriage was never consummated. A graphic diary that Gloria eventually found and read but later returned to Woolrich (who destroyed it) indicates that he had been homosexual for some time prior to the marriage, which he had entered as a sort of sick joke, or perhaps for cover. In the middle of the night he would put on a sailor outfit that he kept in a locked suitcase and prowl the waterfront for partners. The marriage soon ended and Woolrich fled to New York and mother. "I was born to be solitary," he said in his autobiography, "and I liked it that way." But the pages of his novels and stories are haunted by the shadow of his desperate need for a relationship with a woman who never was and never could have been.

After the breakup of his marriage, Woolrich and his mother traveled extensively in Europe. His sixth novel, *Manhattan Love Song* (1932), is the best of his youthful books and the only one that, if published a few decades later, would have been called a crime novel. It begins with a quintessential Woolrich moment.

> FIRST SHE WAS JUST A FIGURE MOVING TOWARD ME IN THE DISTANCE, AMONG A GREAT MANY OTHERS DOING THE SAME THING. A SECOND LATER SHE WAS A GIRL. THEN SHE BECAME A PRETTY GIRL, EXQUISITELY DRESSED. NEXT A RESPONSIVE GIRL, WHOSE EYES SAID "ARE YOU LONELY?", WHOSE SHADOW OF A SMILE SAID, "THEN SPEAK." AND BY THAT TIME WE HAD REACHED AND WERE ALMOST PASSING ONE ANOTHER. OUR GLANCES SEEMED TO STRIKE A SPARK BETWEEN US IN MID-AIR.

Wade, the narrator, soon becomes a helpless slave to his passion for the enigmatic Bernice. Under her spell he abandons his job, assaults and robs a homosexual actor for money to spend on her, abuses his wife Maxine who still loves him desperately. Bernice in some mysterious way is controlled by unseen powers in the city but responds so passionately to Wade's abject passion for her that she's ready to sacrifice everything and risk the powers' vengeance to start life over again with him. But as usual in Woolrich, love opens the door to horror and those who manage to survive have nothing left but to wait for the merciful release of death.

For the next two years Woolrich sold next to nothing. He had moved out of the house on 113th Street and into a cheap hotel, determined to make it as a writer without his mother's help, but was soon deep in debt and reduced to sneaking into movie houses by the fire doors for entertainment. Frantically he tried to complete and find a publisher for a novel he'd begun two years earlier, a story of ballroom dancers in 1912 Paris for which he hoped some Hollywood studio would pay him enough to liberate him from the Depression. No one was interested in the book and finally Woolrich tossed the entire manuscript of *I Love You, Paris* into the garbage. But at that moment he was on the brink of a new life as a writer, one so different from his earlier literary career that decades later he said it would have been better if all his presuspense fiction "had been written in invisible ink and the reagent had been thrown away." He was about to become the Poe of the twentieth century and the poet of its shadows.

⟫·⟪

"There was another patient ahead of me in the waiting-room. He was sitting there quietly, humbly, with all the terrible resignation of the very poor." Woolrich's first crime story, "Death Sits in the Dentist's Chair" (*Detective Fiction Weekly*, August 4, 1934), offers a vivid picture of New York City during the worst of the Depression, a bizarre murder method (cyanide in a temporary filling), and a race against the clock to save the poisoned protagonist—elements which would soon become Woolrich hallmarks. In his next dozen tales (all of them plus his debut story included in my 1985 collection *Darkness at Dawn*) we find the invasion of nightmare into the viewpoint character's workaday existence, a Hollywood movie-making background, first-person narration by a woman, casual police brutality, intuition passed off as reasoning, terror in a milieu of jazz musicians, the use of Manhattan landmarks as settings, inexplicable evil powers that prey on man, set-pieces of nail-biting suspense, whirlwind physical action, the James M. Cain theme of the guy who gets away with the murder he did commit but is nailed for one he didn't—in short, the first appearances of countless motifs and beliefs and devices that would recur throughout his later fiction, including the stories collected here.

Between 1936 and 1939 Woolrich sold at least 105 more stories as well as two book-length magazine serials, and by the end of the decade he had become a fixture in mystery pulps of all levels of quality from *Black Mask* and *Detective Fiction Weekly* to cheapies like *Thrilling Mystery* and *Black Book Detective* and had also appeared in Whit Burnett's prestigious general fiction magazine *Story*. His stories of this period include historical adventures, Runyonesque comedies, gems of Grand Guignol, even an occasional tale of pure detection, and range in quality from magnificent to abysmal, but very few lack the unique Woolrich mood, tone and preoccupations. Among those that remain fresh today are the oscillation thrillers, the races against time and death, the fast-action whizbangs, the portraits of scratching for survival in the Depression, the haunting evocations of the world's malevolence. Woolrich is at his best when he sets a protagonist in a hopeless situation and forces us to share that person's ordeal, dying a thousand small deaths as the man or woman in whose shoes we are trapped flails through streets that, in Raymond Chandler's immortal phrase, are dark with something more than night. "Two doomed things, running away. From nothingness, into nothingness. . . . Turn back we dare not, stand still they wouldn't let us, and to go forward was destruction at our own hands." Even his titles tend to reflect the tension and anguish. "The Night I Died." "Dusk to Dawn." "I Wouldn't Be in Your Shoes." "Three O'clock." "Charlie Won't Be Home Tonight." In his tales of 1934–39 Woolrich created, almost from scratch, the building-blocks of the literature we have come to call *noir*.

The best physical description of the man who spun these bleak visions comes from his pulp contemporary Steve Fisher (1912–1980), who used Woolrich as the model for the brutal and love-tormented homicide detective Cornell in *I Wake Up Screaming* (1941). "He had red hair and thin white skin and red eyebrows and blue eyes. He looked sick. He looked like a corpse. His clothes didn't fit him. . . . He was frail, grey-faced and bitter. He was possessed with a macabre humor. His voice was nasal. You'd think he was crying. He might have had T.B. He looked like he couldn't stand up in a wind." Imagine a painfully introverted man, living in hotels with his mother, going out almost never, the torments of his fictional characters mirroring his own. That in a nutshell is Woolrich.

⋙◆⋘

In 1940 he joined the migration of pulp detective writers from lurid-covered magazines to hardcover books. In his first overt crime novel, *The Bride Wore Black* (1940), he writes in cool unemotional prose of a mysterious woman named Julie who enters the lives of various men and, for reasons never explained until the climax, murders them. Woolrich divides the book into five freestanding episodes, each built around a symbolic three-step dance. First a chapter showing Julie, each time in a new persona, preparing the trap for her current target; then the execution of her plan, each victim being ensnared in his own romantic image of the perfect woman; finally some pages dealing with the faceless homicide cop who's stalking the huntress through the years.

This first in Woolrich's so-called Black Series was followed by *The Black Curtain* (1941), the masterpiece on the overworked subject of amnesia. Frank Townsend recovers from a three years' loss of memory, becomes obsessed with learning who and what he was during those missing years, and finds love, hate, and a murder charge waiting for him behind the curtain.

Black Alibi (1942) is a terror novel about a killer jaguar menacing a South American city while a lone Anglo hunts a human murderer who may be hiding behind the jaguar's claws. This time Woolrich dropped his quintessential themes of loneliness and despair and concentrated on pure suspense, and the result is a thriller with menace breathing on every page.

The Black Angel (1943) deals with a terrified young wife's race against time to prove that her convicted husband did not murder his girlfriend and that some other man in the dead woman's life is guilty. Like Julie in *The Bride Wore Black*, she enters the lives of several such men, of whom one at most is the killer she's looking for, and in one way or another destroys them all and herself too. Writing in first person from the wife's viewpoint—a huge risk for an introverted loner who never knew a woman intimately—Woolrich makes us feel her love and anguish, her terror and desperation, her obsessions that grow to madness inside her like a cancer as she flails the world like a destroying angel to save her man from Mister Death.

The Black Path of Fear (1944) tells of a man who runs away to Havana with an American gangster's wife, followed by the vengeful husband, who kills the woman and frames her lover, leaving him a stranger in a strange land, menaced on all sides and fighting for his life. The earlier chapters, with their evocations of love discovered and love destroyed, their sense of what it must be like to be alone and hunted through a nightmare city of the mind, demonstrate vividly Woolrich's claim to be called the Hitchcock of the written word.

In *Rendezvous in Black* (1948) grief-crazed Johnny Marr holds one among a small group of people responsible for his fiancee's death and devotes his life to entering the lives of each of that group in turn, finding out whom each one most loves and murdering these loved ones so that the person who killed his fiancee will live the grief he lives. This is *The Bride Wore Black* with the sexes reversed and the structure as it should have been: with the explanation of the serial murders at the beginning so that we have some clue how to respond; with a genuine noir cop instead of a cipher in the role of hunter stalking the killer through the years; with a wealth of heart-stopping suspense and anguish instead of cool objective narration; with the forces of chance and fate kept in perfect balance; with a strong climax lacking *The Bride*'s monkey tricks of plot manipulation. Woolrich as usual punches ridiculous holes in the continuity, but on the visceral level where his work stands or falls this is a masterpiece.

Among his finest shorter crime fiction of the early 1940s are the annihilation stories "All at Once, No Alice" (*Argosy*, March 22, 1940) and "Finger of Doom" (*Detective Fiction Weekly*, June 22, 1940), which share one of the most powerful premises in *noir* literature. A lonely young man has miraculously found the one right woman but just before they are to marry she vanishes into nothingness. Everyone who apparently had known or seen the woman denies she ever existed, and the police to whom the man frantically appeals for help can't find the slightest proof she walked the earth. Convinced that she's a figment of his lunatic imagination, they kick him out with contempt and abandon him to despair—all but one lone-wolf cop who's willing to believe that the young man just might be telling the truth. The living nightmare stories "C-Jag" (*Black Mask*, October 1940) and "And So to Death" (*Argosy*, March 1, 1941), better known respectively under their reprint titles "Cocaine" and "Nightmare," form another matched pair of *noir* classics. The protagonist comes to after a blackout episode of one sort or another and is haunted by the memory of having done something horrible while out of himself. Back in the waking world he tries to shrug off the memory as the residue of a bad dream, hangover, drug dose or whatever. Then he finds on his person an objective fragment from the nightmare, and then another, and before long he's on the edge of madness. Desperately he appeals to his brother-in-law, who is a cop and, like most Woolrich cops, as ready to hang those in need of aid as to help them. The two men go back together into the shadows, hunting for the answer.

In the early forties the entrepreneurs of dramatic radio discovered that countless Woolrich stories were naturals for audio adaptation and began buying from him the rights to adapt his tales for broadcast on series like *Suspense* and *Molle Mystery Theatre*. The 30-minute version of *The Black Curtain* (*Suspense*, December 3, 1943, starring Cary Grant), which may have been scripted by Woolrich himself, ranks among the most powerful radio dramas ever written. "I tried to put it all behind me, to resume my life where it left off over three years ago. . . . I don't want to find out anything anymore. I want it all to die away and be still. And it will. All except Ruth. *Because somewhere behind that black curtain I was loved, and loved someone!* We must have known a love I'll never know again."

Woolrich continued to write more novels—too many for publication under a single byline—and soon needed to come up with a pseudonym. The name that he and *Story* magazine editor Whit Burnett hit upon was William Irish. Had Woolrich known that obscure First National title writer back in the twenties, and had he been carrying the man's name in the back of his mind ever since? The first novel published under the Irish byline was *Phantom Lady* (1942). Scott Henderson quarrels with his wife, goes out and picks up a woman in a bar, spends the evening with her, and comes home to find his wife dead and himself accused of her murder. All the evidence is against him and his only hope is to find the woman who was with him when his wife was killed. But she seems to have vanished into thin air, and everyone in a position to know swears that no such woman ever existed. He is sentenced to die, and as the hours rush toward execution day, the woman who loves him and his best friend race the clock to find the phantom. The plot is so involuted that final explanations require two dozen closely printed and none too plausible pages, but the emotional torment and suspense are unforgettable.

Deadline at Dawn (1944) takes place on a single night in the bleak streets and concrete caves of New York as we follow a desperate young couple who have until sunrise to clear themselves of a murder charge and escape the web of the city. The storyline is loose and relaxed, with many characters and incidents in no way connected to the main plot. But the cliffhanger crosscutting between Quinn's and Bricky's searches through the night streets keeps tension high, and the two-pronged quest is punctuated by touches of the deepest *noir*. Woolrich evokes New York after dark and the despair of those who walk its streets with a pathos unmatched in the genre.

Of all his novels the one most completely dominated by death and fate is *Night Has a Thousand Eyes* (1945), which was published as by George Hopley (Woolrich's middle names). A simple-minded recluse with apparently uncanny powers predicts that millionaire Harlan Reid will die in three weeks, precisely at midnight, at the jaws of a lion, and the tension rises to unbearable pitch as the doomed man's daughter and a sympathetic cop struggle to avert a destiny which they suspect and soon come to hope was conceived by a human power. Woolrich makes us live the emotional torment of this waking nightmare until we are literally shivering in our seats.

Waltz into Darkness (1947), again as by Irish, is set in New Orleans around 1880 and begins as much of Woolrich begins, with a man being eaten alive by loneliness. "Any love, from anywhere, on any terms. Quick, before it was too late! Only not to be alone any longer." Enter *la femme fatale*, the nameless woman who is Louis Durand's destiny, whom he comes to love with such maniacal intensity that for her he will degrade himself to any extent, cheat, kill, endure torture and even death. Like several Woolrich men before him, Louis is an acolyte worshipping at the altar of love, and the woman is his goddess. Woolrich describes her in overwhelmingly religious and maternal language. She is God the Mother, unknowable and cruel as life. Louis is caught in her as in a whirlpool and we are trapped in his skin. In the cold light of reason the book is ludicrous, but no one can read Woolrich and be reasonable.

In *I Married a Dead Man* (1948) a woman with nothing to live for and in flight from her sadistic husband is injured in a train wreck. She wakes up in a hospital bed surrounded by luxuries because, as she eventually realizes, she's been wrongly identified as another woman, one who had had everything to live for but had died in the train disaster. Helen grasps what seems to be a heaven-sent chance to start over and even falls in love again, but her new life proves to be a gift from the dark god who rules the Woolrich world. At the climax she and we are confronted with two and only two possibilities, neither of which makes the least sense, each of which will destroy innocent lives. "I don't know what the game was. . . . I only know we must have played it wrong, somewhere along the way. . . . We've lost. That's all I know. We've lost. And now the game is through." Woolrich's last major novel is one of the finest and bleakest of his works.

The success of his novels led to publication of several collections of his shorter work in hardcover and paperback volumes, which are extremely rare today. His stories were staple items in the endless anthologies of short mystery fiction published during the Forties. In addition to the dozens of radio plays adapted from his work, fifteen movies were made from Woolrich material between 1942 and 1950 alone. And his influence pervaded the culture of the forties so extensively that many *film noir* classics of that period give the sense of having been adapted from his work even though he had nothing to do with them.

⇒•◆•⇐

Woolrich published little new after 1948, apparently because his long absent father's death and his mother's prolonged illnesses paralyzed his ability to write. That he was remembered during the fifties is largely due to Ellery Queen (Frederic Dannay), who reprinted in his magazine a host of Woolrich pulp tales, and to Alfred Hitchcock, whose *Rear Window* (1954) was based on a Woolrich story. His magazine work proved as adaptable to television as it had to radio a decade earlier, and series like *Mirror Theater, Ford Theater, Alfred Hitchcock Presents,* and *Schlitz Playhouse of Stars* frequently presented 30-minute filmed versions of his material. Even the prestigious *Playhouse 90* made use of Woolrich, presenting a 90-minute adaptation of *Rendezvous in Black* (CBS, October 25, 1956) starring Franchot Tone, Laraine Day, and Boris Karloff. The finest adaptation of Woolrich in any form is Hitchcock's 60-minute version of "Three O'clock," starring E.G. Marshall and broadcast on the series *Suspicion* (NBC, September 30, 1957) as *Four O'clock*. It's pure Hitchcock, pure Woolrich, and perhaps the most totally suspenseful film the master ever directed.

Woolrich's personal situation remained wretched, and more than once he sank to passing off slightly updated old stories as new work, fooling book and magazine publishers as well as readers. Not long after his mother's death in 1957 came *Hotel Room* (1958), a collection of tales set in a single room of a New York City hotel at various times from the building's years of sumptuous fashionableness to the last days before its demolition. The St. Anselm was an amalgam of the desiccated residential hotels in which mother and son had lived and the stories set there mark the beginning of Woolrich's end. Yet once in a while he could still conjure up the old power. "The Penny-a-Worder" (*Ellery Queen's Mystery Magazine*, September 1958) is a wry downbeat tale of a pulp mystery writer of the 1930s desperately trying to crank out a complete novelet overnight. And "The Number's Up" (in *Beyond the Night*, 1959) is a bitter little account of gangland executioners mistakenly taking an innocent couple out to be shot.

Diabetic, alcoholic, wracked by self-contempt, and alone, Woolrich dragged out his life. He would come to a party, bringing his own bottle of cheap wine in a paper bag, and stand in a corner the whole evening. If someone approached and tried to tell him how much he or she admired his work, he would growl "You don't mean that" and find another corner. In 1965 he moved into a spartan suite of rooms on the second floor of the Sheraton Russell, at Park Avenue and 37th Street, and continued the slow process of dying by inches. He wrote a little, left unfinished much more than he completed, but publishers continued to issue collections of his stories. The last such book published in his lifetime was *The Dark Side of Love* (1965), which brought together eight of the author's recent "tales of love and despair," among them that dark gem "Too Nice a Day to Die." A desperately lonely woman turns on the gas in her apartment one morning, ready to end her life. The phone rings. From force of habit she picks up the receiver. It's a wrong number, someone wanting Schultz's Delicatessen. The absurdity gives her the will to live one day longer. She goes out, walks about the city and, thanks to the long arm of chance or fate, meets in Rockefeller Plaza a man who seems to be as right for her as she seems to be for him. As they're on their way to her place for dinner, she's run down while crossing the street and dies. The world according to Woolrich has rarely been rendered in such fitting form.

During 1967 his slow march to the grave quickened into a fast walk. He developed a bad case of gangrene in one leg but put off seeing a doctor for so long that, in January 1968, it had to be amputated above the knee. He returned to the Sheraton Russell with an artificial leg on which he could never learn to walk and spent his final months in a wheelchair, alone and immobilized much like the protagonist of his 1926 novel *Cover Charge*. But the best of his late stories still hold the magic touch that chills the heart, and his last two suspense tales are among his finest. "For the Rest of Her Life" (*Ellery Queen's Mystery Magazine*, May 1968) follows a young woman whose husband has turned out to be a sadistic abuser of women. She meets another man, confesses the truth, and together they try to escape. Every move they make throughout this excruciating story is precisely the wrong thing to do, and Woolrich keeps tightening the screws until we're screaming at them to change their course before it's too late. But each wrong move has also been foreordained in the womb of destiny, and Linda and Garry are the last of the doomed couples whose shattered remains fill the Woolrich world.

In the late sixties Woolrich had plenty of money and his critical reputation was secure not only in America but in Europe, where Francois Truffaut had recently filmed both *The Bride Wore Black* and *Waltz into Darkness*, but his physical and emotional condition remained hopeless. He died of a stroke on September 25, 1968, leaving unfinished two novels (*Into the Night* and *The Loser*), an autobiography (*Blues of a Lifetime*), a collection of short stories (*I Was Waiting for You*), and a long list of titles for stories he had never begun, one of which captures his bleak world in a single phrase: *First You Dream, Then You Die*. He left no survivors and only a handful of people attended his funeral. His estate was willed in trust to Columbia University for the establishment of a scholarship fund for students of creative writing. The fund is named for Woolrich's mother.

———◆———

In Woolrich's crime fiction there is a gradual development from pulp to *noir*. The earlier a story, the more likely it stresses pulp elements: one-dimensional macho protagonists, preposterous methods of murder, hordes of cardboard gangsters, dialogue full of whiny insults, blistering fast action. But even in some of his earliest crime stories one finds aspects of *noir*, and over time the stream works itself pure.

In mature Woolrich the world is an incomprehensible place where beams happen to fall, and are predestined to fall, and are toppled over by malevolent powers; a world ruled by chance, fate and God the malign thug. But the everyday life he portrays is just as terrifying and treacherous. The dominant economic reality is the Depression, which for Woolrich usually means a frightened little guy in a rundown apartment with a hungry wife and children, no money, no job, and desperation eating him like a cancer. The dominant political reality is a police force made up of a few decent cops and a horde of sociopaths licensed to torture and kill, whose outrages are casually accepted by all concerned, not least by the victims. The prevailing emotional states are loneliness and fear. Events take place in darkness, menace breathes out of every corner of the night, the bleak cityscape comes alive on the page and in our hearts.

Woolrich had a genius for creating types of story perfectly consonant with his world: the *noir* cop story, the clock race story, the waking nightmare, the oscillation thriller, the headlong through the night story, the annihilation story, the last hours story. These situations, and variations on them, and others like them, are paradigms of our position in the world as Woolrich sees it. His mastery of suspense, his genius (like that of his spiritual brother Alfred Hitchcock) for keeping us on the edge of our seats and gasping with fright, stems not only from the nightmarish situations he conjured up but from his prose, which is compulsively readable, cinematically vivid, highstrung almost to the point of hysteria, forcing us into the skins of the hunted and doomed where we live their agonies and die with them a thousand small deaths. In his finest work every detail serves this purpose, even the chapter headings. Chapter 1 of *Phantom Lady* is entitled "The Hundred and Fiftieth Day Before the Execution" so that even before Marcella Henderson is strangled the countdown to the day of her innocent husband's electrocution for the murder has begun. In *Deadline at Dawn* Woolrich replaces the customary chapter titles or numbers with clock faces so that like Quinn and Bricky we feel in our bones the coming of the dreaded sunrise.

But suspense presupposes uncertainty. No matter how nightmarish the situation, real suspense is impossible when we know in advance that the protagonist will prevail (as we would if Woolrich had used series characters) or will be destroyed. This is why, despite his congenital pessimism, Woolrich manages any number of times to squeeze out an upbeat resolution. Precisely because we can never know whether a particular novel or story will be light or dark, *allegre* or *noir,* his work remains hauntingly suspenseful.

The viewpoint character in each story is usually someone trapped in a living nightmare, but this doesn't guarantee that we and the protagonist are at one. In fact Woolrich often makes us pull away from the person at the center of the storm, splitting our reaction in two, stripping his protagonist of moral authority, denying us the luxury of unequivocal identification, drawing characters so psychologically warped and sometimes so despicable that a part of us wants to see them suffer. Woolrich also denies us the luxury of total disidentification with all sorts of sociopaths, especially those who wear badges. His Noir Cop tales are crammed with acts of police sadism, usually committed or at least endorsed by the detective protagonist. These monstrosities are explicitly condemned almost never and the moral outrage we feel has no internal support in the stories except the objective horror of what is shown, so that one might almost believe that a part of Woolrich wants us to enjoy the spectacles. If so, it's yet another instance of how his most powerful novels and stories are divided against themselves so as to evoke in us a divided response that mirrors his own self-division.

Even on the subject of love he tends to divide our reaction. Often of course he identifies unambiguously with whoever is lonely, whoever is in love, or needs love or has lost it. From the absence of love in his own life springs much of the poignancy with which he portrayed its power and joys and risks and pains and much of the piercing sadness with which he described its corrosion and loss. There's a haunting moment in *Phantom Lady* when the morgue attendants are carrying out the body of Scott Henderson's wife. "Hands riveted to him, holding him there. The outer door closed muffledly. A little sachet came drifting out of the empty bedroom, seeming to whisper: 'Remember? Remember when I was your love? Remember?' " On the other hand, several Woolrich classics are precisely about protagonists—Julie in *The Bride Wore Black*, Alberta in *The Black Angel*, Johnny Marr in *Rendezvous in Black*—who destroy their own lives and the lives of others in a mad quest to save a loved one from death or avenge one who has already died.

Woolrich does invariably unite himself and us with his people at one moment. In the face of the specter of Anahuac nothing matters anymore: saint or beast, sane or mad, if any person is on the brink of death Woolrich becomes that person and makes us do likewise. In "Three O'clock" we sit bound and gagged and paralyzed with the morally warped Stapp while the bomb ticks closer and closer to the moment of destruction, and Woolrich punctuates the unbearable suspense with language and imagery clearly echoing the story of the crucifixion of Jesus, whose agony also ended at three o'clock. During the brief electrocution scene of "3 Kills for 1," which is included in the present collection, the cold steel hood falls over the head of the murderer Gates and he whispers: "Helen, I love you." No character named Helen ever appears in the story. At the point of death we are forgiven much, and if we love we are forgiven everything.

The intense, feverish, irrational nature of the Woolrich world is mirrored in his literary faults. His plots are full of outlandish contrivances, outrageous coincidences, "surprise" developments that require us to suspend not only our disbelief but our knowledge of elementary real-world facts, chains of so-called reasoning that a two-year-old could pull apart. But in his most powerful work these are not gaffes but functional elements that enable him to integrate contradiction and existential absurdity into his dark fabric. Long before the Theater of the Absurd, Woolrich discovered that an incomprehensible universe is best reflected in an incomprehensible story. The same holds true for his style, which is often undisciplined, hysterical, sprawling with phrases and clauses crying out to be cut and sentences without subjects or predicates or rhyme or reason and words that simply don't mean what Woolrich guesses they mean. But many (by no means all) of these features are functional in Woolrich's doom-shrouded world, just like many (by no means all) of his plot flubs. Without the sentences rushing out of control across the page like his hunted characters across the nightscape, without the manic emotionalism and indifference to grammatical niceties, the form and content of the Woolrich world would be at odds. Between his style and his substance Woolrich achieved the perfect union that he never came within a mile of in his private life.

"I was only trying to cheat death," he wrote in a fragment found among his papers. "I was only trying to surmount for a little while the darkness that all my life I surely knew was going to come rolling in on me some day and obliterate me. I was only trying to stay alive a little brief while longer, after I was already gone." Trapped in a wretched psychological environment and gifted or cursed with an understanding that being trapped is *par excellence* the human condition, he took his decades of solitude and shaped them into a haunting body of work. He tried to escape the specter of Anahuac, and he couldn't, and he couldn't, and he couldn't. The world he imagined, will.

Cigarette

CHAPTER I

The Errand Boy

Tommy the Twitch came out and said, "Okay, the Boss is ready for you, you can go ahead in now." He pointed one uncontrollably-shaking hand over his shoulder at the room behind him.

The thin, inoffensive-looking young fellow they both called The Errand Boy dropped the newspaper he had been pretending to read and got up without having to be told twice. He looked a little scared. He always was when the Boss sent for him like this.

"He ain't sore about anything—" he started to ask.

"He ain't sore," said Tommy tersely, "just wants to say hello to you." Tommy the Twitch said that each time, said the Boss just wanted to say hello to him. Then the Boss always had some little thing or other that he wanted The Errand Boy to do for him, never anything much, but almost always it was something The Errand Boy couldn't understand the meaning of.

He knew better than to ask, though. That would have gotten the Boss sore at him, and if the Boss ever got sore he could send him back to jail. He'd said so himself plenty often.

It was in jail that they'd first met, The Errand Boy and the Boss. He'd been in for theft, that time his mother and the kids didn't have anything to eat in the house, and the Boss had been in for being unjustly accused of killing somebody. The Boss got out much sooner of course—as soon as his lawyer got around to

1

proving that it was all a mistake. When The Errand Boy was let out he sort of naturally gravitated toward him. In fact the Boss let him know that it was due to him that The Errand Boy had been let out a little ahead of his full term, and he shouldn't forget it.

After that, by not quite getting the Boss' orders straight once or twice, he had unwittingly made himself liable to another sentence, overstepped the line of the law. The Boss would never explain in what way, though. "Just a technicality," he'd say, and give Tommy the wink. The Errand Boy knew that as long as he stayed in good with the Boss, everything would be okay.

He went in to the Boss' private room and Tommy the Twitch closed the door and came in after him.

The Boss had been rolling cigarettes or something, and was just putting a very small bottle away in the drawer under him when The Errand Boy came in. The Boss usually only smoked the most expensive Havana cigars. It was funny, him rolling cigarettes, but this was another of those things it was wiser not to ask questions about.

On the table in front of the Boss was a flat tin of cigarettes, the ready-made kind that come by fifties, with a handful scooped out. There were also a pair of nail scissors, a small eye-dropper, some wooden toothpicks, a little bottle of mucilage, a great many grains of spilled tobacco, and a quantity of spoiled cigarette papers— which is why The Errand Boy thought the Boss had been rolling cigarettes. Lastly there was a brand new but not very expensive looking flat enamel cigarette case, with The Errand Boy's own initials, E. D., Eddie Dean, stamped up in one corner.

The Boss swept everything off the table into the drawer but the initialed case, then turned to The Errand Boy and held out his hand in his friendly, cheery way like he always did.

"Hello, Eddie," he said. "Glad to see you. Sit down."

Tommy the Twitch, who was always with the Boss, shoved forward a chair, like an executioner, for Eddie. A bullet had done something to his spinal cord and he never stopped shaking. Eddie sat as near to the edge of it as he could without falling off.

The Boss pivoted on one elbow and smiled benignly at Eddie. Then he said, "Eddie, I've got a little present for you," and picked up the flat case from the table and showed it to him. "Notice how you work it."

He pressed the catch with his thumb, and instead of opening up the way most cases do, a single cigarette shot up at the top of it, ready to be pulled out. "Tricky little gadget, isn't it?" the Boss grinned. He opened it with his thumbnail, carefully patted the protruding cigarette back in line, then clicked it shut.

⟞⬥⟝

Eddie stammered his thanks. He didn't smoke, but this was no time to bring that up; the Boss was in good humor, was highly pleased with him, to treat him this way. But it turned out the Boss knew that, anyway, like he knew everything else.

"You don't smoke, do you, Eddie?"

"N-no," Eddie faltered, afraid of getting him sore, "I can't on account of my bellows—"

"I know you don't," the Boss told him enigmatically, "that's why I'm giving you this." He looked down at it for awhile and seemed to change the subject "That guy—that Mr. Miller, that I told you to strike up an acquaintanceship with about a month ago—how you getting along with him?"

"He don't warm up to people very easy. He seems to be sort of—" Eddie groped for the right word, "sort of a suspicious guy; sort of leery of people. Then another thing, he's always got three or four guys with him and they won't let you get very near him."

"He thinks you want some sort of favor out of him," the Boss prodded, "some sort of job or graft, isn't that it?"

"Yeah, like you told me to," Eddie nodded.

The Boss stroked his chin, as though he were anxious to help Eddie solve his problem of getting close to Mr. Miller, when as a matter of fact it had been the Boss' own suggestion to start with.

"He's a big shot, Eddie," he said softly. "You want to get in good with him; get on the right side of him. Did you offer to stand him and his friends a round of drinks last time, like I told you to?"

"They let me," said Eddie simply. "Only they laughed about it, like they knew I didn't have much money. One of them followed me home afterwards, I saw him from my room."

"That's all right. That's just so they could be sure who you were," the Boss reassured him. "Tell you what you do, you go back there again tonight. I want you to keep on being nice to this guy Miller. Stand him and his crowd another round of drinks. Pass around your cigarettes—" he stopped and tapped the case slowly for emphasis, "only whatever you do, *be sure you offer Miller one first before you do the others.* If he's got one in his hand, wait till he's through with it before you offer yours. Don't give anyone ahead of him—he's likely to get sore at that. Got it? And if he refuses, don't offer anybody else, but wait until he'll take one from you later on. Keep offering until he takes one—the first one in the case."

Eddie pondered, screwed up his courage, finally went to the unparalleled length of asking a question on his own hook. "But—but suppose he gets feeling good-natured and asts me what the favor is I'm sucking around for? What'll I say it is? You ain't told me what to ast for?"

A spasm of white rage flickered across the Boss' face for a moment. Eddie, of course, didn't know it wasn't meant for him. "He won't ask you, no danger! If his own mother was drowning he'd pitch a glass of water in her face." He shoved the case at Eddie, stripped a ten-spot off a hefty roll. "This buys the drinks. Now get going and remember what I told you—see that Miller takes a cigarette from you if you gotta stick with him all night, and see that he gets first choice ahead of any of the others. Another thing, if he asks you, you bought the case yourself. You paid two-fifty for it at Dinglemann's. Now stay with all I been telling you and see that you get it right!"

Eddie slipped the case inside his coat, folded the ten-spot to a postage stamp and tucked it into his watch pocket, stood up.

"Gee, thanks, Boss," he stammered. "Thanks a lot for the sawbuck and the present," he murmured gratefully. Aiming to please, to show that he was worthy of the Boss' confidence, he ventured, "Want me to give you a ring after I leave them, so you can be sure I done what you told me?"

A look of saturnine amusement appeared on both their faces, Tommy's and the Boss'. "Okay, lemme hear from you afterwards," the Boss consented, and Tommy added something that sounded like, "if you're not too far away."

As the door closed after Eddie, they both roared with laughter.

"He'll ring up from hell," choked Tommy, "wonder what the toll charges are?"

"That's what's so beautiful about it," agreed the Boss. "There's no use trying to get Miller any other way—you saw what happened those last two times. Since my mouthpiece sprang me out of the pen last year, I don't think Miller even goes to the bathroom without his bodyguard. But this way, you can't even pin it on me afterwards. Instead of stopping to think that maybe they could beat something out of that chump just went out of here if they saved him long enough, the whole bunch is going to lose their heads when they see what happens to Miller and plug him so full of holes it'll set some new kind of a record. Then they'll have a fat chance of getting him to talk!"

He gazed complacently at the chair The Errand Boy had recently been sitting on. "How can anyone be that dumb and live? I hadn't been talking to him five minutes up in the pen, when I knew he was going to come in handy some day. He's even got the right kind of a face to go with this job—so absolutely harmless that even Miller, y'notice, will let him stand next to him taking a drink. He's a natural. And he thanks me yet—for putting him in the way of committing suicide!" He shook with huge enjoyment; so did Tommy, but then he was always shaking anyway.

"C'mon, get your lid," said the Boss, getting up, "We'll kill a coupla hours at the Naughty Club, invite a couple of the dolls to sit with us, break glasses, kick up a row about the service, let everybody know we're there."

"I can hardly wait," smiled Tommy, snapping the brim of his felt down to his mouth, "for the midnight papers to hit the stands. Ain't we going to be surprised!"

———◆———

Eddie Dean was whistling as he trudged along Lorillard Avenue, hands in his pockets, on his errand. He was glowing with self-satisfaction and relief; the Boss was pleased with him, the Boss had shaken his hand and made him a present of a cig-case, he had cheated the axe that was always hanging over him one more time.

It hung by a thread, made his life miserable. Each time he was sent for, he was afraid it was coming down. Each time he came away again, like now, it meant he was spared for another two, three weeks. The summonses never came any more often than that. But of course to earn his new reprieve, to make sure of staying in good with the Boss that much longer, he'd have to carry out his orders to the letter tonight.

He was a simple soul, asking only to stay out of jail for something that he wasn't even sure of having done, much less being able to tell what it was. "A technicality—" the sound of it froze him. Do just what he was told to, that was the only way to ward it off. Each time he came to a street crossing he took one hand out of his trouser and touched the enamel case in his coat pocket and the ten dollars wedged in his watch pocket to make sure they were both still there. Couldn't carry out orders if he lost either one of them.

Once he reached out, wet his thumb, and touched a lamppost in passing; that was to bring him luck. This Miller, whom he had to be nice to tonight, and to whom he must never mention knowing the Boss, lived downtown with those friends of his in a big flashy hotel. Eddie had overheard a bellboy say once that they'd hired an entire floor, to keep other people at a respectable distance, and had made arrangements that only one elevator was ever to stop at that floor—and then only when one of Miller's gang were using it.

Eddie couldn't go up there, of course. But once in awhile they came down to the smaller of the two bars, especially late in the evening when there was no one much in it, and it was there he'd worked up a sort of speaking acquaintance with Miller. After they'd taken a good look at his face they'd laughed and let him stay in there with them when everyone else was sort of hinted out by the barmen. And the last time, when he'd warmed himself up to the point of inviting them all to a drink, it seemed to strike them very funny and they all spoke up and ordered milk and root beer, without, of course, drinking those things.

He turned off Lorillard into Franklin, which led straight down toward the hotel. It had been a little after eleven-thirty when he left the Boss' place, but he still had plenty of time. When Miller came down at all, it was never until well past twelve. No use getting there too soon; he didn't care enough about drinking to stand doing it by himself waiting for them to show up. The more he saved out of the ten-spot, the more he'd have for himself after he carried out the Boss' instructions.

There was plenty of vacant lots this far out; the Boss' place was in a sort of semi-detached suburb. Then after awhile as he went along it started to get more built-up. But it was already pretty late, the streets were dead even when he got down into the heart of town. Twelve o'clock tolled from some church steeple just as he was within two blocks of the hotel; he could already see it rearing up ahead of him in the darkness.

The cigar-store on the next-to-the-last corner was still lighted up inside, but the lights outside flicked out as he came abreast of it. What attracted his attention to it was a man standing outside the locked door pounding angrily on the wire-laced glass and gesticulating to the clerk who was still visible behind the counter. The clerk was shaking his head, wouldn't make a move.

Eddie stopped to watch and the man turned and saw him.

"He couldn't get away with this!" he said wrathfully. "I'm gonna get in there if I have to break the door down! If he hadn't been in such a hurry to lock up, I coulda made it before twelve. He locked up ahead of time, five-to, and now look at him standing there doing nothing!"

The clerk callously snapped off the remaining light and disappeared toward the back. "Can't it wait till the morning?" suggested Eddie mildly.

The man shoved his hat to the back of his head, turned from the door in despair. "I go crazy if I'm stuck like this without a cigarette— can't go to sleep." He jabbed his thumb at three lighted windows on the top floor of a flat opposite. "I live right across the way there; we had company tonight and musta used them all up. Anyway I didn't find I'd run out of cigarettes until five minutes ago. I beat it down here and he puts on the lock right under my nose—" He broke off short. "Say, you haven't got one on you, have you? Just one'll tide me over."

CHAPTER II

THE WRONG VICTIM

Eddie had, for probably the first time in his life, or at least since he'd gotten the con up in jail. He hesitated just momentarily, but since Miller wasn't there to see, there didn't seem to be any danger of offending him by offering anyone else a cigarette ahead of him. Later, in Miller's own presence, of course, he would make sure of giving him first pick, ahead of his friends, so as not to belittle him.

It is, incidentally, the hardest of all requests to refuse—and the anxious look on the man's face showed he had the addiction pretty bad. Eddie took out the new case, pressed the lever, and a cigarette shot up at the end.

The man took it, stowed it in his breast pocket. "You're a life saver," he thanked him.

Eddie looked at him, pressed the lever a second time and another one showed up. "Take a couple with you," he said, "one for the morning." He'd seen how many were in it, there were more than enough left to go around; Miller never had more than four friends with him and Eddie himself didn't smoke.

The second one went to join the first in the man's upper pocket. He said good night, and Eddie watched him cross the street and disappear into the flat with the three lighted windows. He shook his head, put the case away in his pocket and went the rest of the way toward his destination.

They were in the bar already when he got there, Miller and his three cohorts. Everyone else had been switched to the larger bar across the lobby as usual, but Eddie stepped in unhesitatingly. The barman tried to head him off but Miller spoke up:

"Well if it ain't Aloysius! That's all right, let him stay, we need some comic relief in here."

Eddie grinned sheepishly and said, "Good evening, gents. Uh-uh-uh-rye highball, but not too much rye."

The laugh that went up drowned out the rest of it and he had to repeat himself so the barman could hear him. "And find out what the rest of the gents will have."

Miller killed his drink, winked, and said, "Uh-uh-uh-sarsaparilla for me." He banged his hand down. "I don't care if I do get drunk!" Another roar went up.

Eddie went over and deliberately moved in next to him. Miller insolently snapped an imaginary grain of dust off his shoulder, said, "That's all right, screwball, you're all right at that!"

The man on the other side of Eddie coolly patted him all the way down one side, then down the other. Eddie hoisted his elbows, stood perfectly still till he was through.

"What'd you expect to find on him," said Miller, "a water-pistol?"

They all had their drinks on Eddie, and when Miller saw him carefully stowing away the change from the ten-dollar-bill he asked curiously, "What do you do with yourself all day, punch-drunk?"

"N-nothing," said Eddie, "That's what I wanted to talk to you about, Mr. Miller."

Miller said, "See my lawyer," and turned his back on him.

They all ignored Eddie for awhile after that, and when they re-ordered left him out. Eddie waited for awhile, then took out his cigarette case, held it halfway toward Miller.

"Care for a smoke?" he said. Miller turned back toward him brusquely.

"Quit trying to play up to me," he snapped. "It ain't gonna get you a thing—" A cigarette popped up and he took it and put it in his mouth while he was speaking, "—make up your mind to that! Well, how about a light?" Eddie put the case down, struck a match, and Miller smothered his face in a puff of carefully aimed smoke. Eddie had a spasm of coughing that seemed to tear his chest in two; he choked down on it, afraid of antagonizing Miller.

Meanwhile the fellow on the other side of him had picked the case up, helped himself, and passed it on. They all tried the trick mechanism in turn, and by the time it had reached the third one it was already broken. He sent it skating back along the bar toward Eddie with the remark, "Why don't you get yourself a good one?"

Miller took hold of it, looked at it, and said, "Where did you pick this up, outa the ashcan?"

"I got it at Dinglemann's for two-fifty," memorized Eddie.

"Remind me not to go there and get one like it," Miller said to his nearest henchman. He deliberately dropped it on the floor, and when Eddie reached down to get it, his foot sent it coasting along toward the next man. They would have made quite a game out of it, only Eddie quit trying to retrieve it after the first attempt. He straightened up and sighed patiently. "It don't feel playful," commented Miller, and once again they all ignored him.

Miller smoked the cigarette Eddie had given him down to within a half-inch of his thumbnail, dropped it, and stepped on it. "How about adjourning?" he said, and they all filed out, one on each side of him, one in back of him, without saying goodnight to Eddie. The last one to leave, however, in passing behind Eddie, tried to startle him by perpetrating a gesture that doesn't bear repetition. The barman howled appreciatively, then looked at Eddie, whose face bore no resentment, shut up and turned away ashamed.

———◆–◆———

As soon as they were gone Eddie picked up his cigarette case and went out to one of the telephone booths in the lobby. He called the Boss' private number and there was no answer, Tommy and the Boss must be out. He sat down to wait for them to come back. He wanted to report that he'd done just what he'd been told to do before he went back to his room for the night.

Tommy and the Boss came home much earlier than they'd intended to.

"No sense hanging around that lousy joint any longer than we did," the Boss remarked. "We were there, and everybody saw us, so that's all that matters."

Tommy had just turned in on the day-bed outside his chief's door, when the phone buzzed. He got up again swearing and went over to it. Annoyance became stupefaction; he nearly dropped the receiver in surprise. It was Eddie. The guy was still alive!

"The Boss there?" Eddie asked humbly. "I just wanted him to know I did what he told me to. I'm going home now."

Tommy had to park the phone and sit down in front of it to hold it straight. "Why you—what'd you do, fumble it?" he snarled.

"I bought 'em all a round of drinks and I offered Miller a cigarette first, and then all the others helped themselves," wailed Eddie, "just like I was supposed to."

"And Miller smoked his?" Tommy snapped.

"Down to the end, I watched him with my own eyes—"

"How long ago was this?" Tommy interrupted, his face a livid grimace. It was just as well Eddie couldn't see it at the other end.

"About ten minutes ago," Eddie insisted. Something was wrong, and he could feel the axe dangling over his head again just when he thought he'd staved it off.

Tommy asked just one more question. "And what happened to Miller after he smoked it?" he snarled.

"He finished it, stepped on it, and went upstairs—"

"You lousy stumblebum, you're lying through your teeth!" Tommy roared out, and rage at what he considered the underling's transparent deceit getting the better of discretion, he added: "D'you know what was in that cigarette? Cyanide of potassium!"

Eddie gave a heave at the other end that carried clear across the wire. "Now are ya going to tell me what you did with it? The Boss is asleep in there, but wait'll he hears about this! I wouldn't want to be in your shoes. He'll make you wish you hadn't been born!"

Eddie was nearly going insane at the other end. "As God is my witness, I saw him take it and I even lit it for him my—"

"Don't try to tell me he got the right one! He woulda dropped like a log right at your feet long before he finished it! The cyanide was in a gelatin capsule in with the tobacco and the heat woulda melted it and the suction carried it into his mouth. You crummy, double-crossing punk, what'd you do with it?"

"I—I—" Only the narrowness of the booth kept Eddie from falling to his knees with fright. Terror of Tommy and the Boss was still uppermost in his mind though, ahead of another terror that hadn't been identified yet. Anything was better than admitting he'd given the cigarette away of his own accord, bungled the thing by a positive action.

"—I musta dropped it going over," he panted desperately. "I— I tried the catch on the thing to see how it worked, I remember now. Maybe it's still there, maybe I can find it again—I'll go back and look. Gimme a chance, will ya, Tommy? Don't tell him! Gimme a little time! It must be lying there yet, nobody would pick up a cig'ret off the sidewalk—" Even while he spoke he knew he was lying, but he was half-hysterical. He didn't care what he said if only he could postpone retribution.

"You better see that you get hold of it quick!" Tommy said in a cruel, grating voice that seemed to flay the wincing Eddie alive. "And bring it back here if you wanta square yourself! You know what that means, don'tcha?" he warned somewhat illogically but with enormous punishing-power. "If anyone gets hold of that cigarette, that makes you into a first-class murderer!"

He heard Eddie moan through chattering teeth. What he really meant was that they wanted it safely back in their hands where it couldn't be used against them as evidence.

Eddie was in no condition to think clearly. Even an hour's delay was better than hearing doom pronounced on him right now at the moment.

"I—I'll get it for you!" he promised hoarsely, "I'll find it and bring it back, I swear I will! I know just where it must be—only don't tell him yet. For God's sake let me look for it first and then tell him if you hafta!" His voice trailed off into a groan and he replaced the receiver with an arm that was shaking more than Tommy ever had in his life.

CHAPTER III

THE FUGITIVE IS DEATH

Eddie was sweating like a mule when he staggered out of the booth and his face was the color of clay. That guy in front of the cigar store half an hour ago—that poor harmless guy—was carrying around loaded death in his pocket—and Eddie had handed it to him!

This second terror now became uppermost, displacing the first, the minute Tommy was no longer snarling in his ear. He didn't want to kill anyone; he didn't want to become a murderer. He wouldn't even have given it to Miller if he'd known ahead of time.

He had to get hold of that guy; maybe there was still time! It was only half-an-hour ago, only two blocks from here and he mightn't have smoked it yet. Thank God, he'd given him two, one was probably harmless (although he wasn't sure even of that). "One for the morning," he'd said to him. And, thank God again, he knew where the fellow lived—those three lighted windows on the top floor of the building across the way; two breaks, anyway. All he asked was a third; that if the guy had finished one already, it was the harmless one. If there was any mercy in heaven at all, then let it be that way!

He brushed the sweat out of his eyes and started running, down the steps of the hotel out to the sidewalk and up the street in the direction from which he'd strolled whistling awhile ago. He knew that if he showed up too late he was putting his own neck in a noose, giving himself away as the anonymous killer whom otherwise they might have hunted for for weeks and months without finding.

But it didn't deter him; Eddie was yellow about a lot of little things, but he wasn't yellow when it came to a big thing like this.

There was the locked cigar store just ahead. He cut diagonally across Franklin Avenue without waiting to get to the corner, and groaned as his eyes sought out the top floor windows of the flat. They were dark. Only for a minute, though, until he realized that might be a good sign, that might mean everything was all right instead of otherwise. If it had happened already, the place would be blazing with light, wouldn't it?

But ominous or reassuring, the blank windows had flashed past over his head already and he was in the dimly-lit vestibule. He danced back and forth in front of the mailboxes. Top-floor front, there it was—Adams. He ground the bell in with the ball of his thumb, leaned on it with his whole weight. They must be hearing that, anyone would hear that, he wasn't giving the battery a minute to breathe. Why didn't somebody answer?

And then he looked down and saw that it didn't ring. The card that he or somebody before him had displaced lay there under his shoe where it had fallen. He could read it from where he was. *Bell out of order."*

He gave a whimper like a small animal caught in a trap, flung himself against the thick glass inner door, began to pound on it with the heels of both hands. He visualized the man Adams lying there in the dark, reaching out to the side of his bed, picking up a cigarette, striking a match—and him down below here, unable to get to him. Wait a minute, the janitor or superintendent, should have rung his bell, that must be working!

Just as he turned to do it, the street door opened behind him and a man came in, key in hand. One of the other tenants. But he was very drunk and very loquacious, and he dropped the key once before fitting it into the lock and twice more after he'd already had it in.

Eddie gave him a maddened push that sent him sprawling back, jammed the key in with force enough to break it, opened the door with a sweep, and went hurtling up the inside stairs. The drunk's indignant remonstrance pursued him up the stairwell.

"You sure must be henpecked—ish only a little after one!"

Eddie was already pummeling Adams' door far above with both fists and one knee.

"Lemme in!" he called. "Lemme in, can't you hear me! For God's sake, open this door!"

A chain clashed faintly, the door edged narrowly open, and Adams' nose showed, two frightened eyes alongside of it. At least they were living eyes! Eddie nearly folded up with relief for a minute, he had to open his mouth to let all the air out before he could say a word.

The man inside spoke first.

"Get away from here, what is this, a hold-up?" the man behind the door rapped out sharply. "I'm warning you I've got a gun. Who are you anyway, what d'ya want?"

"On the street just now—you remember?" Eddie panted. "I gave you a coupla cigarettes! I come to tell you—not to smoke 'em—not to touch 'em—you better let me have 'em back!"

"What're you driving at anyway?" said the man suspiciously.

"I found out something about 'em—never mind, give 'em back, I tell you!" He wrung his hands together frantically. "For Pete's sake, open up. Can't you see I'm alone out here; this is not a stick-up! Hand me those cigarettes back."

Adams said, "I'm going to telephone the hospital and have 'em come around and get you."

"There's something the matter with the cigarettes. Don't you understand English?" Eddie shouted. He brushed a hand before his eyes trying to think clearly; mustn't tell him the whole story. "They were given to me by a doctor. Somep'n got on 'em, one of 'em anyway—it'll kill you if you touch 'em. He warned me and I come chasing all the way back to find you—"

A woman inside the flat gave a yip of fright. The chain clanged loose and Adams flung the door open; his face was green. He put his hand to his throat. "I—I—"

"No, you're all right If you'd smoked the poisoned one it wouldn't take this long to happen," Eddie said impatiently, brushing by him. "Where's the other cigarette?"

Adams pointed limply toward a bedroom door behind him. His wife was just inside in a kimono, trying to make up her mind whether to scream or just faint. Eddie reached in back of her, snapped on the light. Next to the disturbed bed, just as he'd visualized it in his headlong rush over here was a stand, on the stand a tray, on the tray a pinched-out butt lying on a brown little bed of ashes. He picked it up, slit it open with his thumbnail. Nothing but brown tobacco fell out.

"I told you you were all right. You smoked the good one—but you don't know how lucky you are!" He held out his hand impatiently. "Where's the second one—hurry up, let me have it! Don't leave it lying around loose!"

Adams hadn't quite gotten over the shock yet, he kept running his hand through his tangled hair over and over again as if he was trying to think.

"Mildred," he appealed to his wife in a scared voice, "you were here when I came in that time, you must have seen me—what'd I do with it?"

This time she did scream, then choked it off with both hands. "You gave it to Fred! I saw you! Oh Lord! Don't you remember, they were just leaving when you came in; he said he didn't have any either. You said something about sharing the wealth, and I remember you handed one to him at the door—"

"Then he got the bum one," groaned Eddie. He grabbed Adams by the shoulder and tried to shake some presence of mind into him. "Tell me where he lives. Maybe I can still head him off!"

"It's too late already," Adams told him. "They live way out. It's a long drive. He'd smoke it in the car—he told me he wanted it for that, now that I think of it!"

His wife exclaimed: "The telephone!" and darted over to it, began to dial.

"It can't be too late. Where does he live?" shrilled Eddie.

"Forty-seven Palmer Road," Adams stuttered, "that's out near Westbury."

His wife said, "They don't answer; that means they haven't gotten in yet. Maybe you can still catch up with them on the road—it's only a Ford."

Eddie nearly turned her completely around getting out of the flat. "Keep phoning, his life depends on it!" he said over his shoulder.

———◆———

Eddie was nearly run over by a taxi passing the door. Another of those breaks, like with Adams. "47 Palmer Road," he shouted as he stumbled in. "And don't slow up until you see a Ford heading the same way we are!"

He sat back for awhile and coughed until he thought his lungs would burst; too much exertion. The spasm wore itself out and he edged forward, watching the road ahead across the driver's shoulder.

It occurred to him he didn't even know the guy's name, had forgotten to ask them—just "Fred," that was all.

The houses had petered out long ago; they were in open country already.

"That it?" said the driver suddenly. A Ford was running along meekly in front of them, hugging the outside of the road.

"Get up next to 'em," said Eddie, "and I'll find out."

The taxi drew abreast, swerved in, hubs nearly interlocking with those of the other car.

Eddie leaned his head out, shouted, "Fred? Your name Fred?"

The Ford, two wheels off the concrete, began to wobble crazily. Its five occupants all squalled in alarm.

"Iss no Fred," the man at the wheel jabbered excitably, "iss Antonio! What you make?"

The taxi veered off again, shot ahead.

The suburb of Westbury showed up, in clumps of little bungalows.

"Palmer Road," the driver said, and turned down a side thoroughfare. It had arc lights only every half mile or so.

"Take that side and I'll take this!" Eddie ordered. "43—41—39—Wait a minute, you're passing it!"

The brakes squealed like stuck pigs. The house was back from the road and there wasn't a light showing. But in the split-second it took him to jump out, the porch light suddenly went on and outlined a Ford standing there still pulsing in the driveway in front of the entrance.

"I think I hear our telephone ringing," a woman's voice said. "Got your key?"

Eddie began to run across the lawn yelling: "Hold it! Hold it! Fred!"

They froze where they were standing, in a sort of tableau. The woman was up on the porch, her hand on the door knob. The man was standing beside the machine with the door still open, holding his hands cupped to a cigarette; they showed up transparent, salmon-color against the match flame they shielded. It went out while he was staring, but Eddie could see the haze already coming from his lips.

"Drop that cigarette!" he shrieked. "Get that out of your mouth!"

And almost colliding with the man, he tore the little white cylinder from his face, threw it smoldering on the grass over his shoulder.

"I just came from the Adamses'—been trying to warn you—that cigarette he gave you—something the matter with it—another half-minute, and it woulda been all up!" Eddie gasped it all out and stopped breathless.

Fred didn't wait to hear any more; he began to spit all over the place like an infuriated cat and brush his sleeve across his mouth.

The wife suddenly came running down off the porch and over to them. "That isn't the one Ad gave you, Fred," she proclaimed. "Don't you remember, you stopped off just now and bought a pack at that lunch-wagon just as we got into Westbury? The one Ad gave you fell in between the seats when you were trying to fish it out with one hand, don't you remember, and you said never mind, let it go—"

"That's right, I did, didn't I?" Fred said doubtfully and wiped his perspiring face, then "Wait, I better make sure—" He took out a freshly-opened pack and examined it; only an edge of the foil had been torn off, only one hole showed in its tightly-pressed contents. "Yep," he said elatedly, "it came out of this new deck. Wow, what a close shave!"

"Then the bad cigarette is somewhere in your car," Eddie summed up, and reached for the latch.

"Oh, no," the wife answered simply, "I felt for it and found it while he was in the lunch wagon—I like to keep the car as tidy as possible—I threw it out of the car—"

CHAPTER IV

DEATH'S VICTIM

Eddie closed his eyes, reeled slightly; there didn't seem to be any end to this thing. It was like a game of tag gotten up by a playful devil. He pulled himself together again.

"That was only a minute or two ago, wasn't it? And right in front of the lunch wagon, you sure about that?" He was already starting away as he spoke.

"Yes, just before we got to the door here. It's around the turn, on the main highway—you can't miss it. I even saw it, it landed on the sidewalk right in front of the two little steps going into the wagon—"

Eddie was back in the taxi again, which had turned and was standing waiting.

"Back to the grub wagon we passed!" he yelped to the driver. The long chase had blunted some of the edge off his terror, but he was still worried and plenty scared. He was no longer at the pitch of frenzy in which he'd torn from the hotel to the Adams flat. But he had to get that cigarette back to the Boss.

He vaulted out of the cab before it had even stopped and began to hop all over the sidewalk in front of the lunch wagon, bent double like a frog, chin nearly touching the ground. The windows of the wagon threw big bright yellow squares across the pavement, and if it was there he would have seen it. It was gone! It wasn't in front of the steps where she said she'd seen it land, and it wasn't under them, and it wasn't out near the curbing, and it wasn't beyond in the gutter.

He lit matches borrowed from the driver in places where the reflection wasn't strong enough. He straightened up, pulled open the screen door, and stuck his head inside the wagon.

"When was the last you swept that walk outside?" he asked the counterman. There was no one else in the place.

"I never do that till six—just before the day man comes on," the man answered.

Eddie said, "Do you remember a guy in a Ford stopping in for a pack of cigarettes about ten minutes ago?"

"Sure."

"Anyone been in or out of here since?"

"There was a big coon in here at the time," said the counterman, "nursing along a cup of Java. He left just before you showed up—"

"I gotta find him!" said Eddie. "Which way'd he go?"

"Got me," the counterman said.

Eddie was back alongside the driver again. "See anyone up or down the street?" he asked.

"What am I, an eagle ?" the latter asked wearily, sick of all the shenanigans by now. "Do we ever get finished?"

Eddie got on the running-board without getting in. "Drive slow, follow the highway down a block or two, we may pick him up—if not we'll have to beat it back up the other way!"

———◆◆◆———

They went a couple of blocks, then Eddie gave up.

"All right, turn. He couldn'ta come this far. The guy said he just left before I showed up."

The driver executed an about-face, muttering audibly. As they swept up toward the lighted wagon again a slow-moving figure came in sight around the corner of it, pausing to peer cautiously in at the windows.

Eddie pointed. "That's him now, as big as life! He musta been skulking in back of it the whole time we were here!"

Eddie left the side of the machine with a swoop. The impetus of the moving cab carried him across the sidewalk, face to face with the big vagrant, who towered above him. The latter whirled, crouched a little; his first impulse was evidently to duck and run, but Eddie had him crowded too close to the side of the lunch wagon.

"You picked up a cig'ret when you came out just now—let's have it," Eddie said briefly. He had at last come across someone whom he felt he could dominate mentally, if not physically.

"Who did?" said the big fellow surlily. "Whut you talking about?"

"I can see it sticking outa your shirt-pocket right now; I'm telling you to come across with it."

———◆◆◆———

The big black man put a finger on it possessively. "You ain't gonna git this," he said. "Old man with the whiskers give it to me, thass who. He take keer of me. I buy me cup coffee, and hot diggity, old man with the whiskers put cig'ret under my shoe to go with it!" He started to edge away from Eddie sidewise, his back to the lunch wagon.

The counterman had come to the door, stood looking out; the driver was watching from the wheel of his cab; neither one of them made a move to help him. Eddie fumbled for the change from the ten-dollar-bill. "I'll buy you a whole new pack, inside there, if you lemme have that one—" He turned to the counterman. "Go in and get him a pack, any kind he says—"

Eddie stripped off a dollar bill, held it out toward him, gingerly ready to jump back at the first hostile move. The green oblong fluttered temptingly between his fingers, held only by one corner. The round white eyeballs protruded toward it, as though it were a magnet drawing them half out of the roustabout's skull. Two fingers of his free hand flexed tentatively back and forth close up against his overalls. Suddenly, with a snakelike quickness, the whole hand had darted out and back again. The dollar was gone, and he was scuttling around the corner of the lunch wagon. But he had dropped the coveted cigarette at Eddie's feet.

———⊷◆⊶———

Tommy the Twitch came to the door with an orange dressing gown on his quaking form and an ugly look on his face.

"So ya got here at last, did ya?" he growled through the cigarette that vibrated with his breath. "It's about time, ya mangy squirt!" He ushered the ashen-faced Eddie in by jerking his head backwards. He closed the door, swung venomously at Eddie with one fist, and then went on toward the door that led to the Boss' sleeping quarters.

Eddie dodged the blow by rearing back, then stood there palpitating, his face white with fear.

"Ya—ya haven't told him yet, have ya, Tommy?" he quavered. "Ya said ya wouldn't—honest, I couldn't help it. I didn't mean to muff it like that!"

Tommy put a palsied hand to the Boss' doorknob. "Have you got it?" he said.

Eddie nodded, incoherent with fright, raised his own hand to his inner pocket.

"Just wait'll you hear what he says when I tell him," promised Tommy balefully. "I wouldn't give two cents for your life! Just wait'll you hear—" The tortures of anticipation he was purposely inflicting on the cringing figure standing there behind him seemed to add to his enjoyment.

"Wait, Tommy, don't! Gimme a break!" Eddie gasped in a strangled voice. All his original terror of the Boss and what the Boss could do to him had come back in full force long before he had even entered the place. He was nearly insane with fright.

Tommy turned the knob, pushed the door open, and stepped into the dark room. He reached out to one side, snapped on the light, and then partly closed the door after him. A moment later the Boss' voice boomed out angrily:

"What the hell is this? What's the idea!" Then Tommy, saying something in an undertone, telling him about it. Then the Boss again, "Well where is he? Did he come back with it? Wait a minute—" and the sound of bed-springs creaking.

With that the tension that had gripped Eddie suddenly snapped. His terror became fluid instead of static, released him from the spot he was standing on. He whipped the carefully guarded cigarette out of his pocket, flung it wildly out before him, turned and fled as if pursued by devils, nearly stumbling all over himself in his hurry to get out of the place. The cigarette described an arc, fell athwart the handful left in the tin box that Tommy had been smoking all night long. When Tommy came back, followed by the Boss, the room was empty.

The Boss slammed the door angrily.

"Lammed, did he?" Tommy said. "I mighta figured he'd do that, the minute I turned my back. Probably didn't even have it with him! If I had my pants on I'd go out after him—!" He pounded on the butt he was smoking, took a fresh one from the box, lit it.

The Boss was pacing angrily back and forth; he appeared less put out about The Errand Boy's disappearance than about the miscarriage of his plans.

"A great night's work!" he seethed. He turned, went back into the bedroom, came out again. "Haven't even got a corona left in the house, I was in such a hurry to pass 'em all out at the club and set myself an alibi!" He reached down to the tin and took one of the cigarettes, lit it with a fuming swoop of the arm.

"Yeah," agreed Tommy, puffing away morbidly. "Tonight was all alibi and no job!"

"I'll get him yet," swore the Boss. "I'll think up another way, but I'll get him. And this time I'll get The Errand Boy too—he knows too much now!"

"Aw, these fancy ways are none of 'em ever any good," scowled Tommy the Twitch. "Why don'cha just send a bullet troo—" He stopped speaking abruptly.

An instant before the Boss had been sitting there on a level with his eyes, now he lay face down on the floor. The thing had happened as swiftly, as silently, as a "break" in a jerky motion picture film. An inch or two away the cigarette the Boss had been puffing on just now was still lazily sending up smoke at one end; at the other, a grain or two of whitish substance had spilled from it in falling, showed up against the carpet.

AFTERWORD TO "CIGARETTE"

"Cigarette" (*Detective Fiction Weekly*, January 11, 1936) is one of the earliest crime stories Woolrich wrote after the first thirteen collected in *Darkness at Dawn* and one of my favorites among those that have never been collected before now. With its bizarre murder method, its race against time and death as Eddie pounds headlong through the night trying to find and stop Adams before he lights up, its tension stretched drum-tight as the frantic protagonist chases the poisoned cigarette from one tobacco addict to another, this is one of those gems that only Woolrich (who was a compulsive smoker all his life) could have written.

Double Feature

Merrill stirred uncomfortably at the prolonged osculation taking place on the screen. "Break!" he muttered unromantically. "Come up for air!" He fanned himself mockingly with his hat. He took out his watch. "Two solid minutes they been at it," he remarked.

"Sh, Bill!" His fair companion favored him also with a stab of the eyes and a sharp dig of the elbow. "Let somebody else enjoy it, even if you can't! You don't have to look at it if it hurts that bad. Close your eyes till it's over."

He promptly carried out the suggestion, effacing the two gigantic heads still pressed tightly together on the silver screen. "I don't hafta come here to sleep. I can sleep at home, free of charge," he mumbled rebelliously.

"It's a double feature," she reminded him tartly. "Maybe the second one'll be better."

He sighed sightlessly. "It couldn't be worse." He gave a cavernous yawn, genuine this time and not pretended. He sank a little lower in his seat, eyes still closed. His features relaxed. Soon a burbling sound like coffee in a percolator came from him. His head slipped sideways by notches, until it came to rest on the girl's slim shoulder. Somebody in the row behind them snickered.

Her attitude, now that he was no longer a witness to it, was entirely different from what might have been expected. A smile dimpled her pretty cheeks. She sloped her shoulder to make him more comfortable, reached around and gave the other side of his head a little pat. "Poor kid," she said to herself, "dead for sleep!"

Betty Weaver was a good sport; you have to be when you're an ace detective's best girl.

The nip of a hefty heel coming down on one of his pet toes jolted Merrill awake with a grunt. There was a man trying to worm his way past him to the vacant seat on the other side of Betty. The usher with the torch standing helpfully by hadn't been much help showing him where to step and where not to. Merrill jerked his foot back and screwed up his face.

"I'm sorry," said the man softly, and edged through with his back to them. Merrill doubled his leg up in front of him and held onto his throbbing toe with both hands.

He put it back on the floor again, and leaned out across Betty to give the man a dirty look. The latter's eyes weren't used to the dark yet; he didn't seem to notice it, but sat squinting straight ahead at the screen. He'd kept his coat on, with the collar up in back, although the way the place was jammed, it was pretty stuffy.

Merrill sat back again, his indignation evaporating as long as there had been no answering look for it to feed on. The five-minute kiss had finally faded out and they were showing trailers now. He shifted his attention to the program, determined to get his forty-cents-worth of show even if it was next week's.

A lion showed up, burped at the audience, and the newsreel came on. Merrill liked newsreels. Betty evidently didn't. She took out her mirror and began to inspect her face by the fairly strong gleam coming from the screen. It was a snow scene, skiers on a mountain, flashing down runways that were steep and dazzling white.

It changed abruptly to a group of prison officials, posing with a convict in their midst, seemingly in the greatest of friendliness. The picture was a "still," snapped by a newspaper photographer nearly two years before, incorporated now in the newsreel because of its timeliness. That convict standing there beside that numskull warden had escaped since then, had made a name for himself by his later exploits that topped Jesse James', and was the object of the biggest man-hunt in the history of the country. Nobody in that theater needed the voice of the announcer to tell them who that was, but he did anyway. A sort of shudder passed through the audience at the sound of the name; it had become a household word all over America.

"Take a good look at this man, ladies and gentlemen," the sound track pattered. "You've been hearing a lot about him lately, and you don't need to be told who he is. Chink-eyes Harriman— and they're still out looking for him!"

"Harriman," sounded in suppressed whispers from all parts of the house. "Harriman—see him?" The audience rustled like a flock of uneasy doves.

———⋙⋅⬩⋅⋘———

Merrill became cold and tense all at once, every nerve taut as piano wiring. The hand that suddenly gripped the wrist with which Betty was replacing her mirror in her handbag was like an iron clamp. She gave a nervous start, but had presence of mind enough not to cry out. He was beckoning for the glass with his other hand, but keeping it close to his body. The little quick-silvered oblong passed between them unobtrusively. She still didn't know what it was all about; glanced at him inquiringly, but remained still as a mouse.

"Keep looking straight ahead," he breathed out of the corner of his mouth. "Sit back a little in your seat." She closed the inch gap between her shoulders and the back of the seat, so he knew she'd heard him.

He palmed the glass with his right hand, the hand that dangled out over the aisle; it just fitted between second-joints and heel. Then he brought it up sidewise, unobtrusively, to the level of his face, and turned his eyes toward it. He was looking out toward the aisle. The glass was turned inward toward the row of seats. Betty's little nose intruded on the edge of the reflection for a second, then almost instinctively her head retreated still further and carried it back out of the way. The profile of the man next to her had the glass to itself.

He was still squinting, and he'd been in ten minutes now, so the squint was habitual and not because of the darkness of the theater. It gave his face a Mongolian cast.

Merrill shifted his eyes to the screen for purposes of comparison, then back to the mirror again. One was full-face, the other a profile, and so identification couldn't be established instantly, not even by a trained eye like Merrill's. But the eyes, the squinting, slitted, malicious eyes, were the connecting link. They were a perfect match to those on the screen. That was Chink-eyes Harriman sitting two seats away, staring with perfect composure at his own picture! In fact, he was even enjoying himself a little, to judge by the canine curl of his upper lip.

Just as the "still" on the screen dissolved, but while it was still printed impalpably on Merrill's retinas, he seemed to feel the latter's indirect gaze on him via the mirror, because he turned inquiringly that way for an unguarded moment and presented himself full-face. Nose, mouth, chin, cheekbones, width of brows and facial oval all clicked simultaneously, reproducing what had just been on the screen like a positive matching a negative. So, in spite of the stories going around, he hadn't gone in for facial surgery.

He must have seen the mirror. Merrill just had time to grimace hideously and pretend to be digging between his teeth for a morsel of food. It was a bad slip, and a question of who had beaten the other to it: Harriman's glance over or his own pantomime. The killer turned his head incuriously front again, so that seemed to answer it. He stirred a little in his seat, the better to enjoy a row of half-clad bathing girls parading up and down a Florida beach.

Merrill could hear Betty breathing a little faster, as though she knew something was up but couldn't figure out what it was. He saw her shut her eyes for a minute, then open them again.

He slipped the mirror back to her under her arm, and her handbag swallowed it. Then he plucked at her sleeve and jerked his thumb at the aisle. The first step was to get her out of there and to the back of the theater. The guy was probably loaded down with equalizers, while he himself didn't have a thing on him—which was what you got for thinking you were ever really off duty in his racket.

He had no idea of jumping on him where he sat. There'd be pandemonium in the middle of all these people, and the dump was lousy with unguarded exits. The thing to do was to phone in, have the place surrounded, and pick him up as he came out. Merrill planned even to come back and sit down again where he was so he could keep his eye on the guy until the pay-off.

Betty sat staring straight ahead with a face like marble. Merrill wondered what was the matter with her—she was usually very quick on the pick-up. He tugged at her again and thumbed the aisle. Her eyes flicked toward him but she didn't turn her head. You couldn't hear her breathing any more. She sat deathly still.

They had, fortunately, come in ahead of the desperado, so he had no way of checking on them. Merrill found her small foot with his, prodded it, then said audibly: "This is where we came in, isn't it?"

All she did was shake her head, but without looking at him.

———❦———

He had to get word out without another minute's delay; the show wouldn't break for another forty minutes or so, but that couldn't be taken into consideration in this case. Harriman wasn't just an ordinary movie patron, staying to the end. He might get restive any minute. Something might arouse his suspicions. He might light out before a cordon had been thrown around the building.

"I'm dying for a smoke," Merrill said. "I'm going back and grab one off. Be right with you again." Now he'd have to clear her out after he'd lit the fuse.

She sat there like a statue, rigid, without answering. But suddenly, as he braced his legs under him to get up, she clawed at his coat sleeve with her hand, between their two bodies. She twisted the goods around, caught up all the slack there was, until the sleeve was almost as tight as a tourniquet. It was as though she wanted desperately to tell him something, without being able to.

He tensed at that. A momentary sense of immediate danger swept over him. But when he thrust his head slightly back across her shoulders, Harriman seemed lost to the world, devouring the screen with vacant, moronic enjoyment, mouth idiotically ajar, beady eyes shining. He was a million miles from nowhere!

"Bill—" She spoke in a furred voice, kneading his sleeve frantically, but stopped abruptly. He could hear her give a sudden intake of breath. She didn't go ahead. He waited. When it came, the rest of it, it was flat, toneless. "I'm thirsty. Bring me a drink of water from the cooler when you come back—"

It was just the way anybody would ask for a drink of water, casually, off-hand. But when that "Bill—" and that stranglehold on his coat sleeve didn't match the rest of it; it was as though the request had been improvised, to cover up what she had originally started to say. When he glanced at her, she kept staring at the screen, eyes slightly dilated; wouldn't look at him.

He got up and left the seat without another word, made his way soundlessly up the thick-carpeted aisle, not walking too fast lest the man in the seat next to her turn around and look after him. He turned and looked back at the two of them from the head of the aisle. Their heads were there side by side, amidst all the other heads. Everything was still under control. Harriman had made no move following his own departure; seemed not to have even noticed it. He'd have to get back there quick, though, and get her out of the way. He cursed the sudden stubborn streak that had cropped out in her just now; she'd hear plenty from him when this was over! She ought to know by now that everything he did, he knew just what he was doing!

The moderate up-grade walk changed to a quick lope as he crossed the inner foyer behind the orchestra pit, buttonholed the usher on duty. "The telephones—where are they, quick!"

"Downstairs in the smoking lounge."

A small electric sign pointed the way through the gloom. He streaked down the stair-well to sub-basement-level, came out into a room crammed with modernistic furniture and stuffy. It was somebody's idea of luxury, at four jits a throw. A vintage of flapper was sitting there puffing, using the place as an up-to-date club room.

There was only one phone, but the fact that it was already in use didn't deter him for a minute. He sandwiched in between this second flapper and the wall, said something about police business, took the receiver away from her, and got rid of her party by sinking the hook. He cut her cheeps short by unslinging the glass panel between them, scraping about an inch of talcum off her.

"I'm at the Cortelyou Theatre, on the North Side," he told headquarters, "and Chink-eyes Harriman is here in the audience. Am I sure?" he echoed caustically. "I'm sitting two seats away from him, and he lounged all over my dogs just now getting in! Of course, if you want me to ask him, I'll hear what he has to say!"

"Don't get wise," he was told dryly. "No one said they're not taking your word for it. Now get this, Merrill."

"Yes, sir."

"We'll have a dragnet thrown around the whole block in less than five minutes. In the meantime, these are your instructions and see that you follow them: keep your eye on him, but don't give yourself away—not even if he gets up to leave before we've closed in. Just tail him if he does. Don't try to take him on single-handed, you understand? We'll only lose him again, and the whole damn thing'll start over—"

"I'm not in a fix to dispute that with you," Merrill said, coloring. "I'm here unheeled."

A low whistle sounded at the other end. Then the voice became impersonal again. "We'll get him when he comes out. If he stays till the end, do what you can to protect the audience. We're taking him dead, of course. Now get back and don't lose sight of him for a minute. You can consider yourself personally responsible if there's a slip-up!"

"I'm right on his neck!" Merrill broke the connection, came out to find one flapper yanking the other bodily toward the stairs by one arm. She had evidently been eavesdropping. "Harriman's in the audience! Hurry up!"

II

Merrill beat them to the foot of the stairs, blocked the way. "No y' don't! Go up there and start a riot, wouldje? You're staying until it's over now. You know too much, both of you!" He motioned toward a door. "G'wan, get in there—nothing'll happen to you!"

He pushed the pair of them toward it and through it, and closed it on them. He knew they'd slip out again the minute the coast was clear, but he slid one of the bulky modernistic divans over in front of the door to block it from the outside and hold them as long as possible. He rocketed up to the top of the stairs, flagged the usher, palmed his badge.

"You go down there, son, and sit on that divan you'll see in front of the ladies' door. Don't let anybody out until I tell you to," he whispered. "I'm holding a couple of janes in there. Don't listen to what they'll try to tell you—they're dips, pickpockets. You're my deputy—I'll square it with the manager for you!"

The boy gave him a thrilled look, disappeared below.

He filled a paper cup at one of the filters, took out a pencil stub and scrawled on the outside of it: "Get the hell out of here and home, explain later," in an annoyed scowl.

He started down the aisle none too slowly, splashing a little water as he went. Instantly, the moment the slight dip of the orchestra floor set in and long before he came abreast of the row he had left them in, he knew something was wrong. There was a double gap there in the ranks of heads—two were missing. And the vacant aisle seat that had been his own told which two it was.

He squeezed the paper cup flat. Water spurted out of both ends, and he ran the rest of the way.

Her coat was still draped across the back of the seat she'd been in. Like a mute distress signal. There was no sign that Harriman had ever sat there beside her. His seat was folded up flat.

Merrill nearly threw himself on top of the spectacled matron occupying the fourth seat in from the aisle, shaking her by the shoulder. "The two people next to you—how long ago—did they get up together?"

"Just now," she said stupidly. "Just before you got here. They'll be back. She left her coat—"

He knew better. He knew they wouldn't. He knew a lot of things all at once—and too late. Why she'd sat there so rigid, refusing to budge, afraid to turn and look at him. Harriman had caught onto the mirror stunt at a glance; must have been sitting there with his gun digging into her from that moment on.

He knew what that despairing clutch at his sleeve meant now, and that quickly stifled "Bill—" that had ended so lamely in a request for a drink of water. And he, like a fool, had thought he was putting one over on the sleepy-eyed menace beside her. Now Harriman had taken her with him as a hostage; was using her as a living safe-conduct to see him out of the theater.

———◆◆◆———

He fled up the aisle to the rear of the house again, like someone pursued by devils. One usher he'd sent downstairs, but there was another one on duty inside the main door. Merrill grabbed at him like a drowning man at a straw. "A man and a girl—man with sleepy eyes and a gray coat turned up in back—did they go out this way? Have you seen them?"

"Yeah, just couple minutes ago."

"Oh, Lord!" he groaned, and cracked open one of the opaque

swinging doors that gave onto the outer lobby. In the instant that it swayed open he had a bird's-eye view of the vestibule and the street beyond. The light had gone out in the ticket seller's kiosk and her blond head was missing, yet it was not empty. He saw a form silhouetted through it against the marquee lights beyond. And on each side of the entrance, where there were tinselled sandwich boards advertising coming attractions, idle individuals stood killing time, as if reading the display copy over and over. He recognized both of them. The cordon surrounding the place had already been formed.

The usher was saying behind him, "But they didn't go out. They came as far as here and I opened the door for them, then they changed their minds and went upstairs to the balcony—"

So the cordon had just beaten him to it. But he'd seen them before they saw him, and had doubled back in again—with her! Merrill didn't feel any relief at the knowledge that he was still in the theater with her. Quite the opposite. She was almost certainly a goner, now that the man was trapped!

"I think she'd been taken sick," the usher was babbling unasked. "She looked pretty white, and she kept sort of leaning against him wherever they went. I tried to ask her if she wanted a doctor, but they'd gone upstairs before I had a chance—"

Merrill wasn't listening. "The roof—he can get up there from the balcony, can't he? There must be some way up!"

He gave a short, surreptitious whistle through the crack of the door, and one of the rubbernecks down by the display boards was suddenly vis-a-vis to him, as though he moved on invisible wires.

"He's hep," Merrill breathed through the slit. "The roof—tell them to throw men into the adjoining buildings quick and head him off. The roof is only two stories high and he can get out that way! I think that's where he's heading for—" And then a sort of choked cry broke from him against his will. "And if they see somebody with him up there in the dark, tell them—it's my girl—will ya?" Instantly he pulled himself together again. "Lend me a gun, will you? I'm clean in here. I'm going after him inside!"

It was still warm from the other's body. He pocketed it and went running up the branch of the stairs the usher had pointed to before.

Above, they deployed onto a mezzanine gallery, a long narrow space between the back of the theater and the sloping balcony seats, but walled off from the latter. Two arched openings, one at each end, led out to the seats, and in the middle, but set high up near the ceiling, was the squat, ponderous metal door guarding the projecting room, with just an ordinary, vertical iron ladder reaching to it.

The balcony usher who had been stealing a look at the picture as closing time neared, materialized guiltily at the far end; came running at the vicious swing of Merrill's arm. "Two people just come up here from below, man and a woman?"

"No, nobody's shown up here. They wouldn't this late any more—"

"Then you missed 'em!" Merrill barked. "Show me how to get up to the roof!"

"Patrons aren't allowed—"

"Show, or I'll hang one on you!" He stiff-armed him for a head-start, and the brass-buttoned juvenile went stumbling at nearly a forty-five degree angle toward a panel stenciled No Admittance, just within one of the lateral passageways, leading toward the seats. It worked neither on hinges nor a knob, but on a vertical bolt running from top to bottom the entire length of it. Merrill hitched this up and shoved, but the way the thing resisted and the metallic snarling it rewarded him with was pretty conclusive evidence it hadn't been opened recently.

"I'm going up and take a look anyway," he instructed. "Stay here and hold it open for me so I can get in again!"

⪻◆⪼

A short, steeply-tilted flight of iron stairs led to a duplicate of the first hatchway, and there was a decrepit bulb lighting the space between the two. He went back to the latter, and took the precaution of giving it a couple of turns to the left; it expired and made him less of a target from the roof outside when he'd forced open the second door.

It was just as well he had. The squeaking and grating of the second door boomed out all over the roof, with the tall surrounding buildings to help it along acoustically. Instantly a handful of angry bees, steel jacketed, seemed to swarm at it as he swung it cautiously out, and it clicked and popped in a half-dozen places at once. But the flashes of yellow and the bangs that accompanied them came not from the roof itself but from the various windows overlooking it. The reception committee was greeting the wrong guy, that was all.

"That would've been one for the record, if—" he thought grimly. Still, it wouldn't have been their fault any more than his. He'd flattened himself on the steps like a caterpillar, chin resting on the top one, while he held the door on a crack with one hand. Threadlike as the slit was, something whistled and plopped into the plaster *behind* him instead of hitting the side of the door. "That's Ober, showing off how good he is!" he scowled resentfully. "He oughta be in a sideshow with those eyes of his!"

The thought of what would have happened if it had been Harriman, with Betty in front of him, wasn't a pretty one. But it was a pushover Harriman hadn't come up here, or if he had, had doubled back again in a hurry, like at the downstairs door. Otherwise he'd be lying stretched out on the tar out there right now, and they wouldn't be wasting time trying to riddle still another.

He was reaching behind him with his free hand, trying to get his handkerchief out of his back pocket and flap it at them in some way, when a voice boomed out: "Hold it, men, for God's sake! He's got a girl with him—" They'd just sent word up, and that would have been a big consolation to Betty, turned into a human lead pencil.

Merrill straightened up, gave the door a kick outward with his foot, and bellowed forth: "It's Merrill, you bunch of clodhoppers! Why don't'cha use a little self-control!" A figure poised on one of the window sills and jumped down to the theater roof below with a sound like a bass drum. But Merrill had already turned and gone skittering down the stairs again, to where the usher was calling up to him: "Hey, you! Quick, you up there—"

He missed the last few steps entirely, but there was no room to fall in—just landed smotheringly on the uniformed figure below him. The show must have "broken" in those few minutes while he was up on the roof. The blaze of light coming through from the auditorium inside told him that, and the peaceful humming and shuffling from belowstairs as the audience filtered out and dispersed, all unaware of what had been going on in their midst. It was just a "neighborhood" show house, it hadn't been a big crowd, and the balcony was already empty and still. But the usher, as they both picked themselves up, was pointing a trembling hand out into the gallery.

Merrill took in three things at once: the motion picture operator lying flat on his back groaning, as though he'd just been thrown down bodily out of the projection room; the projection room door above, momentarily open and blazing with incandescence to reveal Harriman's head and shoulders; and the iron ladder swinging out from the wall as it toppled and fell, pushed down by Harriman.

Merrill had the bead on him already, and it wouldn't have taken a dead shot like Ober to plug him with all that blaze of light behind him, but Betty's head showed just behind him and her scream came winging down. Merrill's finger joint stayed despairingly, and the slamming tight of the door cut short her scream and effaced the single opportunity that had been given him.

He just stood there staring sickly upward at where the opening had been, as the full implication hit him. They had him now, sure—trapped, cornered at last, after one of the bloodiest chases in criminal history. But he had them too! He had Merrill, anyway. And that was just the trouble; Merrill was under orders, wasn't alone in this.

The audience safely out of the way, his fellows came pouring up the stairs from below, and another group came clattering down from the roof. The cordon had tightened into a knot gathered there under the projection room door. Merrill, very white and still, just pointed to it without a word.

III

The captain took the situation in at a glance. "Okay, it's all over now but the shouting," he nodded grimly. "But it's going to be pretty messy." He began spitting orders right and left. "Close up all those side exits. Bring up those gas bombs. Spread yourselves out. Don't gang up here. He's liable to pop out again and take half of you with him."

The whole place started to swim in front of Merrill's eyes. He saw them pick up the operator, announce he had a broken collar-bone, and carry him downstairs. He saw them bring up two Tommy-guns, set one up on each arm of the stairs at floor level, tilted to command the projection room door from each side of the mezzanine.

The captain said: "Lug that acetylene torch up on the roof. Cut a hole down on top of him. Take the manager with you—he'll be able to locate the right spot for you."

A livid little man was hustled toward the companionway Merrill had climbed earlier, protesting: "My house! My beautiful house! What'll the owners say when they hear?"

"You, Ober, you're supposed to be good," was the next command. "Go down on the main floor and when I give the word have yourself a pot-shot at the camera sights or whatever other openings there are in front. We might be able to let a little ventilation into him from that side. And now you two with the Tommies, have a try at this door from where you are. Let's see if it's bullet proof or not. Back, everyone—"

It was the man whose gun Merrill had borrowed, who stepped up and said, "He's got Bill's girl in there with him. For God's sake, Cap, you're not gonna—"

The captain whirled on Merrill furiously. "What's the matter with you anyway? Why didn't you speak up? Is that what you been standing there looking so scared about?"

Merrill's knees were about ready to buckle under him; he ran his hand through his hair a couple of times as though he couldn't think straight any more. "We were gonna be married in June," he said wildly. "I thought I was only bringing her to a movie show—" His voice died away forlornly.

"Ahrr, damn wimmen anyway!" the captain snapped unreasonably.

There was a sudden silence. None of the men moved. The orders hung fire. Then abruptly a bell jangled somewhere nearby. A second time, then a third.

"What's that?" said the captain, looking all around him.

The manager, held under duress at the roof steps, came forward frightenedly. "That's him! That's the projection room trying to get me in my office, not the house phone: Three rings—he must have read the signal on the wall in there! He must want to tell you some—"

"All right, get in there and show us how it works!" The captain gave him a push behind the shoulder. He and Merrill and one of the others followed him into his private sanctum and stood watching, while he unhooked a hand set and pressed a button on the edge of his desk. He held the phone frightenedly out toward the captain as though afraid it would bite him. "Here—you—you better talk to him!"

The captain snatched the instrument away from him. They all stood waiting tensely. "Can you hear me in there?" he snapped.

His jaw set at the answer. He muffled the thing against the desk top with a bang. "Safe conduct or he'll bump the doll," he repeated for their benefit.

Merrill looked haggard. His breath sang in his chest like a wind-storm. The captain stole a sidewise look at him. "All right," he muttered to the other man, "he wins. We'll get him the minute he lets go of her, anyway!"

But the three of them shared a single unspoken thought: "He won't let go of her—alive."

The captain lifted the phone again. He was stony faced, and couldn't bring himself to speak for a minute. Finally he swallowed hard, gritted out: "So you want a safe conduct, Chink-eyes!"

The answering voice was audible but indistinguishable; like a file rasping against metal.

The captain's face was red with humiliation; he turned his back on the three standing listening. "I see—as far as the storm canopy over the sidewalk out front," he said in a trembling voice. "And I'm to call my men off—"

"This is hard to take," muttered the detective standing beside Merrill.

"And how do we know you'll keep your word?" the captain said.

"He won't, and we all know he won't!" Merrill groaned. "He'll drag her off with him some place and shoot her down like a dog the minute he gets in the clear, to pay us back for a close shave like this! We're bargaining over a corpse; she's been dead from the minute I left her alone in that seat next to him!"

The captain muttered, scarcely above a choked whisper, "Okay, Chink-eyes, you win this round—we're pulling in our horns." He threw down the instrument and slumped into a chair for a moment, shading his eyes with one hand. "This is my finish," he breathed. "I'll be broken for this!" And then his voice rose to a roar. "But what else could I do? Answer that, will you? What else could *anyone* do?"

He stood up again, pounded his fist on the desk. "There's still one chance we got left of outsmarting him in the long run! He ain't letting go of her out there. He'll get her out in front, and he'll flag a cab and yank her in it with him, that's his only way of making a clean getaway, of shaking us off. That's what we gotta figure on, anyway; he's a rat, and you don't bank on a rat's promises. All right, Merrill, this'll be your job! You get out there now ahead of him, rake up a cab, and be waiting down the street in it—in the driver's seat.

"Watch your timing at that wheel. If you can be coasting along slow when he comes out, instead of standing still waiting, it'll look that much better. Don't try nothing on your own, now—you'll only lose him for us! Hop to it! He'll bleed for this—later."

He turned and marched out, gave crisp orders to the men outside, his face expressionless as though this wouldn't go down as the blackest night in police annals for all time to come. "Call them down off the roof with that blow torch. Get down to the main floor with those Tommies. Clear the mezzanine! Everybody down to the orchestra floor. Line up down there by the stairs. Put your guns away and don't anybody raise a hand. There's a girl's life at stake!" He called in to the manager behind him: "Put the house lights on, every last one of 'em. We don't want any shadows hanging around to bungle things up for us."

The manager scurried across to a control box; frantically pulled down switches right and left. The theater outside blazed to a noonday brightness.

Merrill had vanished.

The faces that met the captain's and turned away to carry out the incredible orders, were pictures of amazement, stifled by discipline. Not a word was said. The bitterness of the pill he was having to swallow was only too evident on the "old man's" countenance.

"Must be some kind of a come-on, to get him out of there," one of the policemen breathed, backing a machine-gun downstairs.

"Na, it's the girl."

"But she's a goner anyway! He'll only do it out on the street afterwards—"

They all knew it instinctively, even the "old man" himself. But she had to have her chance. She was a girl, and she was Bill's girl. The almost certainty of her death mustn't be turned into a dead certainty, not while there was the slightest means within their power of pulling her through. Which didn't prevent the lot of them from wishing heartily she'd never been born at all. Or had been born in China.

IV

The captain was the last one down off the stairs. "All right, fall in there, along these stairs. Face the lobby out front. Fold your arms behind you."

They stiffened. A look of resentment that grew to burning hate kindled, swept across their faces, but they held their tongues. The blazing lights beating all around on them, turned the thing into a parody of the line, with themselves in the part of the suspects, for once. They were swearing softly, some of them, under their breaths, a sort of hissing sound like steam escaping from a valve.

Their captain sized up the long, helpless line strung across from right to left, and then he closed his eyes as though he couldn't bear the sight.

"Where's Merrill?" someone asked his neighbor out of the corner of his mouth.

"Probably gone off somewhere to bump himself off!" was the scathing answer.

"He should have waited," groaned the captain, "and I'd be ready to join him after this night's work!"

The captain turned to face the way they were. "Attention," he said almost inaudibly. Then he raised his voice and called to the manager up above: "All right, go back in there and ring him—tell him he's in the clear!" Then he just stood there after that, beside his men, like a very old man, chin down, shoulders bowed, waiting.

The inner doors to the lobby had all been folded back, giving an unobstructed view from where some of them were all the way to the silent, deserted street out front. At the far end, like a marker beyond which the safe-conduct expired, stood the tenantless ticket booth, door thrown open to show it was empty and a light burning inside it. Beyond was a ribbon of yellow sidewalk under the marquee lights, and the darkness of the street, with once in a while a car skirting by, never dreaming what was going on inside. From out there it must have seemed just a movie house thrown open for ventilation after the last audience had left it.

A breathless silence engulfed the whole place from top to bottom after the captain's last order. They could hear the manager slam down some window that had been left open in his office. Then the faraway triple buzz of his signal sounded in the nearly sound-proof projection room. His voice came down to them clearly, through his open office door. "You're in the clear, they're all down below!" Then the office door banged as he locked himself in up there, out of harm's way.

There wasn't another sound throughout the house for maybe five minutes.

The pall of silence lay heavier and heavier upon the waiting, listening men, until their nerves were ready to snap with the increasing tension. Every eye was on the stairs that came down from the mezzanine.

Suddenly a heavy door grated open somewhere out of sight, up above them, and they tensed. He was reconnoitering. Then there was an impact, as though somebody had jumped, immediately followed by a second, lighter one. Then nothing more for awhile, while seconds that were like hours ticked themselves leadenly off into eternity, and the tension had become almost unbearable. One or two faces showed gleaming threads of sweat coursing down them.

Then, like a flash, something appeared on the topmost step, just under where the ceiling cut the staircase off from view, and they all saw it at once, and they all stiffened uncontrollably in unison. A woman's foot, in a patent leather pump, had come down slowly onto the step, as though it were feeling its way.

That was all for a minute. Then its mate came down on the step below it, showing a short section of ankle this time. Then the first one moved past it, down to the third step. And behind them both, as the perspective lengthened following each move they made as closely as in a lock-step, came a man's two feet. The sinister quadruple extremities advanced as slowly as some horrible paralytic thing descending a staircase, slowly lengthening.

The heads only came in view when they were near the bottom. He had his right arm around the girl, holding her clamped to him in an embrace from behind. Her head leaned back against his shoulder, as though she were incapable of standing upright any longer.

She didn't look out at them; it was he who did, and nodded grimly. His free arm, dangling in a straight line from his shoulder, ended in a wink of burnished metal—another gun, for surely there was one already pressed menacingly close to her sagging body.

They came down off the stairs and for a moment presented a perfect double target, broadside to the deathlike row of policemen ranged across the width of the orchestra. The captain held them in leash with a single glance of his dilated eyes, and not one stirred. "Steady!" he breathed. "For God's sake, steady!"

Slowly the double target telescoped itself into a single one—the girl—as Harriman turned the two of them to face his enemies, then began to back up a step at a time through the long mirrored lobby toward the street.

His voice suddenly shattered the almost unbearable stillness. "I hope you raked 'em all in from out there—for her sake! If I get it in the back, she goes with me!"

"I've kept my word, Harriman!" the captain shouted back. "See that you keep yours. That ticket-booth's the deadline!"

"Back!" snarled Harriman suddenly. "Ba-ack!" The line of men had begun to inch forward, trying to keep the distance between from widening too hopelessly as Chink-eyes retreated through the long funnel of the lobby.

Harriman came abreast of the ticket booth, veered off to one side of it after a single flick of his eyes had shown him it was harmless. He moved a step beyond it, a second step, was out on the open sidewalk now under the marquee. He gave a swift glance up one way, down the other.

"Turn that girl loose, you're in the clear now!" the captain roared out to him.

He had reached the edge of the curb now with her. His arm went up, signalling off to one side, and a faint droning sounded, coming nearer.

"Merrill!" the captain breathed fervently. "Don't spoil it, now, boys—there's still a chance of saving that girl. Hold it," he pleaded, "hold it!"

The oncoming hum suddenly burst into a sleek, yellow cab body, braking to a halt directly behind Harriman and the girl, so close it almost seemed to graze him. "Open the door!" they heard him growl, without taking his eyes off them.

A gasp went up from them as they watched.

In the full glare of the lights overhead, the grinning bronzed face of a negro flashed around as he turned to carry out the order. The cab door swung free. Harriman had already found the running board with the back of one foot. "D'ye want her?" he snarled back. "Then there she is, come and get her!"

The sudden widening of the space between their two bodies as he stepped back to avoid his own bullet, without dropping the encircling arm, showed what his intent was—murder and not release.

<hr />

A form suddenly dropped from above, like something loosened from the rim of the marquee, and flattened Harriman with a swiftness impossible for the eye to follow, even in all that bright glare. It was Merrill's hurtling body, rounded into a ball.

There was a flash in front of the girl, but *out* from her as the impact jerked Harriman's curved arm straight. A sprinkling of glass trickled from the canopy overhead.

She went down in the struggle and a moment later emerged unharmed from the squirming tarantula that had formed on the sidewalk, crawling away on her hands and knees toward the sanctuary of the ticket booth. The cab driver, frightened, sped onward with his empty machine without waiting.

What remained as she drew away had two heads, four arms, four legs, all mixed inextricably together, threshing around, tearing itself to pieces. Metal glinted from it, and one head reared above the other. Only a lunatic could have risked a shot at such a target from back in the inner foyer of the theater. Yet a shot roared from inside, and the upper head dropped flat. For a moment the whole thing lay still, as the line of police broke and came rushing out toward it.

Ober came out last, blowing smoke out of his gun.

Merrill slurred Harriman's body off his gun, and stood up shakily in the middle of all of them. The desperado lay squinting up at the marquee overhead, a black trickle threading out of one ear.

The captain was almost incoherent with rage. He shook his fist in Merrill's face; acted like he was going to throw himself at him bodily. "I oughta demote you for insubordination! What the devil do you mean by deliberately disobeying my orders? I told you to commandeer a cab and tail him, not pull off a flying-trapeze act out here on the sidewalk!"

It was mostly relief—blowing off high-pressure steam after the terrible suspense.

"We got him, didn't we?" Merrill blazed. "It was a cock-eyed idea, getting a cab. He could've pinged me from the back the minute he got suspicious and then where'd—" He stopped. Betty was squeezing his arm warningly. He caught on what the squeeze meant: we'll be needing your salary after next June, so shut up.

He did. And he looked up at the marquee while the captain went ahead getting things off his chest and they all stood around and listened. It said up there in screamy fiery letters: Double Feature, Most Exciting Show in Town, Your Money's Worth for 40c.

"Yeah," he thought grimly, "that was no lie, either."

AFTERWORD TO "DOUBLE FEATURE"

"Double Feature" (*Detective Fiction Weekly*, May 16, 1936) is one of the earliest and most vivid and breathless of Woolrich's action whizbangs. A memorable thriller hung on a simple peg of plot, with a big-city movie palace as the setting and with emotions and action in perfect counterpoint—who but Woolrich could have pulled it off?

THE HEAVY SUGAR

"Gee, the coffee in this dump is sure rank!" Tom Keogh thought to himself, putting down the cup and running a dubious tongue about the lining of his mouth. The stuff tasted as if they'd lowered one bean on a thread into the whole boiler, held it there a minute, then pulled it out again. And if he didn't like it he could leave it there and go somewhere else. They didn't care.

Which was why he sat there nursing it, with both hands around the hot cup. There wasn't any place else he could go, whether he liked it or not. This mug of so-called java had taken his last nickel. The jitney was still in his pocket, the etiquette of cafeterias being what it is, but that punched-out 5 on his check meant it didn't belong to him any more.

Outside it was raw and drizzling. In here there was steam heat— a little of it over in the corner by the radiator, where he was. As long as he could make the coffee last he could stay.

He took another gulp, and this time the flavor was that of an old inner-tube soaked in boiling water. It was scalding hot, which was all you could say.

"That guy over there," he told himself dully, "doesn't seem to mind it. He's going back for more."

The only other customer in the place looked too well-dressed to be drinking terrible coffee in a joint like this. But he had emptied his first cup hastily and gone back to the counter for another. He left the first one where it was, wet spoon sticking up out of the hefty sugar bowl that each greasy table was provided with. When he came back again with the fresh cup he sat down at a different table.

Keogh, watching idly, saw him plunge his spoon into the new sugar bowl, stir it around vigorously, and bring up a little.

"He wants his sugar from underneath, to be sure no dust has gotten on it," Keogh thought, and quit watching for a while. He had his own troubles to think about.

An abrupt movement brought his eyes back that way again in less than two minutes. The guy was on his way back to the counter for a third cup! The second one stayed on the table, still about a quarter full, to judge by the steam threading up from it.

"Maybe his sense of taste is shot!" Tom Keogh thought. On the way back to a table, the fellow shot a glance over him, as if to see whether he was being watched or not. Keogh dropped his eyes. He wasn't afraid to be caught watching, but people don't like to be stared at. He didn't himself.

When he looked again, the other had chosen still a third table to go to with his new cup. Again he stirred up the contents of the sugar bowl until it threatened to overflow the edges.

This time Keogh watched him closely when he put the cup to his lips. He gulped as though he couldn't get rid of it quickly enough, but there was no real enjoyment on his face. A wry expression, like there had been on Keogh's own, accompanied the act.

"Why, he doesn't really want to drink it; he's only pretending to!" Keogh exclaimed to himself. And in addition, he saw, the man was beginning to look worried, tense.

A minute later he saw this peculiar coffee fiend move his cup out beyond the edge of the table, look to see if the counterman was watching, and then deliberately tilt it and let most of the liquid trickle noiselessly to the floor. The counterman went back behind the steam kitchen just then. The night manager, up front by the cash register, had his face buried in a paper and wasn't giving attention to anybody unless they tried to get out the door without paying.

The man with the coffee cup slipped quickly out of his seat and moved to a fourth table, cup and all, this time without getting a refill. Again he churned the sugar bowl hectically, as though he had a gnawing sweet tooth. But the worry on his face was beginning to look like dismay.

Keogh got it finally, just about as quickly as any one else would have, barring a professional detective.

"He isn't interested in drinking coffee!" he told himself knowingly. "He's looking for something in those sugar bowls, working his way around the room table by table!"

———◆———

He didn't care much for sugar himself. He'd only been interested in getting something warm inside him when he first sat down. He'd just scraped a little sugar lightly off the top of the bowl. Now he picked up his spoon second time and gripped it purposefully. No reason why he shouldn't join in the treasure hunt himself, and try to find out what the fellow was after.

Maybe it was only a love note left for him by some sweetie with a jealous husband, using a sugar bowl for a post office. The other customer didn't look like a ladies' man, though, and there were better ways than that.

Maybe it was something else, something that wouldn't be any use to him, Keogh, even if he did find it—a little packet of cocaine, for instance. The guy didn't have that pasty look, though. Ugly and tough and healthy described him better. And then again, maybe it wasn't even in here, whatever it was. Maybe this wasn't the place where it was hid at all. Still, there was nothing like taking a crack at it for oneself.

He folded back the metal flap in the lid of the bowl. Waiting until he was sure the other guy wasn't looking at him, he spaded his spoon deeply in. It hit the bottom. He stirred surreptitiously, as he'd seen the other do. The grains of sugar swirled, coruscated under the light, gleamed, twinkled, all but sparkled. Wait—they had sparkled, here and there!

Little lumps showed up, a whole coil of them. He dredged one out with the tip of his spoon, and all the rest came after it. Sugar rolled off, the lumps caught fire one by one, and he was holding a necklace of priceless diamonds dangling in the air!

———◆———

For just a split second the light got to it, in all its glory, and he forgot to breathe in or out. Then instinctively he whipped it out of sight into his lap and crouched protectively forward above it, hiding it with the upper part of his body.

He knew enough not to take time off even to stuff it into his pocket. He just had time to slap down the flap of the bowl, before the searching man looked over at him. Had he seen him fish the diamonds out? Keogh looked sleepily down at the floor, seemed to be drowsing over his coffee. The other fellow moved again. Now he was just one table away, facing Keogh.

"He has a gun on him," Keogh thought. "Ten to one he has. He didn't come after a thing like that without one. If he catches on I've already found it, he'll use it on me first, and ask for his trinket back later. If I get up and try to walk out, he may suspect what happened. But if I wait, he'll run out of tables—and then he'll be sure!"

It was hot, of course. Either smuggled or stolen. And it was pretty easy to guess what must have happened. The other had had the necklace on him earlier in the day—no longer ago than that, for the sugar in these bowls was renewed about once every twenty-four hours.

He'd found out he was being shadowed by dicks along the mangy avenue outside. He had to get rid of the gems in a hurry, knowing he was apt to be pinched and caught red-handed with them at any moment. Afraid that if he jumped into a cab or car he'd be overhauled and searched before he could get to some place he'd be safe, he'd popped in here, the first doorway that offered itself, and cached the necklace in one of the sugar bowls in the instant he had before they sized him up through the glass front.

Then when they'd made their pinch and hauled him away, he was clean. They'd had no evidence on which they could hold him, so he'd gotten himself sprung almost at once. Making good and sure he wasn't tailed a second time, he'd come back here to get his loot. It was a desperate expedient, but not as bad as dropping the diamonds down a sidewalk grating or letting them be found on him.

He'd had to hide the thing in such a hurry, with his eyes on the plate-glass front, that he probably wasn't sure now just which table it had been. Or else he thought the bowls had gotten transposed during the course of the day's hash-slinging. Right now he must be sweating blood!

But Keogh would be doing more than sweating it. He would be

bleeding it from a couple of bullet punctures if he didn't get out of here pretty fast, he knew. He'd located the bulge now, under the guy's left arm. It was not very noticeable, but it wasn't just made by a pack of old letters, either!

As for turning the necklace back, walking up to the guy and saying, "Here, I found this and you seem to be hunting for it. I'm hard up. Is it worth forty or fifty bucks to you—" He wasn't that much of a fool.

He might get the fifty, sure, on loan for about five minutes. Then he'd get a couple of slugs in addition at the first dark corner he came to after leaving, just as insurance that he really kept his mouth shut. No, thanks!

———◆———

The other man had finished dredging the tureen at the table where he was, and Keogh's was the next in line. Fortunately, the counterman had showed up again, and the hunter didn't seem to want to make the move without any excuse. It was easy to see the people in this place weren't in on it with him, and he didn't want to arouse their curiosity or suspicion.

By now he apparently couldn't stomach any more of their putrid coffee, so this time for an excuse he got up and went over to the water filter. And when he came back, it was going to be to Keogh's table.

The riskiest place to carry the diamonds would be the safest in the long run, Tom Keogh decided quickly. Pockets were a dead giveaway, and it would take too long to put them in his sock. The water ran out of that cooler into the glass awfully fast, and the outfit was some kind of polished metal that reflected the whole room behind the fellow's back almost as well as a mirror. Keogh couldn't make any suspicious moves. The necklace was bunched up in Keogh's lap, and he had one hand sheltering it sidewise from observation. He gathered it into the hollow of that hand, then tucked it in and folded his fingers down over it without moving another muscle of his body.

Then he yawned, as if coming out of his lethargy. He brought his arms up, elbows out, and stretched in his chair. He kept the backs of his hands turned toward the gunman at the filter. Then he opened his clenched fingers a little, with his hands up in full sight. Not much, but enough to guide the string of jewels in the right direction.

His cuff was baggy and shapeless, as wide open as a firemen's net. He felt the thing go wriggling down his wrist like a cold, rough-edged little snake, and his sleeve swallowed it. It fell all the way down to the crook of his arm, bringing up against his biceps.

He got a good grip on the bottom of his cuff with that same hand, doubling it back on itself and tucking it shut tight around his wrist. Then he brought his arms down again, and yawned.

The necklace dropped right back down his sleeve again, of course, but it couldn't get out. There wasn't any slack left in the cloth now, the way he was holding it. The jewels stayed in. The awkward position of his fingers was barely noticeable, and then only if you looked closely down at the hand. Most people carry their fingers curving loosely inward a bit anyway, not stretched out stiffly like an Egyptian bas-relief.

The hard guy was coming toward the table with his glass of water. Tom Keogh scraped his chair back, picked up his check with his free hand and sauntered aimlessly toward the cashier. He put the check down, reached in his pants and dug out his last nickel, dropping it on top of the slip of cardboard. The cashier, interrupted halfway down Walter Winchell's column, gave him a dirty look for staying that long on a five-cent check and banged the coin into the till.

Out on the sidewalk, Keogh turned his head slightly and glanced back in. This time the guy was *not* messing the sugar bowl at the table Keogh had just left. Instead he was staring intently at it as if something about it seemed to show it had already been searched.

Keogh struck a quicker gait, but had hardly gotten started when the voice behind him stopped him with a sickening fear. He'd only gotten one doorway down the street, but luckily that was a good dark one.

"Just a minute, buddy! Hey, you! Take it easy!"

———◆———

There was a feline softness about the voice, almost a purr, that was somehow more menacing than the loudest shout. The fellow stood revealed for a moment outside the lighted cafeteria doorway, as Keogh turned, then suddenly was standing next to him, without seeming to have moved at all.

"Trouble you for a light, buddy?" he asked, still purring.

Keogh knew better than to run for it. He tapped his pocket half-heartedly. "Didn't they have one in there?"

"Couldn't say, buddy, didn't ask them," was the answering drawl. "Lemme help you look, I'm good at finding things. Just move back a little closer to this doorway, out of the drafts."

There was a maddening quality about that smooth, silky tone of voice. Perhaps it was intentional, to provoke men to their deaths. Keogh, goaded, would have grappled with him then and there, but the gun had come out.

"What is this, a holdup?" he asked bitterly. "I haven't anything on me. Why don'tcha pick some one that—"

The other's pronunciation became even slower and softer.

"Ju-ust relax, buddy. Don't say anything you'll be sorry for. There's nothing to get excited about."

Keogh didn't argue the point. The other had him now with his back pressed flat against the closed doorway behind him. The gunman held his gun hand back a little, and hidden close up against his own body. You couldn't have noticed what was going on from a yard away.

He threw a quick look up one way, then down the other, but too quickly for Keogh to take advantage of it. Keogh wasn't in a chancey mood, anyway. Diamonds don't cure bullet wounds.

With his free hand the guy started in at Keogh's outside breast pocket and worked his way all over him. He didn't miss a seam. Keogh was holding his cuff in now by no more than three fingers, letting the others hang stiffly downward. Every second the stones felt as though they were going to come slipping out of their own weight and clash to the pavement beside him. They were bunched there right at the mouth of his cuff, held in only by the slightest of pressure.

"Hunh!" the guy laughed shortly, when not even an Indian-head penny had shown up anywhere in Keogh's clothes. "You're sure flat, all right!" he said, with contempt.

He backed away a step. "Now bend down, undo your kicks, and step out of them!" he ordered.

Keogh did so, desperately hanging on to his cuff and only using two fingers of that hand to do the unlacing. The other didn't seem to notice in the darkness. He snatched up one shoe, then the other, shook them out, tossed them back.

"All right, stick your leg up against the side of the doorway and hoist up the bottom of your pants!" he snapped, crisply now.

He examined the top of Keogh's sock, feeling for bulges. Then he repeated with the other leg. He wasn't missing a trick. The sweat stood out on Keogh's forehead like raindrops.

The stick-up guy stood there for a full minute, swearing deep down in his throat. He searched every spot but the right one— Keogh's bare left hand. Keogh took a chance, just to see if the other would give himself away.

"What is it y' think I've got?" he asked querulously.

But the searcher was too cagey to be tripped. "I'm an anatomy student and I just wanted to see what makes you tick!" he snarled. He was probably remembering that there were still a couple of tables in there with sugar bowls he hadn't searched. And somebody else might walk in while he was standing out here.

"Keep your mouth shut about this if you know what's good for you," he warned, and turned to go back to the cafeteria.

At that instant the laws of gravity finally had their way. The heavy jewelry at last found the outlet it had been looking for. There was a prismatic flash at Keogh's wrist. The diamonds rolled down over his hand like a jet of water and fell at his feet, glittering even in the faint illumination from the corner arc light. Instantly he put one stockinged sole over the necklace and blotted it out.

The tough guy, still within arm's length, turned and looked back over his shoulder. "Here, catch," he said jeeringly. "Just to prove that wasn't a holdup." Then he flipped a quarter at Keogh. His own footstep just then must have covered the slight sound the necklace made in falling, for he seemed not to have heard it.

The coin, though, fell far more noisily, and went rolling out of reach. The other went back to the cafeteria without waiting to see Keogh pick it up. Which was a good thing, for Keogh couldn't have moved without uncovering what lay under his foot.

Sweat dripped from his bent-down face onto the sidewalk as he crouched, shoveled on his shoes, scooped the stones into his pocket, and made tracks away from there, without bothering to look for the coin that only a few short minutes before would have been such a life-saver to him.

He was remembering that, although he'd gotten away with it just now, there were still those two other guys inside—the counterman and the cashier—either of whom might possibly have seen him take something out of the sugar bowl and might mention it if this guy asked them when he went in again. A thing that didn't occur to him until too late was that the quarter he had left lying on the sidewalk would be a dead giveaway if the guy came out looking for him a second time, and spotted it there. Broke, without a red cent on him, and he left two-bits lying there without even stopping to pick it up? A sure sign he'd had those diamonds on him and wanted to get away in a hurry!

Keogh got away from that side of the street, cutting across it diagonally to the next corner. Just before turning up the nearest side street he looked back, from behind the shelter of an empty glass show case on the corner. The hard egg had already come outside again, much faster than he'd gone in.

So one of them had already told him! Maybe they'd only seen Keogh messing up the sugar in his bowl, but that was all the other needed to know.

Keogh saw him stoop and pick something up. The quarter! And now he knew that he'd betrayed himself after all, in spite of the marvelous run of luck he'd had until now. That quarter had been lying in full sight. Keogh couldn't have helped finding it if he'd looked at all.

Now the man with the gun knew beyond the shadow of a doubt who had found those diamonds!

——⬦——

Keogh didn't linger there to watch what his next move would be. He lit down the side street as if devils pursued him, hugging the shadow of the building line, his breath rattling like dry leaves, until he'd put blocks between them. His pursuer must have turned the other way for there wasn't a sign of his being followed.

But the fellow knew what Keogh looked like now. That was the worst of it! He'd be on the look-out for him, and Keogh might run into him when he least expected it. From to-night on his life would be a hunted, haunted misery, with never a moment's peace.

If he kept the necklace, they'd be after him until they got it back. And if he turned it over to the police, they'd still be after him anyway, until they got even with him. Asking the police for protection wouldn't be any good. They didn't worry their heads about drifters like him. Even if they offered it to him, he couldn't spend the rest of his life sleeping in some precinct-house basement.

And furthermore, if he went near them with these jewels, they might implicate him in the theft. Certainly they'd never believe his story of finding a necklace like that in a hash-house sugar bowl. Nobody would. They'd take him for a go-between who was double-crossing the rest.

Without money, friends, influence, anything to back him up, he'd have a hell of a time clearing himself—and he might not be able to at all. He was beginning to wish he'd never found the thing. For a moment he was tempted to drop it in an ash can. But that wouldn't do any good either. He was stuck with it, and he had to stay with it, come what might.

He trudged along, taking a precautionary look behind him at every crossing, skulking slowly Boweryward. Misguided people think that there is a sort of birdlike freedom of movement that goes with destitution and vagrancy. They're entirely wrong. A man with a dollar or two in his pockets has the run of the entire city, no matter what the time of night. No cop can tell him where to go or where not to, provided he minds his business. But a down-and-outer is severely restricted to a few neighborhoods if he wants to avoid questioning and detention after dark.

The parks are closed to him, the police clearing them after midnight. Up on the better thoroughfares like Fifth, Madison and Park avenues, he is liable to be picked up for vagrancy or panhandling. Even on the less savory ones like Third, Sixth and Ninth he is apt to be run in as a suspicious character. There remain only a few refuges for the homeless in New York, in the early-morning hours. Those are the subways, the flop-houses for some who have the price, and the Bowery.

Keogh didn't have a nickel to get into the subway. Anyway, helpers were being rounded up over there as an aftermath of several recent lush-murders. So there was only the Bowery left, and the Bowery was an old friend of his. He had tramped it many a night.

He knew just where to go, even at this hour, to raise two-bits on the metal links that joined these stones he had found—enough to enable him to hole up in a room in one of the twenty-five-cent "hotels." That would get him off the streets before they caught up with him. He was sure the links must be silver, at the very least. Maybe they were even gold silvered over, or even platinum. He knew better than to show the stones themselves. That was asking for swift and sudden death, on the Bowery.

When Keogh was opposite City Hall Park, he cut across from the West Side, where the thing had happened, and plunged into the blackness under the sheltering El pillars of Park Row. A few blocks north was the Bowery. But he had to find some way of loosening the stones from their setting before he reached it. Too many prying eyes might be watching up there.

He stopped outside the wire-mesh grating of the powerhouse of the Third Avenue El, on the west side of Park Row. The attendant on the early-morning shift there knew him by sight and had exchanged a word or two with him before now, when he came close to the grating to get a moment's breath of air and found Keogh standing on the other side of it watching the machinery.

Keogh called to him. "Say, Mac, have you got a small pair of pliers I could borrow for a minute? Give 'em right back to you."

"What d'you want with 'em?" the machinist asked suspiciously.

Keogh thought fast. "There's a nail in my shoe killing me," he said. "I can't stand it any more. Just gimme something so I can break it off short."

The mechanic dug a small pair of wire-cutters out of his overalls and passed them through the grating. "Don't walk off with them now," he warned, "if that's what you're thinking of, because you won't get anything on them."

"I'll be back with them in a jiffy." Keogh limped artistically out of sight into the nearest doorway. He took out of his pocket a folded newspaper that he'd picked from a trash can, spreading it across his lap. There was hardly any light to see by, but he couldn't risk doing this where it was any brighter.

He had to feel the links with the tips of his fingers, hardly able to see them. The stones were fortunately all hung from one main chain that fastened at the back of the neck. The metal, silver or whatever it was, was soft and the clippers severed it easily.

Even so, it was almost a half hour before he showed up in front of the lighted powerhouse grating once more to give them back. The machinist's expression showed plainly that he'd been thinking the worst in the meantime.

"What'd you do, try to trade 'em in for a shot of 'smoke'?" he wanted to know sullenly. "Now don't come around here no more, understand?"

But Keogh didn't intend to, if he could help it. All he wanted was a sanctuary, to get in out of the open for a while, where they couldn't find him. Those denuded links of gleaming metal carefully collected in a scrap of newspaper in his pocket would be a means toward that. The loosened diamonds, wrapped up in another piece of paper, were in his other pocket. Once he got into some kind of a room, he could think of a better hiding place for them.

He went walking up Park Row with almost enough wealth in his shabby coat to have bought the street out, and went into the Federal Bar. Unfortunately the pawnshops weren't open now, but they knew him there in the Federal. He wasn't a drinker, but they'd let him sit in the back until closing time more than once on a cold night.

There were only two or three glassy-eyed barflies left at the bar at this hour, but he didn't want even them for an audience. He went all the way to the end and signaled the barman.

The latter sensed a touch, or an attempt to promote a free drink. "Whaddya want?" he asked without moving.

"I wanna show you something," Keogh answered in as low a voice as would serve his purpose. Even so, the three barflies, glassy-eyed though they were, turned and gandered down at him to see what it was.

Keogh turned his back to them when the barman had joined him and nervously took the wad of newspaper out of his pocket. He was under a strain, trying too hard not to let the barflies see, and worrying too much about whether the barman would let him have fifty cents on what he was going to show him. Without realizing what he was doing he had opened the wrong package! The barman, snapping from professional boredom to electrified incredulity, had a glimpse of fifteen or more loosely pressed diamonds in the hollow of the newspaper before Keogh quickly bunched it up again.

The barman's eyes were like half moons. "Wait a minute; what was that again? Lemme see, don't be in such a hurry!"

But Keogh, his face pale at the ghastly blunder, had already crammed them back in his pocket. He didn't attempt to take the other package out now. The least spiffed of the barflies took a tentative step up toward him, to see what had made the bartender goggle so.

Keogh backed away toward the door. "Look real, don't they?" he stammered. "Just glass—found 'em in an ash can just now. Well, so long!"

"Lemme have a closer look. I can tell you if they're glass or not," the barman said craftily. Then as Keogh turned and bolted out he called after him futilely, "C'mon, have a drink on the house! What's your rush?" Trying to get him cockeyed and kill him if the stones turned out to be real!

Keogh hurried away from the place, cursing himself. Now he *had* to get off the streets in a hurry. He hadn't kidded that barman any. Unlike pearls, it wasn't very hard to tell real diamonds from glass, even at a brief glance. The fellow would talk his head off within the next few hours to any one that came into the place. And the wrong guy might just happen to come in!

Keogh plunged into the next dive, a block up, the Silver Flash. He was known in there, too. The place was empty under the pair of dismal, icy-white reflectors that gave it its name. This time he didn't make any mistake in opening the right package, but his hands were shaking so he could hardly unfold the paper. A man could have all the wealth of Golconda on him and still remain as broke and homeless as ever, he was finding out.

The new barman studied the links and remained unimpressed. "What good are these to me?" he asked. And then, inevitably, "Where'd you get 'em?"

"A guy gave 'em to me," Keogh improvised. "Lemme have

fifty cents on 'em just until morning. They're silver," he added desperately.

"How do I know they're silver? I ain't in the loan business, anyway." The barman handed the outspread paper back.

The owner had come out from the back while they were talking. He picked up one of the pieces now and looked at it, with a sort of remote professional interest, as though he had once been a jeweler himself or a jeweler's assistant. Then he looked more closely, taking the whole paperful under the light to study them better.

When he came back he said to the bartender, with crafty casualness, "Naw, it's not silver, but give him fifty cents anyway, Joe." They exchanged a look, and the bartender punched the register. The owner had just seen *14K* stamped on the back of one of the links and knew it was white gold.

Keogh, outside with money in his hand, took a deep breath. Now at last sanctuary was within reach! And none too soon. He was giving them—by them he meant the gang involved in the original theft, for, of course, there were more of them implicated than just that one tough who had held him up outside the cafeteria— credit for sense enough to know where to come looking for him.

He hadn't had a cent on him, so the Bowery was the logical place to search for him. But now he could get in out of the open, until morning at least, so let them look! For thirty-five cents he could get a room all to himself.

He went into the nearest lighted doorway that had a sign, "Rooms for Men," over it and got one. He wasn't shown up, just handed a key and told where to find it. He climbed the stairs, the pounding of his heart slowly quieting. The lights were out in the second-floor "reading room," with its long bare tables and benches, like a meeting house, and its two or three newspapers that passed from hand to hand through the dragging, hopeless hours of the day and evening. But he stepped in and found one of the papers, taking it up to his room to see if he could find any mention of the necklace in it.

———◆◆◆———

The story would have been hard to miss. It was right on the front page—"Daring Jewel Robbery in Broad Daylight." At nine yesterday, the day that had ended a few hours ago at midnight, a rich dame had been held up in her West End Avenue apartment, and she and her maid had been tied up and stacked in a closet.

But the details didn't interest him as much as the words—"a diamond necklace valued at $25,000." That was it, sure! But he nearly fell over at sight of the figures staring him in the face like that, in cold print.

Keogh suddenly got all weak and wobbly, his hands became cold and his knees started to shake. He'd thought vaguely until now in terms of a thousand or two dollars, but the realization that he'd been carrying around twenty-five thousand dollars' worth of diamonds half the night nearly paralyzed him with terror. For long minutes he just sat there on the edge of the crummy bed, panting and perspiring.

All his carefully built-up reasons for not turning the find over to the police collapsed. Let them implicate him. Anything was better than this suspense! The longer he held onto the jewels, the deeper they'd implicate him, anyway. He should have gone right to the nearest station house with them when he'd found them. Now he'd broken the necklace up and sold the settings. But maybe they wouldn't be too hard on him as long as he gave the stones themselves back.

What good would keeping them do him, anyway? If he needed to sell them, he'd probably be arrested in the act, or within a few hours. And he couldn't keep the things hidden around him indefinitely, skulking, afraid of every shadow. That bartender already knew he had them. Pretty soon half the Bowery would know.

With a sudden decision he jumped up, unlocked the door, and ran down the stairs. He had fifteen cents left. He'd tell the cops about it over the phone and then wait for them to come and get him. That took less courage than going to them himself.

There wasn't any phone in the place, and he had to go out on the streets to look for one. That was his undoing. He failed to notice the long, ominous black car parked directly in front of the Federal, the first bar he'd gone into. The Federal's customers didn't usually drive up in cars like that. But his mind was now finding one of those little blue-and-white enamel disks that verify a pay station inside the premises, few and far between on the Bowery, and he missed the significance of the car's presence.

He turned up the other way and finally found a phone in an all-night one-arm joint. It was just his luck it had to be on the open wall, not in a booth at all. And there were a couple of guys within earshot. But it was the only one for blocks around, and he had no choice. He shrank from the idea of hunting up a cop on the beat and telling him. It might be an hour before he located one, and then the cop might turn around and say that he'd caught Keogh with the stones and take all the credit to himself.

Keogh dropped his nickel in and made a protective funnel around the mouthpiece with his hand, to keep what he had to say from those in the room. He asked for Spring 7-3100. He supposed that was the way you did it; he'd never called the police before.

A voice answered, "Police Headquarters," and he took a deep breath, afraid to go on, but even more afraid not to, now that he'd gone this far. He said, "Uh—I wanted to tell you about that necklace that was stolen from that lady. You know—that diamond one worth twenty-five thousand dollars?"

Another voice got on the wire abruptly, a more authoritative voice. "What about it?" the new voice demanded brusquely, sapping the little self-confidence he had left.

"I—I think I got it," he quavered.

"You think you've got it! Who are you?"

He had visions of cops taking off by plane to land on his neck, while he was kept talking at the phone and the call was being traced.

"My name's Keogh." He hadn't used his given name in so long he actually forgot it for a moment in his excitement! "I— Has it got fifteen diamonds in it? I found it in a sugar bowl up on Eighth Avenue."

He was sweating again, all over, profusely. That sounded terrible. They'd never believe it. They'd arrest him, sure!

"I'm—I mean, I'll be in a room on the third floor front of the Little America Hotel, here on the Bowery." And then, supreme inaninity, "Should I wait there for you?"

The voice grew crushingly ironic. "Maybe you'd better."

He hung up and went out. He had forebodings of what his immediate future was going to be like, yet in one way he was strangely relieved. He'd gotten the damn thing off his mind at last.

In five or ten minutes more he wouldn't have to worry what to do with it or where to hide it, any more. Even if the cops held him for it, at least those others couldn't get to him.

The inscrutable black car had moved when he got back in sight of his lodgings. It wasn't in front of the Federal any more. Now it was outside the Silver Flash. But he hadn't noticed its position clearly enough the first time to be aware of the change. It never occurred to him that he was in a position to watch himself being traced. To his harassed gaze it was just a car, maybe belonging to some slumming party going the rounds bar by bar.

He turned in at the lighted doorway and started climbing. The second-floor "reception desk"—a board across an open alcove— was vacant and dark now, but that wasn't surprising, considering the hour. He went past it and on up to the third floor.

It was when he got outside the door of his room that something cold came over him. First it was just a sixth sense, with nothing to base it on. Then a couple of the other senses came quickly to support that feeling. His eyes saw a three-sided line of light outlining the warped door. He was sure he'd put the light out when he left just now, for they bawled you out in these places if you didn't. And his ears caught a subdued murmur of voices that rose to a snarl.

"He wouldn't leave it around in here any place. You could look all night and not find it. He must 'a' lamped us coming and powdered with it all over again."

"You heard what that bartender said, din'cha? He saw him come in here! He'll be back. And then there are ways of finding out—"

<hr />

But Keogh didn't wait to hear any more. Those weren't the cops in that room, and that was all he cared about! His decision to go out and phone them had saved him from immediate capture, but now he had to flee again. Was there to be no end to his hobgoblin nightmare?

He started backing down the stairs, his heart hammering in his chest, afraid at first even to turn and face the other way for fear of making the steps creak under him. His breath labored in his throat. He would have moaned aloud if he hadn't known the least sound meant his death.

Halfway down he steadied himself against the wall and slowly pivoted, to finish the descent the natural way and get out. But at the turn of the stairs there seemed to be a deeper shadow than there had been the first time, and suddenly it moved, came out behind him, blocked him, spoke. That same soft, maddening purr fell again on his ears.

"Thought I saw you from the car. Reg'lar night owl, ain't you? Well, come on back up. We're gonna put you to bed!"

And the gun was out once more and urging him up ahead of it, boring into the middle of his back. This was the end, and Keogh knew it, and acted it, there in the dark. The first bartender had seen the stones, the second one the links, and now they had him dead to rights. As soon as they got the diamonds from him they'd shoot him.

Repeatedly, as he tottered up that short remaining flight to his room, Keogh clasped both hands to the lower part of his face in mortal terror, and his jaws moved convulsively as if with hopeless prayers for mercy that he knew it was useless to utter.

A few steps more and, "I've got him," purred the silk-voiced killer outside the door. A sudden square of orange opened noiselessly to swallow the two of them, then was blotted out again.

<hr />

The blast of gunfire that would signal Keogh's end was a strangely long time coming. Eight minutes passed, and then ten, and the short, sharp, barking coughs of an automatic that would mean they had found the diamonds and had no more use for Keogh, alive, did not come. And then, when the gunfire did come at last, it seemed more prolonged and violent than was necessary to finish off just one helpless man.

One bullet, one muffled explosion from a gun muzzle jammed cruelly into his ear would have been enough for that. But there was more than one shot, many of them, and they didn't come from within the room itself, but from up and down those long, narrow stairs, shattering the sleeping lodging house awake from top to bottom.

And the shots came from two directions simultaneously, streaking downward from the top of the stairs and hurtling upward from the bottom, while yellow flashes winked and blinked in the darkness and the booming echoes of the shots rolled back and forth along the corridors.

In the first burst of fiery venom a policeman crumpled in the street entryway, and seconds later the body of a man came hurtling, turning, twisting down from above to join it, like something dropped from the sky down a long chute. He was dead by the time he hit the last step.

There was a deep snarl from below, a sudden rush of heavy feet up the stairs, and the firing went up a flight, retreating along the corridor that led past the room Keogh had hired. The feet came after it, gaining on it. Not a door in the whole ramshackle building opened. Iron bedsteads clashed as bodies ducked blindly under them, and glass popped in one of the unseen front windows as some one sought out without waiting to open it the right way.

A detective suddenly flattened out at the very top of the stairs, as they went up that last flight one by one, but over his prostrate, bleeding form there passed such a withering hail of light flashes, all going the same way, that nothing could have lived in that dead-end corridor afterward.

The one they stumbled over hadn't. Then they were outside Keogh's room door, which was open again. But before the foremost of them could get to it, a soft feline voice on the other side of it caterwauled, "Y' don't get *me!*" and a single, final gunshot exploded somewhere inside the room.

⬥

The soft-voiced one was folded neatly across the foot of the bed, like a clothespin, when they came in and ringed up around him.

"He didn't muff," somebody said sourly. "He should 'a' done it the day he was born!"

There was somebody else in the room, too—Keogh, his eyes pleading with them for release, lashed to the head of the bed with strips torn from a pillowcase. His shirt had been pulled down from his shoulders without being taken off. There were cigarette ashes all over one shoulder, as though he'd tried to smoke without the use of his hands. Somebody slashed the bonds with a pocketknife, and he folded up and groaned.

"Who are you?" a cop asked.

"I'm the guy that phoned you," he said faintly.

They straightened him up again. "What'd they do to you?"

He winced, lifted one elbow, and a cigarette butt dropped out of his armpit, where it had adhered. It was out now.

"The works, huh?" some one commented.

"They held my arm down tight." He showed them a blister the size of a quarter. But he kept writhing, doubling up and straightening out again like a concertina.

"It can't hurt *that* much," one of the detectives said skeptically.

An ambulance had come for the two of their own who had been hurt. The doctor came in to take a look at Keogh after he'd had them carried down.

Keogh kept squirming on the floor while they were trying to question him. One of the detectives was getting sore. "Will ya stay still a minute and answer?" he snarled. "Ya said ya had 'em! The insurance company's offered a reward, and so has the woman they belonged to. You stand to collect $5,000 if you hand 'em over of your own free will. Now don't make me get rough with ya!"

"I wanna hand 'em over!" protested Keogh weakly, "but how can I? I had to hide 'em and I—oooh!" he groaned, unable to continue.

The doctor squatted down to examine him. Keogh groaned something into his ear. The doctor got up again.

"One of you run out and buy a bottle of citrate of magnesia," he directed. "No wonder he's got the bends! This man's got fifteen assorted diamonds in his stomach!"

AFTERWORD TO "THE HEAVY SUGAR"

"The Heavy Sugar" (*Pocket Detective*, January 1937) is a suspense masterpiece, full of tension and anguish and the look and feel of Depression-era New York, its hunted protagonist flailing through night's empty canyons, unable to call the police or even to hide in the subways or a flophouse yet wealthier than almost anyone else in the city. It's a perfect *noir* situation and, whether he read this particular tale or not, the kind of story that inspired the parallel sequences in Richard Wright's classic novel *Native Son* (1940), where the doomed protagonist thrust into a similar urban nightmare is black.

BLUE IS FOR BRAVERY

He was on late duty that week, which was why his face was so long as he came down the steps of the precinct house in the middle of all his shift-mates a quarter of an hour before midnight. He hated that late racket—couldn't get used to it. Midnight to 8:00 A.M. The dregs of time. You had to sleep in broad daylight— try to, you mean, around where he lived. Loaf around all afternoon when other people worked. Didn't know whether to call it breakfast he ate before he reported in at 11:30 P.M. or midnight-lunch or what.

And such a totally-forsaken beat: Lincoln to Main, Halsted to Spring. Trying store-fronts to make sure they were locked up. Picking them up and putting them down. Ringing the House twice an hour. Then you came off, went home to bed when the rest of the world was waking up. Got up at noon and the whole thing started over once more.

"Cheer up," Dinty Falvey said at his elbow, "think of all the nice fresh air you get."

"Every dog has his day," O'Dare answered. "I'll be having mine—one of these fine nights!"

They formed a double column on the sidewalk, tramping along two by two. Not in drill-formation by any means, just roughly symmetrical, to avoid ganging up. The two green lamps dwindled to the size of peas behind them, lost themselves in the night-murk. They started thinning out, dropping off one by one to relieve the men going off duty. O'Dare's beat was the farthest out of them all. "S'long, Danny, see you tomorrow!"

"Right," said Danny O'Dare, and went on alone. Just a cop.

Just a cog in a machine. He reached his beat, opened the call-box, phoned in:

"O'Dare taking over, corner of Lincoln and Rogers."

Keefer, the man he was relieving, had a drunk on his hands. A drunk and a taxi-driver and an accusing meter. One of the pesty kind of drunks that persecute cops. It's that way more often than not, public belief to the contrary. A cop loathes running in a drunk, will lean over backward if he can possibly avoid it. For one thing, they're rarely held the next day, unless they've done something particularly overt. For another, it takes up the cop's time, he's got to appear to press the charge. It's a nuisance.

Keefer had a disgusted air, as though this had been going on a good ten minutes or more. "C'mon now," he said weariedly, "which pocket did you put it in? It must be in there somewhere! Give the man his money."

The drunk, legs splayed, hat teetering on the back of his head, was digging a thumb into a vest-pocket with somnambulistic slowness. Three or four others had their linings turned inside out. The taxi-driver sat by at his wheel, mum as a clam, aware that the gentry in dark-blue have no great love for his kind.

The drunk pulled the exploring thumb out, smote himself a devastating blow on the chest, bellowed indignantly: "I been robbed!" The dramatic emphasis was too great, he went off balance, sat down abruptly from the effect of his own Tarzan-wallop.

"I got a better idea," said O'Dare quietly. He picked him up by the feet instead of the collar, held his legs straight up in the air. "Catch his head so it don't bump," he warned his brother-officer. "Now, shake!" The drunk began to vibrate like someone with the palsy. Something chinked musically to the sidewalk under him, something else followed; there was a succession of pleasant tinkling metallic sounds.

"Holding out, huh?" Keefer said with feigned ferocity as they stood him up. "I oughta run you in!"

The drunk heaved with exaggerated dignity. "Never wash so insulted in my life!" he glowered.

"Now pay the man and get outa here, before I haul you in!" Keefer took a threatening step forward. The drunk scurried around the corner as though he were worked on pulleys. When Keefer turned to the cab-driver, however, his truculence was no longer assumed, it was the real thing. "Now y' got paid, get out o' here, gyp-artist! Y'oughta know better than take on a drunk for a fare in the first place! Don't lemme see y' around here no more, chiseler!"

The driver, meek as a lamb, took off his brake, glided away without a word.

"What's new?" O'Dare asked when they were alone.

———⋙✦⋘———

Keefer jerked his head despondently after the disappearing tail-light. "That's all I ever get. And I hadda get somebody's pet cat out of a flue for them around at 40 Spring awhile ago. I'd almost be willing to trade places with either of those guys." Which wasn't exactly true, and wasn't meant to be taken as such. O'Dare understood. Blowing off steam, they called it.

"Well, be good, Danny—see you t'morra."

"Yep." The footfalls died away. The night-silence descended, unbroken blocks of it, an occasional machine in the distance, a trolley taking a curve in High-C, only adding emphasis to it. The quiet of a sleeping city, that for complete suspension beats any country-quiet hollow.

Danny O'Dare was on duty.

He started down Lincoln, in and out of the store-entryways, testing the locks, peering through the glass fronts. He got to the other end of his beat, turned right, followed that street. A window was thrown up high above him, a window that showed black directly over one that showed orange. A lady of uncertain years thrust her head out, exclaimed with shattering audibility: "There's one now! Officer, officer—will you come up here please?"

He knew right away it wasn't going to be important; a cop can tell about those things—sometimes. She wasn't frightened, just sore. "What's the trouble, lady?"

"I want those people under me arrested! They keep playing their radio until all hours of the night. It's an outrage !"

"Sh, quiet, lady!" O'Dare reminded her. "You're making more noise than any radio yourself right this minute."

He sighed, went into the building, climbed two flights of stairs, knocked on a door. You could hardly hear it, she probably had a grudge. He liked the people at a glance, screwed up the side of his face good-naturedly. "Just tone it down a little," he advised. They offered him a drink. "I'll hold you to that when I'm off duty," he grinned, went down to the street again. A clock chimed the half-hour and he rang in from the call-box at the next intersection. "O'Dare, 25th and Main, nothing to report."

And then right away, as though just to give him the lie, there was.

It didn't seem like anything at first glance, anything at all. Just a car parked half-way down one of the side-streets, lights out. For all the life it showed, it might have been there all night. No violation in that. It wasn't on the main thoroughfare, wasn't near a hydrant or anything. If its owner lived in that building, he had a perfect right to leave it out all night instead of bedding it at a garage.

But, somehow, it didn't blend with its surroundings, with the building it was standing in front of, with the neighborhood as a whole. Even in the dimness, it was too high-class, too expensive a job, to look right hanging around here any length of time. It would have been more in keeping with Heinie Muller's beat, over around Rivercrest Heights.

I'm not trying to make a swami out of Danny O'Dare, but it's a fact that a cop has a definite instinct about that sort of thing, maybe even without realizing it. Just as he had known that that lady-crank had had nothing worth hearing to say to him out of the window just now, something about this car struck him as not being quite as guileless as it let on to be.

He had been in full sight of it when he rang the House just now from the corner. Had only spotted it as he finished closing the call-box. Some sort of a tension got to him from it, as he looked down toward it from where he was. As though somebody, either in it or nearby, were holding their breath, metaphorically speaking, waiting to see what his next move would be.

He continued on the way he'd been heading, crossed the mouth of the side-street and passed from view behind the opposite corner. Then he stopped, got up close to it, and stuck about half of one eye out beyond the building-line. He could have been dead wrong. It could have belonged to a swell who had a wren tucked away in this part of town. Its presence could have been explained by any one of a half-a-dozen things that were none of Danny O'Dare's business.

Then, while he hinged like that, a portion of a doorway-shadow detached itself and came further out into the open, became the out-line of a man who had been watching O'Dare, himself, from there—and now wanted to make sure he had gone! O'Dare drew that tiny sliver of his head back, paying him out a little more rope as it were.

The silhouette went over to the car; a brief, almost unnoticeable blat of its horn sounded. *Pip!* like that. Not just a signal of impa-tience, too short and quick for that—a warning signal, for some-body unseen within that building.

It was O'Dare's meat now. He had been the cause of that warning, and anyone that's afraid of a cop must have some reason for being afraid of a cop.

———◆———

The set-up was a particularly bad one; he realized that as he breasted the corner, came into full sight, and headed down on that car and its look-out. An ordinary man would have thought twice about bucking it, and then not bucked it. Which is why cops wear blue uniforms to distinguish them from ordinary men. He and the car and the street-light across the way formed a triangle. As he advanced, the street-light fell behind him. He had half a block to cover as a looming silhouette, silver radiance behind him, a target that a blind-man could hit. They—the car and its watchers—stayed safely shrouded in gloom. They could stop him long before he got there and he couldn't do a thing about it, wasn't even entitled to fire first until he was given the provocation. Tension had switched over to him now, had hold of every nerve. He thought of Molly, waiting at home, alone, helpless, going to present him with a Danny O'Dare Junior one of these fine days real soon now. Thought, but that was all. He didn't even try to protect himself by feigning casualness as he bore down. He wasn't using his beat-gait, was coming on at the quick pace of aroused suspicions.

Half-way to it now. The look-out had gotten in the car long ago, when he first revealed himself around the corner. But the door stayed invitingly open—like an invitation to sudden death. Metal glinted momentarily behind the glass above the dash, highlighted by the rays of the street-light far behind O'Dare. You couldn't even see the guy's face, just that warning glint of deadly weapon.

O'Dare had partially unlimbered himself, though the act was begging for the death-flash that was to come, closed in with his hand to his hip-bone. The odds, climbing as high against him as they could possibly have gone, now suddenly began to drop down again in his favor. He was in close now where he could do some damage himself; the guy had waited too long to drop him.

The car's gleaming bumper flashed past behind him, he was up to the door. The guy's face came into focus—and a little round knob pierced by a hole sighted over the top of that door into the middle of O'Dare's stomach. He was going to take him the hard way.

"Can it, Detroit!" a commanding voice cried warningly from the doorway, "I'll handle it, you jerk!"

The round knob with the black hole vanished, the door-top was just a straight line as though it had never been there. The glimmer of white face under the car-ceiling went "S-s-s!" through puckered lips and pinched nostrils like something letting off steam through a safety-valve. That's very bad for a killer's nerves, to be at firing-point and then be checked abruptly. Fiction-writers like to say they haven't any. It's really just the other way around; they're all nerves. O'Dare whirled, careless of whether he got it in the back or not.

Two men were hurrying out of the doorway, across the sidewalk to the pulsing car. O'Dare drew first, looked second to see if there was menace coming from that direction. There wasn't, at least not on the surface. The one in advance was stocky, short, matched the car. Sleek like it, glossy, important-looking. Fleecy vicuña coat with big headlight pearl-buttons flapping open as he strove to get there before anything regrettable happened. Furious, apparently, that it so very nearly had. Or maybe for other reasons that O'Dare hadn't divined as yet, having to do with his own happening along just when he had. At any rate—this sleek pudge—had his brakes off for a moment, spoke without thinking—as though O'Dare weren't present.

"Never one of *them!*" he barked hoarsely. "Don't you know any better than that? Never one of *them!*" He reached the running-board, swung a short right hook in under the low-slung roof of the car. The impact sounded as it hit the dim face lurking below.

Whock! "There's never anything that can't be straightened out if you use your head!" he raged on. A dark line was bisecting the chin of the face he had hit.

It was now O'Dare's turn. He saw no one else was coming out of the doorway. Neither of the two new arrivals made the slightest threat toward him. The second man, less conspicuously-dressed than the shorter one, stayed in the background, lighting a cigarette with four hands—the way they shook he seemed to have at least that many. But O'Dare wasn't forgetting that surreptitious gleam of metal behind the windshield, that bored knob atop the door. "Put up your hands!" he rasped into the car. "Step out here where I can get a look at you, and identify yourself! What was that you had sighted on me just now when I was coming up? Where is it?" His own gun was in the open now; not exactly pointed, but just there, ready.

<hr />

The man in the vicuña coat spoke, as though that were a short-cut out of an unpleasant misunderstanding. "He's my driver, brother, that's all," he explained blandly. "His name is Emmons, we call him Detroit because he comes from—"

O'Dare cut him short like a knife with: "I didn't ask you, I asked him!" The man had stepped out, palms up like somebody carrying a cafeteria-tray. The blood down the cleft of his chin had widened but was drying. He glanced at Vicuña-Coat quizzically, as though asking: "Why don't you stop this cop's foolishness?"

Vicuña-Coat seemed to think it was about time to. "I'm Benny Benuto," he said softly, and waited for that to get its work in.

It didn't seem to. O'Dare didn't even flick his eyes over at him, kept them on the driver. "Where is it?" he growled. He missed seeing the brief pantomime. The second man gave Benuto a brief, inquiring look, hand idly fingering the lapel of his coat within grabbing distance of his own left shoulder. The look might have meant: "Want me to give it to him? He's holding us up." Benuto answered with a negative shake of the head, a contemptuous curl of the lip, as though: "What, this harness cop? Leave him to me!"

He said aloud to O'Dare, "You don't seem to understand, brother. I said I'm Benny Benuto."

Again O'Dare didn't hear, apparently. The driver had handed over the gun, a brutal-looking thing all steel and a yard wide. O'Dare pocketed it. "License?" he snapped.

Benuto cut in reassuringly, "He's got one, brother. I wouldn't let him carry it if he—"

"He better have!"

He did. O'Dare scanned it by the light of the dash, which he had ordered cut on. All Jake, nothing phony about it. He jabbed it back to him reluctantly.

Benuto was soaping him, "You see, he's a sort of bodyguard of mine as well as driver; a little fidgety like all such guys are. Must have mistook you for some kind of footpad in the dark and—"

O'Dare at long last gave him his undivided attention. If he'd placed him by now, you wouldn't have known it by any change in his voice or manner, any creeping-in of deference. "The corner-light was on me the whole way up," he said tersely. "He saw me at the call-box even before that! I take it you don't live here, Mr. Benuto? You can explain your presence in this building at this hour, can you?"

Benuto seemed to be trying hard to control himself. "Would you mind giving me your name, officer?"

"Answer my question!" O'Dare yelled loudly in his face. "I don't care who you are, if you're the biggest big-shot in town!"

"Oh, then you *do* know who I am." Benuto smiled a little dangerously. "That should make it much simpler. Sure, glad to answer your question, Officer 4432." He repeated the numerals on O'Dare's shield aloud. The other man in the background was scribbling them down. "I just dropped in to visit an old friend. Well, I found out he doesn't live here any more—"

O'Dare's eyes involuntarily went up the face of the house. It was changing right while he looked. A whole half-floor went suddenly orange, or rather the windows did. A minute later the other half followed suit. Then the one below. It was waking up from top to bottom. One of the sashes went up and a frightened-looking young woman peered down at the group by the car. She seemed to be about to say something, when abruptly a man standing behind her in the room clasped his hand to her mouth, pulled her in again. His voice carried down to the sidewalk just before he slapped the sash down again: "Stay out of it! What's matter wit' yuh? Wanna get in trouble?"

A woman suddenly appeared in the street-doorway, distracted, dazed, staggering, clad only in her night-dress, blood down the front of it. "Johnny!" she was groaning, hands pressed to her forehead. "Johnny! What've they done to you?"

O'Dare took a step toward her. A steely-grip suddenly shot out, held him fast by the upper arm. "I wanna talk to you!" All the suavity was gone from Benuto. He meant business.

The woman had sat down on the top doorstep just as she was, huddled there clasping her knees, rocking back and forth like some lost soul. "Johnny! I knew this would happen to you! You wouldn't listen to me! Johnny!"

———◆———

Benuto's voice was a harsh whisper in his ear. "Now, before you get any ideas in your head, listen to me, brother! Use the old bean. We heard some trouble going on in one of the flats up there— somebody getting his from somebody. That's why we got out in a hurry. We didn't want to get mixed up in it. I *still* don't—do you get me? And here's how much I don't—step down this way." He led O'Dare a step or two to the rear of the car, just out of the line of vision of his two henchmen. "Tact" is what Benny Benuto would have called that if asked for a definition.

Danny O'Dare had never seen a thousand-dollar bill before. He saw five of them now, as they went into his uniform-pocket one by one. Benuto took good care that he should, let each one focus without blurring, yet without being too blatant about it. "Just a token of good-will," he said. "You know where you can find me, drop around tomorrow or next day, and I'll match them for you. All you gotta do is just forget I happened to drop around here at the same time this was happening. Everybody else is getting theirs. Get yours, brother. Be up-to-date. Your looey is a pretty good pal of mine. Maybe I can do you some good, 4432."

He thought of Molly and the kid they were expecting, for the second time that night. What a lot of difference ten-grand can make in this world! Get his, everybody else was—Through the blur of his thoughts he heard himself saying: "There's blood on your shirtfront, Benuto. There's blood on that other guy's hand too, I saw it when he lit a butt—"

"That's from hitting my driver in the nose," Benuto said softly, "You saw me do it." He flicked the back of his hand familiarly against the pocket that held the five-thousand. "You saw me do it," he repeated slowly. "Ask the jane. Call her over here and ask her—and then let me get out of this mess."

O'Dare had to drag her forward bodily. She kept trying to dig her naked feet into the sidewalk intersection-lines, resisting, holding back in mortal terror. "What happened upstairs? Who got hurt?"

She was almost incoherent with grief—and something else besides. "My Johnny! They came after him! He went to the door, I stayed in bed. They locked me in there. I heard them, I heard them doing it! Right in my arms he—" She spread out her nightdress like a pitiful child showing a mud-stain. "Look."

"Who?" O'Dare said.

"Somebody. I don't know."

"Look at these two men. Was it either of these two men?" Benuto and the other one just stood there, smiling slightly.

She went nearly wild with fear, began to thresh about trying to free herself, swung all the way around O'Dare backwards until she faced the other way, straining away from him like something on a leash. "Lemme go! Lemme go, oh please! No, I never saw them before! I don't know who it was! I tell you I don't know!"

Benuto said "See?" You could hardly hear the word, just a lisp on his tongue. He turned, took an abrupt step; the other man went with him. The car-door cracked smartly. The tuned-up engine bellowed out. Benuto's voice topped it. "Be seeing you, brother!" The Isotta-Fraschini telescoped itself into a swirling red tail-light that seemed to spin concentrically as it receded.

O'Dare half-raised his gun at it; held it that way at a forty-five-degree angle from the ground. One foot stamped forward a pace. The other wouldn't follow. $10,000. Three and a third weary years of pounding pavements, trying door-latches, that represented. Forty solid months of it, twelve-hundred days. In rain and snow and slush; in below-zero numbness and blistering dog-days. And the accrued earnings of all that plodding drudgery were his in the space of five minutes, without lifting a finger. Just by forgetting a name. A name that it wouldn't do him any good to remember, a name that counted for more than the numerals 4432 in high places. A name that could send him to a worse beat than this one even, out by the river shore where the ash heaps were. A wife home that he didn't want to watch grow ugly and old, wrestling with pots all her life. A kid coming that he wanted to be someone, to send to college some day. Who gave a rap about them, but him? Who gave a rap about him, but himself? Others were getting theirs, why shouldn't he get his? The modern way, the up-to-date way.

He ground the heel of his left hand in, above his eyes, letting go of the woman. She slumped down like a clawing, groveling animal, around the leg that hadn't moved forward. The red tail elongated into a comet, turned the corner. A prowl car passed it, going slowly the other way, ebbed from sight.

O'Dare yanked out his whistle, gave it a blast. He put his gun away and picked the woman up with both arms. "You *do* know who did it, don't you?" he asked without looking down into her face. "You're afraid to tell!"

"Johnny!" she moaned. "Johnny!" Her head was hanging downwards over his elbow. "What's the difference who did it? He's gone now! *You* can't bring him back, you guy with the badge!"

The prowl-car backed up, turned in, shot down toward them, stopped on a dime. The one on O'Dare's side leaned out. "There's a guy just been beaten to death in that building," O'Dare said with a jerk of his head. He carried her in without waiting, up the stairs. "Which door is it?" he panted.

The house was unnaturally still from top to bottom; light threading from under every door, floor-boards creaking under tip-toed footsteps, but not a face showing outside. Self-preservation working overtime.

He set her down on her feet and she groped along the wall, wavering toward the right door. It was open, anyway.

"Those guys did it, didn't they?" he said a second time.

"Why should I tell you?" she shuddered. "Who can help me? Who? Everyone in the house must have heard him groaning, must have heard me pleading for him through that locked door. Nobody would come near us to help us. What a world this is!"

"Why didn't you scream for help?"

"I was afraid that would kill him even quicker."

He turned and went in. The lights were on, from when the dead man had answered the door. It was pretty fierce. The assistant medical examiner's full report, later, was to be something unique in the municipal records: there was not an unfractured bone or group of bones in the man's entire body! All the legs were off four otherwise undamaged chairs, and all sixteen of those, in turn, were broken—some of them three or four times. They must have stayed in there quite some time.

<hr/>

The woman kept trying to come in and he wouldn't let her, kept her out in the hall. Finally one of the neighbors got up enough courage to show up outside, took her in with them, gave her some whiskey or something. Her sobs, when she finally thawed, came thinly through the door—a little bit like that cat must have sounded Keefer said he'd rescued from a flue. O'Dare thought: "I got someone loves me like that too." He touched his pocket; paper crackled.

One of the prowl-car men's name was Anderson, the other was Josephs. O'Dare knew them both. "Some job," Anderson remarked. O'Dare kept looking down at what was left of the guy. Maybe it was that. The woman's mewing kept coming in. Maybe it was that. Or maybe it was that he hadn't thought quickly, clearly enough down below on the street when that red tail spurted for the corner. Just before the decks got there he blurted out: "Benny Benuto and one of his hoods were leaving just as I got to the door."

They both looked at him, looked away, again. Anderson said warningly out of the corner of his mouth: "Pipe down! Are you crazy, O'Dare?" They glanced at each other understandingly. "Who are you, to buck—things? D'ya want your beat shoved so far out y' gotta commute to get to it? D'ya want just empty pin-marks left on your coat? You're no rookie, kid. Take a tip from us, shut your yap. Don't tackle—"

Two dicks came hustling up the stairs into the room. "Whew! Hamburger!" one let out. An inspector arrived, minutes later. O'Dare said in answer to his questioning: "I didn't hear anything, but there was a suspicious-looking car standing out front, numbered 6M58-4O. A man who identified himself as Benny Benuto came running out of the house with another man just as I got up to it. There was blood on his shirt-front."

"Then why did you let him get away?" asked the inspector.

O'Dare looked unflinchingly at him. He said slowly, "He gave me five thousand dollars to forget I'd seen him here, jumped in the car. Here it is." He opened his hand. It held ten pieces of paper, five bills torn in half. They all fell down on the floor as he dropped his hand to his side.

The inspector said, "Send out an alarm for Benny Benuto. He's to be picked up for questioning, on suspicion of murder, along with two other men, Detroit Emmons and Wally Furst." He pointed to the torn bills. "Pick that up and seal it in an envelope, to be presented as evidence at the arraignment—if there is one."

"If," somebody unidentifiable in the room piped very low.

One of the dicks murmured dryly as he brushed by O'Dare: "I wouldn't want to be in *your* shoes, cop!"

Josephs, going down the stairs with O'Dare, said: "You'll find out. He'll meet himself coming out, he'll spring so fast! He bounces like a tennis-ball off a racket." When they got to the prowl, he picked a newspaper out of the door pocket; handed it to him. "Better start getting familiar with the Help-Wanted ads."

O'Dare said grimly: "He'll bounce like a cannon-ball, once I get my two-cents-worth in. The woman up there can identify him, if they'll only get it out of her. There's a man and woman on the floor below must have seen something too. She tried to—" Something started coming over the car-set right while they were standing there talking next to it. "Calling Cars 15 and 8, Cars 15 and 8. Go to 50 Diversey Place. 50 Diversey Place. Third floor front. A woman has been reported abducted. A woman has been reported abducted. That is—"

The unintentional irony of it, that: "That is all!"

"Not our party," Anderson was saying.

O'Dare had hold of the car-door in a funny way, as if he were drunk or had just tripped over something against the curb.

"What's matter with you?" A peculiar hollow sound came from his chest. "I live there. That's my wife's and my—flat."

"Hang on!" Josephs snapped. They swung off so quick they nearly took him off his feet along with them. He jumped, clung there on the running-board, crouched a little to meet the wind. Just before they skidded around the corner, two of the dicks came out of the house, bringing with them the dead man's wife and the couple from the floor below, all of whom O'Dare had indicated as possible witnesses. He wouldn't have known them at the moment if they'd stared him in the face. "Make it a mistake," he prayed in the teeth of the wind. "Not Molly!"

<hr>

They screeched to a stop in front of where he'd started out from four hours before, with her waving goodby from the third-floor window. There were too many lights lit for three in the morning. The whole face of the building was blinking with them, like that other house they'd just come away from. He knew then, beyond shadow of a doubt. Something was wrong, something had happened here. It was written all over the place to his cop's-eye. One of the assigned cars was there already ahead of them.

He jumped down and went at the door like someone stumbling off-balance, shoulders way ahead of his feet. Josephs and Anderson—who'd come out of bounds to bring him here—lit out again around the next corner. Mrs. Kramer, a floor below his, head a mass of curl-papers, was standing in her doorway discussing it with the woman across the hall. Their voices dropped as tragedy in a blue uniform went hurtling by. Not low enough.

"That's him now. Poor soul, they were going to—"

"Did you see that look in his eye? He'll kill them if he ever—"

The two men from Car 15 were talking to the super, who had a sweater over his pajamas, just outside O'Dare's own door. He elbowed the two aside, grabbed the man by the shoulders, began to shake the life out of him. "How'd it happen? What'd they look like?"

The other two pried his hands away tactfully. "He don't know, he didn't see them. How can he talk anyway when you're turning him into an egg-nog?"

"Say that when it happens to you, McKee." O'Dare said bitterly.

"I happened to be up, reading. I heard her call out in the hall, just once. Your name, 'Danny!' Like that. My wife had told me about—and I thought maybe she was sick, needed help. Right down by the street-door, it sounded. Time I got there, I didn't see anyone, just heard a car driving away outside, that was all."

O'Dare brushed by them, went in to look. There wasn't anything to see, but he didn't want them to see his eyes. They dried right up again, from the slow, fine rage that was beginning to set in. The super sidled up to him, sidestepping the others momentarily.

"And there was this," he whispered. "On the sill. I thought I better show it to you first, by yourself."

YOUR MEMORY PLAYED YOU A BAD TRICK, DIDN'T IT, TONIGHT?
MAYBE THIS WILL HELP IT SOME

the note said. O'Dare turned slowly and showed it to the others. "Benuto did it." And shaking with a terrible, quiet sort of intensity, "If they bring him in tonight—!"

The inspector who had been over at the other place had shown up. "They just brought him in. I got the flash on my way over here."

"Where've they got him? Where've they got him?" O'Dare cried out wildly.

"Holding him over at one of the outlying precincts, without booking him, so his mouth can't jump right in and haul him out—"

The phone started ringing in the room there with them. The inspector motioned to O'Dare to go ahead.

"Yeah, this is Patrolman O'Dare," they heard him say.

The voice said, "It's ten minutes past three, O'Dare. We'll give you one hour. If the gent you've framed isn't released from wherever it is he's being held by ten past four, you know the answer, don't you?"

O'Dare said, "No, I don't—" Suddenly his face went the color of clay, he jolted there as though the instrument had short-circuited him. Molly's voice sobbed in his ear: "Dan, what're they doing this for? What've we done to them—?"

A line of beads came out across his eyebrows. "Where are you, quick, where are you?" he said rabidly. But she was gone already. "Not a chance," the first voice said. "Still claim you don't know the answer?"

O'Dare said, "I'm only a cop. What can I do? He's in the hands of the homicide squad—"

"You put him there, you—!" the voice snarled. "You better correct that identification of yours in a hurry. Or maybe you'd like some changes made around the house—a crepe on the door, f'rinstance? One hour." The connection broke.

———◈———

The inspector, when he'd told him, said: "We'd better get over there in a hurry, see that he's turned out. Always can pick him up again later."

"Not always," thought O'Dare bitterly. And the next time he'd have a whole battery of legal talent short-stopping him. This wasn't the way to bring her back, anyway. He'd never be able to look her in the face again if he let himself be blackmailed into— He went running down the stairs after the inspector, sprinted for the running-board; they didn't say anything. He was a man before he was a cop, after all.

Benuto was in the basement of an out-of-the-way suburban precinct-house, where they rarely handled anything more than traffic violations. If they'd begun sweating him already, he didn't look it; sat there glowering in the corner on a stool. He was, they admitted to the inspector, a hard nut to crack. They hadn't gotten anywhere much.

"His crowd are holding this man's wife, we have reason to believe," the inspector said. "Afraid we'll have to pull in our horns for the time being."

"Lemme talk to him," O'Dare pleaded. "Lemme talk to him alone! Lemme just find out where they've got her! Gimme a break."

The inspector nodded. One of the dicks took the precaution of slipping O'Dare's gun out of its holster first, then they let him go in there by himself. He closed the door. The walls were thick down in that basement. That was why they brought suspects down there for questioning. They couldn't hear a sound for awhile. In about ten minutes O'Dare stuck his disheveled-head out and asked for the loan of a fountain-pen. One of the dicks passed him his.

"You mean you're getting him to sign?"

"I'm not asking him about the murder," O'Dare said quietly. "Just my wife, now." He went in again. When he came out a second time he was wiping off the gold nib of the pen by pinching it between his fingers. He returned it to the lender. Beyond him, in the murky room, Benuto lay on the floor in a dead faint. Ink discolored his fingernails, there was a purple blob of it in underneath each one. It was O'Dare, not he, who was doing the shaking, as though it had been pretty much of a strain.

Three pairs of eyes sought his questioningly.

"He told me," he said very low, and wiped the back of his hand across his forehead. "They've got her in a refrigerating-plant out at Brierfield. He told them to take her there, in case he was picked up."

"How d'ya know he told you the truth?" one of them said, which was just the dick in him being superior to a mere cop in matters of this kind.

"I let him tell me three times before I paid any attention," O'Dare explained simply. "Three times running it must be the truth; his brain was too busy blowing out fuses to think up a stall, anyway. I read about some Japs doing that, only yesterday in the paper. Gimme back my gun," he wound up somberly, "I'm going over there and get her back."

"We'll get her back for you," one of the dicks promised, "now that we know where—"

"I'll do my own getting back." O'Dare's voice rose. "Gimme back my gun. I'm facing suspension anyway, for going off my beat while on duty. Don't try to stop me, any of you; I'm going, with my gun or without it—!"

"We're not trying to stop you," the inspector said. "Give him his gun. Go with him, McKee. The rest of us'll follow. Wait there out of sight for further orders, you two. Don't make a move until we size the place up. This woman's life is at stake."

"And we've got thirty-five minutes," O'Dare said bitterly.

Brierfield lay across the river—which made it an interstate

death-penalty kidnaping and put her in just that much more jeopardy of her life. Since they got top prices whether they killed her or not, there was every inducement for them to do away with her rather than be caught with the goods. O'Dare was cursing the day they were born.

⟾◆⟸

McKee ran the car out along the river-drive, with its siren cut off; past the stony cliff-dwellings where Benuto himself lived and had been picked up, past the desolate ash-dumps further on that were the rewards of demotion on the force. They crossed the interstate bridge, slithered through four o'clock, dead-to-the-world, downtown Brierfield, which was just a little annex to the Big Town, and came out beyond in a barren region of scattered breweries, warehouses, and packing-plants. The side-streets quit but the main highway ran on. McKee slowed a little, doused the lights. They skimmed along like a little mechanical metal beetle over the macadam. "They coming?" he asked.

O'Dare wasn't interested, didn't even bother looking to see. "Acme Refrigerating Plant it's called," he said. "Keep watching. He owns it—one of his lousy rackets."

McKee slowed to a crawl as the outline of a sprawling concrete structure up ahead began topping a rise of the road. A single dreary arc-light shining down on the highway, bleached one side of it; the rest was just a black cut-out against the equally-black night-sky. Stenciled lettering ran the length of the side that faced the highroad, but too foreshortened by the angle at which they were looking to be decipherable. McKee went over to the side with a neat little loop of the wheel, stopped dead—and soundlessly. O'Dare gestured to him, got out, went up ahead to look. "Keep out of that arc-light," McKee whispered.

The cop came back again in a minute. "Sure," he said. "I can make out the first two letters, A and C, and that's enough." He looked back the other way, for the first time. "What'd they do, lose their way?"

McKee got out, eased the car-door closed after him. O'Dare couldn't stand still, took his gun out, put it away, took it out, put it away. "What time y'got?" he almost whimpered. Not a moving thing showed on the long arc-lit ribbon of road they had come over.

McKee hadn't been there when the phone-call was made to O'Dare. "Five after four," he answered incautiously.

"Damn them! They'll kill her!" the agonized cop rasped out. He meant the strangely-delayed follow-up party. He lurched away from the car, struck out alone toward the ominously-quiet building up ahead.

"Hey! Wait!" McKee hissed after him desperately, "Don't do that, you fool—!" He took a quick step after him, grabbed him, tried to haul him back to the car. They had a brief, wordless struggle there by the roadside, gravel spitting out from under their scuffling shoes. O'Dare, crazed, swung out with all his might at the dick. The blow caught him on the under-side of the jaw. McKee went down, sprawling on his back. O'Dare's gun was out again, he stood there crouched over him for an instant. "I'm going in there—*now*, d'ya hear me? I'll put a bullet in you if you try to stop me again!" He turned and went toward the concrete hulk, bent double, moving along the roadside with surprising swiftness for a man his weight and height. Like an Indian runner.

Caution, concealment, was a thing of the past. His stumbling footfalls echoed in the stillness of that place like drumbeats. Behind him the road, which he could no longer see, stretched empty all the way back into Brierfield. What was that to him, whether they came now or didn't? In, that was all he wanted, in! He came up to the cold, rough walls, padded against them with one bare hand outstretched to guide himself as he ran along beside them.

The entrance was around on the side, a darker patch in the dark wall that turned solid as he got up to it. Vast and huge, to admit and disgorge trucks, impregnably barred, the lidded bulb over it screwed off so that it was dark. He was like a tormented pygmy dancing up and down there, raging helpless in front of its huge dimensions. Even McKee didn't come up to help him. Maybe he'd knocked him out.

There weren't any openings at all within reach of the ground. Higher up, at about third-story level, there was a row of embrasures paned with corrugated glass. He ran down the rest of its length, turned the corner to the back, looking desperately for an outside ammonia-pipe, drain-pipe, anything that would offer a way up. Nothing broke the cream-smooth surface of the concrete, for a length of half a city-block. But there was something else there, a black shape standing out from it. The car in which they'd brought her here, left outside ready for their quick get-away once Benuto was turned loose and they'd gotten rid of their encumbering hostage. O'Dare recognized it. The same hefty Isotta Benuto had gone out to do murder in earlier that night! They must have dropped him off at his own place, then gone straight to O'Dare's flat to get her, then come direct out here.

———◆———

He got up on the convexed roof, balanced there erect, saw that even that way he couldn't reach the height of those embrasures. He jumped down again, got in. They'd left the key in it, so ready were they to start at hair-trigger timing—maybe pick up Benuto at some prearranged place along the way to save time.

He turned it up, roared out away from the walls in a big semi-circle, careless whether they heard or not. Over grass and sliding sand and stones, that rocked but didn't impede it. You only had to handle it to understand why some cars are made in Turin too. Not all are made in Detroit. He wheeled in toward the plant again, straightened out, came at that door diagonally from away off there in the open, fifty yards away, in high. He slid down the seat onto his kidneys, braced his feet. There was a jar that went up his back, exploding in his brain like a blue flash, a boom like a cannon; glass went flying up like powdered sugar from the headlights or something, came down again on the read-end of the roof with a sound like rain—but the car ducked in away from it before it was even finished falling. There was electric light inside, rows of dim spaced bulbs that showed an inner wall rushing at him. He was still stunned, but managed to kick his foot down. The car bucked, went into the wall anyway, but with a less severe jolt than the first time. Behind him, the big doorway looked somewhat like those beaded string-curtains used in the tropics.

He wanted to stay there, sit there under the front wheel, and just ache. He had a headache and a sprained back and the pit of his stomach felt like a mule had kicked him, and his mouth was gritty with tooth-enamel. A disembodied thought, "Molly!" came to him from far away. He didn't know what it meant just then, but did what it seemed to want him to. Got one of the buckled doors open and crawled out hands-first. Just as his chin got to the ground and his feet came clear, a gorgeous sunburst of yellow beamed out from the car-engine, and an instant later a towering pillar of flame was shooting sky-high from it. It stung him and he jerked away from it side-wise along the floor, but the pain brought him to, he got up on his knees.

Feet came pounding, but not from the busted front door, from another direction, going toward it. On the opposite side of the curtain of flame. A voice cried shrilly about its hum: "I don't know who was in it, don't bother looking! Get out quick—give it to 'em with the tommy if they try to stop us outside!"

A figure flashed by from behind the furnace-glow heading for the open door, carrying something in front of it. A second one was right behind it. O'Dare snatched his gun out, did his best to steady his wrist but couldn't wait to make sure. "Hold it!" he yelled. Both figures whirled. The second one, with a bared revolver, slightly telescoping the first, with a sub-machine! He saw then that the warning had just been a medieval anachronism on his part, instantly fired first before they had, from where he was, on his knees. It was the second one went down, not the one with the tommy. He'd cleared the way for it, that was all. He dropped flat on his face in a nose-dive, as though there were water under him, not cement-flooring.

It was popping, and something that sounded like horizontal rain was hissing by above him. Then it broke off again after about two rounds, and he raised his face from the little pool of blood the nose-bleed he'd given himself had formed under it. The guy was on top of the weapon, shaped like a tent, bending too far forward over it, blocking it with his own body from O'Dare. Then he straightened out in a flat line along the floor, and McKee came in from outside holding a feather of smoke in his fist. He spread his legs and stepped over him.

"Got him, didn't I ?" he said almost absent-mindedly. "First time I ever shot a man in the back!" Then taking in O'Dare's blood-filmed face, "Great guns! you're a goner! Shot your puss off—"

"I hit it on the floor ducking!" snapped the cop impatiently. "What was you doing, picking daisies out there the last two hours ?"

McKee held the side of his jaw. "I took a nap on the road. Next time don't be so—"

⬥

The blaze from the car was collapsing into itself, turning red. O'Dare ran around it, past the dick and in toward where they had come from just now. An arctic blast hit him in the face. There was a long corridor, it seemed to stretch for miles, lined on both sides with gleaming white refrigerator-doors. Dazzling, like a snow-scene, each door big enough to take whole beeves in at a time. He ran down to the far end of it, turned, came back along a second one. "Molly!" he yelled, "Molly!" and then a sudden premonition freezing him, screamed it like an inmate of a madhouse. "Molly!" The sound of his own voice rang mockingly back in the vast, cold, empty place. "They've done away with her! She's in one of these things, I know it!"

There was a sudden scampering of fugitive footsteps somewhere nearby. He heard McKee, in the next aisle over, stop short, call out, and dart back the other way, as though chasing someone. O'Dare's yells changed as he too raced toward the sound, hidden from him by the towering row of refrigerators. "McKee! Don't shoot him—whoever he is! He's the only one can tell us where she—! *Don't shoot!*"

And then, in despairing finality, a gun cracked out there where the car was. Just once.

There was a third prostrate figure this side of the other two when he got there, head toward the door in arrested flight. McKee was standing stock-still, looking down. The inspector and the rest, who had just gotten there, were coming in from outside.

O'Dare flung himself down on the still form like a long-lost brother, tried to sit it up.

"He's dead," a voice said, "Whaddya wanta do that for?"

"I didn't do it," McKee said, white, "they got him from outside, like I did the first one."

"She's in one of them ice-boxes, I tell ya!" O'Dare screeched, "Now we'll never find out which one—!"

The inspector barked, "Get in there quick, you men! Open 'em up—" A sudden mass-panic gripped them, horror was on their faces as they rushed forward in a body.

It was O'Dare who sighted the thing, with seconds that were centuries pounding at his maddened brain. Didn't know how he had for the rest of his life. A little fleck of color down the long dazzling-white of that vista, a tiny thing, a mote, a dot. Green. Smaller than the smallest new leaf in May. The edge of a dress caught in the airtight crevice between ponderous refrigerator-door and refrigerator. A thing that in another age they would have called a miracle; that still was a miracle in this 1937, call it what they might.

They got it open and she slumped into their arms, lips blue, fingernails broken, in the bright-green dress he'd kidded her so for buying only a week before. (She still has it; he won't let her wear it, but he won't let her give it away either. He touches it to bring him luck, keep them from misfortune, every time he goes out on duty—as a *detective, third grade.*)

She opened her eyes in the car, going back, and smiled up at the blood-caked face bending over her. "It was so cold in there and dark, and I couldn't breathe any more. It was just a dream, wasn't it, Danny? Just a dream and I'm awake now?"

"It was just a dream," Officer 4432 said, holding his wife close in his arms.

AFTERWORD TO "BLUE IS FOR BRAVERY"

"Blue Is for Bravery" (*Detective Fiction Weekly*, February 27, 1937), which had been submitted as "The Police Are Always With Us," is rather short and almost plotless but full of action and desperate urgency and with a viewpoint rare indeed for Woolrich. As Danny goes berserk and careens across the nightscape in a race against time and death, for once our reaction to a Noir Cop is undivided and we are completely and uncritically behind torture, mayhem and whatever else is done by a protagonist with a badge.

You Bet Your Life

He was a wise guy. He'd had one Collins too many, but even without that he still would have been a wise guy. He had too much money, that was the whole trouble with him. No, that wasn't it either; he had an offensive way of showing he had too much money. Get the difference? Always knew everything. That type. Ready to bet any amount on anything, at the drop of a hat. On whether the next pretty girl to come down the street would be a blonde or a brunette. On which of two given lumps of sugar would attract a fly first.

Money talks, they say. His always drowned out the other fellow's argument. He'd put up stakes he knew the other fellow couldn't afford, most of the time. Leaving him a choice of backing down or being taken for a thorough cleaning. His money had a habit of putting the other fellow in the wrong either way; making a liar out of him or showing him up for a welsher. I'm convinced he would have caught cold without a big fat overstuffed wallet for a chest-protector. He was always making round trips in and out of his pocket, with a flourish and a hard slap down and a challenging bellow. And the way he hounded them afterwards until he'd collected what was coming to him, you'd think he really needed the money. He was the one usually on the collecting end too, poetic justice to the contrary. He didn't have a real gambler's instincts. Apart from a few side-bets of the type I've mentioned above, he almost always picked a sure thing. Not much of a sport, when it came right down to it. The dislike, the spark of animosity his overbearing ways always aroused, was what got his bets taken up for him more often than not. Case of the poor slobs cutting their noses to spite their faces, just because they hated his insides so. He steered clear of professionals, seldom bet on sporting events. If I hadn't known he'd been born wealthy; was lousy with money— and lousy without it too—I would have suspected him of making a nice living out of this nasty little pastime of his. But there wasn't even that excuse for it. And yet he put the screws on worse than a loan shark, using a man's reputation and self-respect among his friends as a bludgeon to make them pay through the nose.

There was a story around town, never substantiated, that he was indirectly to blame for one high-strung young chap putting an end to himself, to forestall discovery of a defalcation that had been the result of his topheavy "obligation" to this Fredericks. I wouldn't have put it past him.

I'm one of those lucky people that nothing ever happens to; that are always the bystander. I was the bystander that night that this happened, at the 22 Club, too. Fredericks had never tackled me. Maybe he sensed a detached amusement that baffled him. He could have waved that famous wallet in front of my nose till it wore out and it wouldn't have done him any good. He knew enough not to try it.

———◆◆◆———

I came into the 22 with Trainor, and we saw Fredericks there swilling Collinses. He came over to our table, and there was a minimum of conversation for a while. I wanted to walk out again, but he was between the two of us and I couldn't get Trainor's eye.

The radio over the bar was giving dramatized news events, and the highlight of them was the description of the capture of a long-wanted murderer, cornered at last after being hunted high and low for months. The case, which we all remembered well, was finally closed.

The commentator was good, played it up for all it was worth. It got you. You couldn't hear a sound in the place until he'd finished. Then we all took a deep breath together.

"There, but for the grace of God," Fredericks remarked drily, "go you or I or any one of us."

Trainor gave him a look. "Thanks for the compliment, but I don't class myself as a potential murderer. Nor does Evans here, I'm sure."

"Everyone is," Fredericks said loftily. "Every man you see standing around you in this bar is. It's the commonest impulse there is, we all have it. It's latent in all of us, every man-jack. All it's waiting for is a strong enough motive to come to the surface and—bang!" He drained his glass, started to warm up. "Why, I can pick any two men at random, outside on the street, who have nothing against each other, who've never even seen each other before; you give them a powerful enough motive, and one'll turn into a potential murderer, the other his potential victim, right before your eyes!"

He was feeling his drinks, I guess. He wasn't showing them, but he must have been feeling them, or he'd never have said a thing like that.

I tried to catch Trainor's eye, via the bar mirror, to pull him out of it. But his dislike was already showing in his face. He was past the extrication stage.

"You're crazy," he said, with white showing around his mouth. "Normal people aren't murderers, and you can't make them into murderers, I don't care what motive, what provocation, you give them! Understand me, I'm talking about cold-blooded, premeditated murderers now, like this beauty we were just hearing about. What the law recognizes as intentional premeditated murder. Crimes of passion, committed in the heat of the moment, aren't on the carpet right now. What it takes to perpetrate a premeditated murder is a diseased mind. That's what this guy they just caught had; that's what every murderer always has. That's why normal people cannot be made into murderers. I don't care what motive you give them. Your two hypothetical men on the street, who have nothing against each other, don't even know each other, would knock your theory into a cocked hat!"

I spoke for the first time. "Let's change the subject," I suggested mildly. "Murder is nothing to talk about on a lovely evening like this."

They neither of them paid any attention. There was a current of antagonism flowing between them that wouldn't let either one back down.

Fredericks fumbled in his inner pocket. I knew what was coming next. I'd seen the gesture often enough before to know it by heart. I tried to hold his arm down, and he shook my hand off.

Out came the well known wallet with the gold clips on each corner; down it whipped on top of the bar. People looked over at us. Fredericks said, "I'll bet you a thousand dollars right now any two men picked at random on the street outside can be turned into potential murderer and potential victim, by me, right while you're looking on! I'll let you do the selecting, and I'll let you name the time-limit. And I'll give you any odds you want on it."

I knew Trainor's financial position. I gave him the eye across the back of Fredericks' neck. "Hundred-to-one shot, ten bucks," I suggested flippantly, trying to keep the thing theoretical.

Maybe Fredericks knew Trainor's financial position too. "I don't make ten-dollar bets," he said nastily. "What are you trying to do, find an easy out for him? People that haven't the courage to back up their conviction shouldn't be so quick to air their opinions. I'll give him two-to-one, his thousand against two of mine. Well, how about it?" he sneered. "Are you in—or have you suddenly decided that maybe you agree with me after all?"

That was no way to put it. Trainor could have refused to have any part in the fantastic proposition, without it necessarily meaning that he retracted his opinions. But Fredericks always managed to put it in that false light. I'd seen it happen time and again. This time I happened to be the only witness, instead of the usual group, but it had the same effect as far as Trainor was concerned. If there's one thing any man detests it's seeming to back down.

"I'll take you up on that," he growled. "This is one time I'm going to show you up! It may take you down a little to lose a couple of grand, and it's certainly worth it! You've bet on a sure thing again—but for once you've picked the wrong end of it!"

<hr />

Fredericks was shuffling hundred-dollar bills out of the moire lining of his wallet, as though he was dealing cards. He put his empty Collins glass down on top of them. "This says I haven't!"

Trainor said cuttingly, "I haven't that much on me, I don't usually walk around as though I expected to have to bail myself out of jail. I'll make out a check, will that be all right? Endorse it to you, if—and when."

I hadn't thought they'd go this far. "Say, listen," I protested, "you don't want to win that money, Fredericks. If you do, it means a human life's been taken. Isn't that the test?"

"We can keep it from going quite that far," he assured me. "Just so long as the *intention* to commit murder is unmistakably shown by one or the other of our two hypothetical men. We can interfere at the last minute to prevent it being carried out. But there must be no reasonable doubt, before we do so, that it's already fairly under way, premeditated by one of the two. Is that satisfactory to you, Trainor?"

"Why shouldn't it be? There's absolutely no danger of things going that far—always providing these two have never seen one another before; have no long-standing grievance or bad blood between them. And to keep you from building up any grudge between them, that might fester, corrode and sicken their minds, which would invalidate my argument, I'm going to give you the shortest possible time: one week from tonight. This is Tuesday. Next Tuesday night, at this same time, you and I and Evans will meet here. If one of the two men whom I am about to select—with your approval—has in the mean-time made an attempt to take the life of the second one, and there is no possible mistaking it as such, I'll endorse this check over to you. If not, that two thousand dollars is mine. And I'm sorry, but any move you make, any contact you have with these two, by way of injecting what you call a 'motive' between them, must take place in the pres-ence of Evans and myself, or the bet is off."

"You'll both be eyewitnesses to the mechanics of the thing," Fredericks promised. "Nothing will be done behind your back. There won't be any bad faith in this. We're all gentlemen, I hope."

I spoke up sourly. "I got my doubts. You're both vultures in tuxedos, if you ask me! I keep feeling like I ate welsh rarebit before going to bed, and ought to wake up any minute. And you're as bad as he is," I added bluntly to Trainor. "I thought you had more sense. You're both a pair of bloodthirsty fools. Before you're through, you're liable to get two poor devils that never did you any harm in some kind of serious trouble, with all your theories. Why don't you both put your money away, skip the whole thing?"

They turned deaf ears to me. Trainor waved his check in the air to let it dry, then dropped it on top of the twenty hundred-dollar bills.

Fredericks was smiling, pleased with himself, like a cat that expected to lap up a lot of easy cream. "We'll let Evans here hold the stakes."

"I won't have any part of such a dirty, underhanded bet!" I flared.

"All right, if you won't, then I'll call the barman."

He started to raise his hand. I slapped it down just in time. "What you're doing's bad enough as it is so try to keep it to yourselves! Haven't you got any sense of decency at all? He'll talk his head off to everyone that comes in the place. Here, give me the money, I'll hold it for you." I glanced up at the wall. "Next Tuesday at exactly midnight, one or the other of you gets it."

I put it away in my own wallet. Then I called the barman, myself. "Bring me a shot of straight whiskey, I've got a bad taste in my mouth. And something for these two gents. My suggestion is chloroform!"

We drank in silence. I had the impression Trainor was already feeling ashamed of himself; would have crawled out of it if there was any self-respecting way he could have. At that, his side of the contention was the least offensive of the two. Fredericks had a smug, wise-guy look on his face, that made you want to plant a fist right in the middle of it.

He rang down his glass. "Let's get going. Pick your street corner," he said tersely to Trainor.

The latter said, "The busier the corner, the higher the ratio of average men. And the busiest one I know, night or day, is the corner of Seventh Avenue and 42nd Street."

Fredericks said, "All right, let's go there. And a very good choice too. But before we start," he added, "I've got to have a single thousand-dollar bill."

"Money, eh?" I remarked. "So that's how you're going to work it."

"The root of all evil," he smiled unpleasantly. "The sure-fire motive that never missed yet, since the world began." He tried to pay for the drinks we'd had.

"Mr. Fredericks' money's no good as far as I'm concerned," I let the barman know, without any of the joviality usually associated with that remark. "It's the wrong color." I meant it was bloody.

He took it with good grace. "Very well," he said. "Then this'll pay for three Collinses in advance. See that you have 'em ready and waiting for us when we come in next Tuesday at midnight. Let's see how good your memory is, now."

———◆———

He hailed a cab at the door and the three of us got in. "I think I know where to get a grand-note," he remarked. A stony silence answered him. I couldn't tell whether Trainor's conscience was bothering him or he had already developed cold feet because of risking more than he could afford—maybe even more than he actually had. One thing was sure, Fredericks was the kind would prosecute criminally if he won and that check bounced back stamped "Insufficient Funds." It was no joking matter. I happened to know that Trainor was keeping company with a certain girl, intended to marry her in the fall. His whole future, you might say, was the dotted line of that check.

We stopped off first at a fashionable gambling place. Fredericks told us what it was, I wouldn't have known otherwise. It looked like any other swank apartment building. Well, for that matter it was, all but one certain apartment, that paid heavily for protection. We waited for him in the cab, as we weren't known in the place.

The minute he'd gone in, I said to Trainor: "You're not kidding me any. Can you cover that check, in case you have to endorse it next Tuesday night?"

"I won't have to endorse it next Tuesday night. I'm winning this little pot."

"That doesn't answer my question! Nothing's sure, and this whole set-up depends on the human equation, the most doubtful quantity there is. Well—have you got a thousand dollars?"

"I can just about raise it if I have to," he admitted glumly, "by hocking my shirt and borrowing on my salary."

"I thought so! You ought to have your head examined!" I took the check out of my wallet. "Here, take this back while you've still got the chance. I'll tell him the whole thing's off."

"You open your mouth to him, about what I just told you," he warned in a cold rage, "and I'll punch your head in. D'you think

I'd crawl to him, go begging for leniency? He'd rub it in every time he met me, never let me forget it. I'm going to take that two thousand of his and smear it all over his kisser, to show him what I think of him!"

I saw there was nothing I could do to dissuade him. "That's sure an expensive way of expressing an opinion," was all I said to that.

—◆—

Fredericks came back again with a thousand-dollar bill they'd given him in exchange for ten hundreds.

"Now let's get the ground-work laid. 42nd Street and Seventh," he told the driver, "northwest corner."

He showed it to us in the cab, by the flame of his cigar-lighter. It was new, crisp as lettuce. Notes that big don't pass from hand to hand much, I guess. "You sure it's not fake?" I couldn't help asking. "That'd be a nice ironic twist, bring two people to the verge of murder over a phony bill."

"It's as good as though I got it at a bank. Their games may be fixed, but they don't go in for queer money."

"How you gonna work it?" Trainor wanted to know coldly.

"I'll show you. Watch this." He folded it neatly in half, edge to edge and carefully creased it by running his fingers back and forth over it. He took out a gold cigar-cutter and inserted the blade under the crease. He carefully severed the bill into two equal parts. "It's valueless this way, isn't it?" he told us. "There's your motive right there. Two different people, each one gets half. Neither half's worth anything without the other. Neither one will give up his half. A deadlock. Whichever one is the more aggressive and daring of the two will do something about it. That spells murder. Maybe both will at once. Tonight we plant the first half, with whoever Trainor here selects. You follow him, Evans, and get his name and address and all about him for the record. Tomorrow night, same time and place, we plant the second half. Then we make known to each party the identity of the other, who is all that is standing between him and a neat little windfall. Then you'll see Nature take its course. And *you say,*" he sneered at Trainor, "that you can't make a murderer out of any chance passerby on a street corner! Well, watch, between now and next Tuesday night—and learn something!"

"It's a filthy scheme," I said hotly. "Treating human beings like flies stuck on a pin! You're going to start something that you won't be able to stop in time, mark my words! There'll be blood on both your heads."

Our driver coasted down past the Rialto Theater entrance, looked around questioningly.

"How long are you allowed to park here?" Fredericks asked him.

"I ain't allowed to park here at all. I can park around on the 42nd Street side with you, though, just past the corner, if I don't stay too long."

"That'll be all right. We'd better stay in the cab," he said to us in an undertone. "If we stand out on the sidewalk in full sight, it mayn't work. Pick someone coming from that direction, 8th Avenue, so we can see them before they get here."

<hr />

We braked to a stop alongside the curb. That particular stretch of sidewalk is plenty bright, any time of the night. In addition, there was a street light just far enough ahead to give us a sort of preview of anyone who passed under it coming our way. We all three had good eyes. It was anything but deserted even at this hour, but the passersby were spaced now, not coming along in droves.

Trainor sat peering intently ahead through the partly-opened cab door. "I suppose," Fredericks observed drily, "you'll make every effort to pick someone who looks prosperous enough not to need a thousand dollars badly enough to kill for it."

"Not at all," snapped Trainor. "I'm not loading the dice. I'm here to pick an average man. And the average man on the street hasn't very much money—not these days. But neither does he kill for what he hasn't got."

"You'll find out," was the purring answer.

There was a long wait, while people drifted by, by ones and twos and threes, but mostly by ones. I kept thinking, contemptuously and yet a little admiringly too, "Every cent he's got in the world, risked on the imponderable reactions of some chance passerby out there. It must be great to have that much confidence in your fellow-men."

"See any that look average enough yet? You're hard to please," mocked Fredericks softly.

Trainor said, "If I'm any good at reading faces, the last few that have gone by would cheerfully cut anyone's throat for a toothpick, let alone a thousand bucks. I wouldn't call these flashy Broadway lizards an average type of man, would you?" Then he said suddenly, "Here's someone now—quick! This fellow walking along near the outer edge of the sidewalk."

I just had time for a quick, comprehensive glimpse of the candidate, through the windshield, as he passed under the street light. Trainor was a good picker. The guy was so average he would have been invisible in a crowd. Clothes, face, gait, everything were commonplace. You couldn't feature him killing anyone, or doing anything but just breathing all his life long. Fredericks shied the half-bill out of the cab window.

He came abreast a minute later, missed seeing it, went on his way. That was in character too, the type nothing ever happened to, even when it was thrust right at his feet.

Fredericks snapped his fingers, swore, stepped out and picked it up again. The three of us laughed a little, nervously. We were all under a strain.

<hr>

Another wait. "All right, this one, then," Trainor said abruptly. "He looks decent and harmless enough." Again one of those colorless "supers" of the New York mob-scene.

Fredericks flipped his wrist again, and the bait fell out. Again it missed fire. The pedestrian looked down, saw it, went a step beyond, turned, came back and picked it up. He stood looking at it, turning it over from side to side, while we held our breaths, hidden in the cab, close enough to have reached out and touched him. I could see a skeptical frown on his face. Finally he deliberately threw it away again, brushed his hands, and went on his way.

"Suspicious," Fredericks catalogued him drily. "Thinks it's too good to be true, there must be a catch to it. Queer money, or an advertising scheme. Typical New Yorker for you."

He retrieved it a second time. This human-interest byplay, though, had managed to dull my objections to the scheme, made me overlook its dark implications for awhile. When people acted so naturally, so comically even, as these passersby, there didn't seem to be much risk of getting them to kill one another, as Fredericks insisted. It was like watching frisky half-grown jungle cats at play with one another inside a zoo, and forgetting they have claws.

Trainor went on scrutinizing everyone that came along singly, eliminating couples and trios. "Here's some—" he started to say, then checked himself. "No, he's had a drink, that doesn't make for normalcy."

After that, there was a complete cessation of motion on the street for a minute or two, as sometimes happens on even the busiest thoroughfares. As though activity were being fed to it on a belt, and there had been a temporary break in it.

Then a figure came into sight. His isolation gave Trainor a good chance to size him up without distraction. I had a feeling he was going to finger him, even before he did. I think I would have myself. A quick snapshot of him, under the light-rays, showed a fellow of medium height, stocky build, high Celtic cheekbones, dressed in a tidy but not expensive gray suit.

"This is the ticket," Trainor said decisively.

Fredericks skimmed the bait out and a ghost of a breeze carried it a little further away from the cab than before.

He picked it up, scratched the back of his neck. Then he looked all around him, as though wondering how it could have gotten there. He glanced once at the cab, searchingly, but we were flattened back out of sight in the dark interior of it. He evidently took it for an empty one standing waiting for fares, didn't look a second time.

It took him a good four, five minutes to decide the second half of the bill wasn't lying around anywhere. What made him desist, chiefly, was an unwelcome offer of help from a second passerby.

"Lose something, bud?"

"Mind ya business!" was the retort.

Fredericks breathed in the direction of my ear: "Trainor's average man is pugnacious. You mean he won't kill for the other half of that?"

"That's just Manhattan manners, not a bad sign at all, shows he's completely average," Trainor contradicted.

⟫⟪

Our man moved away with what he'd found, receding toward the 7th Avenue corner. Watching through the back window of the cab, we saw him stop at the curb, glance back at where he'd found the unlikely token, as though he still couldn't get over it. Then he crossed to the Times Building "island," skirted that, and crossed Broadway.

"There's one half of our murder team," Fredericks said. "Whether he turns out to be the murderer or the victim, depends on how aggressive the party of the second part is. All right, Evans, go after him, keep him in sight. Find out his name, where he lives, all about him—only don't accost him yourself, of course. It may make him leery."

I opened the cab door, stepped out, and started briskly out after our unsuspecting guinea pig. "Fine thing to turn into," I thought. "A private detective!"

It was easy to keep him in sight, because of the sparsity of other pedestrians. In the day time he'd have been swallowed up in a minute in this teeming part of town. He kept going straight east along 42nd and made for the 6th Avenue El. When I saw him start up the stairs to the platform I had to close in on him, as a train might have come along and separated us before I could get there.

I passed through the turnstile right behind him, and when the train came in, got in the same car he did. He sat on one of the side seats, giving me the opportunity of keeping him in sight from behind without his being aware of it. At one point, I could tell by the downward tilt of his head that he had taken the severed bill out again and was studying it under the car lights. He evidently couldn't quite make up his mind whether it was genuine or not. He looked around to see if anyone had been watching, put it away again.

"He's got a guilt-complex about it, for one thing," I decided. "That's not so good from Trainor's point of view. If he feels guilty about it, he's liable to kill for it, too, before he's through."

He straightened and walked out at the 99th Street station, in the heart of the teeming, jostled Upper West Side district. I left by the opposite end of the car, to avoid being too noticeable about it. I gave him a headstart by pretending to stop and tie a shoe lace, so I wouldn't be treading on his heels.

He plunged from the stair-shed straight into his favorite bar. So he wasn't going to any bank to verify its genuineness. He was going to put it up to that Solomon of the lowly, the saloon-keeper. I suppose a professional sleuth would have carefully stayed outside, to attract as little attention to himself as possible. I was no professional, however, and I had no great hankering to hang around on a street corner in that strange neighborhood waiting for him to come out again. I barged right in after him.

———◆—◆———

It seemed the right move to have made. It was within an hour of closing time, and the two of us were the only customers. It was an empty barn of a place with swell acoustics; you couldn't whisper if you tried. I was just in time to hear the barman boom out sociably: "Lo, there, Casey, where've you been keeping yourself?" So that gave me his name.

I had a beer and regretted it even at six inches away from my nose. I became very interested in the slot machine, to give myself something to do, but timed the noise so it wouldn't interfere with their husky undertones.

"Where'd you find it, bejazes?" The barman was holding it up to the light, shutting one eye at it. I got that in the machine mirror.

Then after he had been told, and the inevitable question put to him, "I nivver saw them that big before, but it looks rail to me."

"But waddya suppose it's cut in two like that for? 'Tis no tear, it's a clane-cut edge."

Casey's bosom friend in the white apron was doing some mental double-crossing. I could read it on his face in the mirror. Or maybe he just thought it would look nice framed on his wall. "I'll stand ye a drink for it!" he offered with sudden fake heartiness.

I started to get uneasy. I hadn't bargained on the thing passing from hand-to-hand all over town. And if a saloon-keeper took over, that was piling the odds against Trainor too high for my liking. They aren't the most unmurderous breed in the world. I made up my mind, "If Casey parts with it, I spill the beans to the two of them right here and now!"

But Casey wasn't parting with it that easy. The barkeep's argument that it was unredeemable, no good, not worth a cent as it was, fell on deaf ears. The ante rose to fifty cents, then a dollar, finally a two-dollar bottle of rye. Casey finally stalked out with the parting shot, "I'll kape it. Who can tell, I might come acrosth the other part of it yet."

"Ouch!" I said to myself. "You're going to, before the week's out. Then what?"

On an impulse, I stayed behind instead of following him. The cagier way to find out everything about him was to remain behind, at this fountainhead of gossip, instead of tracking him home through the deserted streets.

The barman drifted over, brought the subject up himself. I was the only one left in the place to talk to. "That fellow that was just in here, found half a thousand-dollar bill on 42nd Street just now."

I showed proper astonishment. "Yeah? Who is he?"

"Name of John Casey. He comes in here all the time. Lives right around the corner, the brownstone house, second from corner of 99th. He's an electrician's helper." Not all at once like that, of course. I spaced my questions, making them those of a man obligingly keeping up his end of a conversation in which he has no real interest.

"He'll take me up on it yet," he wound up. "As soon as he finds out it's no good, he'll be glad to take me up on it." But there was a glint in his piggy eyes, as though if Casey didn't, he'd do something about it himself.

I went out of there telling myself, "Brother, if you're this steamed up about half a bill, what you won't do when you find out who has the other half!" Trainor's thousand was as good as gone. There was certainly going to be a murder somewhere within this triangle before the week was out. And no matter who committed it, the barman or Casey or tomorrow night's unknown finder, Fredericks would be the actual murderer. And Trainor and I the accessories.

<hr />

If I'd been dealing with a square guy, I might have persuaded him to drop it, after what I told him next day. There would have still been plenty time enough, But I found out how skunkish he was when I put it up to him. Trainor of course was present.

"The bet isn't with you," he told me. "If Trainor wants to call it off—because he can't possibly win—I'll play ball with him. All he has to do is refund me the thousand dollars, the amount of the bill I sacrificed. Are you ready to do that, Trainor?"

Trainor just looked at me and I looked at him, and the three of us went back to 42nd Street and 7th Avenue. Somebody's death warrant had been signed. Just barely possibly that avaricious crooked barman's. More likely Casey's. Most likely still, somebody we hadn't even set eyes on so far, walking unsuspectingly along the midnight streets at this very moment to his doom. It gave me the creeps. I hated Fredericks—and I almost hated Trainor too. Too stubborn to back down. Playing the gods of the machine. Thinking they'd be able to stop it in time.

We were in a cab again, almost over the same spot as the night before. It happened quicker this time. For one thing, it was drizzling lightly and there were far fewer people passing. There were no trials and errors like the night before. Trainor bided his time, made his choice carefully. He had to be careful whom he pitted against Casey, for his own sake, and he knew it. He'd gone a little wrong on Casey. His answer to the man that had asked him if he'd lost anything, and what had occurred in the barroom, showed Casey had a well-developed streak of stubbornness in him, that might easily turn into pugnacity. Trainor had to be careful whom he matched against him now.

Presently a reedy-looking individual, coat collar turned up against the rain, came shambling along. Probably the weather and the turned-up collar and his soggy hat-brim made him look more dejected than he was. A single glance, as they come walking down a street, is no way to judge character, anyway. But his face was wan, and whatever his inner disposition, he looked frail enough to be harmless.

"Drop it," signalled Trainor under his breath. The second half-bill fell on the gleaming sidewalk.

I couldn't help feeling I was looking at a dead man, as he came on toward us, so unaware. Almost wanted to yell out to him in frantic warning, "Don't pick anything up from the sidewalk, whatever you do, or you're a goner!"

He saw it and he stopped in his tracks. He brought it up to face-level. His mouth dropped open. We were so close we could even hear what he muttered. "Holy smoke!" he ejaculated hoarsely, and pushed his water-waved hat to the back of his head.

He stood there a long time, looking stunned. He went on uncertainly after awhile, and the mist started to veil his figure.

"Hurry up, before you lose him," Fredericks said, and unlatched the door for me.

"Why do I have to do all the dirty work in this?" I grunted, stepping out.

"Because you have no stake in it. Not to put too fine a point on it, Trainor doesn't altogether trust me, and I'm not sure I altogether trust him. We both trust you implicitly. You're the contact-man in this."

"Malarkey!" I growled, and belted up my waterproof. The taxi went one way, I went the other way after my quarry.

———◆———

This time instead of beer I had to sit drinking vile coffee in a cheap cafeteria, while he took the bill out from time to time and studied it surreptitiously below table-level, across the room from me.

"Planning what you'd like to get with it, if it was only whole," I thought pityingly. "Little knowing what you're *likely* to get, because of it."

I could see him day-dreaming there under the lights. I could almost see the girl and the bungalow and the frigidaire—or maybe it was a radio—in his eyes.

"Damn Trainor!" I seethed. "Damn Fredericks!" Why didn't they drop a whole bill with no murder-strings attached, and make someone happy! One thing was sure, if there was going to be any killing in this, it wouldn't be through him. You could read goodness in his face. Trainor had shown good judgment in his choice this time.

I followed him home through the rain at two that morning, and if his thoughts hadn't been so preoccupied with what he'd found, I'm sure he would have caught on easily enough. The jaunty cut of the waterproof, and the rustling noise it made, were too damn easy to identify. But he was walking on air. A troop of elephants could have followed him and he wouldn't have known it.

He went to a little hole-in-the-wall flat in the Chelsea part of town, and me twenty yards behind him. And then I was in for a bad jolt! He had his own key, so I couldn't get his name from the mail-boxes in the grubby little foyer. To avoid having to come around the next day and ask questions of the janitor, I deliberately went up the inner stairs after him (the street-door was unlocked) to ascertain what his flat number was in that way, if I could. I heard a door on the third floor close after him, and when I got up to the landing it was 25, since that was the only one had voices coming from inside it. You could hear everything out there where I was.

I heard a kiss, and a sweetly solicitous voice asked: "Tired, dear?" Then he told her about what he'd found, and they stood there just the other side of the door, planning what they could have done with it if it had only been intact.

"Maybe," she suggested wistfully, "if you take it around to the bank, they'd give you something on it in partial redemption, a hundred or even fifty. Even that would be a Godsend!"

Then an infant started whimpering somewhere in the back of the flat, and I crept downstairs again all choked up. Married, and with a young baby! It was inhuman to torture people like that. And to place them in danger of being murdered was bestial.

25, the mailbox said, was rented by Noble Dreyer.

I jotted the name and address down. I said, as I girded my waterproof up and went out into the wet again, "Well, Dreyer, you don't know it, but I'm your guardian angel from now on."

I met Fredericks and Trainor by appointment at the former's club, at cocktail time next afternoon. I had very little to say, only "The guy's name is Noble Dreyer." And I gave them the address. I didn't mention the wife, I didn't mention the kid, I didn't mention the guardian angel.

Fredericks said, with about as much emotion as an oyster, "Good. Now all that remains is to inform the two parties of one another's existence and whereabouts, and the test is under way."

⋙◆⋘

We followed him into the club's writing room, and he sat down and addressed two envelopes, one to Casey, 99th Street, the other to Dreyer, 24th Street. Then he put them aside and wrote two identical notes, on club stationery.

THE OTHER HALF OF WHAT YOU PICKED UP AT 7TH AVENUE, 42ND STREET, IS AT THIS MOMENT IN THE POSSESSION OF *(HE*

INSERTED CASEY'S NAME AND ADDRESS ON ONE, DREYER'S ON THE OTHER). HE FOUND IT IN THE SAME WAY YOU DID YOURS. YOU HAVE AS MUCH RIGHT TO THE WHOLE BILL AS HE HAS!

The come-on, of course, was that last sentence. It was an invitation to murder if there ever was one. But Trainor made no objection. "The average, decent, normal man," he said, "will not be incited to murder even by getting information like this. He'll envy maybe, or even try to strike a bargain with his co-holder, but he won't kill."

Was Trainor right?

Fredericks left the notes unsigned, of course. He blotted, folded each one over. I was holding the two addressed envelopes in my hand. "I'll seal them for you," I said quietly and took them from him before he could object. I put each one in an envelope, moistened and closed the flap and sent the steward for stamps. "Mail these for Mr. Fredericks," I said.

Then I took a good long drink, and I felt better than I'd felt yet since the devilish bet had been made.

"That's that," Fredericks said, gleefully rubbing his hands. "Now, of course, we must be ready with some sort of preventive measure, or at least some form of supervision, to keep them from going whole hog. Although I don't suppose you two'll give me credit for it, I don't want either of them to lose their lives—if I can help it."

The way he said that burned me, as though he were talking about some form of insect life. "Oh no-o, of course not," I drawled, "it's all just in the spirit of good clean fun, that's understood. And now, what precaution do you propose taking? Sending them each a bullet-proof vest? Or maybe just a rabbit's foot will do."

I smiled tightly.

He'd never had much sense of humor. If he had, he'd have been in hysterics his whole life—at himself. "The idea will take a while to ferment," he said seriously. "Premeditated murder always does. Probably nothing much will happen for a day or two, while they digest the thought that the other half-bill is theirs for the taking. Suppose Trainor and I keep an eye on this Dreyer, and you sort of stay close to our friend Casey. That way we can keep one another posted, the minute an overt move gets under way. Just give them rope enough to leave no doubt of their intentions, but be prepared to step in between as a buffer before the act is actually carried out. It shouldn't be necessary to drag the police in at any time. The mere knowledge that three outsiders have read their minds and know what's going on, should be enough to scotch the inclination once and for all. Nobody commits murder before an audience.

Trainor said: "I want one thing understood. I want positive evidence of murderous intent on the part of either one of them before I'll consent to your claiming the money. I won't have you jumping to the conclusion that just because Casey, let's say, set out to look up Dreyer, he's going to take his life. If he goes there provided ahead of time with a weapon, that's another matter; you've won the bet. If he doesn't, you haven't proved anything. There's nothing more normal than for him to seek out the other man, try to strike a bargain or come to some agreement with him, or even just talk the thing over with him out of curiosity. I want proof of a murderous intention, and, my friend, many a prosecutor has found out that's the hardest thing there is to get!"

He could have saved his breath. I could have told both of them I didn't think there was much chance of Casey or Dreyer approaching one another at all within the next few days. But I didn't. They might have asked me why I was so sure, and I was in no position to answer. Ethically, I wasn't troubled in the slightest. In reality the bet would end in a stalemate. In appearance, it would be decided in Trainor's favor. That was all to the good. He could use that two thousand better than Fredericks, who was a louse anyway.

⊰⊱

This was Thursday evening. They wouldn't get the notes Fredericks had sent them until Friday morning so there was no reason to start keeping an eye on them until Friday evening. Since they both worked daytimes, Dreyer as manager of a chain grocery branch-store, it was only after working hours that they needed to be kept under observation. I may have felt privately that there was no reason for it even then, but I went through with it for form's sake.

We established, as points of contact by which to get in touch with one another in case of necessity, the saloon Casey frequented and an all-night drugstore on the corner below Dreyer's flat. They were to call me or I was to call them, if anything got under way at either end that required quick action.

The wear and tear was pretty bad at my end, because of the quantities of rancid beer I had to keep drinking to "pay my rent." The place was fairly well-filled up to about midnight, then the customers thinned until there finally remained only Casey and myself. He had been in there from eight on. I was obsessed with the slot machine again.

It was the barkeep who brought up the subject, after maneuvering his barcloth around for awhile. "Still got that thousand-dollar scrap ye found?" he asked, sleepy-lidded.

"Yeah, but not on me, don't worry," was the shrewd answer.

"What'd you do, put it in the bank?" asked the barman, scornfully.

"I tried to turn it in there, but they wouldn't take it," Casey admitted.

"What'd I tell ye! Why don't you listen to reason? I'll give you two bottles of rye for it, you pick the brand."

"If it's no good, what do you want it so bad for?" Casey asked, not unreasonably.

The white-aproned one tripped slightly over the answer. "I want it for a curayosity. Sure, what else would I be wanting it for?"

"Well, I'm hanging onto it, now more than ever! Take a look at this. This was in my mailbox when I left the house this morning." I recognized the note Fredericks had sent him, in the mirror.

The barman bent over the counter, laboriously read it through with lip motions. "Hunh," he said, "this must be meant for someone else. It's got your own name down. What would they be telling you you found it for? You know that already."

"It got in the wrong envelope," Casey said angrily, like a man who's been cheated. "They must have sent one to somebody else, and I got his by mistake, worse luck! Anyway, it shows there's another half to the bill, somebody picked it up just like I did, so I'm keeping mine."

The barkeeper scratched his chin. He was doing lots and lots of mental double-crossing, I could see that in the mirror. "I'd be careful, Casey," he said with friendly concern. "Have you got it in a good place? Somebody might try to take it away from you."

"Let 'em try!" said Casey belligerently. 'I've got it stuck away good, no fear. They'll not get their hands on it in a hurry!"

The barman swatted a fly with his cloth. "I wouldn't carry it around with me or anything like that, if I was you," he advised by way of finding out.

"Don't worry, I've got it hidden in my room, where no one'll find it."

"Have ye, now?" The barman scratched his sandpapery jaw some more. "Have another, Casey," he offered amiably. "This is on the house." I made a point of carefully watching his hands as he drew the suds, but he didn't try anything, just filled the glass, knocked its head off, set it up. Then he sort of drifted to the back, by easy stages. There was a telephone on the wall, just outside the washroom door. I watched him fiddling around with it, dusting off the dial slots. Who ever heard of anyone dusting off a telephone at that hour of the morning? He looked around to see if either of us was looking. Casey was squatting down playing with the tavern cat. I'd just put my fiftieth coin into the spiked machine.

A bell jingled back there, and then the barman fiddled around some more with the dial slots. You couldn't hear what he said, through his funneled hand. Then he came back again up the bar by easy stages. Nice pleasant tarantula, he was.

———◆◇◆———

Three beers later a couple of hard-looking customers came in. "Now, isn't that a coincidence!" I jeered to myself. The barman didn't make any further attempts to detain Casey after that. The latter had been saying for the past ten minutes or more that he was full as a pig and had to work tomorrow. He floundered out, and the two hard-looking customers went after him as promptly as a tail following a kite. I seemed to feel like leaving, myself, right around then. Who could object? That was my privilege.

There was beer coming out of Casey's ears, so he wouldn't have known it if a regiment had been at his heels. For my part, however, I overlooked the fact that the other two had only just about wet their whistles, and had all their faculties about them. Not that they glanced back or seemed to be aware of me or anything like that.

They turned in after Casey, at the dismal-looking 99th Street tenement entrance, and I did likewise. There was a spark of green gas flickering in a bowl at the back of the ground floor hall, and a cautious creaking coming from somewhere above on the stairs. I put my foot on the bottom step, and suddenly a shadow detached itself from the wall. The side of my face exploded into atoms, and it felt like the whole roof had fallen down on top of me. I grabbed at a leg, going down, folded it over my chest, and brought him down after me. A lot of noisy kicking, threshing and grunting went on all over the dirty hallway. It served its purpose. Even on 99th Street sounds of combat don't belong inside houses. Doors began to open here and there on the floors above.

Somebody came down off the stairs in a hurry, jumped over the two of us, and made for the street, with a grunted admonition, "Beat it, Patsy, the whole house is awake!" Patsy tore himself from my embrace, stood up, kicked out viciously in the direction of my head just on general principle, then scampered out. Upstairs on one of the landings Casey was howling belligerently: "Come back and fight like a man, ye dirty snaik-thief, whoever ye are!"

It sounded like he still had his thousand-dollar bill which was all that really interested me. I picked myself up, then slipped away to avoid meeting the riot squad. So much for Friday night.

<hr />

Saturday, at cocktail time, Fredericks was already acting a little less sure of himself. Even slightly worried, you might say. I told them what had happened, with just a slight distortion of the facts. I let them think I'd watched Casey put the two thugs to rout from across the street, instead of actually entering the building and taking a hand in it myself, so to speak.

Fredericks said, "That's all right, but what I can't understand is why neither Casey nor Dreyer have made a move toward one another. They've had nearly forty-eight hours now to think it over. We know that they both got the notes I sent. Dreyer's a spineless jellyfish, he'll dream and plan with his wife, but he won't do anything about it. And she's one of these goody-goodies herself—

which is your luck, Trainor. I've really been counting on this Casey fellow, but he seems to be more inclined to passive resistance than aggression. Maybe," he said hopefully, "he's got the idea already, and it's taking time to cook. If he doesn't do something about it before Tuesday night, I'm out two grand!"

"Attaboy, Shylock!" I couldn't help remarking.

⟫⋄⟪

Saturday night was a big night at the tavern. I took a chance and went back, even after what had happened the night before in Casey's hallway. I felt pretty sure the two footpads wouldn't show their faces there, and they didn't. I stayed fairly close to the door, however, to reduce the risk of being ganged up on.

Casey however, did show up as though too dense to connect the attempt on him with his friend the bartender. Or maybe not so dense as he let on to be. When the crowd thinned out and he had the latter's undivided attention, he related what had happened.

The barkeep was all innocent surprise. "And ye think 'twas that they were after, the thing ye found?"

"Think? I know damn well it was! I don't mind telling you I've got myself a gun, and the next party that tries to break in my room like that is going to be a sorry man!" And he turned around and went out again, without saying good-night.

I didn't linger myself. I didn't want to be handed any mickey finns for my timely interference the night before.

⟫⋄⟪

We compared notes again Sunday. Fredericks was biting his nails to the quick, figuratively speaking, at the lack of initiative the two parties were showing. "Only forty-eight hours left!" he mourned.

"I'm not even sure Casey actually did get a gun," I said, rubbing it in. "I think he just said it for a bluff, to scare the bartender off. He must know he engineered Friday night's visit. He saw the two fellows there in the place before he left. And whether he has or not, he's keeping it for defensive purposes only, I could tell by the way he spoke."

"Which is no consolation to you, is it Fredericks?" Trainor jeered. It didn't, to judge by the disgusted look on his face, seem to be.

⋙◆⋘

Sunday night Casey took no chances. He brought a bottle up to his room with him and stayed in close to his mutilated treasure, keeping an eye on it. I could see a dim light burning in his window from where I watched, pacing back and forth between corners on the opposite side of the street. I didn't knock off until 4 A.M., when the lights went out in the *Lucky Shamrock* and I saw the bartender come out, lock up, and go home. He was alone, and he steered clear of Casey's flat, so I figured the latter's gun-talk had had a salutary effect. Everything was peaceful and under control; Sunday seemed to be everyone's night of rest, the way it should be. The lull before the storm, maybe. I went home grumbling to myself about not being cut out for a night-watchman.

⋙◆⋘

Monday night was the last full night left. If anything was going to happen, it was then or never. That being the case, I was on the job early. Casey's electrical repair shop closed up at about 10:30. He stopped off for something to eat, and then went straight up to his room again—without any bottle this time. Probably still had some left in last night's. I girded myself up for a long vigil.

At eleven a messenger boy showed up and went in the building. It struck me as odd for a moment that anyone living in a dump like that should be on the receiving-end of a telegram, but I didn't think twice about it. The lad came out again, and almost immediately the gaslight went out behind Casey's window. A moment later he showed up at the street door himself, bound for somewhere. The message had unmistakably been for him just now. I saw him stop under a streetlight and read it over a second time, as though it puzzled him. Then he went on his way.

I had no choice but to tail him, and after the number of times he'd seen me in the *Shamrock*, it was no easy matter. I had to stay completely out of sight and yet not lose him. Luckily he didn't ride to his destination, but went on foot. He walked a vast distance down Broadway to a certain well-lighted corner, then abruptly stopped there and went no further, as though expecting to meet someone.

I shrank back behind a protruding showcase just in time and watched him narrowly along the edge of it without sticking my nose too far out. He took the telegram out, read it for the third time, looked up at the nearest street sign as though to verify the location and nodded to himself. Fifteen, twenty minutes went by. He began to get more and more impatient, turning his head this way and that, shifting his feet. I could see him getting sorer by the minute. Finally he blew up altogether, balled the message up, slung it viciously away from him, stuck his hands in his pockets, and started back the way he'd come.

"Good work, boy," I commended, "I've been dying to get a look at that myself!" I turned around and studied necktie patterns in the case until he'd gone by, then went over, picked it up, and smoothed it out.

JOHN CASEY
—99TH STREET.
ON RECEIPT OF THIS GO TO NORTHEAST CORNER BROADWAY AND—STREET YOU WILL RECEIVE VALUABLE INFORMATION ABOUT OTHER HALF BILL.

A FRIEND.

"A stall!" I thought. "And the fool fell for it—went out and left the bill unguarded in his room! I bet it's gone by now!"

That tricky barman must have engineered it, of course. But after all, what did I care whether he'd lost it or not? If the stunt had worked, at least it had worked without the aid of murder, so Trainor's money was safe, and Dreyer was safe too—those were the only two angles I was interested in.

A belated suspicion of what was up must have dawned on Casey himself on his way back. He walked so fast that I never quite caught up with him after he left that corner. But I knew where he was headed, so it didn't trouble me.

The light was shining silverly in his room when I turned down 99th Street again. For just one moment more the street clung to its slumbering serenity, then it came to life right before my eyes. The thing itself must have been over already, must have happened just before I turned the corner. Whole rows of windows lighted up suddenly in Casey's building, heads were stuck out. A patrol car was already shrieking up the nearest avenue. It rocketed around the corner, dove at the building entrance as though it were going to crash its way through into the hallway. Just before it got there a figure came tearing out, saw it, swerved, and bolted up the other way. Some woman or other helpfully brayed down from one of the open windows, "Stop that man! Stop him! He just shot somebody!"

The figure threw something from it as it ran, and there was a metallic impact from an ashcan. A cop took a jump off the prowl car running-board, fired warningly into the air, yelled something. The second shot wasn't into the air. The figure went on scampering, leaned over too far, finally slumped down flat and rolled over on its back. It was Casey.

An ambulance showed up with wailing siren and screeched to a stop. Casey was shoved into it with a busted kneecap. But the other figure that was carried out to it under a sheet didn't have a move left in it. I tried to edge it, tilt the sheet, and get a look, and I was nearly knocked down for my pains.

"He's dead—wanner make something of it?" I was told.

I backed out.

Well, if he was, that was all that mattered. I'd done my best, but Trainor's thousand had gone up the flue and he was behind the eight ball now. At least nothing had happened to that poor cuss with the wife and baby.

"How'd it happen?" I asked one of the neighbors, standing next to me.

"He came home and caught somebody in his room. I passed two suspicious-looking characters on the stairs meself when I came home earlier. The other one must've got away over the roof."

I'd figured that that slimy bartender had been at the bottom of it all along. This proved it. It must have been the same two hoods as the first time.

I was the first one to get to 22 the next night. I had the check and Fredericks' cash with me, to turn over to him. I got there about ten to twelve, and wondered how Trainor was going to take it. He came in alone about five minutes later. I could tell by his face he didn't know yet, thought he was coming into two thousand bucks. I decided not to tell him until Fredericks had showed up; spare him the ax until the last minute.

"Well," he said, "Mr. Wise Guy is going to be twice as sick at having to eat crow."

The barman had a good memory. He parked the three Collinses ordered the week before in a row on the bar before us.

"Whaddye mean, twice as sick?" I asked.

"Oh, he got a cramp or something last night, went home to bed about eleven and left me holding down the sidewalk there in front of Dreyer's."

The minute-hand of the clock hit twelve. I said, "I'm going to call his club, find out what's holding him up."

Trainor said maliciously, "Ask him if he's afraid to face the music."

I was at the phone a long time. When I came back he could read on my face that I had bad news for him. I took out the check and the twenty hundreds and laid them on the bar. "Well," I said, "it looks like he won the bet after all. He *did* cause someone to be murdered by someone else, like he said he could."

His mouth just dropped open, and his face went kind of white and sick.

I picked up his check and started to tear it up into small pieces. "But there doesn't seem to be anyone to collect it for him. That was him that was shot dead in Casey's room on 99th Street last night. They couldn't identify him until late this afternoon. He went there to double-cross us. Maybe to make sure Casey learned who had the other half, or maybe even to take it away from him because he wasn't getting results, give it to someone else. It must have been already missing, the bartender's two side-kicks got there first and swiped it, and Casey shot him down in cold blood believing he took it."

Trainor picked up the third Collins and spilled it slowly out on the floor. Then he turned the glass upside-down on the bar with a knell-like sound. He said, without any bitterness now, "They always said he'd only bet on a sure thing. Well he lived up to his name, all right!"

AFTERWORD TO "YOU BET YOUR LIFE"

"You Bet Your Life" (*Detective Fiction Weekly*, September 25, 1937) is one of Woolrich's most off-trail stories. The bizarre wager between the ruthless cynic Fredericks and the idealist Trainor harks back to the bet between the Lord and Satan in the book of Job, although what happens next as the three godlike principals invisibly spy on the two mortals and wait to see which will first set out to kill the other has no counterpart in the biblical tale. The point of this cockeyed philosophic parable, as usual in Woolrich, is that the most powerful god of all is Chance.

DEATH IN THE YOSHIWARA

I

Jack Hollinger, U. S. N., up from Yokohama on a forty-eight-hour liberty junket, said, "Shoo!" He swung his arms wildly in a mosquito-squatting gesture. He was squatting cross-legged on the floor in a little paper-walled compartment of the House of Stolen Hours, which was situated in one of the more pungent alleys of the Yoshiwara, Tokyo's tenderloin. Before him were an array of thimble-sized saki cups. All of them were empty, but Hollinger hadn't worked up much of a glow over them. A warm spot that felt no bigger than a dime floated pleasantly but without any particular zest behind the waistband of his bell-bottomed white ducks.

He tipped his Bob Davis cap down over one eye and wigwagged his arms some more.

"Outside," he said. "Party no good. Party plenty terrible." He made a face.

The geisha ceased her stylized posturing, bowed low and, edging back the paper slide, retreated through it. The geisha who had been kneeling, to twang shrill discords on her samisen let her hands fall from the strings. "Me, too?" she inquired. And giggled. Geishas, he had discovered, giggled at nearly everything.

"Yeah, you too," said the ungallant Hollinger. "Music very bad, *capish?* Send the girl back with some more saki. And try to find something bigger I can drink it out of!"

The slide eased back into place after her. Hollinger, left alone

114

with his saki-cups and the dancer's discarded outer kimono neatly rolled up in the corner—they seemed to wear layers of them— scowled at the paper walls. Presently he lit a cigarette and blew a thick blue smoke-spiral into the air. It hung there heavily as if it was too tired to move against the heavy staleness of the room's atmosphere. Hollinger frowned.

"Twenty-four hours shore-leave left and not a laugh on the horizon," he complained. "What a town! I shoulda stayed on the ol' battle-wagon and boned up on my course on how to be a detective. Wonder if I passed the exam I sent in from Manila?"

The racket in the public rooms up front, where they had been playing billiards all evening, seemed to have grown louder. He could hear excited shouts, jabbering voices that topped the raucous blend of phonograph-music, clicking roulette-wheels, rattling dice-cups, and clinking beer-glasses. Somebody had started a fight, he guessed. Those Japs sure lost their heads easy. Still a good fight might take some of the boredom out of his bones. Maybe he'd just— Nix. He'd been warned to stay out of trouble this trip.

They were taking a long time with that saki. He picked up a little gong-mallet, and began to swing it against the round bronze disk dangling between two crosspieces. He liked the low sweet noise.

———◆———

There was a sound of feet hurrying across the wooden flooring now, as though a lot of people were running from one place to another. But it remained a considerable distance away, at the front of the big sprawling establishment.

Something whisked by against the outside of the paper screen walling him in. Like the loose edges of somebody's clothes flirting past. The light was on his side, it was dark out there, so he couldn't see any shadow to go with it. Just that rustling sound and the hasty pat-pat of running feet accompanying it. Whoever it was, was in a big hurry—

The pat-pat went on past until it had nearly died out, then turned, started back again quicker than before. Then it stopped right opposite where he was. There was an instant's breathless pause. . . .

Then the slide whirred back and a blond girl stumbled in toward him, both arms stretched out in mute appeal for help. He was on his feet by the time she'd covered the short space between them. He got a blurred impression of what she looked like as she threw herself against him, and stood panting and trembling within the circle of his arms.

She was all in. Two or three flecks of red splattered the front of her gold evening gown—even her dress was out of place in a spot like this. She hadn't any shoes on, but you always had to leave your footgear at the door when you came in. Her blond hair made a tangled shimmer around her head and her attractive face was contorted with sheer panic. Her breathing was the quick, agonized panting of a hunted thing.

Hollinger looked down into her eyes—and whistled. He could tell by the contraction of the pupils that she'd been drugged. An opium pill, maybe, or morphine. He couldn't be sure whether it hadn't taken effect yet or she was just coming out of it.

Sound suddenly broke from her lips and she sobbed against his shoulder. "Say you're real. Tell me I'm not seeing things!" Her fingers pressed against his chest. "Hide me! Don't let them get me! They're after me but I didn't do it. . . . I *know* I didn't do it!"

He had squared off toward the opening in the slide, because the trampling of feet was coming this way now and he wanted to be ready.

She pulled at his blouse wrinkling it in her fingers. "No, don't fight them. Don't you see—that would be the worst thing you could do. It's not just people, it's the police—!"

Police? Hollinger swore. He took a quick step over and slammed the slide shut. He kept his hand on it tentatively, as though not sure of what he was going to do yet. He'd get the brig sure if he tangled with them, after the warning they'd been given on shipboard. But—this girl. Well, she was a girl, she was American, she was in a jam. He had to help her—he wasn't any heel.

"What're they after you for?" he asked. "What did you do?"

"They think I—murdered the man I came in with. I found him stabbed to death—just now—right in the room with me when I— I woke up. I know—it sounds silly. They'll never believe it." She gestured helplessly toward the crimson flecks on her bodice. "This blood all over me—and the dagger in my lap when they came in— Oh please, get me out of this awful place! I *know* I didn't do it. I know I *couldn't* have—"

He eyed her ruefully.

She seemed to sense what was passing in his mind. She smiled wanly. "No," she said. "It wasn't anything like that. I'm not—The man was my fiancé. We were going to be married tomorrow. We were slumming. We stopped in here—"

———⊰♦⊱———

His indecision didn't last long. There wasn't time. The oncoming shuffle of feet had stopped right next door. Hollinger grabbed up the geisha's discarded robe. "Get into that kimono quick. They'll be here in a second—maybe we can swing it." He jumped back to where he'd been sitting originally, collapsed cross-legged on the floor. When she'd wrapped the garment around her, he pulled her down beside him, snatched off his white cap, poked it inside-out and jammed it down over her telltale golden hair.

He pulled her against him. "Pardon me," he said with a tight grin. "It's our only chance. Keep your face turned over my shoulder. Don't let that dress show through the kimono."

"What'll I do if they talk Japanese to me?"

"I'll do the talking. You just giggle the way all these gals do." His arm tightened around. "Okay, lady. This is it. Here they are!"

The slide hissed back. Three bandy-legged little policemen stood squinting into the lantern-light at them. Behind them was a fourth little yellow man in plain clothes. And in back of him, huddled a group of customers, craning and goggling.

Hollinger put down one of the saki-cups, and wiped his mouth with his free hand. "Well," he said slowly, "where's the fire? What's the attraction? We're not giving any show in here." No one budged. "Scram!"

"You see gal?" the detective demanded. "You see yellow-hair gal run by here—'Merican gal like you?"

"Haven't you got eyes?" Hollinger growled. "This is the only gal in here— Mitsu-san. Go away, won't you?"

The plainclothesman snapped something in Japanese at the huddled figure. Hollinger's growl turned nasty. "Skip it!" The girl, quaking against him, managed to produce a high-pitched giggle. Hollinger warmed inside. A good girl that. Scared, sure. But nervy. A fine girl . . .

"Fool gal," the detective snapped contemptuously. His gaze rested on the saki-cups. He smiled drily, made a sign of wheels going around close to his head, bowed elaborately. "So sorry to disturb. Pliss overlook." The three policemen bowed likewise, like stooges.

"Sayonara," said Hollinger pointedly. "Goodbye."

The screen slammed shut again. Someone barked a curt order, and the trampling feet moved on. The crowd continued to stop every few yards, looking into the other cubicles.

"Don't move yet a while," Hollinger said out of the corner of his mouth, close to her ear. "Wait'll they get further away." Just as she was about to straighten up, he caught her quickly, held her fast. "Darn it, stay put!"

The screen eased back again, with less noise than before, and one of the geishas peered in. "I bring saki you order—" She glanced in slant-eyed surprise at the form nestled against him. "You find other girl?" She set the tray down on the floor. There was suspicion peering through the thick orange, green and purple make-up that masked her face.

"Yeah. I found new girl. I like better than girl I had before. So long." He jabbed his thumb at the screen.

The geisha backed out submissively, still peering curiously at the other girl.

The slide closed again. Hollinger let his arms fall. "All right now." The girl straightened and her fingertips pressed tight against her mouth.

"Come on. We've got to step on it. I think she's on to us. She's going to give us away. He jumped to his feet, took a quick look out, then motioned to her to follow. She obeyed, holding herself very stiff and straight.

II

The clamor at the front hadn't abated any. Through a gap in the partitions he caught a glimpse of two white-garbed internes bringing in a stretcher. There was no out that way.

The girl looked at him in terror. "We're trapped back here. We'll never be able to get through all these people. I'm sorry I ever got you into this."

"There's got to be a back way out." He threw an arm protectively about her. "Lean up against me, like you were dizzy. We're going out for a breath of air, if they ask us. Take little pigeon-toed steps like you were going to fall flat on your face any minute. Buckle your knees a little, you're too tall. Keep your head down—"

They wavered through the maze of paper-walled passageways, sometimes in darkness, sometimes in reflected lantern-light. The place was a labyrinth; all you had to do to make new walls was push a little. The only permanent structure was the four corner-posts and the topheavy tile roof.

They managed to side-step the police who were returning from the back, by detouring around one of the slides, and waiting until they'd gone by. A hurrying geisha or two, carrying refreshment-trays, brushed against them, apologized.

"Don't weaken," he kept whispering. "We'll make it yet." The stampeding suddenly started back again behind them. Evidently the geisha had voiced her suspicions. They went a little faster. The wavering gait became a run, the run became tearing, headlong flight. He slashed one more of the never-ending screens back into its socket, and they were looking out on a rear garden.

Apple-green and vermilion lanterns bobbed in the breeze; a little hump-backed bridge crossing a midget brook; dwarf fir-trees made showy splashes of deeper darkness. It all looked unreal and very pretty—all but the policeman posted there to see that no one left. He turned to face them. They'd come to a dead stop. The policeman was swinging a short, wicked-looking little club on a leather strap.

Hollinger said into her ear: "I'll handle him. Don't wait—just keep going across that bridge. There must be a way of getting through to the next street over. Be right with you—"

The cop said something that sounded like, *"Boydao, boydao!"* and motioned them back with his club.

"Take it!" Hollinger snapped at the girl and gave her a scooting shove that sent her up one side of the sharply-tilted bridge and down the other. She almost tumbled off into the water.

Hollinger and the Japanese policeman were locked and strug-gling, silent but for the crunching of their feet on the fine sand that surfaced the garden path. The sailor had a sort of awkward head-lock on the Jap, left hand clamped across his mouth to keep him quiet. His right fist was pounding the bristle-haired skull, while the policeman's club was spattering him all over with dull, brutal thuds. The cop bit Hollinger's muffling hand. Hollinger threw his head back in the lantern-light, opened his mouth like the entrance to the Mammoth Caves—but did not yell.

The girl hovered there across the bridge, her hand held against lips once more, her body bent forward in the darkness. Hollinger knew that every minute counted. Lanterns were wavering nearer in the interior of the house, filtering through the paper like blurred, interlocked moons. Their flight had been discovered.

Hollinger sucked a deep breath into his toiling lungs, lifted the squirming cop up bodily off the ground and tossed him like a sack into the stream. The bulge of his chest and the sudden strain of his back and shoulder muscles split the tight middy from throat to waist. There was a petal-shaped splash and the little brown man swiveled there in the sanded hollow, half stunned by the impact, water coursing shallowly across his abdomen and cutting him in half.

Hollinger vaulted across to the girl with a single stretch of his long legs, caught at her as he went by, and pulled her after him. "I told you not to hang around— Come on, willya?" He glared at her fiercely. She was a fine girl, all right. Scared to death and sticking around that way anyhow. . . .

———◆———

They found the mouth of an alley giving onto the rear of the garden behind a clump of dwarf firs that were streaked single-file along its narrow black length between the walls. Hollinger pushed the hobbling girl in front of him. They came out at the other end into the brazierlike brightness of one of the Yoshiwara streets.

It was strangely deserted; seemed so, at least, until Hollinger remembered that most of the usual crowd must have been drawn around to the front of the Stolen Hours by the hubbub. They ran down it to the end of the block, then turned a corner into another that was even more dismal. But this one was more normally crowded. Heads turned after them, kimonoed passersby stopped to stare. A zigzagging bicycle-rider tried to get out of their way, ran into them instead and was toppled over.

"If the alarm spreads before we can get out of this part of town, we're sunk," he panted. "They'll gang up on us. Faster, lady, faster—"

"I can't," she whimpered. "It's—it's this pavement—the ground's cutting my feet to pieces—" He was without shoes, too, but his soles were calloused from deck-scrubbing. He was two arms' length in front of her, hauling her after him by the combined span of his own arms and hers. Betraying flashes of gold peeped out from under the parachuting kimono, were blazing a trail of identification behind them.

She stumbled and bit her lips to keep from crying out. So he grabbed her up in both arms, plunged onward with her. The extra weight hardly slowed him at all. A paper streamer hanging downward across the lane got snared in some way by their passage, ripped off its wire and flared out behind his neck like a long loose muffler. The shopkeeper whose stall it had advertised came out sputtering, both arms raised high in denunciation.

"There's our dish!" he muttered, winded. A taxi had just dropped a couple of fares in front of a dancehall ahead. Hollinger hailed it with a hoarse shout and it came slowly backward. Hollinger let the girl fall on the seat, ran along beside the cab for a minute as the driver went forward again, then hopped in after her.

"Drive like blazes," he panted. "Ginza—anywhere at all—only get us out of here. Fast, savvy?"

"I go like wind," the driver agreed cheerfully. He wore a kimono and a golf-cap.

The girl was all in; the sudden release of all the pent-up tension finished the last of her control. She just lay inertly, hiding her face with both her hands. He didn't speak to her or try to touch her. His head back against the cushion he pulled in eight long, shuddering breaths—slowly, tasting each one like a sip of icy wine. After that, he began to lick the ugly teeth-gashes on his hand.

A sudden diminution of the light around them—a change to the more dignified pearly glow of solitary streetlights—marked the end of the Yoshiwara.

At the end of a long five minutes, the girl pulled herself up. "I don't know how to thank you," she said weakly. "I mean"—she smiled just a little, wearily—"there just aren't any words."

"Who does things for thanks?" he said, spading his hand at her.

She said what she'd said before: "I didn't do it. I know I didn't do it! Why, I was going to marry Bob. I loved him—" She stopped suddenly, confused.

He looked at her sharply, but he didn't ask any questions. He started, though, to reach for her hand, then drew back.

———◆———

They were coming into the long broad reaches of the Ginza now, Tokyo's Broadway. The lights brightened again, but with a difference: This was downtown, the show-part of town, modern, conventional, safe. Safe for those who weren't wanted for murder, anyway.

"I suppose I ought to give myself up to the police," she said, her eyes restless, like an animal in a trap. "The longer I keep running away, the more they'll think I did do it—I lost my head in that dreadful place—the knife on my lap and his blood on my dress, and that horrible manager yelling at me."

"Suppose you tell it to me first," he urged, gently. "I'm sticking with you, see? I didn't go through all that trouble just to have you put into jail. You say you didn't do it. All right—that's good enough for me. I don't know who you are—"

"Brainard," she said. "Evelyn Brainard. I'm from San Francisco."

He said something that should have been very funny, after what had gone on during the half hour, but she didn't laugh. "Pleased to meet you, Miss Brainard," said he, and blanketed one of her hands in the enormous expanse of his. Etiquette.

"If you give yourself up now, I won't have time to do anything for you. I'm due back on shipboard tomorrow noon, and we're pulling out for Chefoo right away after that. You'd just stay cooped up until the American consul gets good and ready to ask what they're going to do about you, and that might be a week—ten days. And then he probably wouldn't take as much personal interest in you as"—he faltered awkwardly—"as a fellow like me would, that has met you socially."

This time she managed a warm smile, "Socially? Well, that's one way to put it, I guess."

"I ought to be able to straighten it out for you between now and the time I go back," he said earnestly. "Look, I've answered four questionnaires already on how to be a detective. I only have one more to go before I'm finished the course. And I've passed three of 'em, I know for a fact."

They had reached the lower end of the Ginza already, were heading slowly back again.

"The first thing we've got to do is get you off the streets, otherwise you'll be picked up in no time. Know anyone at all here you could hole up with?"

"Not a living soul. Bob Mallory was the only one. I just got off the *Empress* yesterday afternoon. I've a room at the Imperial— "

"No, you better not go back there. They're either there already looking for you or they will be any minute. What about this Mallory—where did he hang out?"

"I don't know, he wouldn't tell me. He gave me an evasive answer when I asked him. Somehow I got the idea he didn't want me to find out—"

He gave her another look. "It wouldn't be much help, even if you did know. It's probably the first place they'd look for you." They drove on in silence for a minute. Finally he said, "Look, don't be offended, but—I've had a room since yesterday. It's not much of a place—it's run by a crazy darn' Russian. But it would be somewhere for you to be safe in while I'm trying to see what I can do for you."

"You're swell."

———⟫◆⟪———

He gave the driver the address. It was a western-style building in one of the downtown reaches of the city, little better than a shack, really—clapboard under a corrugated tin roof. But at least it had wooden doors and walls. And windows with shades on them.

He said: "Wait in the cab a minute, I'll get the Russian out of the way. Just as well if no one sees you going up."

After he'd gone in, she caught sight of the driver slyly watching her in his rear-view mirror. She quickly lowered her head, but with the creepy feeling that he already knew she was white, even in the dimness of the vehicle's interior. Hollinger came back and helped her out. "Hurry up, I sent him out to the back on a stall—"

Going up the unpainted wooden stairs—the place had an upper

story—she whispered: "The driver saw I wasn't Japanese. He may remember later, if he hears—"

He made a move to turn and go down again. The sound of the taxi driving off outside reached them, and it was too late to do anything about it.

"We'll have to take a chance," he said.

There was nothing Japanese about the room upstairs. Just a typical cheap lodging-house room, the same as you'd find the world over. An electric bulb under a tin shade. Flaked white-painted iron bedstead, wooden dresser.

She sat on the edge of the bed, wearily pulled off the white cap. Her golden hair came out and made her beautiful again. He drew up a chair, leaned toward her, arms akimbo, poised on his knees. He said, "What happened? Tell me the whole thing from the beginning. See if I can get the hang of it. Talk low."

III

I hadn't seen him (she said) in three years. We were engaged before he left the States. He came out to work for one of the big oil companies here. I was to follow just as soon as he'd saved up enough money to send for me. Then, when he should have had enough laid aside, he started putting me off. Finally I got tired waiting, booked my own passage, came out without letting him know. I didn't tell him I was arriving until night before last when I sent him a cable from the ship. He met me yesterday at Yokohama.

He'd changed. He wasn't glad to see me, I could tell that right away. He was afraid of something. Even down there on the pier, while he was helping me to pass through the customs-inspection, he kept glancing nervously at the crowd around us, as if he was being watched or something.

When we got here it was even worse. He didn't seem to want to tell me where he lived. He wouldn't talk about himself at all. I'd been sending my letters to the company-office, you see. . . . I couldn't make head or tail of it. This morning when I woke up there was a piece of white goods tied around the knob of my door—like a long streamer or scarf. When I happened to mention it to him later on, he turned the ghastliest white. But I couldn't make him talk about that, either.

(Hollinger explained: "White's the color of mourning in this country. It means the same thing as crepe.")

I know that now (she went on). . . . I'll spare you all the little details. My love for him curled up, withered, died. I could feel that happening. You can't love a man that's frightened all the time. Anyway, I can't. Tonight we were sitting in one of the big modern restaurants on the Ginza. I happened to say: "Bob, this is deadly dull—can't you take me to one of the more exciting places?" He didn't seem to want to do that either—as though he were afraid to stray very far off the beaten path.

We argued about it a little—the girl who was waiting on us must have heard. Because not long after that he was called to the phone and as soon as his back was turned, this waitress came up to me. She hadn't been able to help overhearing, she said. If I wanted to see the real sights, I ought to get him to take me to the Yoshi. The House of Stolen Hours, she said, was a very agreeable place. Then Bob came back. And although he'd looked scared when he went to the phone, he was all right now. He said there'd been a mistake— no call for him at all.

It never occurred to me that there could be anything pre-arranged, sinister, about this sequence of events—that it might be a trick to get us in an out-of-the-way place where we couldn't easily get help.

Like a fool, I didn't tell Bob where I'd found out about the Yoshiwara. I let him think it was my own idea. I had a hard time talking him into taking me there, but finally he gave in.

We were shown into one of the little rooms and told just where to sit, to enjoy the entertainment—

(Hollinger interrupted: "There's something, right there. What difference would it have been *where* you sat, when you just unroll mats on the floor? Who told you?")

———⬤———

The manager, I guess it was (she answered). He spread out one mat for me, pointed to it, and I sat down. Then he spread the one for Bob *opposite* mine, instead of alongside it. My back was to one partition, his to the other. They spread the tea things between us. Mine tasted bitter, but I thought maybe that was on account of drinking it without cream and sugar.

There was a lantern shining right in my face. My eyes felt small, like pinheads, and the lantern light dazzled them. I began to get terribly sleepy. I asked Bob to change places with me, so I'd have my back to the light. He sat where I'd been, and I moved over to his side.

Then—the—thing happened—a minute later. Even I saw a faint gleam of light, shining through the screen from the next compartment behind Bob's back—as though someone had opened a slide and gone in there. A big looming shadow hovered over him, like a genie let out of a bottle in the Arabian Nights. Know what I mean? Sort of cloud like, blurred, bigger than life-size. Then it vanished, and the screen went blank. I was already feeling so numb, with a ringing in my ears. I couldn't be sure I'd really seen it.

Bob never made a sound. I thought he was bending over to pick up his cup at first, but he never straightened up again. Just kept going lower and lower. I thought blearily, "What's he putting his head all the way down like that for, is he going to try to drink it without using his hands?" Then the cup smashed under his chin and he just stayed that way. And then I could see this ivory knob sticking out between his shoulder blades, like—like a handle to lift him by. And red ribbons swirling out all around it, ribbons that *ran!* And the last thing I saw was a slit—a two or three-inch gash in the paper screen behind him. My own head got too heavy to hold up and I just fell over sideways on the floor and passed out.

But I *know*, I know I was sitting on the opposite side of the room from him, I *know* I didn't touch him—

When I opened my eyes, I was still there in that horrible place, in the flickering lantern light, and he was dead there opposite me, so I knew I hadn't dreamed it. The dream was from then on, until I met you. A nightmare.

The slide was just closing, as though someone had been in there with me. I struggled up on one elbow. There was a weight on my hands, and I looked down to see what it was, and there was the knife! The blood-smeared blade was resting flat across the palm of one, the fingers of the other were folded tight around the ivory hilt. There was blood on the front of my dress, as though the knife had been wiped on it.

("That's the symbol of transferring the guilt of the crime to you," he told her.)

The slide was shoved back, as though they'd been timing me, waiting for me to come to before breaking in and confronting me. The manager came in alone first. He flew into a fury. The way he kept yelling at me—it was awful. I couldn't think or say anything at all. He pulled me up by one arm and kept bellowing into my face: "You kill! You kill in my house! You make me big disgrace—you make me lose face before customers!"

I tried to tell him that Bob had been stabbed through the paper screen from the next compartment, and when I pointed to where the gash had been—it was gone! The paper was perfectly whole.

He kept pointing to the blood on my dress, the knife at my feet, kept shaking me back and forth like a terrier. Finally he stamped out to call the police. That was my only chance. I got up and ran, I ran the other way, toward the back. I couldn't find my way out, I thought I'd go mad there in that place with fright and horror, but—I'd heard your voice when we first went in, saying "Here's looking at you, kids!" I knew there was an American somewhere under the same roof, if I could only find him—

IV

"That's the story, Hollinger. And here I am, and here you are."

"Not on your life, lady," he grinned, getting up and shoving his chair back. "Here you are, maybe, but I'm on my way back there, to do a little housecleaning." He cupped his hands, blew into them, rubbed them together like a kid going to a circus.

"But they know you helped me get away. They must be looking for *you* by this time. If I let you go back there again—"

"Sure they know. And sure they're looking for me. But that's the one place they're *not* looking for me. Don't you see that? I'm going back there and find out what happened to that slashed paper. The first lesson in that detective book said that when evidence either for or against a suspect disappears from the scene of the crime, look for collusion. First I thought that was some kind of a train smash-up, but one of the officers on the battle-wagon told me it means people getting together to put something over on somebody. You say you saw a slit in the paper. When you came to it was gone. The answer is there's a trick somewhere. Maybe the manager is in on it. Because I don't see how they could do that in his house without his knowing it.

"Now, I've got to locate the exact compartment you were in, and that's not going to be an easy job, the way those places are all alike."

"Wait," she said, "I think I can help you. It's not much of a thing to go by, but—Those lanterns in each cubicle—did you notice that they all have a character heavily inked in on them?"

"Yeah, I couldn't tell one from the other. They're laundry-tickets to me."

"I don't mean that. The one in our booth was finished in a hurry or something, the craftsman inked his brush too heavily. Anyway, a single drop of ink came to a head at the bottom of the character, with the slope of the lantern. It ran down a little way, left a blurred track ending in a dark blob. It was staring me in the face in the beginning, before I changed places, that's how I know. Here, give me a pencil—all right this burnt match-stick will do. It's very easy to remember, you don't need to know what it means. Two seagulls with bent wings, one above the other. Under them simply a pot-hook. Then this blot of dried ink hanging down from that like a pendulum. Look for that, and you'll have the cubicle we were in. I don't think they've bothered to remove the lantern, because they wouldn't expect a foreigner to notice a little thing like that."

"Neither would I," he said and nodded approvingly at her. He picked up a razor blade from the edge of the washstand, carefully sheathed it in a fragment of newspaper.

"What's that for?"

"To let myself in with. In some ways, paper houses are pretty handy. Lock yourself in here behind me, just to be on the safe side. I'll give you the high sign when I come back. Don't open up for anybody else at all."

She moved after him to the door. "You'll never make it in that uniform. It's all torn."

"I'll take care of that, borrow something from the Roosky down-stairs. Try to get some sleep and get that dope out of your system."

The last thing she murmured through the crack of the door as he slid out into the hallway was, "Please be careful."

"Okay, lady," he said with a grin, saluting jauntily from the eyebrow.

———◆———

The Russian, behind the shelf that served for an accommodation desk, growled, "Eh, tzailor! Is no fight by back of house, why you tell me to *go* look?" He pointed to the split middy. "I tink you fight youself."

"Never been known to. Listen, I gotta go out and it's cold. Lend me a hat and coat."

"Sure, bott you leaf deposit. How I know you come back?"

"Here's your deposit, suspicious guy." It felt funny to have something with a brim to it on his head, after two years. The bell-bottomed pants were a give-away, but he counted on the darkness to take care of that. He had to fasten the coat's top button over his bare neck, where civilians wore collars and ties.

A quarter of an hour later he was casually strolling past the front of the Stolen Hours again, hands in pockets, hat-brim tipped down to his nose. The place was shut up tight, whether by police order or at its owner's discretion he couldn't tell. Probably the latter, for no policeman had been left posted outside the premises. The Yoshi had quieted down. Lights still peered out up and down its byways, but the dance halls and pool-parlors had closed up shop for the night, and the only wayfarers in the streets now were homeward-bound drunks and an occasional pickpocket or lush-worker sidling past in the shadows.

He didn't try to get in the Stolen Hours from the front, but went around the block to the next street over, located the lane they'd escaped through and threaded his way along it. There was a bamboo wicket barring it at the inner end. He didn't bother with it—just climbed up over with a seaman's agility and dropped soundlessly down on the inside.

The lanterns were out and the garden was lifeless. The faint gurgle of the brook was the only sound there was. Hollinger stole over the bridge, a looming, top-heavy figure out of all proportion to its microscopic measurements; he was still without shoes, never having recovered his footgear after that first flight. He obliterated himself under the uptilted roof-projection that shadowed the rear of the house, with only the heels of his torn white socks showing in the gloom.

Only taut paper faced him. They didn't use locks or bolts apparently but hitched the frames up fast in some way on the inside. He took out the razor blade and made a neat hair-line gash down alongside the frame, then another close to the ground, making an L around the lower corner. He lifted it up like a tent-flap and ducked through. It cracked a little, but not much, fell stiffly into place again.

The house seemed deserted. Hollinger couldn't be sure whether or not the manager slept here after hours. The geishas and other employees probably didn't. He could hear bottled crickets chirping and clacking rhythmically somewhere ahead and didn't, unfortunately, realize that crickets are used as watchdogs in Japan. They stop chirping whenever a stranger enters the house. They did that now. The sound broke off short almost at the first tentative steps he took, and didn't resume.

———◆———

He worked his way forward feeling his way along the cool slippery wooden flooring with a prehensile toe-and-heel grip, shuffling the multiple deck of screens aside with a little upward hitch that kept them from clicking in their grooves. He waited until he was nearly midway through the house, as far as he could judge, before he lighted his first match. He guarded it carefully with the hollow of his hand, reduced the light to a pink glow. The place seemed deserted.

He tried six of the cubicles before he got the right place. There it was. Traces of Mallory's blood still showed black on the floor. The smeared ink-track on the lantern was just a confirmation. He lit the wick and the lantern bloomed out orange at him, like a newly risen sun.

The location of the blood smears told him which of the four sides to case. The screen out in place at the moment was, as she had said, intact. He ran his fingers questioningly along its frame, to see if it felt sticky, damp, with newly-applied paste. It was dry and gave no signs of having been recently inserted. He could see, now, that the inserts weren't glued into the frame at all, they were caught between the lips of a long, continuous split in the bamboo and held fast by the pressure of the two halves of the wood closing over them again, helped out by an occasional little wooden nail or peg. They couldn't be put in in a hurry.

But they could be taken out in a hurry, couldn't they? He shoved it all the way back flush with the two lateral screens, and squinted into the socket it had receded into. There were two frame-edges visible, not just one. He caught at the second one, and it slid out empty, bare of paper! But there were tell tale little strips and slivers of white all up and down it where the paper had been hastily slashed away.

He just stood there and nodded grimly at it. "Unh-hunh," he said.

Probably the frame itself would be unslung tomorrow and sent out to have a new filler put in. Or destroyed. They hadn't had the opportunity tonight, with the place buzzing with police. He didn't think the rest of the staff had been in on it—just the manager and the murderer. The fact that the girl's last-minute change of position hadn't been revealed to them in time showed that. The geishas waiting on the couple would have tipped them off if they'd been accessories. They hadn't, and Mallory had been killed by mistake. But she'd only arrived the day before—why did they want her out of the way, not him? . . .

Hollinger pondered.

———◆◆◆———

There was no audible warning. But his shifting of the slide had exposed the assassin's compartment beyond the one he was in, and the lantern-light reaching wanly to the far screen of that threw up a faint gray blur overlapping his own shadow—a shadow with upraised arm ending in a sharp downward-projected point. Seeing that shadow saved his life.

The dagger came down behind him with no whisper of sound and he flung himself flat on the floor under it, rolled as he hit. It nailed down the loose overlapping width of the Russian's coat, bit through it into the plank, skewered it there. His assailant, thrown off balance, came floundering down on him.

They both had sense enough not to try for the knife, which was jammed in the floor halfway up to the hilt.

Hollinger couldn't have chosen a worse position if he'd spent a year beforehand working it out. He was flat on his stomach with what felt like the sacred mountain of Fujiyama on top of him. He couldn't use either arm effectively; and he was pinned down by eight inches of steel through a coat he couldn't work himself out of. He nearly broke his back trying to rear up high enough to swing his shoulders around and get his arms into play.

Apelike hands found his throat, closed in, got to work. Two or three backhand blows glanced harmlessly off a satiny jaw-line. Hollinger gave that up, brought his legs into play instead. He got a scissors-lock on the short thick neck of the Oriental, squeezed.

The throttling hands left his throat to try to pry his legs off. He let them be wrenched apart without much resistance; the hold had been just a stop-gap—too passive to get him anywhere. They broke, jockeyed to get into better positions, blowing like fish on land.

Hollinger rolled over on his back, the razor-edged dagger cut its way free through his coat, remained bedded in the floor. He scrambled to his feet, staying low, resting his knuckles on the floor for a counter-balance till he was ready.

The Japanese had planted his feet wide apart like a croquet-wicket. He crouched low so that his chest was nearly touching the floor. The coppery, rippling muscles of his chest peered through the opening of his flimsy kimono.

Hollinger straightened, came up at him swinging. The right he sent in should have taken care of anyone. But it went wide, streaked upward into the air. The Jap cupped a slapping hand to his elbow, gripped the thumb of that hand at the same time. Hollinger felt himself leaving the floor like a rocket, twisting through the empty frame. He landed with a brutal thud in the compartment behind them, where Mallory had been killed. The fall left Hollinger squirming, half-paralyzed. The Japanese whirled to face him, stamped both feet in a new position, crouched again.

Jiu-jitsu. Hollinger knew he was sunk, unless he got a lucky break. He stumbled up again, weaved around warily, arching all over and with his ears humming. What good were dukes against a system of invisible weights and balances?

The hands shot out at him again, open. His own dizziness saved him; he gave a lurch to one side, his reflexes still stunned. The Japanese wasn't quick enough in shifting position; his legs and shoulders swung, but for a second his flank was exposed. Hollinger didn't waste the opening. He sent in a quick short jab to the vital nerve-center under the ear. That rocked the Japanese for a second, held him long enough for Hollinger to wind up a real one. He sent home one of those once-in-a-lifetime blows. The yellow man's face came around just in time to get it between the eyes. The squat figure went over like a ninepin, and Hollinger stood swaying, his bleary eyes watchful, waiting for the other to come at him again but the Japanese was finished. He lay there gasping, threads of blood leaking from his ear, nose and mouth. His eyes stared stonily, without sight in them, at nothing.

Hollinger let out a groan and then let himself slide to the floor.

A couple of minutes went by. No one else came in. That was all to the good because Hollinger felt that one whack with a flexible fly-swatter would finish him off.

The Japanese began to groan after awhile, twitching his shoulders, arms, legs. But there was a board-like stiffness about his middle that caught the sailor's eye. It had cost the Japanese the fight whatever it was. A wedge of white showed, in the kimono-opening, below the rising and falling coppery chest. Underclothing maybe. Whatever it was had kept the yellow man from pivoting out of the range of Holllinger's finishing blow.

The sailor bent over him, pulled the garment open. Paper. Layer after layer of stiff, board-like paper, rolled around him like a cuirass, extending from ribs to thighs. A sash held it in place.

Hollinger rolled him out of his queer cocoon by pushing him across the floor, like a man laying a carpet. The stuff was in two lengths, one under the other. The Japanese had evidently slashed the whole square out of the screen first, then quickly slit that into two strips to narrow it so that he could wind it around himself. The knife-gash itself showed up in the second section, as it peeled free. The edges driven inward by the knife. Any cop worth his salt ought to be able to figure out what really happened with this to go by.

He riffled it out of the way. Then he flung himself down on the still stunned Japanese and gripped him by the throat. "Who was it?" he said in a low voice. "Who was in there? Who killed American fella?"

"No!" was the only answer he could get. "No!" Again and again.

"Better open up! This is waiting for you!" He showed a fist.

"No see! Man go in, come out again. I no know!"

"After what I just took off your hide? All right, here she comes!"

"Denguchi do! Denguchi do! I no do, he do! He get money for to do, he hired for to do—"

"Who hired him, you—?"

The yellow man's eyes glazed. Then closed. The head rolled over heavily. Hollinger swore. He got up and quickly rolled the paper into a long staff, tucked it under his arm, took it out with him. Nothing more he could do here tonight.

The Russian was snoring in his lighted wall-niche when Hollinger got downtown again. Hollinger chased up the stairs past him, wangled the knob of his door triumphantly. "Hey, lady. Evelyn! It's me, open up and listen to the good news!"

V

There wasn't a sound from within. She must be in a pretty deep sleep, after what she'd been through earlier. He begun to thump subduedly. "Miss Brainard," he said. "Lemme in, will ya?" Finally he went at the door in a way no sleeper could have ignored. He crouched down, looked through the keyhole. The light was still on inside, and he could make out the pear-shape of the key on the inside of the door.

Frightened now, he threw his shoulder against the door. The cheap lock tore off at the fourth onslaught. The Russian, roused, had come up meanwhile and was having epileptic fits at the damage to his premises.

The girl had vanished, with the key still locked from inside. A corner of the bedding trailed off onto the floor. One of the cheap net-curtains inside the window was torn partly off its rod, as though somebody had clutched at it despairingly. The window was all the way open. There was a tin extension-roof just below it, which sloped to within easy reach of the alley.

It wasn't the police. They would have come in by the door, gone out with her by the door. All he had to go on was a name—Denguchi.

"Didn't you hear anything? Didn't you hear her scream out up here?"

The Russian immediately turned professionally indignant. "Oh, so you got girl opstairs! For this is extra charge!"

"I haven't now!" gritted Hollinger, and the lodging-house keeper drew back hastily at sight of the grim lines in his face.

"I no hear. I tzleep. How I know you got somebody op here?"

Hollinger tested the disturbed bed with the back of his hand. It still showed faint traces of warmth. "She hasn't been gone very long—" he muttered. "But every minute I stand here—"

Where would they take her? What could they possibly want with her? Just to hold her as a hostage, shut her up about the first murder? He didn't think so. It was *she* they'd meant to get the first time, and not the man. Now they'd come back to correct the mistake. Then why hadn't they killed her right here, why had they gone to the trouble of smuggling her out the window? The only answer he could find for that was that somebody had sent out after her. Somebody who hadn't come here had wanted to see it done, had wanted to gloat. Who could be that interested in killing a woman? Only another woman. There was another woman in this somewhere, he should have realized that from the beginning—

He had a sudden hunch where to go to look for her. He remembered Evelyn's remark in the taxi: "He didn't seem to want me to know where he lived."

He grabbed the Russian by the shoulder. "How do you find an address in a hurry, an address you don't know? I'm out of my depth now—"

"You osk inflammation-lady at telephone-exchange—"

Not so different from home after all. He started shoving the Russian downstairs ahead of him. "Do it for me, I can't talk the lingo! The name's Robert Mallory—and tell her to steer the police over there fast—"

The Russian came out in a moment and threw a "twenty-five" and a tongue-twisting street-name at him.

"I'm leaving," Hollinger called back. "Take care of that cylinder of paper upstairs for me!" He ran out into the streets saying the unpronounceable name over to himself out loud. If he dropped a syllable, it might cost Evelyn Brainard her life. He got a prowling cab just by luck. He kept on saying it over and over, even after he was in it.

"I hear," sighed the driver finally, "I catch."

—◆—

Mallory had done himself well. His place turned out to be a little bungalow on one of the better-class residential streets, with grounds around it, even a little garage behind it and a driveway for his car. There were no lights in front, but the garage told him his hunch had been right. The reflected square of a lighted rear-window showed up against it, ghostly-pale, thrown over from the house. Someone was in the back of the house. Mallory had died hours ago in the House of Stolen Hours, and if the police were here, they would have been in front of the place, not in back.

He didn't waste time on the front door, just hooded the Russian's coat over his head for padding, bucked one of the ground-floor window-panes head on. It shattered and he climbed in, nicking his hands a little. A scream sounded through the house, then broke off short as though a hand had been thrown over the mouth emitting it. He waded out of the velvety darkness of the room he was in toward a semi-lighted hallway, toppling over something fragile behind him.

He ran down the hallway toward the light at the back. As the room swung into his vision he saw the Brainard girl in there, writhing, clutching at her throat, a darker head peering from behind her blond one. Somebody was strangling her with a scarf, or trying to.

But nearer at hand there was a sense of lurking menace hidden behind the slightly-stirring bead curtains bunched over to one side of the entryway. The girl, half-throttled as she was, tried to warn him with a limply outflung hand in that direction.

He caught up a slim teakwood stand, rammed it head on into the stringy covert, at stomach level. It brought a knife slashing down out at him, as if by reflex action. It cut the air in two before him. He grabbed at the tan fist holding it, brought it all the way out, vised it against him. Then he sent a swift punch home about two feet above it. The beaded strips lacerated his knuckles, but they must have lacerated the face behind them too, acting like cruel little brass-knuckles.

There was a yelp of agony and the man reeled out into the open, a short little demon in a candy-striped blazer. Hollinger twisted the knife out of his hand by shoulder pressure, gave him a second head blow that dropped him. Something white streaked by him, and when he looked over at her, the Brainard girl was alone, coughing as she struggled to unwind the strangling sash from her throat. She staggered toward him, fell into his arms with a jerky backward hitch of the elbows, like something worked on strings.

A door had banged closed upstairs somewhere.

The Japanese didn't know he was finished yet. He was starting to inch over toward where he had dropped the knife. Hollinger jumped in between, kicked it out of his reach once and for all, hauled him to his feet by the collar of his sweater, hauled off and dropped him with a remarkable final blow.

The girl had collapsed into a chair, and was breathing with a pitiful burgeoning-out and sinking-in of her body at the waist. He found a water-tap in a western-style kitchen adjoining the room, filled the hollows of his hands, came back and wetted her throat with it. He did that three or four times until that awful breathing was nearly normal again.

"Attagirl," he said. "You're hard to kill—like me."

She managed a wan smile. "The only reason it wasn't all over with by the time you got here was that she had to get it out of her system first—rub it in that he'd been hers, not mine. She dragged me around on a Cook's Tour of the house, with a speech for every memento—"

"Who was she?"

Her gaze fell before his. "His wife," she said slowly, "poor thing. Legally married to him by the Shinto rites—"

He shook his head at her. "What a rat he was," he said. He turned. "She's still in here someplace—I heard her go upstairs."

She reached out, caught him by the arm. "No," she said with a peculiar look, "I don't think so. She—loved him very much, you see."

He didn't at all. A whiff of sandalwood incense crept down the stairs, floated in to them, as if to punctuate her cryptic remark.

The police-watch came trooping in on them at this point, with a great flourishing and waving of clubs, hemmed them in against the wall.

"Now you get here," Hollinger greeted them ungratefully.

"*Hai!*" said the cocky little detective, and pointed to the professional hatchet-man on the floor. Immediately two of the cops started whacking him with their clubs. Then they turned him over on his face, lashed his hands behind him with rope, and dragged him out by the feet—a nice Oriental touch.

They had, evidently, been playing steeplechase, picking up the traces Hollinger had been leaving all night long. They had the battered Stolen Hours proprietor, the furled wall-paper, the Russian, and the first taxi-driver, the one who must have gone back and betrayed the girl's hiding-place to Denguchi.

The detective, puffing out his chest like a pouter-pigeon, said to her, "So you do not kill this man. Why you not stay and say so, pliss? You put us to great trouble."

"We put *you* to great trouble?" Hollinger yelped.

"Iss grave misdemeanor. Run away from question iss not good. You must come and give explanation before magistrate."

"Why, you little pint-sized—!"

She quickly reached out and braked his twitching arm against his side. "Don't you ever get tired of fighting?" she murmured.

"What fighting? I didn't have one good man-sized fight all night, only guys that bite you, grab your thumbs, and jump you from behind curtains!" he said aggrievedly.

"Where other woman?"

The sandalwood, like the troubled spirit of one departed, hovered in the air about them. They found her upstairs, behind the locked door, kneeling in death on a satin prayer-pillow before a framed photograph of the man Evelyn Brainard had come out to rob her of. A pinch of incense sent a thread of smoke curling up before it. Her god. Forward she toppled, as the ritual prescribed, to show she was not afraid of meeting death. Hands tucked under her, clasping the hari-kari knife.

She looked pathetic and lovely and small—incapable almost of the act of violence that had been necessary in order to die.

To have interfered, the sailor somehow felt, staring in from the doorway, would have been the worst sort of desecration. He looked at the weak mouth and chin pictured inside the frame. Too cowardly to hurt either one, he had hurt both, one unto death. A pair of love birds were twittering in a scarlet bamboo cage. A bottle of charcoal-ink, a writing brush, a long strip of paper with hastily-traced characters, lay behind her on the floor.

The detective picked it up, began to read.

"I, Yugiri-san, Mist of the Evening, most unworthy of wives, go now to keep my honored husband's house in the sky, having unwittingly twice failed to carry out my honored husband's wish—"

The girl had stayed downstairs. "Don't tell her, will you?" Hollinger said when the detective had finished translating the death-scroll for his benefit. "She doesn't have to know. Let her go on thinking the woman was the one tried to get rid of her, through jealousy. Don't tell her the man she came out to marry hired a murderer to get her out of his way, because he didn't have guts enough to tell her to her face. It's tough enough as it is."

The detective sucked in his breath politely. "This was—*fffs*—great crime, to make it seem another had done it."

"It was—*fffs*—great pain-in-the-neck while it lasted," the sailor agreed.

It was getting light in Tokyo when they left the police station, walking slowly side by side. They had their shoes at last, and that was almost the best thing of all.

"I guess," she said ruefully, linking her arm in his, "I pretty well messed-up your shore-leave for you."

"Naw," he assured her, "you made it. Absolutely! That reminds me, keep the night of November third open, will you?"

"November third? But that's six months away!"

"I know, but that's when we get into Frisco Bay."

"I will," she said. "I'll keep November third for you. There isn't any night that I wouldn't keep for you—ever."

"Well, I'll borrow a minute from one night now," Hollinger said. He took her in his arms.

AFTERWORD TO "DEATH IN THE YOSHIWARA"

"Death in the Yoshiwara" (*Argosy*, January 29, 1938) is the only Woolrich pulp story set in Japan and a gem of pure whizbang action writing that will remind older readers of a Republic Pictures cliffhanger serial, while its protagonist will no doubt strike younger generations as a prototype of Indiana Jones. The climax of course comes straight of *Madama Butterfly* and demonstrates yet again how profoundly Woolrich was influenced by seeing Puccini's opera in Mexico City when he was a boy.

ENDICOTT'S GIRL

Jenny hadn't come home by the time we were through our meal. I couldn't wait because I had to get back to the precinct-house. As I left the table, I growled, "Wonder where she is?"

My sister said, "Oh, she's probably having a soda with her girl friends. She only went out a minute or two before you got back." Her school books were there on the radiator, so I didn't have to be told that.

I looked at the books fondly on my way past. "Duncan's Elements of Trigonometry" was the title of the top one. I shook my head and snorted. Now, what earthly good was it filling a pretty eighteen-year-old girl's head with junk like that? In one ear, out the other. Bad enough to ladle it out to boys . . . There was a tiny light-blue handkerchief, so thin you could see through it, caught between the pages. I pulled it out, held it between my thumb and forefinger, and chuckled. Now, that was more like it. That was what a girl should be interested in, not trigo-what-ever-it-was. There was a little colored design of a kitten stitched on one corner, and there was an intermingled odor of honeysuckle and chocolate. She probably took candy to school, wrapped in it, I thought as I laid it back again between the pages of the book. I walked on into my bedroom.

I buttoned up my collar, put on my vest, fixed the rope that I call a tie, and slipped into my coat. I opened the bureau-drawer and felt blindly for my gun. Then I had to open the drawer wider and look, because I couldn't find it. I didn't always carry it around with me, being a captain, since it pulled my suit out of shape.

I disarranged all the shirts my sister had neatly piled up in the drawer, and still I couldn't find it. "What'd you do with my gun?" I called in to her. "I can't find it."

"It's wherever you put it last," she answered. "Don't ask me where that is. You ought to know by now I wouldn't put a hand on it for love nor money."

That was true, for she was afraid of guns. She used to even ask me to pick it up and move it, when she wanted to clean out the drawer.

"Did you take it with you this morning?" she asked. "Maybe you left it down at the precinct-house."

"No," I said short-temperedly, "what do you think I do, go around cannoned-up like an armored-truckman? I simply wanted to turn it over to one of the guys in the lab, have it cleaned and oiled. It's getting a little rusty."

"Well, I'm sure I don't know what *I'd* want with it. Or Jenny either, for that matter. And we're the only other two people living in the house with you."

"There you go," I said. Her bringing Jenny into it was pure whimsy, as far as I was concerned. "I didn't say anything about you wanting it. Can't a man ask a question in his own house? I can't find it, that's all."

I was getting sick of this.

"Well, look in the right place and you will!" And that was all the help I could get out of her.

———⟨∙◇∙⟩———

The front door opened and the kid came in just then. I was in the hall closet by that time, and by the time I could shift around to look, she'd gone by me.

I heard my sister say, "I kept your supper warm, dear. What are you walking like that for?"

"Oh, my heel came off just now, crossing the trolley tracks. I'll have to go around to the shoemaker right after supper."

"*Tsk tsk,* you could have been run over."

I came back into the room and put on my hat. "Well, I'll have to go without it," I said. "Look for it for me, will you, Maggie? I want to turn it over to Kelcey."

But she didn't have any time for me now that the kid was back. She was too busy putting food on the table.

The kid was in my room, but that was understandable, since the mirror in there was the handiest and you know how kids are with mirrors. I happened to glance past the door and she was gazing at herself in it as though for the first time.

She must have heard me for she whirled and said: "I thought you'd gone already! I didn't see you! Where were you?"

"Why, you brushed right by me," I said, laughing. "Where are your eyes?"

She came toward me and first I thought she was going to fall, but I guess it was her shoe. I said, "Got a kiss for your old man?" There was no answer.

"What's the matter?" I asked.

She shook her head quickly.

"Nothing," she said.

My sister called her just then to come in and sit down, and she left me like she couldn't get away fast enough. Just hungry, I guess.

The bureau-drawer was still open so, just for luck, I went over and took another look. And there was the gun, between two of my shirts.

I scratched my head and said to myself, "Well, I'm a great one!" You wouldn't think you could miss anything that size and weight, in such a small drawer.

I hadn't quite finished slinging it away as I came though the doorway, and they both got a glimpse of it. The kid must have been hungry and tired all right for her face was white and drawn.

My sister couldn't let a chance like that go by. "Oh," she said, nodding severely, "so you did find it! What did I tell you?" She continued to prattle on about my carelessness.

In the middle of it, without either of one of us seeing her go, the kid suddenly wasn't there at the table any more. But we heard the bedroom door close and then there was a sound of something heavy dropping on the bed.

I just looked blank. I hadn't been yelling or anything. In fact, I hadn't said a word. But my sister took it out on *me* anyway. "Oh, anyone but a man would understand," she said, and looked wise. What about, I don't know. She picked up the kid's dinner-plate and carried it toward the room, calling, "Jenny dear, finish your supper for Aunt Margaret." Then to me over her shoulder: "Go on to your job!"

Riding down to the precinct-house on the bus, I said to myself: "I'm going to see she eases up a little on her schoolwork, she's been working too hard at it. That damn trigger-whatever-it-is would make anyone nervous."

The desk-sergeant put Holmes through to me at about ten that night. He said, "Cap, we've just turned up a homicide out here at Starrett Avenue. Number twenty-five. Guy shot dead in a bungalow. Want to come out and take a look?" The last was just rhetoric, of course.

"Yep," I said briefly, and hung up.

I got in touch with Prints, Pix, and the examiner, told them where to go, and then I picked up Jordan and we rode out. . . .

It was a cheap little house, the kind that are put up a whole dozen at a time. Each one about ten or twelve yards away from the next. It was the only one in the whole row that was lit up, except one way down at the corner. The whole community must have been out to the movies in a body.

We braked, got out, and went up on the porch. The light over it was lit, and Holmes had the door swung back out of the way, with just a screen-door veiling the lighted room. We went right into the room itself from the porch. The man was there, lying on his face, with an arm thrown up around his head, as though he had tried to ward off the shot.

My instinctive impression of the man, even before I'd even seen the face, was that he had been a no-good.

Holmes and the patrolman from the beat were both there with us. The cop was just waiting to be told what next to do, and Holmes was taking stabs at looking around—which I guessed he had only started after he heard us drive up. There's really nothing to be done until after the experts have had their innings, but the average second-grader hasn't the moral courage to sit there with his hands folded when his captain walks in on him. I was a second-grader once myself. And before that, a harness-cop.

"Who is he?" I asked.

The cop said, "Their name is Trinker. His wife is over at her sister's in Mapledale, who's been down with the flu or something."

He had the details all right.

I said, "How do you know?"

"It's my beat, sir," he said. "She stopped on the sidewalk and told me about it when she was leaving Wednesday. I saw the door open and the room lit up, like it is now, when I first came on duty. Kind of cold for the door to be open these nights. But I went on past the first time, thinking he might have gone out for something and didn't have a key. It was still that way the second time I made my rounds, so I went up the walk and called out to him, and then I stuck my head through the door, and there he was. I happened to run into Holmes down at the call-box—"

"You been relieved on your beat?"

"Yes sir, of course."

"You come on at six, don't you?"

"Yes sir."

"About what time was it when you walked past here the first time?"

"Ten-after at the most, sir."

"That places it for us then," I told Holmes and Jordan. "It wasn't dark enough for lights much before six. And they were turned on, of course, before it happened, while he was still alive. Between six and six-ten."

This needed confirmation, of course. Nothing's ever certain. The lights *could* have been lit long after he was killed, by a sneak-thief stealing in, or the murderer himself, but it was a very slim possibility. The examiner confirmed it as soon as he got there. "About four hours," he said, which carried it back to six—and then the office where this Trinker worked reconfirmed it, if you want to call it that. I had Jordan call the office-manager at his home; Trinker had left there about ten to five. He couldn't have gotten out here in much under thirty minutes, even by bus.

He hadn't been killed right away after he got in. There were four cigarette butts discarded around the living-room—another twenty minutes even if he'd smoked one after another. The soap upstairs in the bathroom was still moist and the ironed folding-lines in a Turkish towel had been erased by recent use. He'd evidently taken a bath and changed after he came home. So the time was figured about right.

———⊰♦⊱———

I sent Holmes out to Mapledale to bring back Trinker's wife. "You don't know what about, until I talk to her," I warned him through the screen door. I like fresh material to work on.

I asked the cop whether there'd been lights in any of the other houses when he went by the first time, or just this one.

"Most of them were lit up. I guess they were all home having their suppers," he said. "The next one beyond is vacant, though."

I said, "Well then I wonder how it is nobody seems to have heard the shot?"

He said, "Well they were getting coal in down one of these long chutes further down the street, and you know what a racket that makes tumbling down."

"What company?" I asked him. "If the murderer left by the front door while they were delivering it there's a chance that truckdriver and his helper got a look at him."

"I didn't notice, Captain Endicott," he said.

"You want to watch those things," I rebuked mildly. "You want to be a detective some day, don't you?" But it was easy enough to find out, there were only three companies in town.

"That's you," I said to Jordan. "Find out which of them delivered a load to this street late today. Get hold of the men that made the delivery, and if they noticed anybody at all come out of here, or even go by on the street, bring them down."

The cameramen took all the pictures worth taking, and then went down to Headquarters to develop. The body was taken out, and I asked for as quick a report on the bullet as Ballistics could give me. Then I was left alone in the house, with the cop cooling his heels by the door while I worked.

The front room, where he had been dropped, was entirely undisturbed. The struggle had taken place in the kitchen behind it. The rear door of that was locked on the inside, so the murderer had left by the front and those coalheavers might just come in very handy.

It had been no slight struggle either, by the looks of it. The chairs and the table were over on their sides, and dishes and things were smashed wholesale all over the floor. Scattered remnants of food showed he'd been sitting down to a meal by himself when his caller arrive. There were also two highball glasses, one drained, one almost untouched. They hadn't been destroyed because both had been set down out of the way on a low shelf.

The signs of struggle in one room, the lack of them in the other, told me it had been a woman right away, even a rookie could have figured that out.

Instead of trying to run *away* from the assailant, he had gone *after* her, from one room into the next. The bullet hole had been in the front, not the back of his head.

There'd been a complete absence of any bruises or welts on his face. If it had been a man there would have been at least a mark or two showing on him.

Confirmation quickly followed. Even my unaided eye could make out a smudge of red on the rim of the undrained glass.

I went upstairs and looked the rooms over more thoroughly than we had the first time. There was plenty of stuff such as letters, memoranda, and belongings, to fill in his background.

He and his wife had been married four years the previous June. Her picture gave me the impression of an honest, straightforward woman who wouldn't try to hide anything. It was smiling a little sadly, like she was making the best of a bad bargain. A bank book showed that they hadn't put away much money. I jotted a reminder down in my notebook to find out what salary he'd been paid.

I went downstairs again. The cop had been sitting down resting his legs but straightened up again when he heard me coming. I was sure of that because I used to do the same thing myself when I was a beat-pounder.

"Spooky after they're gone, isn't it?" I muttered. "Still gets me, and I've been on about a hundred of them by now."

He said, "Yes sir, Captain Endicott." But he didn't sound very definite about it.

The phone rang just as I got down to the bottom step, and I went to it alertly, but it wasn't a private call. It was for me. Jordan, to tell me he had the two coal-heavers down at Headquarters.

"All right, keep them there," I said, "I'll be down shortly, I'm just winding up here."

I went back into the kitchen again and scuffed the china-fragments around aimlessly. And then I kicked aside some dishes and uncovered a heel.

Looking at it reminded me of how Jenny's had come off too; it only showed how insecure the average feminine heel was. It was a wonder they didn't hurt themselves more often than they did.

———◆———

The screen-door opened and Holmes came in with Mrs. Trinker just then, so I put it into my pocket for the time being and went out to talk to her.

"What's happened?" she said in a sort of helpless, pleading voice. The harness-bull by the door loomed bigger than either Holmes or myself to her, the way a uniform usually does to a layman. "What's this officer doing here? Has Paul done something?"

She was a nice wholesome-looking blonde, of the housewife type. Her voice was the nicest thing about her. Soft and soothing, the kind that is seldom raised in anger. She was well-dressed and quite nice looking.

"I had to leave my sister sick in bed," she said.

I hated this part of it that was coming next. "Sit down, won't you?" I flicked my eyes at the staircase, and Holmes ran up it unnoticed to the bathroom to try to find a sedative in case she needed it. He knew what I meant by past experience.

"But where is he? This other man wouldn't tell me anything coming down."

I said, "Your husband's been shot."

"Bad?" She got white, not all in one flash, but slowly.

"He's gone," I said.

I don't need to go into it after that. I could tell in about five minutes that I wouldn't be able to question her any that night. A matron came up to take charge of her as soon as she was able to walk, and took her to a hotel in her custody. There was no need to lock the poor woman up in a cell for the night.

A new cop came up on special duty to keep an eye on the premises from outside, and I started to put the lights out and lock up, to go down to the house and work on what we had. We were about through up here for all present purposes. I was the last one in the place. Holmes had gone out to the car and was chewing the rag with the cop, while he waited for me.

The living-room switch was just inside the front door, and as I crossed toward it, my current cigar butt, which had grown too small to handle adequately, slipped out of my lips and dropped to the floor. I stooped down to get it, naturally, not wanting a fire to start after we'd left the place, and with my line of vision way down low like that, parallel to the floor, I saw this object under the sofa.

People had sat on that sofa all night long, Holmes, the cop, Mrs. Trinker, and their feet must have been just an inch or two away from it, but nobody had seen it. I thought it was just a crumpled piece of paper, or maybe even a ball of gray waste from a vacuum or carpet-sweeper, but I reached in and pulled it out.

It was a handkerchief; a woman's handkerchief, pale-blue and so thin you could almost look through it. It had a little colored design of a kitten stitched on one corner. A faint hint of honeysuckle reached my nose, and when I raised it higher, it got stronger, and there was a whiff of something else; like it had been wrapped around a chocolate bar.

I had a tickling sensation in my memory of smelling, or looking at, or picking up, something just like this, somewhere before. But the rest of my mind was on the job and told me: "She dropped it, all right. It's never Mrs. Trinker's, I know that already."

I started to stuff it into my pocket—until I could go out and show it to Holmes—and my knuckles brushed the heel that was already in there, and the lining of my throat suddenly contracted.

Did you ever get dizzy on your knees? I was on my knees there, upright in front of the sofa, and the four walls of the room suddenly shifted around me. The one opposite me went off to the side, then in back of me, then around to the other side, then they were all back where they started again. But meanwhile I had to reach out and steady myself against the edge of the sofa.

A clock was ticking somewhere in the house. Upstairs in the bedroom, I guess. I could hear it clearly in the stillness.

It had ticked hundreds and hundreds of times, when finally Holmes' voice came in to me from the curb outside: "Coming, Cap? What's holding you up?"

I was still there on my knees, supporting myself with one hand out against the edge of the sofa. I was afraid he'd come in and find me there. I took my hand out of my pocket where it had stayed all this time, and left the handkerchief in there with the heel.

It was a slow business, getting up. I am still only forty, but I knew what it felt like to be sixty. I planted one foot flat and hoisted myself on that, then I dragged the other one up after it, and I groaned with the effort. Or maybe it was a broken mainspring, inside me.

I said something. I heard a sound come out of me that said, "My little girl," and I zig-zagged in the middle and almost went down again.

I dragged myself over to the light-switch and punched it out, and the kindly darkness came around me and hid me. I put the back of my hand against my eyes and held it there. Outside, from the quiet sidewalk, Holmes' voice carried in to me clearly, though he was talking low now. "The guy's as good as fried. Endicott never fumbled one of these things yet. He never misses," he was saying to the new cop.

"What I like about him is, he's so human with it, just like one of us," the cop was saying.

Human was right, if human meant to hurt all over, to be scared all over, to be going under for the third time without a helping hand in sight.

It didn't last very long. It couldn't. I would have gone batty. But it had driven an awful dent in me, left me wide open. I said to myself: "Be a man. You're nuts. It couldn't be. It just *looks* that way now, but it'll straighten itself out. You'll see." I fought it off that way.

Finally I moved out of the dark room into the pale wash of the street light filtering through the screen door. Holmes was coming toward me up the walk, to see what was taking me so long. He had the makings of a good dick. He could tell even by the pale street light. He said, "What's the matter, Cap? You look funny."

I said, "I had a dizzy spell in there just now. That ever happen to you? I bent down too far to pick up my cigar."

He said, "You want to take it easy, Cap. We can always get you a new cigar, we can't always get a new Cap."

———◆◆———

I gave the cop his instructions, and we got in the car and drove down to the house. The death-watch tried to gang up on me in the ante-room, but I brushed through them. "Not now, boys. May have something for you in the morning. Query me then."

One of them called after me, "Our papers can't wait till the morning, give us a hand-out at least—"

Holmes showed his teeth, said: "You heard the captain, didn't you?"

I sat down behind my desk and called Ballistics. Kelcey came on, and I said: "Did you get the pill out of him yet? What sweat-band does it take?"

"We're giving it the screen-test now. Thirty-eight around the waist," he said.

The same caliber as our police positives.

There was a strained pause. But why should there be a hitch in a call like this, when we both ought to know what we wanted to say? He was waiting for me to give him further instructions, I guess. I didn't. Then he said, "Oh, by the way, Ed, I'm still waiting for that gun of yours you asked me to have cleaned and oiled for you."

I said, "I forgot to bring it down with me."

He said, "Hello? Hello? Oh, I thought I heard us being cut off."

The click that he heard had been me cracking my positive open. Did you ever get nauseated from smelling gunpowder? I hadn't fired it in months, ages, that's why it needed cleaning so bad. The smell came up like a breath of hell into my nostrils. One chamber was empty. I always kept it fully loaded.

"All right, Kelcey," I said, "All right, Kelcey." The receiver landed back in its forked support like a hundred-pound weight, dragging down my hand with it.

I got up and went over to the water-filter and drank a cupful of water. I needed it bad.

I opened the door and said, "Tell Jordan I'm ready for those truckmen now." I went back and sat down behind my desk and picked up a report upside-down, as the men were brought in.

One of them was a big stocky guy, the other, his helper, was a little bit of a squirt. They were both half-scared, half-pleased at being the center of interest like this. Jordan came in with them, of course. The thought in my mind was: "I've got to get him out of here. If this is—what I'm afraid it's going to be, I can't take it in front of him."

Jordan saw the reversed report, but he must have thought I was just using it as a screen to overawe them. He looked surprised, like he wondered why I should bother, with small potatoes like these guys.

The first couple of questions brought out that the shrimp had been down in the cellar of the house the whole time, it was the other guy who had been up by the control-lever of the truck. That gave me my out. I said, "Take this other guy out, I don't need him," and motioned Jordan to the door. Then, "Wait'll I send for you." He went out.

I said, "Did you hear anything like a shot?"

"No, boss."

"What house was this you were unloading in front of?"

"Fifteen."

Same side of the street, five houses down. "While you were there, did you see anyone come out of any of the houses to your left, toward Roanoke Boulevard? You know—in a hurry, running, excited, anything like that?"

"No sir, I was too busy tipping and adjusting my truck."

I had no business being so glad. I loved that dirty mug standing there before me, for saying that. Fine captain of detectives. But they must have had some information for us, otherwise Jordan wouldn't have brought them in. "Well, what *did* you see?"

"A girl comes hustling along the sidewalk. I didn't see her come out of no house, but she did come from that direction . . ."

A girl. I thought: don't let him say he got a good look at her.

"A cripple, like. You know, game-legged. Went down lower on one side than the other, every step she took . . ."

The heel. He didn't know what caused the unevenness, attributed it to deformity.

"She was in a hurry, came hustling along, hobbling like that, and looking back behind her every minute . . ."

"Would you know her again if you saw her?" I asked, afraid to hear his answer. "Now answer me truthfully. Here, have a cigarette." Stalling, fighting for a minute more of grace for myself. I passed him a package I kept on the desk for visitors. My hand shook so, in offering it, that I had to pivot my elbow on the desktop to steady it. My other hand was gripping the cloth of my trouser-leg tight, in a bunched-up knot.

"I couldn't see her face," he said. "It was dark, y'know, under them trees along there."

The papers in front of me rippled a little, so I must have blown out my breath without knowing it.

"It was the way she was hustling along on that game leg attracted me attention, and the way she kep' looking behind her. She didn't see the truck until she nearly run into it; we were blocking the sidewalk, y'know. But imagine anyone not seeing a truck in front of 'em! I said, 'Watch it, lady,' so she cut across to the other side of the street."

"Was she young or old?"

"Just a chicken. Not more than eighteen. I couldn't see her face, but her shape was young, if y'know what I mean."

I pulled the knife out of my heart, to make room for him to stick in a few more. "Could you gimme an idea of what she was wearing?"

"On her head one of them round skating-caps, like boys wear." I could see it so well, back there on our hall-table, carelessly thrown down. "And then a leather coat, like a—whaddye-call them things, lumber-jacket, only fancier, for a girl." I could feel the cool crispness of it against me again, like when she bent over me to kiss me . . .

"Damn," I said, deep inside of me.

"Then a minute later"—his voice went on, somewhere outside my private hell—"a guy in a car came cruising along, slow and easy. I guess he was trying to pick her up or follow her home or something. He just stayed back behind her, though, about half a block behind her. Funny to be out on the make after a girl with a game leg. I guess that's why she was in such a hurry and kep' looking back . . ."

He was dead wrong about that, but I grabbed at it like a drowning man does a straw. It didn't do *me* any good, but it eased him and his damnable testimony out of the picture—for the present anyway.

I said slowly, "I guess that lets her out. I guess that's not what we're after. She the only one you saw?"

"Only one."

"Okay, that'll be all." But then as he moved toward the door, "Did you tell the guy that brought you in about this girl? What she was wearing, and all like that?" I felt lower than the boards on the floor.

"Not about what she was wearing, no, they didn't ask me. I just told them about seeing her go by."

"Well, keep what you just told me to yourself, you understand? Don't talk about it to anyone, you understand ?"

"Yes sir," he said, feeling he'd gotten in wrong in some way.

"Now, see that you don't forget that," I added belligerently. "Gimme your name and address. All right, you can go now. And don't forget what I told you."

"Anything?" Jordan wanted to know when I sent for him again.

"No, false alarm. He saw some flapper trying to dodge a pick-up artist, that's all it was." I passed a hand limply across my brow. "I'm going home now. I feel rotten."

"You look kind of worn out," he admitted.

"Not so young as the rest of you guys. Check up on the neighbors first thing in the morning, find out what kind of a reputation he had, who his callers were. We can't really get under way until I have a chance to question Mrs. Trinker, and hear what she can tell us. Holmes, give her movements a going-over, find out if she really was at Mapledale all day yesterday and today. G'night. Call me if anything pops between now and morning."

I trudged wearily out into the street, calling myself a liar, a hypocrite, and a traitor.

I was shivering standing there in the pool of light waiting by the bus-stop. Just a man with his life and hopes all smashed. I let the one for my own street go by, I took the one behind it, that went past Starrett Avenue.

Jogging along on it, on the top deck in the dark, I kept thinking: I've got to shield her, got to cover her. It's not the murder-rap, the trial. It's the implication of her being mixed-up with him. Acquitted or guilty, either way she's finished, she'll never live it down. I'm not going to let her be dragged through the sewer. I'd rather put a bullet through her with my own hand. I've got to protect, got to cover her.

And it wasn't as easy to decide as it sounds. Do you think duty, loyalty to the men over you, the trust of the men under you, don't mean anything after twenty years?

I staggered off the bus at Starrett Avenue and went back to the Trinker house. The cop was lurking there in the shadows under the trees, keeping an eye on it.

"It's me," I said, "I forgot something," when he flashed his torch at my face.

"Yes sir, Captain Endicott," he said, and quickly cut it off again.

I went up the walk to the porch, took out the key, unlocked and put the lights on. He stayed out on the sidewalk, since I hadn't told him to come in with me. I went through into the kitchen, lit that, eased the door shut after me.

I picked up the glass, the one with the rouge-smear on its rim, and looked at it. They'd missed it. They hadn't dusted it. It was one of those flukes. If it stayed here they'd be bound to discover the oversight. Nothing could be done about the prints they had already, and they had plenty, but something could be done about this. I tilted it slowly, hypnotizedly, emptied the stale contents down the sink. Then I stuffed it in my pocket, not caring whether it bulged or not. Then I put out the lights, locked up, and came out again.

"Did you get it, Cap?"

"Yeah," I said, "I got it."

He called after me, "G'night, Cap," as I moved down the street.

"Good night, officer," I said.

I took out the glass and smashed it against the curb, on a quiet corner near my own place. Shoveled the fragments down into the mouth of a sewer with the edge of my foot.

———◆———

They'd both gone to bed long ago. I spent a long time in the kitchen with a piece of rag, scouring my gun. The ashes still glowed red underneath the white linen when I lifted the stove-lid. The handkerchief went right away, with a flare of yellow; the heel, leather-covered wood, more slowly, burning down to a char. A heel, a handkerchief, a highball glass.

Maggie had left a bottle of beer and two slices of rye on the table for me, like other nights. But I couldn't touch it.

I eased open the door of their room, peered in. There was no light behind me but enough in there coming through the window to see them by. Maggie was asleep with her mouth open. *She* wasn't. She was lying perfectly still, but I could tell she was awake. She had her face turned toward the wall, and her two hands were up hiding it, and she was crying into them without making a sound. I could tell by the way her shoulders kept shaking a little. It had been going on so long, it was mostly reflex by now.

When daylight came I was still sitting on the edge of my bed holding onto the back of my neck with both hands, staring— staring at nothing that anyone else could have seen.

———◆———

You'd think hope would have been all gone, but it wouldn't die. It flickered up weaker each time, but somehow it still was there.

She sneezed at the breakfast table and blew her nose on one of those handkerchiefs, a pink one with a rabbit's head on the corner. I said, "Where do you get those handkerchiefs?"

"Kringle's. They come by the set, a half-dozen for a dollar."

"You can't buy them separate?"

"Yes, but you've got to buy them six at a time to get that price. All the girls are going in for them."

All the girls—anyone at all could buy them. But honeysuckle, chocolate—

I said, "Did you take your shoe over to have it repaired?"

"Yes, last night, after you left."

It flickered up again. Maybe she had the heel. Maybe. . . . "How much is he going to charge you?"

"A dollar," she said. She looked down at her plate and closed her eyes. "I lost the heel. He's got to make me a new one. It fell down in that conduit where the trolley transmission-cable is laid."

I said, "Where—what were you doing at six yesterday, what kept you out that long?" Trying to make my voice sound kindly, casual.

"I was having a soda at Gruntley's. . . . She suddenly threw her hands over her ears. "Don't! Don't ask me, any more questions! I can't stand it!" She got up and ran out, with a stricken look.

Maggie started to lace it into me. "What are you trying to do, practice up for your duties on her? The poor child didn't sleep a wink all night!"

She pulled herself together in about five minutes, came out again, picked up her books, went past me into the hall. I said "Jenny," got up and went out there after her. She was standing by the clothes-tree, getting her jacket. I said, "Don't—wear that leather jacket any more, leave it here where it was."

She didn't ask me why not. I noticed that; as though she didn't have to be told. I reached out and took the knitted cap off her head too. I let them both drop on the floor behind me. "Don't go out in these things any more," I said helplessly.

I half-stretched my arms out toward her, dropping them again. I said huskily, "Isn't there—is there anything you want to tell me? You can tell me anything. Is there—any way you want me to help you?"

She just gave me a stricken look, turned and ran out with a sort of choked sob.

I went over to the window and stood there looking out after her. I watched her go down the street. A minute later a car came drifting along—very slowly, at a snail's pace. It was going the same way she was. There was just a young guy in it, a sleek-looking young guy with a mustache. It was hard to tell exactly how old he was. He was inching along so slowly, you had an impression he was stalking somebody. If I'd seen him try to close in on her, I would have rushed out. But he didn't, just kept his distance, creeping along so slow the spokes of his wheels didn't even blur. I grabbed out my notebook and jotted down his license number.

I opened the bureau drawer where she kept her things and looked into the box of handkerchiefs. There were three left in it, two whites and a pink. The lid said they came two to each color. She'd taken one pink with her just now. The blue I'd seen between her books yesterday was in the laundry-bag. It was the only one in it. One blue was missing entirely.

I stopped in at Gruntley's on my way to the precinct-house. I said to the soda-jerker, "Do you know my daughter, son?" When he nodded, I went on. "What was that sweet stuff you gave her last night just before supper-time? It came near ruining her appetite."

He looked surprised. "She didn't come in here last night, sir. First time in weeks, too. I had her special kind of a sundae all made up waiting for her, but she didn't show up. Had to finish it off myself."

I started off with the usual, "Do you know of any reason why your husband should have been killed?" Holmes had already established Mrs. Trinker's alibi, she hadn't budged from her sister's house in Mapledale for two whole days.

"No, Captain," she said dully, "I don't."

This was only beating around the bush, and we both knew it. "Were there any other women in his life?" I blurted out.

"Yes," she said mournfully, "I'm afraid there were."

"He was killed by a woman, you know."

"I was afraid of that," she admitted.

"Can you tell me who they were?"

"I tried—not to find out," was her answer. "I did my best not to know."

"You want to see justice done, don't you? Then you've got to help me."

"Several times there were folders of matches in his pocket, from that road-house out at Beechwood, the Beechwood Inn. I never went with him there. I suppose somebody else may have." She smiled a little. What a smile! "I tried not to look, I tried not to find things like that, I kept my eyes closed. That's something to be grateful for: I don't have to try—not to know—any more."

She was a fine character. That didn't make things any easier all around, either. . . .

I had Jordan go out to the Beechwood Inn and lay the groundwork. "Find out just who the interest was out there, who he was seen with. When you've got that, call me for further instructions before you tip your hand."

Prints called, all elated. "We've got the finest set of trade-marks you ever saw, clear as a bell. If you don't go to town on 'em, Ed, you're losing your grip."

"Outside of his?"

"Sure outside of his. What're you trying to do, be funny?"

Holmes reported in, after spending all morning casing the neighbors. "He had a bad rep. They all had a hammer handy when I brought up the name. The one next door told me a blonde dame rung her doorbell by mistake one morning about two months ago, asking if he lived there."

It was the first good news I'd had all day long. Even if it was two months old, at least it meant another candidate.

I needed another candidate, even if it was only a straw one.

"Let's have her," I said eagerly.

He opened his notebook, read hieroglyphics that didn't mean anything to anyone but him. "Tall, blonde, flashy-dressed, night-life type. Blue eyes. Mole on chin. There was a man waiting outside for her in a car."

"Did she give you anything on him?"

"Being a dame, she was only interested in this other dame."

I said, "We've got to get that jane, I don't care if she was only the Fuller Brush lady making her rounds. That the only time she saw her?"

"Only time."

When I was alone in the room again I called up the license-registration bureau, read from my book: "060210." That was the car that had dawdled past our place this morning. There had also been a car escorting the blonde, you see.

They gave me: Charles T. Baron, such-and-such an address, resort operator, height 6-1 (well, the guy following Jenny had been sitting down), weight 190 (well, he'd still been sitting down), age 45 (he'd looked younger than that to me, but maybe he'd just had a shave), and so on. . . .

Jordon called me about five, from the Beechwood Inn. He said, "The party is a hostess here, name of Benita Lane."

"Got any idea what she looks like?"

"I ought to, I'm sitting out there with her right now."

"Tall, blonde, blue eyes, mole on chin?"

He gasped, "For pete's sake, what are you, a wizard?"

"No, I'm a captain. You stay with her, get me?"

"I've got her going," he said cheerfully.

"I want her prints," I said, "and I want 'em as quick as I can get 'em. I'm going to send Holmes out there for contact-man. You get them across to him. Now here's what else I want, I don't care how you manage it, but these're the things I gotta have: I want to know what perfume she goes in for. I want to know if she owns any colored handkerchiefs with animals' heads on the corners. I want to know if she's got a weakness for chocolate bars. I want to know if she's short a pair of shoes, and why. I'll hold off until I hear from you. If I'm not here, phone me at my house. If you want me to send out somebody to double up on it with you, say so."

He whined, almost like a kid, "Aw, don't make me divvy this up with anyone, Cap; this is too good to split."

"Well, see that you don't muff it," I warned him.

She'd be good for weeks, to wave in front of my men and the commissioner. I could get something to hold her on, even if it was only knowing Trinker, and hold—and hold—maybe until the case curled up and died of old age. It was a dirty trick but—place yourself in my shoes.

—❖—

Holmes was back in under an hour. He must have just stuck his head in the place, gulped a beer, and beat it out again. He had a burnished metal mirror from her kit, about the most perfect surface for taking prints there is.

It seemed another hour before I got the report from Prints. It must have been much less than that, since all they had to do was compare the two sets under the slide. In the meantime I'd walked five miles around my desk.

The phone rang and I jumped.

"Doesn't check," Prints said. "Not at all similar to the ones we got up at Trinker's place."

Jordan's second call came right on top of that, to give me the knockout-blow. "I'm up in her place now, Cap, upstairs over the Inn. She's down there doing a number for the supper-trade, and she's bringing up sandwiches and drinks."

"I'm not interested in your social life," I snapped.

He went on:

"The kind of gas she uses on her engine is called: gardenia. I promised to buy her a bottle. She can't eat anything sweet, her teeth are on the blink. All her hanks are white with just her initials on 'em. The only thing I haven't turned up yet is about the kicks. She admits she knows Trinker, but she doesn't know he's dead yet, I can tell that by the way she talks. Furthermore, she was singing downstairs here at six last night, like she is now, I found that out from the waiters. How'm I doing, Cap?"

I felt like saying, "You're cutting my heart out." But I managed a hollow, "Great stuff. Stick with it. Maybe we'll pull her shortly, just on general principle."

He sounded dubious. "Gee, I hope you pull her soon. I'm a married man, and I'm practically down for the count now." He hung up abruptly, as though he'd heard her coming back.

I couldn't stand it around the precinct any more after that. I flung them the usual, "Call me home if there are any new developments," and got out. That got me home ahead of my usual time, so they weren't expecting me. Maggie must have been out marketing. The kid was there, standing where the phone was, with her back to me. The front door didn't make any noise opening. I could see her in there, in the room, from where I was, standing in the door. Her voice reached me; it sounded strained, furry with panic. "What do you want to see me about?"

Blackmail! That was the thought that exploded in my brain like a ghastly star-shell. Somebody had seen her—last night; somebody was threatening her with exposure.

Her voice dropped in defeated acquiescence. "The bandstand

beside the lake, in the park. . . . Yes, I know where it is. . . . All right—I'll come."

She must have sensed me standing there out in the hall. Her elbow hitched abruptly and there was a click. I heard her give a frightened intake of breath. She didn't turn around, just stood there with her head averted.

I walked slowly up behind her. I rested both my hands on her shoulders. I could feel the spasmodic shiver course up her spine.

"Who was that?"

"A boy I know in school."

I made her turn around and look at me—but not roughly, gently. She didn't want to, resisted, but I made her. I said, "Let me help you, little Jenny. That's what I'm for."

I couldn't get a word out of her. A greater terror held her mute. Just a haunted look on her face, of one on the edge of an abyss. I dropped my arms finally, turned away. Maybe she was right. Maybe it was better not to talk about it, maybe it was better to finish it out in pantomime. To put it into words between us was to give it an even more ghastly reality than it already had.

Maggie came in, bustled around. The meal was an awful thing. We just sat there like two people in the line-up. I would have given any-thing for Maggie's obliviousness, peace of mind. She said, "I don't know what's the matter with you two, after I go to all the trouble of cooking. . . ." Afterwards she filled a basket full of jellies and things, said she was going to help out at her church bazaar or something like that.

I heard her go but it was like being in a trance. And then Endi-cott and his girl were left alone. An old war-horse who had had the tables turned on him, by some dirty trick of fate.

———⊰◆⊱———

The phone rang again, and she heaved above her chair. Well, I kind of jolted too, why should I lie about it? I went over to it, but it was only Holmes. "Hey, Cap, Jordan hasn't called back any more from the Beechwood. Don't you think we should have heard from him again by now? He may be in a jam."

"He's probably in bed," I said crossly.

"Hell, he don't have to be that realistic. He's on an assignment."

"All right, see if you can get in touch with him then. Get word to him to bring the dame in, we've kibitzed around enough with her." I wondered what I was going to hold her on. But I had to have somebody; it was her tough luck she'd once asked the way to Trinker's house two months ago.

But all this was just a side issue now to the main problem. I kept saying to myself: "The bandstand—by the lake—in the park. I've got to get him. I've got to get him and shut him up." I only knew of one way to shut him up, to shut him up so that he could never menace her again. I only had to look at her, sitting there gripping her chair, suffering the tortures of the damned, to know that I was going to take that way.

I moved with pretended casualness into my own room. She didn't seem to be watching, didn't seem to be aware of what I was doing. I took my gun out and pocketed it. I came out again, still casual, moved past her toward the door. I mumbled something like: "Got to go down to the job again. Stay here until Maggie comes back. . . ."

I don't know whether I'm not a good actor or whether it was feminine intuition. But suddenly she was up, her arms were around me like barnacles, trying to hold me, trying to keep me back. "No! I know where you're going! I know what you're going to do! I can tell by the look in your eyes! You took your gun! Daddy . . ."

I thrust her aside, but she tried to hang on. I just kept stomping forward, with my face expressionless, dragging her after me down the hall like so much dead-weight. She was going wild now, hysterical. I reached up over my shoulder, pried her hands off me, held the two of them together by the wrists with one hand, pulled her into a little windowless spare-room we had off the hall. I locked the door on her in there, took the key out. She was beating a frantic tattoo on it, almost incoherent, calling for help from someone who wasn't there. "Aunt Margaret, stop him! He's going to kill someone!"

The phone started up again, just as I opened the outside door. That wouldn't be the precinct, so soon again. There was, I remembered, a hot-dog concession at the park entrance, open until midnight every night. It provided refreshment for homeward-bound spooners. It provided a pay-phone, too.

"Coming, damn you, coming," I growled as I closed the door after me and lurched heavily out into the street. Everyone protects their own, even police-captains.

The lake came into view as I followed the curving driveway, and the deserted bandstand was outlined against the stars. There were no more leaves on the trees, no boats on the water, no cars in motion along the driveway. It was too late in the year for the park to be used for anything—but blackmail and murder.

Two things glowed red ahead of me as I came along; the ruby tail-light of the car standing motionless in front of the band-stand, and the smaller gleam of a cigarette under the black sheltering roof of the structure. The number checked with the one I had in my notebook, the one I had taken from the car that had gone slowly past our place this morning. I didn't have to refer to it, I knew it by heart. 060210. So his name was Charles T. Baron, was it?

I kept the motionless car between me and the bandstand as I soft-shoed up on him. So he wouldn't catch on, break and run. Then when I was up to its rear fender, I came out around from behind it, went up the two steps into the bandstand, with my gun out. I said, "Come here, you."

He was a silhouette against the lake through the open sides of the structure. I saw him jump with shock, and his cigarette fell down in a little gush of red sparks on the floor.

I didn't wait for him to come to me. I went to him. I said, "Is your name Charles T. Baron?" He didn't have to answer if he didn't want to. It wasn't important. The real answer was behind my curved finger-joint, anyway.

I said, "D'you know me? D'you know who I am?" He was too frightened to answer, could only shake his head.

I did want the answer to what I asked him next. My mind was a policeman's mind, not a congenital murderer's; it had to have its confession before it executed justice. "Did you see her last night? Did you see her—with this?" I hitched the gun-muzzle upward to emphasize it. "You know who I mean."

I was gripping him by the shoulder with my other hand, holding him in place in front of me. He could hardly articulate with terror. He'd seen the glint of the gun by now, if he hadn't before. "Yes," he breathed, "I—I saw it go off . . ."

That was his death-warrant.

I pulled the trigger and it flamed out, lighting up his eyes, dilated with unbelieving horror.

It had a terrific kick to it, worse than I'd ever remembered—it was so long since I'd fired it last. Such a kick that it pitched upward, the bullet going off harmlessly over his shoulder instead of into his chest. I tried to right it, bring it down again, so that second shot would take effect, and I'd lost control of my arm. All kinds of hands, that didn't belong to me and didn't belong to him either, were grabbing me all over.

Holding my gun-arm stiffly up and away, twisting the gun out of it, pulling me back away from him, holding my other arm fast at my side.

Holmes' voice was pleading in my ears, like a frightened kid begging off from a licking from his old man: "Don't, Cap! This is murder! What's the matter with you, what're you trying to do? Hang onto him, now, officer, don't let him get that gun." He was almost sobbing the words.

He got around in front of me and all I could see was his face, not the other guy's any more. He didn't actually have wet eyes, but he had the whole screwed-up expression that went with them, like I was breaking his heart.

I growled, "Get out of my way, Holmes—don't do this to me. I'm asking you as your captain, don't do this to me! You don't understand—my little girl . . ."

He kept pushing me back in front of him, not like when you fight, but sort of leaning up against me, crowding me. He crowded me back out of the bandstand, and the running-board of the car caught me below the calves of my legs and I sat down on it involuntarily. He leaned over me, talking low into my face. "It's Holmes, Cap, don't you know me?" he kept saying. "You've nearly killed a man, Cap." He started to shake me a little, as if to bring me to. "What do you want to do, bust my heart? Don't you know how we all look up to you? Endicott, Endicott, what do you want to do?"

All I gave him back was, "My little girl, my little girl . . ."

"But he's just a kid, Cap," he said. "Don't take your gun to him." There was a motionless form lying on the bandstand-floor in there, with the policeman bending over him trying to bring him around. He'd fainted dead away from fright.

"Just a kid?" I said dazedly. "He's a resort-operator, he—"

He kept shaking me slightly, like when you try to wake someone up out of a sleep. "Naw, that's his father," he said disgustedly. "This is just a kid, a high-school senior. Even the car is his old man's. If he didn't go around wearing a misplaced eyebrow on his lip, anyone could see how young he is!"

I ducked my head suddenly, covered my face with both hands. "But you don't understand," I said through them.

"*I* understand," he assured me, hand on my shaking shoulder. "I'm not a parent, but I guess I know how it is—you just naturally get all burnt up the first time they fall in love. But hell, Cap, suppose they *were* sweet on each other, suppose she *did* go around with him after you forbid her to, suppose she *did* sneak your gun out of the house to show it to him and then it went off accidentally while they were jiggling it around and they nearly got hurt—suppose all that? Don't take your gun to the brat, Cap! That's no way. You been working too heard . . ."

I said. "How do you know all this? Who told you?"

"She did. Luckily I beat it out to your house when I couldn't get you on the wire. I was afraid something was wrong. And something came up that couldn't wait. I hadda bust the door down to get her out. You shouldn't have locked her up like that, Cap. She told me about it. They had a row when the gun went off, each one blamed the other. You know how it is when you're that age, they take their love affairs and their rows serious, like we do our cases and our jobs. He's been following her around ever since in his old man's car, trying to get her to make up with him."

⊰━◆━⊱

I've been glad ever since, I didn't blurt out: "Then she didn't do it?" like I wanted to. I looked up at him beseechingly, but he interrupted me before I could get the words out: "Come on, Cap, we've got a busy night ahead of us. Forget these kids. Feel better now? Are you over it now? Then come on, let's get going, this can't wait. The prowl car's right down the drive a way. You didn't hear us coming up—luckily." He turned to the cop. "Send that punk home when he comes around, and have his old man dry him behind the ears and keep him away from Endicott's girl after this. And O'Toole—if you open your mouth about this, I'll take it out of your hide."

He turned back to me. "Come on, Cap. Every minute counts. I've got bad news for you. . . ."

I just looked at him as I straightened up beside him.

"Jordan's been shot to death out at the Beechwood Inn; we found his body in the woman's apartment when we broke in before. Her and her accomplice, the manager, have lammed out. We've got to get those two. They killed Trinker. Her and this guy that runs the Beechwood must have been shaking him down. . . ."

"But Jordan told me himself, just before he was killed, that she had an alibi—and two clues that I was looking for, a heel and a handkerchief, wouldn't click," I faltered.

"Well, they did after we got there. We found a heelless shoe and the remains of five partly-burned colored handkerchiefs in the roadhouse incinerator. And as for the alibi, naturally the employees there would go to bat for their employer and his lady friend. It meant their jobs."

I could see how the rest of it would be; the kid, my kid, must have come limping through that street on her way home, after her spat with her boy friend, and just after losing her own heel in the trolley tracks. But of all the freak coincidences! It nearly made your hair stand up to think of it.

I said, "But doesn't this punk's father run the Beechwood? Baron, or whatever his name is?"

"He's the owner of the whole chain. But he's a respectable man. It's this manager we want. . . ."

I said, "Hang back a minute, and get word to the kid in that other car: if he wants to stop off at my place on his way home and say hello to his girl, Endicott's girl, it's all right with Endicott."

Afterword to "Endicott's Girl"

"Endicott's Girl" (*Detective Fiction Weekly*, February 19, 1938) is one of Woolrich's strongest Noir Cop thrillers and also carries forward the oscillation motif from earlier stories like "The Night Reveals" and "Murder on My Mind." Captain Endicott destroys the clues that seem to link his daughter to the murder, takes steps to jail another woman innocently involved in the case, sets out to murder the man he believes to be blackmailing his child and is even ready to kill Jenny himself rather than see her reputation (and his?) sullied, but at the fadeout his psychotic malfeasance is covered up by his subordinates, who love him for his compassionate heart. What more perfect specimen of the Woolrich cop? Many years after its publication Woolrich picked this tale as his personal favorite among the hundreds he'd written. So why has it never been collected until now?

Detective William Brown

I

Bill Brown, even at fourteen, led the field in everything. He was flashy, brilliant, colorful. Joe Greeley was a plodder, would never be anything but a plodder, an also-ran. He knew it even then, and so did everyone else. He was "Slow Joe" to the fellows. Reliable, steady as a block of concrete, but not very exciting. When the cry of "Batter up!" echoed over the ash-dumps, Bill Brown could be counted on for a homer. If Joe Greeley didn't strike out, the most he could get was a one-bagger.

About the only thing you could say for Joe Greeley was that once he made up his mind about anything, he never changed. A million kids have said they wanted to be policemen, and then dropped the idea when they got a little older. Bill Brown and Joe Greeley said it too, and as far as Joe was concerned, from that moment on his life work was cut out for him. He never veered from his determination. "When I'm on the force—" he'd say, quietly, or "When I've got my shield—"

"I can see Slow Joe spending his whole life pounding a beat, ringing in his station house, stopping runaway horses, until they retire him on a pension," Brown sneered.

"Well, what about you? I thought you were going to join the cops too?"

"Sure, but I'm not going to *stay* a cop! Any fool can do that. I'm going to be an ace detective before I'm through!"

"More power to you," Greeley said. He wasn't jealous.

They'd finished public school together, although Bill Brown had started two full terms after Joe Greeley. Brown got out with a flourish, Greeley just made it by the skin of his teeth. But whatever he'd put down on his final exam papers had come out of his own head, he'd worked hard to hang onto, hadn't asked anyone's help. Brown's answers were a composite; they'd come from the guy in front of him, the guy behind him, and the guys on each side of him. The handwriting, at least, was his own. He got his name up on the school roll-of-honor in the assembly room, in gilt letters. He was selected, because of his rating, to deliver the graduating class' valediction. He made a fine, thrilling speech. It had been fine and thrilling even five years before when it was delivered, word for word, by some visiting dignitary asked to preside at some other graduation somewhere else.

Through with school, they both took temporary jobs to tide themselves over until they could get appointed to the force. Both doing the same thing for the same concern, driving ice trucks. Mechanical refrigeration was fairly new yet. Now for the first and last times in their lives they were on a basis of absolute equality; there isn't much chance to show brilliance or originality driving a truck.

They studied for their police exams and sat down at adjoining desks in a big roomful of other prospective limbs of the law. Bill Brown got through in half the time, and with half the sweat, Joe did, but Joe passed—that was all that mattered.

They went to training school together, listening to lectures, having things chalked for them on blackboards, just as if they were kids all over again. They learned fine points of wrestling in the gym, and how to disarm an adversary, and all the rest of it.

They were rookies together, self-conscious in the blue coats and visored caps and brass buttons. Or rather Joe was; but he was proud too. Prouder than anyone would have guessed just by looking at him.

They were given the assignments rookies are given, quiet out-of-the-way beats, where the most that was liable to happen was that some homecoming householder had forgotten his key and couldn't get in, and had to call on the cop to climb in through a second-story window and open the door from the inside. Which made Joe, at any rate, feel vastly self-important and helpful, and he'd walk down the street again afterward with his chest out even farther than before. Bill, reporting a similar plea for assistance, took a different view of it.

"I told him to climb up himself if he wanted to get in. Wouldn't I have looked great climbing up over a porch like—like a carpenter or housepainter? What do they think we are anyway, their darky servants?"

"What do the regulations say?" asked Joe doubtfully.

"Aw, you and the regulations! If you're gonna live by the regulations, you'll never get anywhere in this racket."

Racket? thought Joe. That wasn't the word he would have used for it. Life work, dedication, something like that.

Finally the day came when they weren't rookies any more; they became full-fledged members of the force. Both on the same day, and both attached to the same precinct-house. They still lived on the same block, a few doors from each other. They walked on-duty and off-duty together whenever their shifts coincided.

Joe was first to get married. He was on the force now, he was set for life, the rest was just a matter of slow advancement up through the ranks, there was no reason to wait any longer. He married a girl that lived on the same block with him, whom he'd known since they were kids. Just a plain girl, but a nice girl, satisfied to be his wife and share a policeman's lot. Bill Brown had been going with one of the girls on the block too, but he held off getting married. He didn't say so of course, but he had an air as if to say, "I can do better than around here. I'm going to be somebody. Why should I be in a hurry?"

Officer and Mrs. Joe Greeley moved into a little flat only a couple of blocks away from where they'd always lived. Bill Brown dropped in to see them once or twice, when he and Joe both happened to be off duty simultaneously, but he had an air of good-natured contempt, of—well, almost of looking down on them, feeling sorry for them. Of Joe, for being Joe; and of his wife, for having hitched her wagon to a mud turtle.

⟨⟩

Equality ended on a day in October after they'd both been on the force a little over a year. Mr. Kasimir Swoboda, storekeeper, of their precinct, had been held up repeatedly in the past few years and was getting sick of it. Always the same technique: he was driven into a back room at the point of a gun; tied up in there, and sometimes it was an hour before he could attract anyone's attention, his store was that dark and inconspicuous. Once the robber had had the gall to impersonate the proprietor and wait on a customer who came in while he was in the act of emptying the till, while Swoboda helplessly chewed on a gag a few yards away. To make it even more aggravating, he wasn't sure but that it had been the same individual each time. Swoboda had been too badly frightened to get a very good look at him.

Swoboda went and beefed long and loudly to the lieutenant about it. "He's living off me!" he complained indignantly. "I pay my taxes and I want yet protection! Each time you come too late after it's over, and what good does that? You look for him everywhere but where he was the last time, and he knows that, so back he comes again some more yet! Now idder you do something about it, mishter, or I write a letter to the mayor!"

The lieutenant and he, between them, concocted this little scheme by which to put an end to the marauder's depredations once and for all. Greeley, because he was already known to be a plodding, patient, dependable sort, was assigned to it. A hole was bored through the store's partition-wall between front and rear, and for three weeks Joe Greeley sat in the back like a hen, sizing up every customer that came in from the time the store opened in the morning until it closed at six. Swoboda was to give him a signal and duck out of range. Joe got so he knew the prices of every article on the shelves. Even his wife, when he told her about it, thought Joe's superiors might have worked it on a shift basis, not kept Joe at it *all* the time, for twenty-one days.

"It's an assignment," he said uncomplainingly. "Somebody's got to do it."

II

On the twenty-second day, at three in the afternoon, a man came in and asked for sugar. Swoboda picked up a large tin measuring-scoop. "Not that kind of sugar," said the man quietly.

Swoboda dropped the ladle with a crash, got down on his hands and knees behind the counter, and stayed there with his head tucked under like an ostrich. The door opened and an elderly lady came in with a shopping basket. The counter was short and she moved up directly beside the man, on Greeley's side of him, where she could watch the scales better.

Greeley, already in the doorway with gun bared, held his fire. He had to—there was too great a risk of hitting her. She was fluctuating, terrified, back and forth in the line of fire, like a chicken with its head cut off.

The hold-up man snapped a shot at Joe that must have singed her hair, and it clunked into one of the cans on the shelf behind Greeley, as he came out, and vegetable soup trickled out. Then the bandit turned tail and broke for the open.

Greeley hit the sidewalk only seconds after him, big as he was and with a panic-stricken woman to detour around. A slice of hindmost heel was all he saw of the man. The store entrance adjoined a corner; that gave the fugitive a few added seconds of shelter, and as Greeley flashed around it in turn, again the breaks were the lawbreaker's.

There was a school midway up the street toward the next avenue. It was a couple of minutes past three now, and a torrent of young humanity came pouring out of the building by every staircase and exit, flooding the street. In through them the sprinting man plunged, knocking over right and left the ones that didn't get out of his way quickly enough. If it had been hazardous to take a shot at him in the store, it would have been criminal out here.

The kids parted, screaming in delighted excitement, as Greeley tore through them after the bandit with uptilted gun, but he couldn't just callously knock them flat like the man before him had. He sidestepped, got out of their way as often as they did his, and he began to fall behind the other, lose ground.

The kids weren't just on that one street—they had dispersed over the entire vicinity by now, for a radius of a block or more in every direction, in frisky, milling, homeward-bound groups. Through them the quarry zigzagged, pulling slowly but surely away. He kept going in a straight line, because it was to his advantage to do so—the presence of these kids made for greater safety—but he was already far enough in the lead so that when he should finally decide to turn off—the answer was pretty obvious; a taxi or a doorway or a basement. Any of them would do.

And then Brown suddenly horned in. It must have been his beat they'd reached by now. Greeley didn't know who it was at the time. Brown was just a blue-coated figure in the distance, cutting in between him and his quarry from the mouth of the transverse street up there.

A shot sounded, topping the kid-screeching, and the blue-coated figure went down on one knee, then got up again with the help of a basement railing. That was to be expected from a cornered rat. What did he care how many kids he hit as long as he saved his own skin? In addition, the sound of the shot had made the children dangerously volatile. They were scattering and breaking for cover in a dozen criss-cross lines of obstruction. A corner loomed directly ahead and the guy was going to get away sure. Joe tried to put on more speed.

And then he saw this second cop, who had already been hit once and therefore must be suffering from nervous shock and impaired muscular control if nothing else, deliberately draw and take a sight on him. The man must be insane.

Greeley bellowed "Hold it! Don't, you fool!" although he was still a good half block behind.

Brown didn't even jockey for a clear line of fire, just squeezed with cold-blooded obliviousness. *Bang!* and the kids squealed wildly, and the fugitive went over like a log and pinned one of them under him.

For a minute Greeley couldn't even tell which one had been hit and which one had stumbled. Then the kid squirmed free and hopped to his feet and lit out for home with the fright of his young life. That didn't alter the facts of the case any.

Greeley came up swearing. The other cop was there ahead of him, holding his own shoulder where he'd been hit, rolling the corpse vindictively over on its back with his foot, and he saw that it was Bill Brown.

"You oughta known better than to try a thing like that!"

Bill Brown just looked at him. All he said was, "I got him, didn't I? And you didn't."

And that, it seemed, was what counted when the reports came in. Bill Brown got a citation and was promoted to detective, third grade.

Joe Greeley stayed right where he was, and got a calling down from his lieutenant in the bargain. Or at least, a displeased cross-questioning.

"How is it when you were planted there right on the spot, and had been for three weeks past, you let him get away from right under your nose, Joe? You didn't doze off back there by any chance, did you?"

Greeley's self-respect wouldn't let him answer this last. "An old lady got in between us and I couldn't take a chance on hitting her."

"That's all right, but she didn't follow the two of you for three solid blocks, did she? How is it he got that far from the store before he was dropped?"

"There were kids ganged up on the sidewalk the whole three blocks. Any man would've had to be a dead shot. And even then, I couldn't take the responsibility—"

"Brown's no better marksman than you," his superior said pointedly. "He got his practice on the same target range than you did."

Joe Greeley lowered his head. But not in retraction, in stubborn refusal to admit he'd been wrong. "I did the best I could Lieutenant," he said quietly.

The lieutenant relented a little. "I know you did, Joe; I can see your point," he admitted. "But it's the results in this business that count."

Bill Brown came around to the flat to show them the clothes he wore to work now. He was on Safes and Lofts now, he mentioned.

Mrs. Joe didn't act dissatisfied or envious, though. "Thirty-two dollars at the best store in town wasn't all that homespun tweed might've cost," she said after he'd gone. "The price might've included a kid with a bullet in his spine. I like you better in blue, Joe."

III

They met again over a dead man several years later. Their paths hadn't crossed again until then.

Bill Brown looked him slowly up and down across the corpse. "So you finally got out of blues, Joe?" He said it as though he hadn't really ever expected him to.

Greeley just grinned a little for an answer.

"Third-grader now, eh?" Brown went on.

"Yeah, just now. This is my first case."

"Like I told you 'way back in the beginning," Brown said patronizingly, "You've got to make your own chances in this game. Otherwise you just gather cobwebs off in some corner."

So now it was a game, was it? It had been a racket to him once, Greeley remembered. Well, to *him* it still was what it had always been—his life's work.

"I suppose you heard what I did to that Ingram business?"

"You tied it up in knots," agreed Joe.

"But you're only as good as your last case in this chain-gang." Brown pointed downward to the floor, to what they were talking back and forth across. "I been praying for something like this to come along. It's just what I need. It's been over a year now. I'll get another boost out of it sure as you live." He actually rubbed his hands together above the corpse. Joe Greeley just looked at him inscrutably.

"I'm working with Bill Brown again," he told Mrs. Joe that evening.

"You may as well save your energy," she remarked mockingly. "The case is practically over already."

But it wasn't, by a long sight. It was a cast-iron, unbreakable witch of a thing.

The man's name was Thomas Allroyd. He was an installment collector, and he had been found bludgeoned to death in the upper hallway of a seemingly respectable and even fairly high-class apartment house on the West Side.

The linings of his pockets told them a good deal of it before they'd done more than search the body. Namely: that he represented a firm marketing sun-lamps called the Sol-Ray Company, that he had visited all but one of the customers on his list (they could tell this by pencil checks next to the names), that he had already collected nearly three hundred dollars up to the time he was set upon and killed (they could tell this because monthly installments on the lamps averaged twenty-five dollars, and he had been to see about a dozen people), and that the money had been taken from him—therefore robbery motive—because he hadn't turned it in at his home office, and his billfold was gone.

The rest should have been fairly simple, but as so often happens in these "fairly simple" cases, appearances were deceptive. The building was not the "walk-in" type, open to the first passerby who chose to enter; there was a doorman posted at the entrance. Which should have meant that anyone who had followed Allroyd in from the street would have had to pass the doorman's scrutiny, state his business, and be remembered later. And that would have been an enormous help. Unfortunately it wasn't anything of the kind, because the doorman insisted no outsider had entered at or around that time.

Allroyd had entered the premises at about four-thirty in the afternoon and his body had been found by one of the tenants about half an hour later. The doorman had not during that time left his post; this was substantiated by a woman tenant who had used him to air her dog at that hour, and at the same time had kept a watchful eye on her pet from the window.

The elevator was self-operative. There was a delivery entrance, but this too had been commanded by the doorman, and he was equally positive no deliveries had been made at or around that time. An exhaustive compilation was made of every grocery, laundry, dry cleaner, and whatnot patronized by every tenant in the building, and each and every employee of them, running into the dozens, was tracked down, questioned and cross-questioned. All were able to furnish satisfactory proof of their movements and whereabouts.

This narrowed it down to somebody who had been living in the house itself, and therefore had never entered or left the premises around that time. It was not, fortunately, an unduly large building. Again an exhaustive series of interrogations, from floor to floor and flat to flat, brought the police nowhere. Almost all the men in the various families, the wage earners, had been still at work. The doormen and their various places of employment, when checked, quickly eliminated them. Of those who hadn't been out, one (a customer of Allroyd's) was a doctor on the ground floor who used one of the firm's lamps for his patients; he not only had his nurse to vouch for him, but also a patient whom he had been treating at the time. The second (again on the installment-man's list) was a semi-invalid confined to a wheel-chair, and he too had an attendant. The party whom Allroyd had still to call on when he was slain, had been conveniently "out" all afternoon—possibly the collector was expected—but in any case the party had certainly been far from home until long past the hour when there was any danger of encountering the collector.

A fourth lamp was discovered in the house, belonging to a Mrs.

Ruth Crosby. She was not down on Allroyd's list because she had bought it outright. She kept late hours, she explained rather nervously, did a lot of entertaining, and needed it to pep herself up the following day. Her apartment was luxuriously furnished and, they discovered, she paid an exorbitant rent for it, nearly twice that of anyone else. Their scrutiny and interrogation seemed to make her strangely ill at ease; she was almost abject in her willingness to placate them, offered them drinks and fawned on them. Be that as it might, she had had two young women friends staying in the place with her the day of the murder, as well as a Negro maid, and all four had been fast asleep at the time it happened; they seemed to be late risers.

So they had gotten exactly nowhere, and fast. Everyone living in the house was exonerated, and no one had been seen to enter it from outside, and yet the man had certainly been slain and robbed in that upper hallway, while he was lingering there waiting for the customers who were "out" to return.

While all this was going on Greeley, being the lowest ranking man on the case and a newcomer to Homicide, had been given all the dirty work to do. The tedious drudgery of reconstructing Allroyd's movements, step by step, from the time he'd first opened his eyes that last day of his on earth. This meant days on end of monotonous, repetitious interviews, asking the same things over and over. "What time did he come here that day? How long did he stay here?" And then counter-checking someone else's statement against that, to see if it would hold up. In other words he built up a laborious time-table for the others to make use of, and it wasn't a very thankful task.

"It's somebody," Brown kept insisting dogmatically, "who is down on that collection list of his. Somebody who knew what his job was, and therefore knew that in all probability he'd have a considerable amount of money on him by the time he neared the end of his rounds. Maybe they'd already gotten a glimpse of his receipts when he called on them themselves, and that worked up their appetite for a little lettuce. If we can't figure out how they got into the building after him, then we can't. Let's skip that altogether, instead of letting it hold us up, and work it the other way around. Go back to it later, after we've already got our possibilities lined up, and fill it in. It may fall into place by itself. Now here's what we want: somebody who owns one of those damn lamps, who Allroyd had already been to see that day, who's plenty hard up for cash, and who can't supply an airtight account of themselves from four to five that afternoon."

They sifted through the customer list exhaustively, with the help of additional data supplied them by the company's records. There wasn't anyone down on it who couldn't have used three hundred dollars. The mere fact that they had bought the appliances on time instead of outright was evidence enough of that. The majority, after a preliminary floundering brought about by nervousness, were able to pass muster on their movements.

Meanwhile the days were adding up to weeks, and suddenly it was a couple of months and still the thing was unsolved.

>——>◆<——<

The captain of detectives under whom they were working gave them all a fight talk one night. Probably his own superiors had been riding him. Moreover, the Sol-Ray Company, Allroyd's firm, had pointedly offered a reward on its own account for the capture of their agent's murder, which looked suspiciously like a dig at the police.

"Now get out after it or there's going to be a shaking-up around here that's gonna change the color of some of you people's clothes before you know it!" He pounded the top of his desk mercilessly. "I want whoever killed that man Allroyd! I want him brought in here, d'ye hear me? If you can't work together, then work separately, but dammit, *work!* The man that brings him in here first stands a good chance of promotion. I'll recommend him for it myself!"

They drifted out of his office grousing in low voices, "You'd think we done nothing but sit and twiddle our thumbs, the way the old man talks. You'd think we were holding out on him purposely. What does he expect us to do—pull the guy out of our hats?"

Bill Brown, for once, had nothing to say, Greeley noticed. He looked glum, like when you see something desirable slipping through your fingers. He had a hard, remorseless glint in his eyes, and a little later he was missing. No one knew where he'd gone.

Greeley, on his part, went and took another shot at the Ruth

Crosby apartment. He had, of course, absolutely no illusions as to just what kind of a place it was, but that had nothing to do with this.

Mrs. Crosby, summoned by the colored girl, greeted him with a mixture of sulky annoyance and patient resignation. He asked her a few routine questions, but there was nothing he could really get his teeth into.

"I've told you men already," she sighed, "I bought the lamp outright, for spot cash. This collector of theirs never had occasion to call here, I never set eyes on the fellow from first to last. Wait a minute—I'll get you the receipted bill."

She'd already shown them that long ago, so he tried to dissuade her, but she seemed to want him to see it again, for some reason that he couldn't fathom. "That's all right, I understand," she said drily as she went out.

She came back again a minute later and handed him the receipt. It was folded around the outside of a small bulky envelope, and there was money in the latter. How much, he didn't trouble to find out.

He said, "You've made a mistake, haven't you?"

"That's for you to say."

"Well, I say you have. Watch yourself or you'll get in trouble. Real trouble!"

She saw that she actually had tipped her hand, and became a little frightened, he could see. Both the bill and the money envelope vanished as if by sleight-of-hand. "I—I thought somebody'd been talking to you," she faltered.

"Who, for instance?" he asked, dangerously intent.

"Oh—er—I don't know, one of your teammates, maybe," she floundered.

He couldn't resist saying, "So you already made another of those little 'mistakes.' Only that time it wasn't."

"It pays to stay in with people," was all he could get out of her.

IV

He got back to the precinct house in time for the bombshell. It burst at the captain's telephone and spread in a widening circle of excitement from mouth to mouth, from room to room.

"Brown's got the Allroyd murderer! Single-handed. He just phoned in! He's on his way over with him now."

"Who is he?" Greeley asked. No one seemed to know.

The captain came hustling through just then with another man, spotted Greeley in the anteroom, jerked his head at him to follow them. They got in a car and streaked off.

"Who is it, Cap?" Greeley asked again.

The captain either didn't know yet himself or was too excited to answer. "If I had a few more like him working under me—" he muttered.

"We'd be too good for just one squad," the other man finished for him.

"Well, no danger of that happening!" the captain squelched him.

They started to taper off in their headlong rush as they neared their destination. It seemed to be a small one-family house occupying just one corner of a big empty plot. It was sparsely built-up out here, and the street lighting was poor. But before they reached it a man suddenly stepped out of the darkness ahead into the path of their lights, flagged them to stop. It was Bill Brown. He was alone.

The police car skidded to a violently broadside to him, braked. The three of them spilled out around him.

"Where is he?" the captain almost screamed. "I thought you said you were bringing him in. Did he get away?"

"No, he didn't get away." Brown spoke with difficulty in a low, panting voice as though he still couldn't get his breath back. He had a dazed or rather a blankly disappointed look, in his eyes. He was holding his gun in one hand, his new hat in the other. It had a bullet hole through the crown.

"He's over there in the lot." Brown said. "He broke out a gun." He held the hat up, looked at it. "It was him or me."

The captain swore. He said, "Well, we got him anyway, and that's something." Then he added hastily, "Are you sure he was our dish, Brown?"

Bill Brown met their eyes unwaveringly in the brightness of the head-beams. "He confessed," he said, "and I found the Allroyd money on the premises."

He turned and struck out into the darkness, across the sidewalk and into the hollows of a weed-grown lot, that had a footpath running through it diagonally, from near the house to the opposite corner. They followed him single file. Greeley thought, as he stumbled over a loose stone, "What'd he bring him through here for? This was asking for something to happen."

The sound of low weeping, of a woman moaning in distress, reached them from the darkness ahead. There was somebody huddled on the ground there, two somebodies. Bill Brown's torch flicked on, and the other man with them raised a distracted woman to her feet. Greeley had never seen her before. There was still somebody on the ground, motionless among the weeds. The torch pointed downward, and it was the doorman from the building where Allroyd had been murdered, with a black thread of blood bisecting his forehead.

Brown spoke, in the unassuming voice of one who expects to be complimented. "I had my eye on him for quite some time. Someone *had* to go in there after Allroyd, and no one had. We proved that. I think we all developed a blind spot in the case of this man, sort of overlooked him from the beginning. Just because a tenant insisted he'd been in sight the whole time, airing her dog below. Well, he had. She was telling the truth of it. Only, the other day I happened to ask her, 'Who returned your dog to you when the airing was over? Did you go down and get it or did he bring it up to you?' 'Why, he brought it up to the door, of course,' she said. Don't you see, that's when he did it—right while the dog was still with him, on his way to return it to its owner. How long would it take? We musta missed that because it was so obvious, and kept looking for something unusual." He reached into his inside coat-pocket. "And here's the money, to cinch it. Where would a doorman get this much, and why would it be hidden where I found it?"

"And he admitted it, you say?"

"Yeah. I'm only sorry there wasn't time to get it down on paper."

"No, no," the woman sobbed.

"Not in front of you, no," Brown said gently. "He didn't want you to know. But he admitted it as soon as I got him out of the house, away from you." He turned back to the captain with modest remorse. "I'm sorry, Cap."

"Sorry?" the captain roared. "If everyone else on this squad had as much to be sorry for as you, my worries would be over! Look after this woman, Greeley," he added. "Take her back to her house. Call in one of the neighbors to stay with her."

Greeley left Bill Brown being symbolically, if not actually, hoisted high on their shoulders in triumph. He guided the newly made widow back along the footpath. He got her back to the house somehow. She was in pitiable condition. She caught at his sleeve with both hands, clung to him pleadingly, as if he could bring the dead back to life. "No, no," she kept moaning, "he murdered him. He murdered my husband, out there in the darkness. He never resisted. Dick went with him willingly. Oh mister, you've got to listen to me! *I was there* when he took him! He purposely wanted to get him outside the house, where I couldn't see what happened. Dick said, 'Sure I'll go with you. Take me there right now. I'm ready to answer any questions they want to ask me. I know I can clear myself.' Those were his very words! He went like a lamb."

Joe Greeley's face was whiter than it had ever been before. "Did he have a gun? Did he own a gun?" He said it so low she could hardly hear him. Afraid to speak his thoughts too loudly, even to himself.

"Yes, yes." She nodded readily. "Oh, it was an old leftover from his army days. But *he* didn't take it. This man of yours took it. He put it in his pocket before he took Dick out of the house with him. I saw him do it!"

"Which pocket?"

She patted her hip. "Here."

That was a careless place to put it, on the side nearest the prisoner. And he hadn't used a manacle. Why, Greeley wondered, hadn't he used his manacle? That was something they'd forgotten to ask him. Did he *want* the prisoner to break and run for it? Was he looking for an excuse to shoot the man down, to distinguish himself even further than he had already? Or had something even worse happened out there on that dark empty lot, with no one watching the two of them but the weeds and stars?

Joe got her a glass of water, but he needed one himself. "How many shots did you hear?" he whispered.

"Two."

"One right after the other, close together, right on top of each other?"

"Not awfully close together. One, and then the other pretty soon after, *but not right away.*"

Maybe—maybe just long enough for a man to change guns. That is, throw down the first, unlimber a second, doff his own hat—and deliberately fire through it, his "assailant" already dead on the ground.

"And the money?" he asked after a long hideous time. "Where did he find the money?"

"Behind the radio, between it and the wall. He stuck his hand down, and it came up holding it." She rocked back and forth, hands pressed to her eyes. "I cleaned there right this morning, and it wasn't there!" Then she said the most horrible of all things she'd had said yet. "He seemed to know right where to look for it." Greeley flinched as though he'd been cut. "Dick didn't hide it there. I could tell by his face. He didn't know it was there any more than I did! He murdered my husband. He's not a policeman, *he's* the murderer!"

⸺◆⸺

He got out of there fast. But the talk followed him along the quiet sidewalk outside, ringing in his ears. He could still hear it all the way down at the next corner—or thought he could: "He murdered my husband! He shot him down in cold blood!"

Joe didn't go back to the precinct house to share in Bill Brown's Roman holiday. Instead he shut himself up in a booth and called the Crosby woman again. His voice was harsh and relentless. "This is Greeley of the detective division. I want to know just one thing out of you. Give me a straight answer, and you've got nothing to worry about—it won't go any further. Try to cover up, and you'll be on your way to the lockup before the night's out!"

She drew in her breath in sudden fright for an answer.

"Who was the guy, the man before me, you made a 'mistake' with, like you tried to with me tonight?"

"I don't know his name, honest I'm not kidding you I don't!"

"Tall, good-looking guy, snappy dresser?"

"Yeah," she said reluctantly.

There was only one man on the squad that applied to.

"How much?"

She lowered her voice uneasily. "Three hundred."

He banged up, but he forgot to leave the booth right away. He seemed to see things in it, vermin on the wall. Three hundred dollars wouldn't buy Bill Brown a promotion. But properly invested—pinned on a badly wanted murderer pulled out of his sleeve—it could get him one. And he'd still be seven hundred ahead on the Sol-Ray Company's thousand dollar reward.

No, he told himself—and it was as much in desperation as conviction—Bill Brown took a bribe from a source that had nothing to do with the work he was assigned to. All right. That's not my speed, but it's not my business either. Other men have done it before him and other men'll do it after him. But beyond that—that's all I know. That's all I want to know. That's all there *is* to know.

V

His name was Danny Halpern, he'd been wanted for a killing in a poolroom, and after about three weeks they caught up with him and brought him in.

No, of course he hadn't done it. He hadn't been near the poolroom in question that night. If they said he had they were lying. He hadn't been near it any other night either. He'd never been near it in his life. He'd never killed anyone, he was as innocent as a newborn babe, he was being unjustly accused, he was being framed, he had an alibi a yard long. And so on.

So they went to work on him. Greeley was allowed to participate in the questioning of suspects by this time. They needed everyone available in this one particular case, anyway; they worked shifts, sent in by relays as the suspect wore them out.

They called Greeley in to take a hand, at about midnight. It had been going on since noon the day before. He passed Brown on the basement stairs, coming up all wilted, with his coat off and looking sore as a pup. "Take him apart and find out what keeps him going," he muttered. "My knuckles are all swollen." Brown wasn't so good at this protracted grilling stuff. He didn't have the patience. It was more in Greeley's line. Tricky questions, in Halpern's case, did no good; he had been born tricky. Knocking him against the walls didn't get them anywhere either; he'd been taking hard knocks all his life. But his vitality was flickering now, and that was all that had been keeping him going.

It was a pretty brutal scene, but he had taken a human life and that had been a pretty brutal scene too. Whether he confessed or not, he couldn't bring that life back again. Moreover, he was no novice. He was suspected of a long string of other crimes. He'd never shown mercy, given a break; he wasn't getting one now.

They kicked the chair out from under him again and again, they tortured him by holding glasses of water before his swollen, bleeding lips, then slowly emptying them out on the floor as he strained forward to drink.

"Water!" he wept. "Water! Oh, if you ever had mothers, just a drop of water—and I'll tell you everything you want."

He'd broken. As unexpectedly as that.

Another glass was brought, poised within his sight, but withheld. "Say it!"

"Yes, I shot Tomasso. I was on dope and I had to have money. I waited until he'd closed up the poolroom that night. I'd purposely left my hat behind in there. I went back pretending I'd forgotten it, and he let me in, and I—

"I'll get the chair for it anyway, and they can't fry you more than once. That Frankie Reynolds thing you were asking me about—yes, I done that too. And Allroyd, the bill collector, that was me too."

There were only two of them left in there with him by this time—Greeley and another man. The captain had already hurried out with the confession that the culprit just finished dictating and signing.

There was an electric pause. The two dicks looked at each other across the prisoner's bowed head. Then Greeley jumped for him, grabbed him by the shoulder, dragged him to his feet. "What'd you just say? Allroyd? How'd you get in the building?"

"I was in it the whole time, from noon on. I must have gone in while the doorman was on relief, having his lunch. I was in the doctor's office. He was treating me for the junk habit. A patient came in that had to have immediate attention, an emergency case, and they told me I'd have to wait. I was getting a sun bath under that lamp of his, in a little cabinet off the waiting room. I was already wanted for something and I was afraid to go back on the street again, so I stayed where I was. They were both too busy inside there, him and the nurse, to keep an eye on me. I saw Allroyd stop by to collect for the lamp, I got a glimpse of his receipts, and that gave me the idea. I slipped my shirt on, eased out and followed him upstairs. Then as soon as I—done it— I came back down, peeled my shirt off, and lay down on the cot under the lamp again. They never even missed me."

His eyes rolled around in his head. He sagged across Greeley's arm, and fainted away on his feet. "Did you hear that? We better get the old man in here again in a hurry!"

But the other dick swept his arm contemptuously, "Don't pay any attention to him. These snowbirds'll confess to anything once you get 'em started. He's having a pipe-dream. We've worn him down till he don't know what he's saying any more." He took the inert prisoner over, started to shake him like a terrier and slap him backhand across the mouth and cheeks to wake him up. "Watch him retract that and the whole string of them, even the Tomasso thing, as soon as he's rested up a little and gotten hold of a mouth. You're new at it, Greeley. That's why you're ready to believe anything they say."

Greeley went out without waiting to argue, and up the basement stairs, looking for the captain. "New at it? Maybe I am," he said to himself. "But people don't confess to things they haven't done. Not things they're *not* being grilled about at the time."

Brown was in the locker room as Joe passed through it. He was shrugging into his coat, getting ready to go home; he'd presumably taken a shower after the ardors of the grilling. He had a cigarette dangling from his mouth.

Greeley stopped, turned and came back to him. "This'll tell me," he thought. "This is one way of finding out." He fixed his eyes on Brown dead-center, locked and held Brown's with them.

"He just said he killed Allroyd," he said quietly.

The cigarette fell out of Brown's mouth, and he took his face down out of range to fumble for the cigarette and pick it up. Then he threw it away anyway. His face was all right again when it came up level with Greeley's once more, but it had had that minute to itself, to straighten out free of observation.

He said with unshakable calmness, "Boy, that's a hot one! He did, did he? He sure must be high." But he wasn't, and they both knew it. He'd been in custody for nearly twenty-four hours now, and no drug lasts that long. Their eyes held magnetically, unbreakably. Brown's refused to waver, to give an inch. ("Swell facial control," thought Greeley.) And then Brown said, "Who was down there with him at the time?" Carefully casual. Too carefully casual.

That did it. "Now I know," thought Greeley, and his stomach caved in.

He turned on his heel, went on his way to look up the captain. Behind him, Brown seemed to have changed his mind about going home after all. He was standing there perfectly motionless, looking for something in his locker. Or at least looking into it, lost in thought.

Greeley got the captain down to the basement with him again, but this Halpern was in a state of collapse. They had to let him alone for awhile. They didn't believe it anyway, Greeley could tell that. Not even the captain.

"Take him out. He's in bad shape," the captain said, and the prisoner was removed to a detention cell in the adjoining building and locked up for the night.

Greeley went home. But Bill Brown was still there when he left— killing time, for there was nothing to keep him there any more.

When Greeley reported back the next day he found them in a welter of excitement. The prisoner had taken his own life in his cell sometime during the night. When they'd come to get him out to take him before the line-up, they'd found him with his wrists and throat slashed. He'd gotten hold of a razor blade in some way. They found it in there by him. It was old and rusted. It was a Jewel, single-edged. His shoelaces, his belt, and everything else by which he could possibly have harmed himself had been taken away from him, and yet he'd gotten hold of a thing like that.

Bill Brown was the last one who had seen him alive. He'd escorted him to the cell, supervised his incarceration. The prisoner had begged for cigarettes after the bars were locked, and Brown had taken pity on him, gotten him a pack, and thrown them in through the bars in the presence of the turnkey. They were found there at his feet, with just one taken out and partly smoked.

The captain had the turnkey in and raked him mercilessly over the coals. "You were responsible for his safekeeping once we turned him over to you! Now he was thoroughly searched, and he didn't have as much as a pin on him! It musta been lying in there on the floor of the cell and he found it! I'm gonna report you for your carelessness, fella."

"I know my job! He didn't get that off no cell floor! That cell was thoroughly swept out before you brung him over."

"Don't give me no buts! He was on stuff, and they're tricky!" the captain roared. "He should have been watched more closely."

Him, and I wonder who else? Greeley thought dismally.

Two weeks after, he came in a little later than usual one day, with an overnight growth of beard, as though he hadn't had time to shave at home, and they all kidded him about it.

Bill Brown—a recommendation for his promotion had gone in and he was feeling good-natured these days—offered to lend him a kit he kept in his locker. Several of the others kept spares on hand like that too.

Mrs. Joe, at about that same time, was replacing the shaving things she'd laid out for him at home and which he hadn't used. "I wonder why not?" she thought.

He was in the precinct house washroom just then, making use of Brown's. It was a Jewel, made to hold single-edged blades.

VI

"Yeah," Brown was saying one night, "promotion's one thing, but it's these long waits in between that give you ants in the pants. How long is it, now, since that Allroyd case?"

"A year, just about." Greeley turned his head aside a little, as though he didn't like to be reminded of it.

"See, that's what I mean. I had to wait a year between the Ingram case and that. Now it's been another year since that one again. It's all right for you, Joe. You're a different type from me. You don't seem to mind staying in a rut. 'Slow Joe.' But me, I could go nuts just thinking about it. It gets me down."

Joe Greeley gave him a look. "You've gone up pretty fast."

"Not fast enough to suit me," Brown insisted. And he got that same hard, calculating glint in his eyes, and seemed to be looking past the other man, into the future. His own future.

A cop stuck his head in. "Brown. Greeley. Report to Captain Hackett's office right away."

"Maybe," said Joe, as they crowded through the doorway together, "this is it now."

They met the captain coming out of his office. He'd snatched his hat up without waiting for them to get there, was making a bee-line for the hallway and the street. "Homicide at Two-ninety-five Russell Street just reported," he snapped over his shoulder at them.

Riding out to it, Greeley wondered: "Where do I fit in? Why me, teamed up with the great Brown, and not one of the other guys?" But he knew the answer without having to be told. Brown for the fireworks; himself for the dirty work, the thousand and one petty details that didn't need much imagination or originality, just a mole-like patience, but were essential just the same. He was as good in his way as Brown was in his. He made a very good cog in the machine. Brown supplied the electric current. They were short-handed just then anyway. The division as a whole was up to its ears in work trying to track down a payroll bandit who was responsible for the deaths of two armed guards and a policeman.

The Russell Street address was a substantial private home, set back from the street on its own plot of ground, with a garage adjoining. It belonged to a middle-aged couple, a retired saloon-keeper named Jerrold Nolan and his wife.

<hr />

When they got out of the car and went up to the entrance, one of the prowl car men who had reported it in came forward to meet them. "It's not in the house, Captain Hackett—it's over in the garage," he explained. They turned and cut across the lawn to the concrete driveway that led to the garage. The garage doors were wide open now and the lights on behind them. A year-old sedan was backed into place, and in the lane between it and the side wall of the garage a man's leg was thrust grotesquely upward from the floor.

They could only see the rest of the crumpled body by getting over close to the wall and peering in. There was a window in the wall directly above it, the only one in the garage, fairly high and narrow, its glass protected by wire mesh. The sash was up as far as it could go. A lean narrow-hipped man could possibly have wriggled out through it; the body, from what could be seen of it, was that of a somewhat stocky, rotund man. He had evidently tried to climb through just the same. There were innumerable evidences of this, even before the car had been jockeyed out of the way. The toes of his shoes were badly scuffed, and yet the heels and uppers had been shined only recently. There was a pad of dust on each knee of his otherwise immaculately pressed and cleaned suit, where he had braced his legs against the wall under the window to try to hoist himself up to the ledge. And lastly there were a number of blackish toe-marks down the wall, where the shoe polish had streaked off on it.

At first sight it almost looked like an accidental death. He had fallen backward into the lane between car and wall in his effort to climb out through the window, and struck the back of his head either on the cement garage-floor or against the steel-rimmed running-board of the car. But Greeley knew they wouldn't have been there if that was all there was to it. When the car had been exhaustively powdered for prints and shunted out of the way and they could get in closer, and Joe knelt down over the man in his turn, after Hackett and Brown, he could see that the ugly wound in the front of his head (and he had fallen backward) had a black core to it that no cement flooring in the world could have caused. Bullet hole.

Greeley straightened up and got out of the light so that the photographers could take the scene.

"Who found him?" asked the captain.

One of the prowl car men answered, "We did, sir. We were cruising past and noticed a woman leaning out of one of the upper-story windows of the house, hollering something. We braked to see if anything was the matter, but she was only calling to her husband to find out why he was taking so long to come in. So I got out and went to take a look in the garage, where she said he was. The doors were jammed fast and the keys were still sticking in them on the outside. I had to call my partner over before we could get them open. We found one of them warped." He led them over and showed them. "See, it hangs unevenly on its hinges, and the wind must have blew them shut after him and got them stuck. When we finally pried them open, all the lights were on and there he was, with one leg sticking up against the wall like that."

"What tipped you off it was a homicide?"

"Well, he landed backward, so I knew the floor couldn't have given him that ugly looking hole in front. I could see it even from out past the car's bumper. I've seen bullet holes before."

"Good work," said the captain crisply, "because that's what you saw this time too. Now just one more question. About those doors: are you sure they were just jammed fast, and not locked on the outside?"

"Yessir. One side hung unevenly, like I said. For half of the distance it slanted in a little further than the other, and for the other half it leaned out a little more than the other. You could see the light coming through up at the top and down near the bottom. All he could do on his side, I guess, was just shove in one direction. That's why he couldn't free them. The way we had to do it, I pulled out at the top and my partner pushed in at the bottom, we evened it with the other wing and that got it loose."

"Take those keys anyway," the captain ordered the print men, "if they're not spoiled already. And all around that window, every square inch of it. I'd like to know if he opened it to try to get out or somebody else opened it to shoot in at him. How long ago do you figure?" This last to the examiner.

"A good hour, maybe even more."

"How do you figure it?" He turned almost instinctively to Brown when he put the question.

"Just roughly, with what we've gotten so far, something like this: the wind blew the doors shut on him and trapped him in here after he drove his car in to put it to bed. He couldn't get them open from the inside, like the radio cops suggest, so he tried to climb out through the window. He either inadvertently attracted someone's attention doing so and they approached him, or he got stuck and called out to someone to give him a hand. Whoever this person was, they almost certainly fired a bullet at him and killed him instead of helping him out."

"I think that's close enough for a starter," the captain agreed. "We'll build on it, anyway, until and unless we find evidence to the contrary. It doesn't give us any motive yet, but we haven't gone far enough to reasonably expect one." He indicated the fat wallet and silver cigarette-case that had been taken from the body. "Whatever it was, it wasn't robbery. Let's go in and talk to her if we're able to."

As they moved up to the house he added, "This thing's going to make a big splash. The sooner we can get a strangle hold on it, the better for us. You know who they are, don't you?"

Greeley saw Brown nod, but he hadn't any idea, for his part.

"Didn't you ever hear of Big Bill Nolan, the politician? This is his brother."

Greeley knew vaguely that he pulled a lot of weight, a sort of district boss of some kind.

"Yeah," Brown added, "we better get it under control fast." But he sounded fairly confident.

Mrs. Nolan was in pretty bad shape, as was to be expected, but managed to give them an outline of her own and her husband's movements just preceding the event.

"Jerry and I had dinner at Big Bill's house tonight," she wept. "He's my brother-in-law, you know. He was giving some kind of a smoker or party for his club-members afterwards, and wanted Jerry to stay—oh, I only wish he had. But he serves such elaborate meals, we'd both had wine at dinner, we weren't used to it, and it made us both sleepy. Jerry wasn't much of a drinker any more than I am, in spite of the fact that he used to be in that business. We got back a little after nine, and I came right into the house and he went to put the car away. I must have dozed off upstairs. The next time I opened my eyes over an hour had gone by and he hadn't come in yet. I wasn't worried about his being overcome or anything like that, because he'd had that window put into the garage especially on that account, only about a year ago. The two officers in the radio car came by while I was calling to him."

"You didn't hear anything like a shot, Mrs. Nolan?"

"I can't tell if I did or not. You see the car had backfired all the way home, its exhaust-pipe needed cleaning badly and Jerry had put off attending to it. It was still going on after he got it into the garage, but I had the windows closed in the bedroom and it wasn't enough to keep me from dozing off."

"Do you know of anyone who had a grudge against your husband, Mrs. Nolan?"

"No one did. Everyone liked him," she said tearfully. "He was very easy-going. Big Bill is the one who has enemies."

"Well, we won't distress you any more tonight," the captain said sympathetically. "We know how you must feel." He motioned his two men out with him.

In the hallway they met Big Bill Nolan as he came storming in in answer to the bad news he had just received. He was still in dinner jacket and lapel flower, a big florid silver-haired man, chewing viciously on a cigar.

"You get that man for me, Captain!" he thundered, pointing his cigar menacingly at Hackett. "You get the man that did this, d'ye hear me? Give me a chance to get my hands on him!"

"We'll get him, Mr. Nolan," the captain answered evenly. "We'll give it everything we've got. I'll put my best men on it. Here's one of them here." He rested a hand on Brown's shoulder. "This is Bill Brown, one of the best men on the squad. D'you remember the Ingram case? D'you remember the Allroyd case? That's this boy."

Nolan studied him a moment, with the swift appraisal of a man used to judging character at sight. Then he swept up Brown's hand, pumped it with ferocious intensity.

"Brown," he grated, "the sky's the limit! I'll shoot you up to the top. I can do it! If you're as good as they say, you get me the dirty sneaking so-and-so that done this to my brother and you're made for life! You can count on Big Bill Nolan!"

Then he barged on past them, to go in and console his sister-in-law, without so much as a glance at Greeley.

"Well, you men heard," Hackett said succinctly as they returned to the garage. "It means our scalps."

Brown said, "The angle, of course, is that it's some enemy of Big Bill's, who couldn't get at him himself and therefore struck at him through his brother."

"That's logical," Hackett conceded. "Big Bill never married, so his brother was his nearest of kin, and he always had a peculiar affection for him anyway. He gave him all this." He waved his hand at the house behind them. "Took him out of the saloon business and pensioned him for life."

※◆※

They had taken Nolan out of the garage by now. "I don't think this place can tell us much more, for the present," Hackett remarked after a final look around. "I want to get down and find out what Ballistics can tell us about that slug. That's going to be important. Get hold of Big Bill as soon as he cools off a little, Brown, and see if you can get a line on anyone who in his opinion might possibly nurse a grievance against him. He's made enough enemies in his time. Case the vicinity, Greeley, and try to find out if anyone was seen loitering around the premises earlier in the evening, if any parked car was noticed that didn't belong in the neighborhood. Stuff like that. Sometimes little things, that don't seem like anything, pack more weight than the biggest leads you can get."

The dirty work again. He went at it without a murmur. Hackett drove off back to headquarters to await the autopsy and ballistics reports. Brown remained puttering around the garage, measuring the window dimensions with a pocket tape, examining the warped doors microscopically. All this was highly pertinent, but it wasn't much in character for him to bother with it. It was more the sort of thing he usually delegated to Greeley. He was hanging around waiting for Big Bill to come out, Joe supposed. The last Joe saw of him he was going over the ground on the outside of the garage window inch by inch, crouched down on his heels with a torch.

Greeley worked his way down the street dwelling by dwelling, on the side nearest the Nolan garage. He got practically nothing. It had been, and still was, an unusually windy night. No one had heard anything like a shot, or if they had they hadn't been able to differentiate it from the incessant banging of loose shutters and rattling of window frames that had gone on. One family, in the house nearest the Nolans', but which was separated from it by one empty building-lot, remembered hearing the backfiring of the car when it arrived home, but this had been going on for days now, so they didn't think anything of it. "I guess he kept forgetting to have the carbon scraped off. He was a lovely man, but he was very absent-minded at times." The woman sighed reminiscently. "Poor soul. Only about a week ago he locked himself out of the house one night—his wife was away or something—and a man in a car stopped and caught him in the act of trying to climb in through the window. It turned out he was a plainclothesman too." She laughed a little, ruefully. "Poor Mr. Nolan had to identify himself, tell who he was, that he was Big Bill's brother and all that, before the policeman would let him go. Then Nolan wanted him to climb up for him and open the door on the inside. He was too stout himself to be very good at it, you know. The man said, 'What do I look like, a sign painter or a monkey in the zoo?' And he drove off and left Nolan there on the sidewalk at two in the morning. I had to send my husband out and have him do it for him, otherwise he'd have stood out there all night." Her smile faded and she sighed again. "And now he's gone. I can't believe it."

The incident reminded Greeley of when he and Brown had been rookies, in uniform, and that was almost the sum total of their duties. Brown had been just like that too in those days, with an exaggerated sense of his own dignity.

VII

When he got back Brown had gone. Big Bill presumably had too, for the two retainers and the battleship of a limousine were missing. A single dim light behind a lowered shade on the upper floor of the death house marked where Mrs. Nolan was under medical supervision. A cop was preparing to lock up the garage.

Greeley came up to him in the dark, his shoddy topcoat ballooning about him, hanging onto his hat with one hand. "Open 'em all the way again," he suggested. "Let's see if the wind'll do the same thing this time."

They swung the two halves back to the full width necessary to admit a car, took their hands off, and watched and waited. Nothing happened for a few minutes; then just when Greeley was starting to get doubtful a sudden gust came along that shot the doors closed with a noise like a giant firecracker. It took the men a good five minutes to pry them apart again.

A young woman in a nurse's cap threw open the window next to the one where the night light burned and hissed down: "Will you men please get away from here! This woman's in a critical condition!"

"Sorry," Greeley whispered back huskily.

But he lingered there by the locked garage. As he watched the cop shove off down the street he wondered, "Why don't I get out of here? What am I trying to do—give an imitation of a detective? I'll never be one."

He drifted around to the side where the window was, playing his torch around the way Brown had his. He wondered if Brown had found anything. Leave it to him, if there was anything to find he'd find it, Joe assured himself. Bill had been looking for the gun, maybe. No, it couldn't have been that; even he, Slow Joe, knew no murderer was going to be dumb enough to discard it right there, yards away from the crime. That would have been leaving his name and address with a vengeance. Brown had probably just been killing time until Big Bill was ready to leave his sister-in-law's house.

All Joe could see, in the little white egg of light he rolled around his feet, was stubble and dried leaves and little stones. He scuffed and prodded around, knowing that if he wasn't doing any good at least he wasn't doing any damage either.

He did see something like a beetle nestling there under one of the little stones he dislodged, that was about all. He poked it indifferently with the tip of his shoe. It shop up at an angle against the garage wall, hit with a little click, and dropped again. He looked for it and found it a second time, and it wasn't a beetle, it was a button.

It was one of those fancy leather-covered ones with a rounded head, not holed through for thread but with a little metal "eye" underneath instead. The kind of button that is sometimes featured on certain extreme types of sports suits. Or uniforms.

Studying it he thought, "Is it possible the great Brown missed this and I got it?" It seemed inconceivable. It could have happened, of course. Brown was only human after all. He might have just missed disturbing the right little stone out of all the dozens strewn around. But it seemed far more likely Brown had lost it himself just now, when he was crouched over exploring around here. Only, on second thought, Greeley remembered he'd had on a dark blue suit, and this button was brown, so that was out too. It was a vest- or cuff-button, judging by its size, rather than a jacket button.

"Maybe it is something after all," he decided. "I better take it down with me and show it."

⎯⎯◆⎯⎯

Hackett wasn't in his office when he got down to the precinct station. Some tip had come in, they told him, on the payroll bandit, and Hackett had chased out again. Brown wasn't there either, and nobody seemed to know where he was. Probably still consulting Big Bill Nolan on a list of possible enemies.

Joe was going to leave the button on Hackett's desk, but that looked silly as hell. He could hear the captain growl, "What do you think you're doing, playing kids' games?" The more he thought about it the sillier he felt, coming in to say: "I found a button on the ground outside the garage up there." He realized fully that just such things had turned out to be highly important clues before. In fact whole cases had been hinged on much less than that—a wisp of nap, a single hair, the broken-off tip of a lead-pencil—but perhaps it was that he lacked self-confidence, he was used to playing second fiddle on any case in which he was teamed with Brown; coming from Joe Greeley, a thing like this seemed bound to be disregarded, laughed at. Or so he thought. It might, for all he knew, turn out to have belonged to Jerrold Nolan himself. He hadn't lost it tonight, for when they found him he too had been in a dark blue suit, but maybe earlier in the week. He decided that before he said anything about it he'd go back tomorrow and check through Nolan's clothing, just to make sure. For the present he returned the button to his vest pocket, in the little scrap of newspaper in which he'd brought it in.

The ballistics and autopsy reports had come in already, were there on Hackett's desk under his eyes. Whether Hackett had read them yet, before he was called out on this other thing, Greeley couldn't tell, of course. He picked them up and glanced through them himself. Being on the case, he was entitled to the information they contained. The bullet that had killed Nolan was from a .45 caliber revolver, and had been fired at very close range, though not quite actual contact. The other typed sheet was less important. The cause of death was a bullet in the brain. Nolan had also received a bad gash at the back of the head from striking against the steel-rimmed running-board of the car, but this was not sufficient to have caused death. Moreover, it had bled only slightly, so the death wound had probably preceded it. Nolan had had a slight amount of alcohol in his system at the time.

Hackett's desk phone rang while Joe was standing there reading, and he took the call. He recognized Brown's voice. That pounding like a dynamo was more noticeable in it than ever. He must be on the way to something already.

"Hackett there?"

"No, he was called out on the Wolf Bernstorff thing. This is Joe Greeley."

"Well, listen, Joe. I've just been talking to Big Bill Nolan and we've shaped up a list of possibilities in this thing. You know, people who have threatened to get even with him at one time or another, who have held long-standing grievances against him, that kind of thing. Some of them look good and I think we're going to town. But it's too big, takes in too much ground, for me to cover single-handed. I want Hackett to get it as soon as he can. He'll have to apportion it, put some other people on it along with me."

"All right, let's have it. I'll take it down for you."

"Number one, Anthony Trusso, ward-heeler up in Italian Harlem, frozen out by Nolan and lost his pull. Number two . . ." When Brown got through he had given six names, with all the requisite information that went with each.

"Which ones are you following up yourself?" Greeley asked unexpectedly.

Brown's voice had been the staccato rapid-firing of a machine gun until now. It suddenly missed fire, faltered, then recovered again. "Er-Trusso and this Little Benny."

"No he isn't," Greeley told himself. "He wasn't ready for that and it tripped him. He isn't going after those two at all. But what's he bothering to stall me for? What's he afraid of, *my* horning in? I'm no competition for him."

"Okay," he said, "I'll underline those two, so he'll know."

"Yeah, fine." Brown's voice lacked enthusiasm, though. (He's not really interested in them, Greeley thought.) "See that he gets it right away, will you? And don't let it get around—it's dynamite."

Brown had hung up before Joe could ask him whether he'd seen the ballistics report yet.

VIII

Hackett came in at two that morning with a face sour as green apples. "Got away again," he commented tersely. "The guy must be an eel. What's this list?"

Greeley explained.

"I haven't got a man to spare, Big Bill or no Big Bill," Hackett told him. "We've got to get Bernstorff, dammit! He's killed a cop and if we let him get away with it, it amounts to waving a white flag of surrender in the face of the entire underworld. Our lives won't be worth a nickel." He handed the list back to Greeley. "You and Brown'll have to cover it between you. Get hold of him and tell him those are my orders."

Greeley couldn't locate Brown any more that night. Brown must have started already. Joe went after two of them on his own hook, and had the satisfaction of eliminating two of the six names pretty conclusively. For the present anyway, unless a dead-heat developed later on. Both had firearms but neither was a .45. Both were willing to admit they hated Big Bill—too willing to admit it, for present purposes—but they were able to lay it on the line and show they hadn't been anywhere near Russell Street that night.

It was the milkman's hour by this time, and still no Brown. Joe was ready to cave in by now himself, so he went home and got a couple of hours sleep before he went ahead. He stretched out fully dressed on the sofa in the living room with an alarm clock under the pillow, in order not to disturb his wife, who had been asleep for hours. By six he was up again.

He thought he might be able to catch Brown on the fly by stopping off at his house on the way down to headquarters, but he'd missed him again. Brown's wife was up already and came to the door instead. She was a tall, stately red-haired girl with an air of breeding. Brown had done himself up right in that direction too.

"He hasn't been home all night," she said. "Phoned about one this morning not to expect him. He's working on a case and"—she shrugged charmingly—"I'm practically a grass widow." She was holding a vest folded under her arm. "I'm amusing myself sewing buttons on his clothes." He could tell she was nutty about the guy, though. "It's great fun until you come up against one that's missing and can't be matched."

"Is there one you can't match?"

"On this. Funny little leather-covered things. What's the matter? You look sick."

His shoulder slumped wearily lower against the door frame. "I am sick, Mrs. Brown. Sicker than I've ever been in my life before."

"Can I get you something?"

He mumbled something that sounded like "Sorry I disturbed you," and suddenly the doorway was empty.

He was standing on a corner, then, somewhere near there, thinking, "I've got to save somebody's life! Somebody whose name isn't down on that list. He wouldn't have turned it in if it was. Somebody who's going to be arrested, who's going to try to bolt at some dark place along the way, and who's going to be shot dead in 'self-defense.' Who, though? How am I to know who?"

Then he was at an open directory, tracing a rubbery finger that wouldn't hold steady across William Francis Xavier Nolan, who'd paid to have all four names listed in full.

It was still only a little after seven when Joe got out of a cab in front of the house. It was a four-story limestone dwelling, and the shades were still down on all the windows. He kept his finger on the doorbell until a half-dressed secretary of some sort opened the door.

"I'm from police headquarters and I've got to see Mr. Nolan."

"You can't at this time of the morning. He's been up half the night. He's just lost his brother, and—"

"Don't try to keep me out of here. I'll take the full responsibility. It can't wait, I tell you." Joe's face was too white and strained not to be convincing.

The secretary gave in. "Have you caught the man yet? Is that what it is?"

He was led up to the second floor, motioned to wait outside a big pair of double doors. He kept pacing back and forth wondering, "What am I going to say to him? How am I going to put it?"

He still didn't know, when the doors slid back once more and the secretary gestured with a thumb. Big Bill's bedroom was fantastic, but Greeley didn't give it half an eye. He got a blurred impression of a canopied bed, a grand piano, a tiger-skin rug, a nightstand with a pearl-handled revolver and a memorial light flickering dimly before a picture of Jerrold Nolan.

Big Bill was sitting up under the canopy in candy-striped pajamas, shading his eyes as remembered grief came flooding back on him from the night before. Greeley just stood there in considerate silence.

"Well, what is it?" Nolan roared finally. "Did you get hold of Schreiber like I suggested?"

That name wasn't down on Brown's list. So that was who it was.

Greeley spoke with difficulty—after that. "I'm assigned to the case with Brown. If you'd mind giving me a few details—"

Big Bill's face got purple with fury. "I gave Brown all the details! Get them from him! Don't you even know your own job? Do they have to send every piddling dick in the division into my bedroom in the middle of the night? You ought to be demoted, whoever you are! What's that?" He scanned the list. "Where's Schreiber? Why isn't his name down here? He's the most important one of the lot. None of these others count! We eliminated them one by one! *He's* the one was heard to say publicly that he'd get even with me. There's been bad blood between us for years! I told Brown all that. I gave him all the details and documents in the case the last thing last night."

Greeley said in a peculiarly muffled voice, "Yes sir. Brown's—after him right now."

"Then what do you want here?" Then, noticing that his caller was already easing the doors shut after him, he boomed, "In *my* day a detective used to have brains!"

"He used to be straight too," said Greeley inaudibly.

———◆◆◆———

It took him an hour, in the Yorkville sector, to locate Gus Schreiber's whereabouts. An earlybird bartender, opening up his tavern, finally admitted knowledge of where Schreiber lived. Greeley went over on foot. Then as he rounded the corner, he stopped dead, a few doors down from the address the barman had given him. Something about it suggested it had been there for some time past, and was going to stay there for a long time to come.

He was too late. The cat-and-mouse play was already in full swing.

He turned and went back the way he'd come. He went midway up the next block over, to a point roughly approximating the location of Schreiber's house. He went into a flat there, and out into the back yard, and climbed the fence over into Schreiber's back yard. He knocked on the rear door until a typical German hausfrau came to open it.

"Lemme in," he said. "I've got to talk to Schreiber. Don't be afraid. I'm a detective."

He thrust his way in without waiting and went up the basement stairs, beating the rain off his hat. The woman was crying now and jabbering behind him. In a back room on the main floor he found a corpulent man with a napkin tucked around his throat drinking coffee with a number of assorted kids.

"Are you Gus Schreiber? Headquarters. I've got to talk to you. Get your family out of here."

The former district-leader stood up, eyes bulging with wrath. "You got a warrant to come in here? Then scram! This persecution stops or I kill somebody!"

"Now wait a minute. I had to do this. If I waited until I caught up with you outside the house, it would have been too late. You own a gun?"

Schreiber nodded belligerently.

"What caliber is it?"

"Forty-fife."

"I was afraid of that," murmured Greeley. "Where is it?"

The question seemed to infuriate Big Bill's enemy. "You ask me where is it? *Nein,* I ask you where is it! I ask you why it was taken away from me!"

"Who took it?"

"Von of your people! I drink a little too much beer von night. He is in there with me, he sees it on me, he says, 'You better let me have that before you get into any trouble with it.' They have told him who I am, how I have said I will kill that Nolan the day I see him, for what he has done to me."

"Why didn't you go around to claim it?"

"I did—and it was neffer turned in! I cannot find the man again. I know if I make too much trouble about it, I get in trouble myself. This Nolan, he would like nothing better than to send me to jail, like he did my oldest boy." He breathed stormily through dilated nostrils. "Wait. Wait. My time comes."

"Well this isn't it. Nolan's brother was killed last night—with your gun. You better get out of here fast! Don't stop to argue or ask questions."

Schreiber's Teutonic stubbornness came to the fore. "I don't move! I was at the club last night. I can proof it!"

"Where? Where you going to prove it?" was all Greeley asked.

"At the police station! Where you think?"

"You'll never get there alive. That's what I'm trying to tell you. You won't show up there any more than your gun did. Come here a minute, to the front window with me. Don't touch the curtains now. See that cab there? There's a man waiting in it to arrest you. He's the same man that impounded your gun. You'll get it back. It'll be found in your pocket, or in your hand, when they come across you in some vacant lot."

Schreiber just stood there staring in hypnotized horror, as though he could see the scene before him. He felt for his own throat, held onto it as though he could feel a noose tightening around it.

"The only thing that saves you is he's alone on it. Take off your bib and follow me. You can get out through the back, the way I came in. Get out of town for the next couple of days and stay there. After that it'll be all right. You can come back again."

He ran down the back stairs, stopped halfway to the bottom to make sure Schreiber was coming after him, then went on down the rest of the way. Schreiber suddenly balked at the yard door. "How I know it ain't you instead of him who does it to me? How I know who you are?"

Greeley, astride the fence already, answered, "Stay here then. I've done my part. I don't much care what you do. I never saw you before in my life."

A doorbell rang somewhere at the front of the house, and it could be heard all the way out here.

Schreiber came out the rest of the way, his arms extended. "Give me a hand up. I ain't so athletic no more."

IX

Greeley didn't go back to headquarters after he left Schreiber at the 125th Street Station. He went out to Brown's house instead. It had to be up there, not at headquarters.

He waited patiently through the long hours, a huddled figure in the outer doorway, hands deep-pocketed, coat collar turned up against the slanting silvery rain. Head down the whole time, never once raised; not lowered in an attempt to avoid recognition, but with the weight of the responsibility upon him.

The shiny sidewalk darkened from pewter to black, and it was night at last. He never moved. He was stiff all over. It seemed like half the night had gone by before tires came whispering up at last and stopped out at the curb before him. He didn't look up. A car door cracked and a man's thick-soled tread came across the sidewalk. A pair of shoes stopped there within the radius of his lowered gaze.

His head came up slowly then, and it was Brown.

"For pete's sake!" was Brown's wry recognition. "Haven't you got sense enough to come in out of the rain?"

He, Greeley, was a coward up to the very last. He couldn't do it down here in the open street either. He said, "Let's go upstairs. I want to talk to you."

Going up, Brown growled, "I was thrown for a terrible loss just now." Greeley didn't ask him what he meant. Didn't have to.

Brown's wife was asleep. Greeley went over and closed the door so she wouldn't hear them. He sat down and took out his gun.

Brown looked at him and smiled. "What're you pointing it at *me* for? Rehearsing what you're going to do to—"

"Finish it," Greeley said. "What I'm going to do to the man that killed Jerry Nolan. This isn't the rehearsal. This is it. Hand over that forty-five you impounded from Gus Schreiber last week. Hand it over. It's on you right now. Your own too. Come out with it. Now don't move. I'll shoot you if you want it that way. I'm in hell already."

"How did you know I—?" Then he tried to say something about having unearthed it just now at Schreiber's house.

"How do I know—the whole thing?" Greeley grimaced in revulsion. "Do we have to talk about it? We've known each other half our lives. Let's shut up, let's shut up."

Brown sat down at long last. "What are you doing this to me for?"

Greeley pitched the leather-covered button at him. "Are you man enough to bring the vest this goes with out here and show it to me? Don't keep looking at me trying to find out how much I know. I know the whole thing. It's been progressive. The Ingram case was on the level. You got a boost. In the Allroyd case, the murder was on the level but you couldn't break it, so you framed a suspect and shot him down in cold blood. You got a boost. Things didn't happen fast enough after that to suit you. You caught the hotheaded Dutchman Schreiber shooting off his mouth what he'd like to do to Big Bill Nolan. You took his gun away. That part of it was in good faith. That was the only part that was. That same night you came through Russell Street and came across Jerry Nolan locked out of his house. It was a devastating coincidence, and it was too much for you. The whole set-up must have come to you then and there. You couldn't do anything right then, because the people in the next house were at their window. You drove through that street again and again, I suppose. And finally it jelled just right. You caught him accidentally imprisoned in his garage, trying to climb out the window, and with a high wind blowing that was making enough racket to muffle any shot.

"You dropped a button. You didn't know just where, but you were worried. I saw you looking for it later that night. I would never have looked myself if you hadn't. Now give me those guns— butts first. Careful."

Brown complied. Joe Greeley pocketed the .45, and started to empty the Police Positive's chambers. "I'm going to get out of here now. I'm going to leave you here—with your wife in there. Say goodby to her or not, whichever you like. I'm going to leave your own gun here with you. It's got one bullet in it."

"I can't, Joe! I can't! I haven't got the nerve. I've got some kinds of courage, but I haven't got that kind."

"Then I'm going in to report," Joe said. "I'm not going to force you with me at the point of a gun—but you better come. What else is there to do? You'd only be a renegade for the rest of your life, hunted and tracked down like the rats *you've* always hunted yourself until now. It's going to blow the roof off the whole division, tear us wide open, this way. There's nothing worse than when a sheep-dog turns wolf."

The door opened and Brown's wife looked in on them. "Would you and your friend like some coffee or beer, Bill?" she smiled.

"No, we're going right away," Brown said. "He's—he's got a report to make. Don't wait up for me. I don't know when I'll be back." And he turned his back to her and hunted for his hat where it wasn't.

——=◆=——

They went on foot, walking side by side as though nothing were the matter. "How many hundreds of guys have been walked in like this," Brown said once. "Now I know what it feels like."

"Quit it!" exploded from Greeley's tight lips. He eyed a car that had recklessly shaved a corner short ahead of them just then. "You don't have to. A step in the wrong direction, without looking behind—"

Brown shook his head. Greeley knew whom he was thinking of.

A block or so beyond, somebody dropped an electric-light bulb in the dim recesses of one of the decrepit rookeries they were passing at the moment, and they both jolted spasmodically, then grinned sheepishly at each other, as if to say, "What a fine pair we turned out to be!"

They went on a few steps farther, and someone coughed behind them. Greeley turned to look and there was a uniformed cop standing there in the entrance they'd just passed, and the cop suddenly keeled over and flattened out and lay there face down across the doorstep.

Lifting a gun, Greeley wheeled, jumped back, Brown a step behind him. Joe crouched down over the man and tilted his head, and a thread of blood came down beside the bluecoat's ear.

"Bernstorff," he whispered. "The one we've been so long—"

The gun was grabbed from Joe Greeley's hand and someone was pounding up the rickety stairs with no attempt at caution or concealment, and Joe stood up. He was alone in the doorway.

"Bill!" he bellowed. "Hold it! That's your gun, and there's only one bullet in it!" But somehow he knew that Brown had thought of that before he sprinted in there.

Joe plunged in after him, but they came before he'd even reached the foot of the stairs. Six slashing, vindictive shots, so fast you couldn't count between them. And then a pause, and then a single shot as if in contemptuous answer, somehow sounding steady, sure, unhurried. Fired by the kind of wrist that could take aim above a flock of school kids and never falter.

Detective William Brown was lying there at the head of the stairs, up on the fourth floor, when Greeley got to him. There was a motionless huddled figure at the other end of the dim hall.

Brown's eyes were still open and they saw Greeley when Joe's face came close in stooping to pass an arm under Brown so the fallen detective's last few breaths could come easier.

"How am I doing?" he panted. "Does that square it?"

Brown lowered his head just once, kept it down.

"You won't tell them?"

"I don't know anything to tell—except you got Bernstorff. Good luck, Bill Brown."

The last thing Brown said, his eyes already lidding closed, was, "I wasn't so smart after all."

Yes, he *was* smart all right, Joe Greeley thought, turning away, and he meant it in sincerest admiration. Smarter than I'll ever be. That was the whole trouble. Just a little bit dumber, a little bit slower, and he would have been all right. Just a little less speed, just a little more control . . .

AFTERWORD TO "DETECTIVE WILLIAM BROWN"

The title character of "Detective William Brown" (*Detective Fiction Weekly*, September 10, 1938) strikes me as the ultimate Noir Cop in the Woolrich canon, a conscienceless opportunist who rises through the ranks of the force thanks to a combination of brutality and raw courage. The story's viewpoint character however is not Brown but his plodding, dedicated and relatively humane boyhood friend Greeley, and the plot takes us through yet another of Woolrich's oscillations as Greeley slowly, by fits and starts but inexorably comes to learn the truth behind Brown's meteoric rise to the top—the truth which, as in "Endicott's Girl," is covered up at the climax. Such, Woolrich tells us, are the men who are licensed to kill us at their whim, and even those who enter the life as decent people are corrupted by the system they serve.

THE CASE OF THE KILLER-DILLER

A SWING-MURDER MYSTERY

CHAPTER ONE

DEATH OF A SANDMAN

In the streets outside it was broad daylight already, but down in the basement-room night shadows still lingered on. Through stratified layers of hours-old cigarette smoke, unable to find its way out of the poorly ventilated place, two motionless forms, both in grotesque postures, were indistinctly visible. One was a girl huddled asleep on a piano bench, her head and arms resting on the keyboard. The other was a man, toes pointed downward, head on chest, finger-tips touching his sides, as though he were staring entranced at something on the floor.

The basement itself was no different from any other sub-street-level space of its kind. Bare whitewashed walls, an oblong vent fitted with opaque wire-meshed glass high up on one side, that looked out at about the level of passersby's insteps, an array of steam and water pipes of varying girths that ran out parallel to the ceiling for half its length, then disappeared through it by means of elbow-joints. It was what the cellar contained that set it apart.

There were numbers of ordinary, unpainted wooden kitchen chairs scattered about, most of them overturned. For nearly every chair there was a complementary gin bottle lying discarded somewhere nearby—empty or with only a finger's width left in it at the most—and a musical instrument: trap-drum, clarinet, sax, and so on. There was a table too, scalloped around the edges with cigarette burns, some of them with ash cylinders still in them. Loose orchestration sheets and more empty bottles littered its surface, bringing the bottle ratio up to nearly two per chair.

A venturesome cockroach traveled across an orchestration-leaf of Ravel's *Bolero* that had fallen to the floor. It didn't look so different from the other notes, except that it was bigger and kept moving slowly along the clef-bars instead of staying in one place. There was a peculiar acrid pungency in the air that didn't come from liquor, and that no ordinary cigarette ever made either.

———◆———

As the daylight filtered in more and more strongly through the clouded sidewalk-level pane, the girl who slept with her arms on top of the yellowed piano-keys, stirred a little, raised her head. Nearly two whole octaves of pressed-down keys, freed of her weight, reared into place with a series of little clashing discords. The sound woke her more fully.

"In the groove," she murmured dreamily, and blinked her eyes open.

Her silky butterscotch-colored hair, worn smooth and long, came tumbling down over her face, and she brushed it back with one hand. Then her eyes went upward, took in the other figure, who seemed to be dancing there before her in the hazy air, to unheard notes. She shot up from the piano-bench.

"Hal!" she exclaimed. "What are you doing up—" She choked it off short. He was being dead up there, hanging by his neck from a thick electric cord that looped down between two of the exposed steam pipes.

She stumbled back against the keyboard and her hand struck it, brought forth another discordant jangle. She sidestepped, terrified even by that harmless sound. The exploring cockroach scampered off the orchestration-sheet, scurried back toward its cranny.

"They've all gone, left me here alone with—it," she sobbed.

She stared distractedly at the overturned chairs, turned and fought her way through the stagnant air toward the closed wooden door at the back of the place.

She threw it open and looked up and down the dim basement passage lit by a single wan bulb. Rows of empty ashcans were pyramided at one end of it. She was on the verge of hysteria by now. It was not alone what she had just seen, it was also partly due to the depression that always set in after the over-stimulation of one of those jam-sessions—a sort of musical hang-over, so to speak. How the men in the outfit must be feeling, she could only imagine. She didn't drink gin or blaze reefers the way they did.

"Fred! Frankie! Dusty!" she whispered hoarsely, standing there in the open doorway. The long brick-walled passage echoed to it hollowly, like a tomb. She shuddered, crouched back against the wall. A black cat slunk out between two of the ashcans and she gave a tinny little bleat, half superstitious reflex, half actual alarm.

A door grated open far down at the other end of the passage and a grizzled old man in overalls looked out at her. Instinctively she reached behind her, pulled shut the door of the room from which she had just come, so he couldn't look in if he should pass by. "Oh, Mr. Hoff, did the boys—did the rest of the crew leave already?" she faltered.

He shrugged as he shuffled down the passage toward her. "If they ain't in there, then they must have gone. I tell you one thing, I be glad when they go undt never come back. Such noise! What the landlord was thinking about to rent them a room down here. With three doors in between I still heard it." He was opposite the closed door now and she was standing in front of it, as though to prevent him from going in. She was loyal to the men she worked with. This was a matter that concerned the entire orchestra. She had to find the others first, consult them, before she let a stranger—

"Have you got a cigarette, Mr. Hoff?"

Her bag was somewhere inside there, with a package of cigarettes in it, but she couldn't bear the thought of going back in again—and facing *that*—to get it. He gave her a loose one from his overall pocket, scraped a kitchen match down the brickwork. The cigarette shook pitifully in her hand and kept on shaking even after she had it lit and between her lips.

"Yah, look at you," he said disapprovingly. "Fine life for a young girl, shtaying up all night banging and hollering with a bunch of drunk musickaners! You bet if you was my daughter—"

He'd often said that to her, but today, for the first time, she was inclined to agree with him.

"I'd like to give it up myself," she said sickly.

He trudged on up the passage toward his daily chores and disappeared around a corner. She threw down the cigarette she had just lit, tried the door to make sure it was securely closed, then fled up the passage in the other direction. She opened a door, ran up a flight of basement steps, came out at the rear of the ground-floor hallway of the cheap "residence club," that was just a rooming-house under another name. A couple of the orchestra members had rooms here in the building.

⟶◆⟵

She ran around to the front, up the main stairs to the second floor—the place had no elevator—and knocked briefly on a door near the head of the stairs. She threw it open—the knock was just for propriety's sake—and looked in.

Fred Armstrong, the outfit's clarinet-player, was lying soddenly on his back on the bed, mouth open to the ceiling, the gin bottle he'd brought up from downstairs still clutched in his hand, as though it were too precious to let go even after everything it had had in it was inside him instead.

She shook him fruitlessly a few times, tried to rouse him by calling "Fred! Fred!" urgently in his ear. His mouth didn't even close. He'd be that way for hours, she realized. She turned and ran out again, closing the door after her.

Halfway to the stairs again she stopped short in her tracks, turned aside. There was a little enamel sign sticking out at right-angles to the wall—*Bath*. A flicker of motion from the partly open door had caught her eye. She pushed it open and saw a pale-faced youth her own age, standing there looking at her. Strings of damp hair straggled down over his forehead. His coat-collar was turned up around his neck, and he had a black eye.

"Frankie!" she breathed. "What are you hiding out like this for up here?"

He had to swallow a couple of times before he could get his voice out. "I'm not—hiding out. What's the matter, Billie?"

"Hal Thatcher's dead down in that room in the basement where we have our jam-sessions! I woke up just now and—he was right there in front of me, hanging from the pipes." She stared at him. "Frankie! Pull yourself together. Didn't you hear what I just said to you?"

He held up three fingers, looked at her with fear-dilated eyes.

She seemed to understand what he meant by the gesture. "Yes, it looks like we're jinxed. But if we once let ourselves believe it, then we *are* jinxed for fair."

"I'm going to get out of this crew," he stammered. "I'm—I'm quitting right now. I'd rather be out of work than—than—"

"This is no time to talk that way! We can't let Dusty down now, of all times. This is when we should stick by him. Don't be a welsher, Frankie. You haven't told me yet why you were skulking up here, peeping out through a crack in the door at me."

His eyes dropped before her scrutiny. "I wandered up here when the session wound up. I tried to get some sleep curled up in the bathtub. It was the only thing I could find for a bed."

"How'd you get your hair all wet like that?"

"My head was splitting. I ran some water from the shower on it just now when I woke up, trying to get it down to its right size again."

⟫◆⟪

Her eyes sought the nickeled dial of the shower fixture. It was dry as sandpaper. Not a drop clung to it. She didn't say anything.

"What're you asking me all kinds of questions for?" he flared out suddenly, nerves on edge.

"Try to pull yourself together, Frankie," she said coldly, turning away. "Run out and drink some black coffee. I thought I was shot, but I'm all in one solid chunk compared to you."

He took out a pocket comb, ran it through his hair. "What're you going to do?" he asked her apprehensively.

"Where did Dusty go? We've got to get hold of him and tell him."

"Back to his hotel, I guess. Or maybe to a Turkish bath."

"If I can't reach him, I'll have to notify the police on my own."

He dropped the comb, picked it up again, blew through its teeth. "It's not going to look so hot for me, y'know."

"Why should it look bad for you? I suppose you mean because he gave you that shiner last night. What do you suggest we do, *not* notify the police? Bury him under the cellar floor or something?"

She dropped her voice and tapped his shirt-front with one finger. "I don't like the way you're acting, Frankie. Before I ring anyone else in on this, you'd better tell me—do you know more about this than you're letting on? Did you know it had happened before I came up and told you just now? Had you already seen him like that? Is that why you ran and hid up here?"

His weak, chalky face twitched spasmodically. His hand started toward her arm, appealingly, then he dropped it again. "N-no," he said, "I didn't."

The girl gave him a skeptical look. "I hope for your own sake that's on the level," she said. "Here goes for the cops."

CHAPTER TWO

TWO OUT OF THREE

A detective named Lindsey was the first one to get there, even before Dusty Detwiller, the band-leader. She'd put in her call direct to headquarters, without bothering to send out for a neighborhood cop. They'd been through this twice before, and she knew by now the policeman was just an intermediate step. Headquarters was always notified in the end anyway.

She was holding the fort alone, down in the jam-session room, when he got there. Armstrong was still stupefied up in his room, Frankie was around the corner trying to steady himself on coffee, Detwiller was getting an alcohol-rub downtown at the Thebes Baths, and she hadn't been able to locate Kershaw, the fifth member of the Sandmen. Her nerves were calmer now, she didn't mind going back in there as much as at first. Besides, she wanted to make sure that nothing was touched. They always seemed to attach a lot of importance to that, though of course that was in cases of murder. This was plainly a suicide.

She had had no reason to like Hal Thatcher while he was still alive, so she couldn't really feel bad about his going. She wondered what had made him do it. She sat with her back to him, on the piano-bench, looking the other way. She kept her face down toward the floor. It was pretty horrible when you looked squarely up at him. It was bad enough just to see his long attenuated shadow on the basement floor, thrown by the light coming in more strongly now through the sidewalk-vent.

The voice of Hoff, the janitor, sounded outside, asking questions, so she knew that her vigil was over at last. "Somebody in the house sent for you? Who? That's the first I know about anyt'ing being wrong. Them musickaners, I bet. I knew it! I'm only surprised it didn't happen already before now—"

The door flung open and this detective came in, a uniformed cop behind him. She looked up relievedly, threw down her cigarette.

He wasn't a particularly handsome individual, but she thought what a relief it was to see a man with healthy brown color in his face for a change, instead of the yeasty night-pallor she was used to. His eyes went up toward the ceiling behind her, came down again. Then they switched over to her.

"You the girl that phoned in?"

"Yes," she said quietly.

"Pretty cool little number, aren't you?" he told her. She couldn't tell whether he meant it admiringly or unfavorably. To tell the truth she didn't care much.

"The boys' instruments are all in here, and I thought I'd better keep an eye on them until you people got here," she explained. "I woke up in here with him, so I didn't think it would hurt to stay a minute or two more."

"All right, let me have his name, please." He took out a little notebook.

"Hal Thatcher."

He scribbled. "You say you found him like this when you woke up, Mrs. Thatcher?"

A circumflex accent etched the corner of her mouth. "No, you don't understand. I'm not married to him. We worked together in the same band, that's all. I'm the canary and he played the slush-pump." She saw his face redden a little, as if he felt he'd made a social error. "Oh, because I said I woke up— No, we were having a jam-session, and I fell asleep there at the piano, that's what I meant. We rent this room from the building-owner, come up here after work about two or three in the morning every once in a while and play for our own amusement—you know, improvise. That's what a jam-session is."

He nodded almost inattentively, but she had a feeling he'd heard every word. "What went on last night, to the best of your recollection? Better let me have your name too, while we're about it."

"Billie Bligh. The formal of that is Wilhelmina. About last night—nothing different from any other time. The way these sessions come up is, Dusty—he's our front man, the leader, you know—will say 'How about having a session tonight?' and so we all agree and have one. We left the Troc, that's the club where we work, about three, and piled into a couple of taxis, instruments and all, and came on up. We sat around chinning and smoking for a while, waiting for the spirit to move us—"

He eyed the gin bottles meaningfully, but didn't say anything.

"Some of the boys had a few nips to warm up," she agreed deprecatingly. "Then finally somebody uncased his instrument and started tootling around, and one by one everyone else joined in, and first thing you know we were all laying it in the groove. That's how those things go. In about two hours we were all burned out, they started dropping out again one by one. That's when I laid my head on the piano and dozed off. The others must have left after that, and Thatcher stayed behind, and the willies got him and—"

"Not the willies," he assured her.

"What do you mean?"

He didn't act as though he intended telling her, anyway, but just then the cop who had been left outside the basement door rapped, stuck his head in, and said: "Two of the others just showed up."

———◆———

Lindsey motioned at random and Dusty Detwiller came in alone, flaring camel's hair coat belted to almost wasp-waisted tightness around him. He didn't look particularly jaunty at the moment, though.

"This is awful," he said to Billie, shoving his hat far back on his head and holding his hand pressed to it. "What'll we do about tonight? Who's this man?"

"Name of Lindsey, headquarters. . . . No, don't pick up any of those chairs. I want everything left just the way it is. You'll have to stand up."

Detwiller started unfastening his coat, then changed his mind, tightened it up again. "Hope I don't catch cold coming out like this right out of a steam-room," he mourned.

"Do I have to stay in here any longer?" Billie asked, with her eyes on the elongated shadow on the floor. Then she looked up, glimpsed Frankie standing just outside the door with the cop. "That's all right," she corrected herself hastily. "I'd better stay. You may need me, I was the only one who wasn't drinking."

Lindsey just looked at her, then at the doorway, but he didn't say anything. "At what time did you leave here?" he asked Detwiller.

"A little before five. It hadn't started to get light yet."

"Who was still here when you left?"

"They all were. I was the first one to break away. Armstrong and Kershaw were still playing, but they couldn't lay it in the groove much any more. Frankie was here too, but he was high on weed. Billie was already falling asleep over the piano. And Hal—Hal seemed all right. He was leaning back there, on two legs of his chair, against the wall. He had a little gin in him, but he seemed all right. He kept shimmying with his hands in his pockets."

"You went where?"

"The Thebes Baths. I always go there after a session."

"That'll be all for just now. Send the other one in, Dugan."

Frankie came in. The coffee didn't seem to have done him much good. He looked nervous and jumpy even before Lindsey had opened his mouth to ask him anything.

"Your name?"

"Frank Bligh."

Lindsey looked at the girl.

"He's my brother," she said, moistening her lips.

"You were under the influence of marihuana, I'm told."

The pallid youth cringed. "So was everyone else except Billie. We all blazed it a little. We always do," he said defensively. "I show it more, that's all."

"Did you stay on to the end?"

"Y-yeah, I guess so."

"Just be definite about it, will you?" Lindsey said tonelessly. "Who'd already left this room and who hadn't?"

"Dusty had left, and Armstrong had gone upstairs to his room already, and Kershaw had stumbled out by that time, too. I don't know where he went." His eyes traveled up toward the ceiling, dropped again. "He was still here," he said reluctantly.

"Then you were the last one out, except Miss Bligh and the dead man—" Lindsey broke off short. "How'd you get the black eye? Bump into something while you were high?"

It was one of those verbal traps. Frankie's head started to go up and down affirmatively.

The girl looked up suddenly from the floor. "No, Frank, don't," she forestalled him. "Tell him the straight of it, that's the wisest way in the end. Thatcher gave it to him," she said to the detective.

"Why?" the latter asked quietly.

"He'd been making passes at me for a long time. That didn't bother me, I can handle myself. I didn't tell Frankie. But he found out about it last night for the first time, and they had a scrap in the taxi coming up here. Thatcher hit him in the eye, but then the rest of us patched it up between them, smoothed it over. Dusty won't stand for any quarreling in the organization. It's bad for our work. We even stopped for a minute outside a lunchroom and they got a little piece of raw meat for Frankie's eye and brought it out to him." She smiled placatingly at the dick. "Frankie's been worried about it, though, ever since he heard Hal did that to himself this morning. I told him not to—" Then as there was no answering smile, her own froze. "Why are you looking at the two of us like that?" she faltered.

"What do you want me to do, smile, Miss Bligh? This man never hung himself up there. He was murdered."

Frankie flinched as though he'd been hit. The girl's face paled.

"I could see that the minute I stepped into the room!" Lindsey snapped. "Either you people are still groggy from your jam-session, or you're trying to cover up something—and not being very good at it either!"

Frankie Bligh's cheeks were hollowing and filling like a fish out of water. He gave a stricken yell at his sister. "Now see what you've done! Now see what you've done! I told you it wasn't going to look good for me!" He turned and bolted out the door.

"Grab that young fellow, Dyer!" the dick shouted remorselessly after him. "Hang onto him!"

A blue-sleeved arm shot out, fastened itself to Frankie's shoulder, twirled him around like a top.

Lindsey walked leisurely out to the two of them. "What'd you do it for, kid?" he asked gruffly.

The terrified Frankie's eyelids fluttered a couple of times, then he sagged limp as a dishcloth into the cop's arms.

Lindsey had all the surviving members of Dusty Detwiller and his Sandmen ushered back into the jam-pot again about an hour later.

Frankie Bligh hadn't been booked for the murder yet and was still with them in a bad state of semi-collapse, his wrists manacled together. Armstrong had been sobered up by now, chiefly by heroic methods that had nothing to do with letting nature take its course. Kershaw, the missing member of the original sextet, had been located by an alarm and brought in from the bar where he had gone in all seriousness to brace up on a lethal mixture compounded of paprika, tomato juice and rye.

"Now, if you people still want to do your chore tonight at the Troc," Lindsey warned them, "you'll cooperate with me in this. You're not getting out of here until I've had this reconstructed to suit me."

And as Detwiller commenced to say something, he cut him off with a curt: "If you try getting in touch with a mouthpiece, we'll simply adjourn someplace else where he can't find you right away."

"You can't do this to us!" Dusty fumed.

"No, but I'm doing it"

Billie looked at him hopefully. If he put them all through their paces like this together, instead of just concentrating on Frankie and grilling him alone, maybe it meant he wasn't altogether convinced of her brother's guilt yet. But then she glanced at the cuffs on his wrists and her hopes died again.

Lindsey had two other dicks working with him now, but they must have been third-graders. Mostly, she noticed, they just did the errands. Thatcher's body had been taken down, of course, and removed to the morgue, after both he and the room had been photographed.

An ominous loop still remained in the heavy, insulated wiring where his neck had been. A stepladder against the wall showed how he had been disengaged without bringing the wire down from the ceiling, simply by expanding the loop a little and pulling his head through it. That loop, Billie recalled, had always been there, ever since they'd begun using the room—a long oval hanging down between two of the pipes, just clear of the tops of their heads, to take up slack in the wire. Otherwise the heavy hundred-watt bulb in which the cord ended on the other side of the pipe would have hung down too low toward the floor, been smashed a dozen times over in the course of their high-jinks.

"Let's talk about this contrivance a little," Lindsey said drily, "before we start getting down to cases. Did a licensed electrician put up such a botched job for a light-extension?"

Several of them shook their heads. "I didn't think so," Lindsey concluded.

"Hoff, the janitor, rigged that up for us," Dusty explained. "You see, there was no wiring for light at all in here when we rented this part of the basement. He tapped the nearest wire, which is outside in the passageway there, clamped on an outlet on the wall by it. Then he had to bore a hole up there over the top of the door to pass the wire through to us on this side. He got hold of a long length of wire, ran it through, put a plug on one end and a socket for a light-bulb on the other.

"To save himself the trouble of having to clamp it up against the ceiling, he just threaded it over the tops of those two pipes and let them do the work. But he's a dope. When he got all through, the wire was long enough to lay the bulb on the floor, like an egg. So instead of taking his pliers and cutting it and taping it together again, he just took this big loop he had between the two pipes that supported it, taking up the slack and lifting the bulb about to where it should go. Then to make sure it would stay that way, he made a big knot in the wire just on the outside of the last pipe, too thick to go through the slit between pipe and ceiling."

"Clear enough," Lindsey complimented him. "In other words that knot held it fast on the outside of the two pipes. But on the inside, toward the door and basement passage, it formed a perfect pulley arrangement. That loop could be drawn tight or relaxed at will by someone standing outside the door there, simply by pulling the plug out of the outlet—thereby plunging this room into darkness—taking a good grip on the wire, and pulling it taut out through that hole above the door. And if someone's head happened to get caught in that loop as it contracted, and he couldn't extricate it again quickly enough, it'd be just too bad. He'd probably corkscrew the loop as he thrashed around, until his neck broke. A perfect case of garrotting. That's how it was done."

"But he was held fast up there between the two pipes, as high as he could go, when I woke up and saw him," Billie said. "How could he stay up there like that, unless the murderer kept pulling the cord taut out there in the passage, held onto it for hours? And there was no one out there when I—"

"No, he wouldn't have to do that. He only had to hold it long enough to get a good thick knot bunched in it just past that bung-hole over the door, to keep it from slipping through again with the weight of Thatcher's body. You may have missed seeing that second knot, but I didn't. It's out there big as life right now."

"Well then, that lets Frankie out, without going any further!" she said decisively. "Thatcher may not have been a heavyweight, but my brother hasn't got enough strength in his arms to hold a cord tight so a man's full weight is kept clear of the floor, and at the same time tie a knot into it."

"That doesn't let your brother or anyone else out," Lindsey let her know firmly. "The pipes acted somewhat on the principle of pulleys, took a lot of the direct strain out of it. And another thing, marihuana like any other narcotic can lend a man abnormal strength temporarily. Overstimulation. We've got the method now. That points equally at any one of you, except you yourself, Miss Bligh. We've got the motive. And that points only at you, so far, Bligh. No one else had one. All we've got to learn now is who had the opportunity. Two out of three rings the bell as far as I'm concerned," he concluded ominously.

He turned to Frankie. "Now, according to your own admission made to me before you supposedly knew it was a murder that was involved and not just suicide, you were the last one to leave here, except your sister and the dead man. I suppose you want to retract that now." He didn't wait to hear whether he did or not. "I don't need your own testimony on that point. I can get it by elimination, from your fellow-bandsmen. Now tell me who was the first to get up and go out of here?"

Detwiller said, almost reluctantly, as though he felt it was taking an unfair advantage: "I was."

"Corroboration?" snapped Lindsey.

They all O.K.'d it. "Yeah." . . . "That's right, he was."

"Then you're out of it," Lindsey told him. The band-leader looked apologetically at the others, as though he would have been glad to take the rap if he could have.

"Who was next?"

"Armstrong," said Kershaw, and the girl nodded.

"I was starting to fall asleep already," she said, "but I remember the sound of his slamming the door roused me for a minute. I looked up and Kersh and Thatcher and—Frankie—were still here with me."

"And after him?" He looked at Kershaw. No answer. He looked at Frankie. The latter's eyes dropped and he stared down at the floor. He looked at the girl finally. "I can't help you out on that one," she said almost defiantly. "I was sound asleep by then. That time the door didn't wake me."

"I was pretty binged," Kershaw drawled unwillingly, kneading the back of his neck. "I wouldn't care to get a pal in Dutch by saying something I ain't one hundred percent sure of. It seems to me Bligh and Thatcher and Billie were still in here, though. I kind of remember saying 'Good-night' three times. That's the only way I can tell."

"Don't be so damn noble on my working-time," Lindsey squelched him. He turned back to Frankie again. "How about it? You want to use the out your pal here is giving you?"

He looked up and met his sister's gaze. She stared at him hard without saying a word. "No," he groaned. "I guess what I told you in the beginning still goes. I was pretty high and hazy, but I remember being alone in here with Thatcher at the very end. Billie, too, of course, but she was asleep." Then his voice rose, he shook his manacled hands pleadingly toward the dick. "But I know I didn't do anything like that! I wasn't in any condition even to figure out that I could snare him by means of the loop in that light cord. It was all I could do to find the stairs and get up them—"

"I'm sorry, Bligh," said Lindsey, "but the opportunity jibes, too. There's my two out of three. I'm going to have to hold you. The rest of you can go."

CHAPTER THREE
KILL CRAZY

As they filed out one by one giving him sympathetic looks, Dusty went to him and rested his hand encouragingly in his bowed shoulder for a minute. "Buck up, kid," he murmured, "we're with you. We'll get you out of this. You'll be back laying it in the groove with us in no time!" Then, all business again, he hurried out, remarking: "I gotta get down to the Mad House* in a hurry and see if the Warden** can find me someone to take his place. That means a rehearsal too, to break him in—"

The door closed and Lindsey saw that the girl was still sitting there on the piano bench, hadn't gone with them. "Wouldn't grasping that wire, pulling it, even though it was heavily insulated, have left burns or marks on the palms of whoever did it? Frankie's hands are smooth and white."

"So are everyone else's. I took a look at them all. That don't amount to a row of pins anyway. It would have been easy enough to slip on a pair of gloves or even twist a folded handkerchief around them."

"I want to talk to my brother alone for a few minutes, won't you let me do that, please?"

He motioned the other two dicks toward the door, and went out after them.

As soon as the door had closed, Billie went over beside Frankie. He was holding his head dejectedly with both hands, even though they were linked. "I'm scared, Sis," he moaned. "I got a feeling I'll never be able to get out of this! And I didn't do it. You gotta believe me!"

"I know you didn't do it. But that's why you've got to answer me. You've got to tell me why you acted so funny this morning, when I caught you behind the bathroom door, hiding up there. You knew about it then, already, didn't you?"

"Yeah," he whispered fearfully. "I came down here again after I left the first time. I was full of weed, but my idea was vaguely to wake you up so we could go back to our own flat together. It must have just happened. I thought I saw a shadow duck behind those empty ashcans, at the end of the passage out there. And then

*Musician's union.
**Secretary of the union.

when I opened the door, the light was out in here. He was already up there. I didn't see him, but I stumbled around and went into him face-first. I could feel his legs hanging limp before me. You know how the weed'll give you the horrors over anything like that. I got 'em bad. I forgot about you being in here. I forgot about calling for help. I only wanted out. I beat it upstairs and hid in that bathtub. That's all it was, sis, just bad kicks from the weed. But I can't tell them that. If I tell them, they'll be surer than ever I did do it. I can't prove I didn't, not even to you, but somehow I know it wasn't me. You see, I wouldn't have been so scared if I had done it. The mere fact that I was so scared shows I had nothing to do with it. I didn't turn on any shower. My hair was that wet from my own cold sweat coming out all over me. What am I going to do?"

"You're pretty badly sewed up," she admitted worriedly. "And with every move you've made, you've only made it look worse for yourself. The way you bolted for that door, when he first said murder, and then fainted dead away in the cop's arms out there."

"Nerves," he said. "You don't know what that weed does to you the day after. And then, knowing that I was the last one down here, and that I'd had that fight with him over you last night when he gave me the black eye—"

The door opened and Lindsey came in again. "Time enough?" he asked the girl. He motioned his assistants. "Take him with you, boys."

Frankie stumbled to his feet, pale and terrified, as though he were going to be executed instantly. "Pull yourself together, Frankie," the girl urged. "The truth'll come out, it's got to. It looks bad now, but remember it's always darkest before the dawn."

Then as the door closed, she turned back to the dick again. "And now it's you that I'd like to talk to."

"Shoot," he consented, eyeing her curiously.

"I know my brother never did that."

"I do too," was the unexpected answer.

It took her a half-minute to get her breath back. "What? Well then, why did you have him taken in for it?"

"There are a couple of good reasons. Officially we've got a swell circumstantial case against him that I can't ignore at this stage of the game. I'd be remiss in my duty if I didn't have him booked for murder, after what's been brought out. Secondly, it'll be a good deal easier to catch whoever did do it, if he thinks he's fooled us, thinks we aren't still on the look-out for him. He'll be off his guard this way."

"How come you're giving Frankie the benefit of the doubt?"

"Simply my knowledge of human nature. He acted so damned, flagrantly guilty, that he couldn't be anything but innocent. That may sound paradoxical but it's true nevertheless. If he'd been guilty, no matter how frightened he was, he'd at least have tried to cover himself up. He didn't even try. He's a nervous wreck, his control all shot. That made him do and say the very things he wanted to avoid most. Now was there anything more you wanted to speak to me about?"

"Yes," she said. "It may be disloyal to Dusty and the boys, it may wash us up as an organization, attach a jinx to us, but I can't help it. My brother's life is at stake. Mr. Lindsey, this thing's happened twice before."

"What?" His jaw dropped. Then he clamped it decisively shut again. "Let's hear about it," he said.

———◈———

She sat down on the bench, thrust the point of her elbow back on the keyboard. It gave an eery little *plink!* "You notice not a word was said about it to you. That's for business reasons. There's been an unspoken understanding among all of us to soft-pedal it. There's nothing I hate worse than a stoolie, but I think the time for keeping it quiet is past. It wasn't written down as murder the first two times, but now that I look back, I think it was. It must have been. The details were too much like today's. The dicks that investigated were easier to fool, that was all."

She drew a deep breath. "There's a murderer among us in the band, and there has been all along. He only strikes at certain unaccountable times."

He was leaning toward her intently, devouring every word. "Give me everything you can on those first two times it happened. Every little detail that you can remember. Our whole hope of getting the right man, of clearing your brother, may lie in some little detail— repeated three times."

She contorted her face remorsefully. "If I'd only realized what it was at the time! I don't think any of us did—except *him*, of course, whoever he is. It's so long ago now—"

———❖———

"Try, try," he urged, jack-knifing a finger at her chest. "Don't give up so easily."

"We all knew each other in school," she began slowly. "There was Dusty and Armstrong and Frankie and Kershaw—and the two who have gone now—Lynn Deering and Freeman. They were the charter-members. They'd already formed the band in school, helped pay their way by playing at prom dances and things like that. I wasn't included yet. That was in the early thirties, when crooners were all the rage. This lad Deering used to whisper huskily through a megaphone, and sweet young things would swoon all over the room.

"We all got out of school and went our separate ways, didn't see each other for about a year and a half. But the depression had hit its full stride just about then, and you can imagine how tough the going was. Then Dusty got in touch with all of us and suggested re-forming the band—professionally this time. Well, we did. That was a little over two and a half years ago. Nothing happened the first six months. Then the summer before last we were playing a resort hotel in Michigan, and we started to hold these jam-sessions down in the basement, just like here. I still wasn't a member, but I was there with them on account of Frankie being in the band. I was present at the jam-sessions too.

"There was a society girl there that had been carrying the torch heavily for Lynn Deering all summer, and just two days before it happened her old man showed up and hauled her off by the scruff of the neck. Of course that gave them a ready-made motive to slap on—after it had happened. But here's the thing. I spoke to Lynn about it only the day before, asked him if he felt bad about it, and he told me he was glad to be rid of her, that she'd been a nuisance. And I could see he was telling the truth.

"Anyway, one morning after a session, he was found down there hanging from the rafters. It wasn't nearly as much of a give-away as you found this one to be. An inquest was held, they handed down a verdict of suicide while of unsound mind, and that was that. The hotel had it hushed up, and the boys took me in to canary in Deering's place.

"Well, just about a year later, that's last summer, we were playing the Nautilus Pier at Atlantic City on a season's contract, and we used to hold our afterwork sessions in a little shack across the railroad tracks on Arctic Avenue. One scorching night in August we went over there to hold a session. The heat had gotten Freeman down, he was picking fights with everyone—and there again, you see, they had a plausible motive at hand. There was a rigged-up light-attachment in the shack, just like there is here. I didn't stay until the end. I got out just before dawn and went over to the Boardwalk to get a breath of air. One by one all the others followed me."

"Who was the last one to leave?"

"Two of them came away together, luckily for them. Frankie and Armstrong with him. Freeman was left there alone. But none of us ran into each other right away. You know how long the Board-walk is down there. Any one of us could have slipped back a moment before joining the rest. Freeman never showed up, and when we went back to try to coax him into a good humor, he was hanging there. Again the coroner's inquest finding was suicide while of unsound mind, due to the heat and too much alcohol. That's about all. We took Thatcher in to replace him. And now—"

———◆———

Lindsey said: "All right, you've given me the general outline of the thing. Now let's get down to cases. Were there any grudges between this Deering and the others?"

"No, all the fellows liked him. He was a swell guy, even if he was a crooner."

"How about Freeman?"

"All of them had trouble with him that night. But nothing serious enough to create any animosity, just grouchiness. Dusty was the only one he was careful not to talk out of turn to, because after all Dusty is the boss."

"Could there have been some private trouble that you didn't know anything about?"

"No. I was like that with all of them." She crossed two fingers.

"I knew the very laundry-marks on their shirts by heart. You have about as much privacy as a goldfish, in our racket."

"How about money?"

"No. We'll none of us die rich and we don't give a rap about money."

"Women?"

"None of them ever stepped on the other boys' toes in that respect."

"No offense, but how about you yourself? Thatcher did annoy you lately. You admit that yourself. Either of the other two do that? Because I've still got to count your brother in on this, after all is said and done."

"Lynn Deering didn't have time enough to tip his hat to anyone while that society deb was around his neck. And Freeman was a man's man, not much of a chaser. Frankie isn't the protective sort. It's the other way around. I've had to look after him half the time."

"Then I'm afraid any rational motive is out, and we're up against the worst kind of thing—irrational homicidal mania. Doesn't care who he kills when the kill-mood is on him. But what brings it on? If we only knew that, we could set a trap for him. There's some link there that we've got to get. Something that aroused it last night, and the time before, and the first time. And didn't operate all the many other times you've held jam-sessions. We can't sit back and wait another six months for it to occur again. He's smart, they always are. We won't know then any more than we know now, unless we're on our guard ahead of time—one up on him.

"I'll send for a copy of the inquest findings both from Atlantic City and the other place, but I know already they won't tell me anything. If they were able to tell me anything now, they would have told the officials on the spot something at the time. Did any of them ever show any signs of being not quite right? I mean act unaccountably at times?"

She shook her head. "Not that I could distinguish. Of course, it could be that I'm with them so much, I've grown so used to all their traits, that I can't tell the difference any more. It would take an outsider."

"Well, were any of them ever in any accidents?"

She looked mournfully down at the floor. "The wrong one was," she said slowly. "Frankie and I were both in a pretty bad car smash-up about a year after we got out of school. His nervous system's never been the same since. But his head wasn't hurt, nothing like that—" She hid her face suddenly behind her hands. "The more that comes out, the more points to him—and yet I'm as sure as I'm sitting here—"

"I can't be, of course," he told her gently, "but I'm hoping. Look, let's not give up yet. I'm afraid he'll have to start going through the mill. It's not in my power to stop that, but if we keep at it, we'll turn up something yet, I'm sure of it. And of course, not a word to any of them that we've had this talk, that the case is still wide open as far as I'm concerned. Do you understand? That would be fatal. Whoever the killer is, he must feel that my colleagues and I are definitely off the scent, are satisfied we have the right man."

"But even so," she whimpered, "he won't show his hand again until—until Frankie's out of the way and it's too late. Maniac or not, he'll realize that if it happens again while Frankie's being held in jail, that's proof-evident that Frankie didn't do it, and the whole thing'll be re-opened. He'll lie low—"

"He'll try to, you mean, if we let him. But remember this is something he can't control. If we can find the link, the right impetus that sets him off, he won't be able to."

"Suppose there isn't any?"

"There has to be. There always is, even in the worst cases of this type."

There was a knock at the door, and Hoff the janitor stuck his head in. "Your boss is on the wire," he told Billie. "They got a new man, he says, and they're down at Dryden Hall, ready to begin rehearsing. They want you down there right away."

"My brother's in jail accused of murder, and I've got to make sweet music." She smiled bitterly at the dick.

"Keep your eyes open, now," Lindsey warned her under his breath. "Watch all of them, watch every little thing that goes on, no matter if it seems important to you or not. And keep in touch with me. Give me your address and phone number, in case I want to reach you."

He took out a pencil stub, jotted down her address and number, stuck the slip in his pocket.

CHAPTER FOUR

BOLERO

The new man supplied by the Mad House to take Thatcher's place was named Cobb. He wouldn't have been a union-member if he hadn't known how to handle his instrument, and the tunes were the tunes of the day, familiar to every professional, so it was just a matter of blending him in with the rest of them, smoothing down the rough edges, and memorizing the order in which the numbers came. Even so, Dusty kept them at it until half an hour before it was time to climb on the shell at the Troc. It was, if nothing else, as good a way as any of taking their minds off what had happened.

"We can't keep it from breaking in the papers," Dusty told them while they grabbed a quick bite on their way over to work, "because it's in New York this time and not out in the sticks, but with a little luck we may be able to keep them from digging up about what happened the other two times. Keep your mouths closed now, all of you. Don't talk to any reporters. The agents'll all wash their hands of us, and we won't be able to get a booking for love or money if we once get tagged as a jinx-band. Those things spread around awful quick, and are hard to live down. People don't want to dance with—with death kind of peering over the musicians' shoulders at them." This was said out of earshot of the new man. "And keep quiet about the first two times in front of Cobb."

The girl just sat there at the end of the counter, sipping her coffee quietly and looking covertly at them one by one. "One of you," she thought, "sitting so close to me I could reach out and touch you, is a killer. But which one?" It seemed so hard to believe, watching them.

There was the strain of what had happened on all their faces, of course, but there was no private guilt, no furtive remorse, no sign of self-consciousness or wariness. "Maybe," she thought, "he doesn't even remember it himself after it happens each time, in which case—Oh Lord, how am I ever going to be able to tell?"

"O. K., ready, folks?" Dusty asked, slipping down from his high stool. "Let's go over and climb in the box."

Everyone paid for himself. There was no Frankie to pay for her now, but just as she was opening her pocketbook, Dusty thoughtfully waved her aside and put the money down for her.

"What'd that dick have to say after we left?" he asked her on the way over.

"Oh, nothing. He's dead sure Frankie did it. Nothing'll change his mind about that."

"I know this sounds like hell, but what do you think yourself?"

"I'm afraid he did, Dusty. Where there's smoke there's fire. He acted too funny about it from beginning to end."

He slipped his arm around her waist, tightened it encouragingly for a moment. "Keep your chin up, pal," he said.

The men climbed right into the box to play for the rather second-rate supper show the Trocadero put on, but Billie, who didn't have to canary until the straight dance-numbers later on, went down to the dressing-room and dispiritedly changed into evening dress. "If I were only a mind-reader," she thought. "If I could only see behind their faces. One of them is a mask hiding death!"

There was a perfunctory rap at the door. "They're starting number one now." She got up and went upstairs, stood in the entryway to one side of the box, out of sight of the tables in front. Number one was *Sing for Your Supper*. It looked funny to see Cobb sitting up there in Thatcher's chair. She watched their faces closely one by one. Nothing showed. Just guys making music.

Dusty looked over to see if she was ready, then they slowed a little to let her come in and pick it up. She stepped out in front of them and a spotlight picked her out.

⊷◆⊷

The phone was ringing when she let herself into her flat at half past three that morning. It was Lindsey. "Did you notice anything?" he asked.

"I couldn't tell. He's good, whoever he is."

"Keep watching. It's too soon yet. Anyone come back with you?"

"Dusty wanted to bring me home, but I told him I'd be all right."

"Nothing else?"

"Nothing else." She hung up the phone and suddenly threw her head down and burst into tears.

⊷◆⊷

Lindsey turned away from the window when Billie started to speak. "We've got to do something soon, Lindsey," she said. "It's six weeks now. Do you know what this is doing to my brother? He'll be bugs by the time we get him out of there. I saw him yesterday, and he's ready to fall apart."

"I know. I've tried everything I can think of, and it's no go," the detective answered. "I've been over those coronary findings until I know them backwards. I've communicated with the officials in Michigan and I've interviewed the ones down in Atlantic City. They couldn't help me. I even went over personally and looked at that shack while I was down there. It's still about the same as when you people used it, but it didn't tell me a thing."

She sat down at the piano and started to play aimlessly.

"I've even dropped in at the Troc more times than you know, watching them while they didn't know it."

"You have?" she said in surprise. "I didn't see you."

"I had a get-up on. I couldn't detect a sign of anything on any one of them. It must be so damn deep, so latent, that he doesn't know he's got it himself."

She went ahead playing. "Then what good is it trying to find it? It may never come out again."

He started pacing back and forth. "It's got to, it always does."

"What makes you so restless, Lindsey?" she asked over her notes. "You're as bad as one of us jitter-bugs. Sit down and relax."

He sank into a chair, immediately got up again, began parading around some more. "It's got my goat!" he seethed. "I know I've got it figured right, I'm dead sure of it, but I've got to sit back with my hands folded until he's good and ready to give himself away again!"

He took out a cigarette, lit it, raised his hand at full arm's length above his head and banged it down on the floor a moment afterwards. Then he took a kick at the chair he'd just been in, so that it swung around in a half-circle.

"Lindsey, this is my flat you're in, not the back room at headquarters," she remonstrated mildly. "I never saw you like this before, what's the matter with you?"

He trod out the sparks on the rug. "I don't know myself," he grunted. "I felt all right until a few minutes ago. I've been plugging away too hard, not getting enough sleep, I guess. I've got a pip of a peeve on right now. I feel like busting someone in the face."

"Not me, I hope." She smiled as her fingers continued traveling over the keys.

He was stalking around the room behind her with his locked hands draped across the back of his neck. He looked over at her a couple of times, started to say something, clamped his mouth shut as though thinking better of it. Finally it got away from him. His voice exploded in an ungovernable shout that nearly hoisted her clear of the bench. "For Pete's sake, can't you quit playing that damn piano for a minute! It's got me on edge, I can't stand it any more!"

She turned and looked at him in undisguised astonishment. There was a sudden silence in the room.

He was already ashamed of the outburst. "Or at least play something else. What is that screwy thing anyway?"

"Ravel's *Bolero*. It's a long-hair number but we swing it once in awhile."

"I didn't think I could stand it for another minute."

"It is a monotonous sort of thing," she agreed. "The same theme over and over and over. You just change keys."

"It sure is an irritant, I know that much! I'm sorry, Billie," he apologized. "I didn't know a little thing like that could get me that way. Shows you how jumpy I must be." He grabbed for his hat. "I better get out of here before I put my foot in it any deeper, get some sleep. This case has me down. I guess. See you tomorrow," he called back from the door.

⊷◆⊶

She stared after him with a puzzled frown on her face. Then she struck three random notes of what she'd just been playing, with one finger. Suddenly the piano-bench toppled over and she was flying toward the door he'd just closed behind him. She tore it open. Luckily he hadn't gone down yet, was still out there waiting for the elevator.

"I've got it! I've got it!" she shrieked, as though she herself has gone insane. "Come back here!"

He came inside again. "What the hell—"

She was too excited to explain. "Have you got a gun?" she asked breathlessly, closing the door after him.

"Sure, I always carry one," he said, mystified.

"Good! You're going to need one if this works out the way I think it may."

She'd taken him into the bedroom. "Here, get into this closet and keep your eyes open. Can you see me at the piano from in here?"

"No, it's not in a straight line with the door."

"Well, we'll shove it over further. I want to make sure your eyes are on me every minute of the time, through the crack of this closet-door, or it's going to be just too bad for me!"

They shifted the piano, then she jumped up on a chair, unslung a heavy framed mirror from the opposite wall. "Hang this from the molding over the piano, Lindsey. It'll give you a view of the rest of the room, from in there. Now get back in there, leave the door open a crack, and have your gun ready. You're going to have to listen to that thing steadily for the next few hours. Can you stand it? Your own nerves were pretty much on edge just now. Better take a good stiff drink before we get in there."

He got what she was driving at finally. "You mean—that piece? You think—"

"I'm sure of it, and this'll prove it. That's our link, our impetus. We jammed it that night. I think we must have the other two times, too, although I can't remember for sure now any more. We never play it for general dancing. You saw what it did to you just now, just from lack of sleep. It's monotonous, insistent, frays the nerves the way it slowly builds to a climax, the same arrangement of notes over and over and over. And he's off-balance to begin with. Conceivably it topples him over completely each time he hears it, starts the wheels going."

"Gin with it, and a few puffs of weed," he suggested, "to give it the same priming as at the jam-sessions."

"There must be a couple of Frankie's muggles still around the place somewhere. I'm going to test them out one at a time, to make sure they don't show any inhibitions. I'll be supposedly alone up here. For heaven's sake, Lindsey, jump out as soon as you see anything. Don't let anything happen to me. It's going to be an awful feeling to sit here at the piano without being able to turn around, not knowing when I'll feel a knife between my shoulders, or a pair of hands around my neck."

"I'll be watching, I'll be on the job, just keep steady."

"Ready?"

"Ready."

She dialed a number on the phone. The closet door ebbed noise-lessly back into its frame, without completely meeting it, in the darkened room beyond.

"Hello, Armstrong? This is Billie. Doing anything? . . . Neither am I. I feel kind of lonely. No one to talk to. Why don't you drop over for a few minutes, see if you can cheer me up. Don't bring anyone else, I don't want a mob around me."

Armstrong said: "Yeah, and do you remember that time we were playing that cruise ship, and ran into a norther down in the Gulf, and had to play fastened to our chairs by our belts, so we wouldn't come flying down out of the box on top of the dancers' heads every time she tipped over?"

"What about me? I wasn't attached to anything. Right in the middle of the second chorus of *I Married an Angel* I go shooting across the ballroom-floor and land square in the fat purser's lap. What a night that was! Have another drink?"

"I've had two already."

She sat down at the keyboard, lightly began the querulous opening measures of the *Bolero*. He was sprawled out in an easy-chair with his back to the bedroom doorway, drink in one hand, half smoked reefer in the other. He fell silent, listening.

She changed keys. It began to come in a little heavier now, but the same torturing sequence of notes, on and on and on. She glanced furtively up into the mirror on the wall before her. She could see him in it. He'd let his eyelids droop closed, but he wasn't asleep, she could tell that. Just listening. He lifted his glass to his mouth, drank, lowered it again, all without opening his eyes. The closet door, dimly discernible in the shadowy interior of the next room, was slanting outward at more of an angle now. Lindsey probably had his gun out in his hand. Wouldn't it be a joke if it got him on edge quicker than the suspect they were both testing? It wouldn't, though, now that he was on guard against it.

The strain on her was terrific. She forced herself to keep her eyes down on the keyboard. She had to go on playing, just stealing an occasional glance upward. But any minute she might see a reared shadow loom on the wall and feel—

It was thundering toward its climax now. It was a good thing this place had thick soundproof walls, especially meant for musicians and vocalists. She stole another look via the glass. Eyes still closed. Wide awake though. He'd finished the marihuana cigarette and ditched it. Did she imagine it or had his hand twitched just then on the arm of the chair? No, there it came again. He'd given it a little spasmodic jerk, sort of shot his cuff back.

Her breath started to come faster. There was moisture seeping through the light dusting of powder on her forehead. She tried not to get tense, to keep her playing even. Was he the one? It was nearing the end now. Was he going to be able to hold out, or would he suddenly spring up and across at her?

She went into the last stretch, fortissimo, mounted to the almost unbearable climax, when—if you were like him—every nerve must be crying out, maddened beyond endurance.

It burst like shrapnel, and then there was suddenly deafening silence in the room, and she just sat there limp, nearly prostrated herself.

He moved, opened his mouth and took a yawn that seemed to stretch from his eyebrows to his chin. "Gee, that was swell," he said lazily. "I guess I'll shove off now. There was a gnat or something bothering me the whole time you were playing." He slapped the back of his own hand viciously. "Got it!"

When she'd closed the door after him, she turned and faced Lindsey, who'd come out. "Whew!" was all she said.

"Whew, is right!" he agreed. "But we've got something there and we're not giving up yet. That thing nearly drives you nuts, especially when you've got to stand still in a closet listening to it."

"Stretch your legs a minute while you've got the chance. Here goes for number two." She started to dial again.

CHAPTER FIVE

KILLER-DILLER

Dusty said kiddingly: "I must think a lot of you. Nobody but you could drag me out of a nice warm steam-room at this ungodly hour of the night, kid."

"You're a life-saver, Dusty. I felt if I didn't have someone to talk to, I'd go crazy. You know it's awfully tough hanging around up here without Frankie."

She sat down at the keyboard. He was in the same chair all the others had been in. She'd fixed it that way, so there was no other handy.

"Have you seen him lately?"

"I saw him yesterday. They let me visit him two or three times a week. The trial doesn't come up until fall." She started to play, as if absentmindedly. Her fingers were nearly coming off by now. "There's a reefer of Frankie's in that box there, if you want one."

"Have one yourself."

"I just finished one before you got here," she lied.

She had to say that, in case he could still detect the fumes from previous ones smoked in the room, although she and Lindsey had opened the windows and aired it out before he got here.

He noticed what she was playing presently, after the first few bars had been gone over. "Don't play that thing," he remonstrated mildly. "I don't like it."

She shot a glance up into the mirror. "Why not, what's the difference?" she said carelessly. "Anything just to keep my hands busy." She went ahead.

"I got hold of a new number today for us to break in. Run over it instead of that one, see how you like it." He came over, put some orchestration-sheets on the rack, went back and sat down again.

She ignored them. "All right, just let me finish this first. I like to finish anything I begin."

Was that a sign of anything, his trying to switch her off the piece! Did he realize himself what it would do to him if she kept it up long enough. Was that why? Or was it just a harmless expression of preference? Anyone is entitled to dislike certain pieces of music and like others without necessarily being a murderer, she realized.

He shifted around a little in the chair, got up again, went over to the window, stood looking out. Then he came back, sat down once more, poured another drink. She quit breathing each time he passed in back of her, but went ahead playing.

He was showing more signs of being affected by it than either Armstrong or Kershaw had. It seemed to be making him restless.

But was it that? She darted another swift glance up at the glass. He was tightening up a good deal, there was no doubt about that. Both his hands were clenched, and the toe of one foot, slung over the other, was twitching a little, almost like a cat's tail does. On the other hand, she reminded herself, she mustn't jump at hasty conclusions. He'd said he didn't like the piece to begin with, and if he was either bored or annoyed by her playing of it in disregard of his request, he might still have shown these very same symptoms, without there being any sinister meaning to them whatever.

And then suddenly, when next she looked, he wasn't moving at all, not even the tip of his foot now. He was sitting there as still as a statue, almost lifeless. His eyes, which had been on her back until then, were on the mirror themselves now. Had he seen something, caught some slight motion or waver on it, reflected by the closet-door? Had he sensed that this was a trap? If he had—

━━◆◆◆━━

She watched at more frequent intervals now. He'd stopped looking up at the mirror after that one time she'd caught him at it, was looking steadily down at the floor now. He conveyed an impression of alert wariness, just the same. It wasn't an abstract, unfocussed look, but a listening, watchful, cagey look.

The thing rose to its crescendo, shattered, stopped dead. The silence was numbing. He didn't move. She didn't breathe. A single bead of sweat glistened on his forehead, but the gin could have made him warm after coming out of a steam-room with all his pores open.

She refused to break the spell. Let him be the first to shatter it—for in that lay the answer.

He started to get up slowly. She could see the move coming long before his muscles carried it into effect. His overslung foot descended to the floor. Then there was a wait. His clenched hands drew back along the chair-arms, to give his body better leverage. Then another wait. His waist ballooned out and his knees drew in, straightened, carried his torso up to a standing position. Through it all, the position of his head alone did not change, remained tilted downward toward the floor. That managed to give an impression of secretive, furtive movement to his getting to his feet, like he was stalking someone.

Her nerves were stretched to the breaking point. She wanted to scream with the suspense of sitting there waiting.

Then his head came up, and he said in the most matter-of-fact way, turning toward the door as he did so: "Guess I'll shove off. My leg went to sleep." He limped out into the hall, slapping at it to get back the circulation.

She reeled there at the piano bench, kept herself from falling by grasping the sides of it for a moment. Then she got up and went out after him.

At the door he chucked her under the chin in a big-brotherly sort of way. "S'-long, sweets," he said. "See you at the barn tomorrow night." The touch of his fingers, she couldn't help noticing, was ice-cold.

She closed the door after him and looked behind her. Lindsey had slipped out of the closet, was coming up behind her. She warned him to silence, head tilted toward the door-seam, listening. "*Sh!* The elevator hasn't taken him down yet."

They waited a moment or two. Finally he eased the door open narrowly, peered through with one eye. "It must have, he's not out there any more."

"I usually can hear it slide shut." She walked back into the living-room. "Well, it was no good, Lindsey," she told him dejectedly, slapping her hands to her sides. "It didn't work. It was the wrong answer. One time I thought he was getting steamed up, but then he subsided again, almost—almost as though he caught on you were in there."

"If he did, he's uncanny. I didn't move a fingerjoint." He kneaded his thatch bafflingly. "Can't figure it at all. It had to be the right answer. I still think it is, but—for some reason it muffed fire. It was the right time too, according to what the psychiatrists say. Just before daylight, when anyone's power of resistance—including a murderer's—is supposed to be at its lowest ebb."

"What is there left? I'm so tired and discouraged. I'll never get Frankie out of there!"

"Yes, you will," he tried to hearten her. "You get some sleep. We'll put our heads together again tomorrow. We're not licked yet."

———※◆※———

She saw him to the door, closed it after him, and went in again. Almost immediately afterward the elevator door down the hall gave a hollow clang that penetrated to where she was. "Funny I didn't hear that the first time," she murmured, but didn't bother any more about it.

She put out the light in the hall, lit up the bedroom, took off her dress, and put on a woollen wrapper. That took about three or four minutes. It was nearly five now, would be getting light in another quarter of an hour. The city, the streets outside, the rest of the building around her, were all silent, dead to the world. She remembered that she'd left the light on in the living-room. She went in there to snap it off. The place was still full of the acrid odor of the weed Dusty had smoked. She opened the window wide to let the fresh air in, stood there a minute, breathing it in.

There was a faint tap at the outside door of the flat, little more than the tick of a nail. She turned her head sharply in that direction to listen, not even sure if she'd heard it herself the first time. It came again, another stealthy little tap.

She moved away from the window and went out there to see. Probably Lindsey, coming back to tell her of some new angle that had just occurred to him. But what a way for him to knock, like an undersized woodpecker. He usually pounded like a pile-driver. He must be getting refined all of a sudden. She wasn't frightened. The test had failed, and she didn't stop to think that it might have delayed after-effect.

She opened the door and Dusty Detwiller was standing there. "Gee, I feel terrible bothering you like this," he apologized softly. "I left the orchestration of that new number I was telling you about on your piano-rack. If you were asleep, I was going away again without disturbing you. That's why I just tapped lightly like that."

"Oh, that's all right, Dusty, I'll bring it right out to you." She walked back into the living-room again, started to gather up the loose orchestration sheets and tamp them together. She thought she heard a slight click from the front-door lock, but didn't pay any attention to it.

Suddenly there was a shadow looming on the wall before her eyes, coming up from behind her, from across her shoulder, the very thing she'd been dreading to see all evening long—and hadn't until now. The loose orchestration sheets fell out of her hands, landed all over the floor around her feet. She couldn't move for a minute, even to turn around.

"Don't scream," a furry voice purred close to her ear, "or you'll only bring it on quicker. It won't do you any good, you're going to get it anyhow."

She turned with paralytic slowness and stared into his dilated eyes. His whole face had changed in the few seconds since he'd come in from the door. He must have been holding the murder-lust in leash by sheer will-power until then. "I would have given it to you the first time, but I had a funny feeling we weren't alone up here. Something told me somebody else was with us. I watched from the stairs going up to the floor above, and I was right. I saw that dick leave."

His hands started to curve up and in toward her throat with horrible slowness, like the claws of a sluggish lobster. "But now you're alone, there's nobody here with you, and I'm going to do it to you. I told you not to play that piece. I don't want to do these things, but that music makes me."

If she could only reason with him long enough to get over to that phone on the opposite side of the room. "Dusty, don't," she said in a low, coaxing voice. "If you kill me, you know what they'll do to you."

His cleverness hadn't deserted him, even now at the end. "The other guys were up here with you tonight too. They must've been— you wouldn't have tried me out if you didn't try them out too—so when they find you they still won't know which of us did it. I got away with it the first three times, and I'll get away with it this time, too."

"But who'll you get to do your canarying for you?" she choked, fighting desperately for time. She glanced once too often toward the phone, gauging its distance. He jumped sideways, like an ungainly dancing-bear on its hind legs, grabbed the phone-wire and tore it bodily out of the control-box.

Then he came back at her again, hands in that pincer-formation aiming at her throat.

———◆◆◆———

She screamed harrowingly, unable to hold it in any longer, shifted madly sideways away from those oncoming, stretching hands, until the far wall blocked her and she was penned up in the angle formed by the two walls, unable to get any further away from him. The window she had opened before he came in was just ahead, in the new direction. "I'll jump out if you come a step nearer," she panted.

He was too quick. He darted in, the hands snaked out, locked around her throat just as she came in line with window-frame. For an instant they formed a writhing mass under one of the curtains.

There was a flash. His protruding eyes lit up yellowly as if he were a tiger, and then there was a deafening detonation beside her face that almost stunned her.

His hands unlocked again, but so slowly that she had to pry them off with her own before she was free of them. Then he went crazily down to the floor. His body fell across one of her feet, pinning her there. She just stood there coughing. A man's leg came over the windowsill alongside of her, and then Lindsey was standing there holding her up with one arm around her, a fuming gun still in his other hand.

"Thank God there's a fire-escape outside that window," he breathed heavily. "I never would have made it in time coming up the inside way!"

He had to step over Detwiller with her in his arms, to get her to the piano-bench and sit her down.

"How'd you know I was in danger up here?" she asked.

"I didn't for sure. I just saw something that struck me as a little strange." He stopped, colored up a little. "I may as well admit I've gone kind of mushy. Every time I leave here I—sort of cross over and stand on the other side of the street watching your window until the lights go out. I was down there, and I saw you open this one and then turn your head quickly and stand there as if you were listening or heard something. I waited, but you didn't come back again, and finally I started on my way. But the more I thought it over, the stronger my hunch got that everything wasn't just the way it should be. I knew it wasn't your phone you'd heard, because you wouldn't have to stand there listening like that. You'd hear it without any trouble. So what else could it be but someone at your front door? By the time I got a block away, it got the better of me. I turned around and came running back—and I took the fire-escape to save time."

"So you call that being mushy. Well you can't be too mushy for me." She looked over at the floor by the window. "Is he gone?" She shuddered.

"No, he's not gone. He'll live to take the blame for what he's done. Only for him it'll be an asylum, not the chair."

Detwiller stared at them vacantly.

"So now we know," she murmured.

"Yes, now we know."

AFTERWORD TO "THE CASE OF THE KILLER-DILLER"

The title is unappetizing but "The Case of the Killer-Diller" (*Dime Detective*, May 1939) is a first-rate pulper, reminiscent of Woolrich's classic "Dime a Dance" (1938) in that its female protagonist, scratching out a living in a vividly rendered low-rent environment, becomes live bait in the trap set for a multiple murderer. With its vivid musical background and effective suspense and surprisingly casual treatment of drug use among jazz people, this is one of many Woolrich stories from the Thirties that deserves to have been resurrected long before the 21st century.

THROUGH A DEAD MAN'S EYE

The idea in swapping is to start out with nothing much and run it up to something. I started out with a buckle without a tongue and a carved peach pit, that day, and swapped it to a kid named Miller for a harmonica that somebody had stepped on. Then I swapped that to another kid for a pen-knife with one blade missing. By an hour after dark, I had run my original capital up to a baseball with its outside cover worn off, so I figured I'd put in a pretty good afternoon. Of course, I should have been indoors long before then, but swapping takes time and makes you cover a lot of ground.

I was just in the middle of a deal with the Scanlon kid, when I saw my old man coming. He was still a block away, but he was walking fast like when he's sore, and it's hard to use good business judgment when you're being rushed like that. I guess that's why I let Scanlon high-pressure me into swapping for a piece of junk like he had. It was just somebody's old castoff glass eye, that he must have picked up off some ash heap.

"You got a nerve!" I squalled. But I looked over my shoulder and I saw Trouble coming up fast, so I didn't have much time to be choosy.

Scanlon knew he had me. "Yes or no?" he insisted.

"All right, here goes," I growled, and I passed him the peeled baseball, and he passed me the glass eye, and I dropped it in my pocket.

That was about all I had time for before Trouble finally caught up with me. I got swung around in the direction in which I live, by

the back of the neck, and I started to move over the ground fast—
but only about fifty per cent under my own speed. I didn't mind
that, only people's Old Men always have to make such long
speeches about everything, I don't know why.

"Haven't I got troubles enough of my own," he said, "without
having to go on scouting expeditions looking for you all over the
neighborhood every time I get home? Your mother's been hanging
out the window calling you for hours. What time d'ye think it is,
anyway?" And all that kind of stuff. I got it for five solid blocks, all
the way back to our house, but I just kept thinking about how I got
swindled just now, so I got out of having to hear most of it.

I'd never seen him so grouchy before. At least not since that
time I busted the candy-store window. Most times when he had to
come after me like this, he'd take a lick at the bat himself, if we
were playing baseball for instance, and then wink at me and only
pretend to bawl me out in front of Ma when we got back. He said
he could remember when he was twelve himself, and that shows
how good he was, because twenty-three years is a pretty long time
to remember, let me tell you. But tonight it was the McCoy. Only I
could tell it wasn't me he was sore at so much, it was something else
entirely. Maybe his feet hurt him, I don't know.

By the time we got through supper my mother noticed it too.
"Frank," she said after a while, "what's eating you? There's something troubling you, and you can't fool me."

He was drawing lines on the tablecloth with the back of his fork.
"I've been demoted," he said.

Like a fool I had to butt in right then, otherwise I could have listened to some more. "What's demoted mean, Pop?" I said. "Is it like
when you're put back in school? How can they do that to you, Pop?"

Ma said, "Frankie, you go inside and do your homework!"

Just before I closed the door I heard her say, kind of scared,
"You haven't been put back into blues, Frank, have you?"

"No," he said, "but it might just as well have been that."

When they came out after a while they both looked kind of
down-hearted. They forgot I was in there or else didn't notice me
reading *Black Mask* behind my geography book. She said, "I guess
now we'll have to move out of here."

"Yeah, there's a big difference in the salary."

I pricked my ears at that. I didn't want to have to move away from here, especially since I was marbles champion of the block.

"What hurts most about it," he said, "is I know they couldn't find a thing against me on my record. I'm like a burnt sacrifice, the captain practically admitted as much. Whenever the Commissioner gets these brain waves about injecting more efficiency into the division, somebody has to be made the goat. He calls that getting rid of the deadwood. If you haven't cracked six cases in a row single-handed, you're deadwood."

"Well," she said, "maybe it'll blow over and they'll reinstate you after a while."

"No," he said, "the only thing that'll save me is a break of some kind, a chance to make a big killing. Once the order goes through, I won't even be on Homicide any more. What chance'll I have then, running in lush-workers and dips? What I need is a flashy, hard-to-crack murder case."

Gee, I thought, I wish I knew where there was one, so I could tell him about it. What chance did a kid like me have of knowing where there was a murder case—at least that no one else knew about and he could have all to himself? I didn't even know how to begin to look for one, except behind billboards and in vacant lots and places, and I knew there wouldn't be any there. Once in a while you found a dead cat, that was all.

Next morning I waited until Ma was out of the room, and I asked him, "Pop, how does somebody know when a murder case has happened?"

He wasn't paying much attention. "Well, they find the body, naturally."

"But suppose the body's been hidden some place where nobody knows about it, then how do they know there was a murder case?"

"Well, if somebody's been missing, hasn't been seen around for some time, that's what first starts them looking."

"But suppose no one even tells 'em somebody's missing, because nobody noticed it yet, *then* how would they know where to look?"

"They wouldn't, they'd have to have some kind of a clue first. A clue is some little thing, that don't seem to belong where it's found. It's tough to explain, Frankie, that's the best I can do. It could be some little thing belonging to someone, but the person it belongs to isn't around; then you wonder why he isn't, and what it's doing where you found it instead of where it ought to be."

Just then Ma came back in again, so he said, "You quit bothering your head about that stuff, and stick to your school work. That last report you brought back wasn't so hot, you know." And then he said, more to himself than to me, "One flop in the family is enough."

Gee, it made me feel bad to hear him say that. Ma must have heard him, too. I saw her rest her hand on his shoulder, and kind of push down hard, without saying anything.

⬅◆➡

I looked the Scanlon kid up after school that afternoon, to ask him about that eye I'd traded off him the night before. It was about the only thing I had in the way of a clue, and I couldn't help wondering. . . .

I took it out and looked it over, and I said, "Scanny, d'you suppose anyone ever *used* this? I mean, really wore it in his puss?"

"I dunno," he said. "I guess somebody musta when it was new; that's what they're made for."

"Well, then, why'd he quit using it, why'd he throw it away?"

"I guess he got a new one, that's why he didn't want the old one no more."

"Naw," I said, "because once you've got one of these, you don't need another, except only if it cracks or breaks or something." And we could both see this wasn't cracked or chipped or anything. "A guy can't see through one of these even when it's new; he just wears it so people won't know his own is missing," I explained. "So why should he change it for a new one, if it's still good?"

He scratched his head without being able to answer. And the more I thought about it, the more excited I started to get.

"D'you suppose something *happened* to the guy that used to own it?" I whispered. I really meant did he suppose the guy used to own it had been murdered, but I didn't tell him that because I was afraid he'd laugh at me. Anyway, I couldn't figure out why anybody would want to swipe a man's glass eye, even if they did murder him, and then throw it away.

I remembered what my old man had said that morning. A clue

is any little thing that don't seem to belong where it's found. If this wasn't a clue, then what was? Maybe I could help him. Find out about somebody being murdered, that nobody else even knew about yet, and tell him about it, and then he could get re— whatever that word was I'd heard him and her use.

But before I could find out who it belonged to, I had to find out where it come from first. I said, "Whereabouts did you find it, Scan?"

"I didn't find it," he said. "Who tole you I found it? I swapped it off a guy, just like you swapped it off me."

"Who was he?"

"How do I know? I never seen him before. Some kid that lives on the other side of the gas works, down in the tough part of town."

"Let's go over there, try and find him. I want to ask him where *he* got it."

"Come on," he said, "I bet I can show him to you easy. He was a little bit of a runt. He was no good at swapping, either. I cleaned him just like I cleaned you. That's why he had to go inside his father's store and bring out this peeper, he didn't have anything else left."

I got sort of disappointed. Maybe this wasn't the right kind of a clue after all. "Oh, does his father sell them kind of glims in his store?"

"Naw, he presses pants."

I got kind of relieved again. Maybe it still was a useful clue.

When we got over there on the other side of the gas works, Scanny said, "Here's where I swapped him. I don't know just where his father's store is, but it must be around here some place, because it didn't take him a minute to go back for that glim." He went as far as the corner and looked down the next street, and then he said, "I see him! There he is!" And he stretched his mouth wide and let out a pip of a whistle.

A minute later a dark, undersized kid came around the corner. The minute he saw Scanlon he started to argue with him. "You gotta gimme that thing back I took out of the shop yesterday. My fodder walloped me for picking it up off the eye-nink board. He says maybe the customer'll come back and ask fer it, and what'll he tell him?"

"Where'd it come from?" I butted in. I tried to sound tough like I imagined my old man did when he questioned suspects.

He made his shoulder go way up until it nearly hit his ear. "I should know. It came out of one of the suts that was brought in to be cleaned."

"From the pocket?"

"Naw. It was sticking in one of the cuffs on the bottom of his pants. They were wide open and needed basting."

"In the *cuff!*" Scanlon piped up. "Gee, that's a funny place to go around carrying a glass eye in!"

"He didn't know it was down there," I said impatiently. "It musta bounced in without his knowing it, and he brought the suit over to be pressed, and it stayed in there the whole time."

"Aw, how could that happen?"

"Sure it could happen. Once my father dropped a quarter, and he never heard it hit the floor; he looked all over for it and couldn't find it. Then when he was taking his pants off that night, it fell out of the cuff. He carried it around with him all day long and never knew it."

Even the tailor's kid backed me up in this. "Sure," he said, "that could happen. Sometimes a thing rolls around to the back where the cuff is tacked up, and the stitching holds it in. People have different ways of taking their pants off; I've watched it in my fodder's shop when they're getting a fitting. If they pull them off by the bottom, like most do, that turns them opside down, and if something was caught in the cuff it falls out again. But if they just let them fall down flat by their feet and step out of them, it might still stay in, like this did." He was a smart kid all right, even if his old man was just a tailor and not a detective. I had to hand it to him.

I thought to myself: The only way a thing like that could fall into a man's trouser cuff without him seeing it would be from low down, like if the owner was lying flat on the floor around his feet and he was bending over him shaking him or something. That made it seem like maybe I *could* dig up a murder in this and help my old man after all. But I had to find out where that eye came from.

I said to the tailor's kid, "Do you think this guy'll come back, that left the suit?" If he'd really murdered someone, maybe he wouldn't. But then if he wasn't coming back, he didn't have to leave the suit to be cleaned in the first place, so that showed he probably was.

"My fodder promised it for him by tonight," he said.

I wondered if there was any blood on it. I guessed not, or the guy wouldn't have left it with a tailor. Maybe it was some other kind of a murder, where wasn't any blood spilled. I said, "Can we come in and look at it?"

Again his shoulder went way up. "It's just a sut," he said. "Didn't you ever see a sut before? All right, come in and look at it if you gotta look at it."

We went around the corner and into his father's shop. It was a little dinky place, down in the basement like most of them are. His father was a short little guy, not much taller than me and Scanlon. He was raising a lot of steam from running a hot iron over something.

"This is it, here," the kid said, and he picked up the sleeve of a gray suit hanging there on a rack with two or three others. The cuff had a little scrap of paper pinned to it: "Paulsen—75c."

"Don't any address go with it?" I said.

"When it's called for and delivered, an address. When it's brought in and left to be picked up, no address, just the name."

His father noticed us handling the suit just then and he got sore all of a sudden and came running at us waving his hands, with the hot iron still left in one. He probably wasn't going to hit us with it, he just forgot to put it down, but it was no time to wait and find out. He hollered, "Kip your hands off those clinink jobs, you hear me, loafers? What you want in here, anyway? Outside!"

When we quit running, outside the door, and he turned back and went in again, I said to Sammy, that was his kid's name, "You want these five immies I got with me?"

He looked them over. They weren't as good as some of my others, but they were probably better than he was used to playing with. "Why should I say no?" he said.

"All right, then here's what you gotta do. When the customer that left that suit comes in to get it, you tip us off. We'll be waiting down at the corner."

"So what do you want from him?" he asked, spreading his hands.

"This feller's father is a—" Scanlon started to say. I just kicked him in time, so he'd shut up.

"We're just playing a game," I changed it to. I was afraid if we told him, he'd tell his father the first thing, and then his father would probably tell the customer.

"Soch a game," he said disgustedly. "All right, when he comes I'll tell you."

He went back inside the shop and we hung around there waiting by the corner. This was about half-past four. At half-past six it was all dark, and we were still waiting there. Scanlon kept wanting to give up and go home. "All right, no one's keeping you here," I told him. "You go home, I'm staying until that guy shows up, I don't care if it takes all night. You can't expect a civillion to show as much forty-tude as a police officer."

"You're not a police officer," he grumbled.

"My father is, so that makes me practic'ly as good as one." I had him there, so he shut up and stuck around.

The thing was, I had to go home for supper sooner or later, I couldn't just stay out and keep watch, or I'd get the tar bawled out of me. And I knew he had to, too.

"Look," I said, "you stay here and keep watching for Sammy's signal. I'll beat it back and get my mother to feed me fast. Then I'll come back here again and relieve you, and you can go back to your house and eat. That way we'll be sure of not missing him if he shows up."

"Will they let you out at nights during school?" he asked.

"No, but I'll slip out without them knowing it. If the man calls for his suit before I get back, follow him wherever he goes, and then come back and meet me here and tell me where it is."

I ran all the way back to our house and I told Ma I had to eat right away. She said, "What's your hurry?"

I explained, "Well, we got an awful important exam coming up tomorrow and I gotta study hard tonight."

She looked at me kind of suspicious and even felt my forehead to see if I was running a temperature. "You're actually *worried* about an exam?" she said. "Well, you may as well eat now. Your poor father's way out at the ends of the earth; he won't be home until all hours."

I could hardly wait until I got through but then I always eat fast so she didn't notice much difference. Then I grabbed up my books for a bluff and said, "I'm going to study upstairs in my room, it's quieter."

As soon as I got up there I locked the door and then I opened the window and got down to the ground easy by way of that old tree. I'd done it plenty of times before. I ran all the way back to where Scan was waiting.

"He didn't come yet," he said.

"All right, now it's your turn," I told him. Parents are an awful handicap when you're working on a case. I mean, a detective shouldn't have to run home to meals right in the middle of something important. "Come back as soon as you get through," I warned him, "if you want to be in on this with me."

But he didn't. I found out later he got caught trying to sneak out.

Well, I waited and I waited and I waited, until it was almost ten o'clock. It looked like he wasn't coming for that suit any more tonight, but as long as there was still a light showing in Sammy's father's shop I wasn't going to give up. Once a cop came strolling by and looked me over, like he wondered what a kid my age was doing standing so still by himself on a corner, and I just about curled up and died, but all he said was, "Whaddye say, son?" and went on his way.

While I was standing there hoping the cop wouldn't come back, Sammy, the tailor's kid, suddenly came up to me in the dark when I least expected it. 'What's the metter with you, didn't you see me culling you with my hend?" he said. "That guy just come in for his sut."

I saw someone come up the steps out of the shop just then, with a folded suit slung over his arm; he turned and went up the street the other way.

"That's him. Now gimme the marbles you said."

I spilled them into his hand with my eyes on the guy's back. Even from the back he didn't look like a guy to monkey around with. "Did your old man say anything to him about the eye that popped out of his cuff?" I asked Sammy.

"Did he ask us? So why should we tell him? In my fodder's business anything that ain't missed, we don't know nothing about."

"Then I guess I'll just keep that old glass eye."

"Oi! Mine fodder forget he esk me for it."

The guy was pretty far down the street by now, so I started after him without waiting to hear any more. I was kind of scared, because now there was a grown-up in it, not just kids any more. I was wishing Scan had come back, so I'd have him along with me. But then I thought maybe it was better he hadn't. The man might notice two kids following him quicker than he would just one.

He kept on going, until we were clear over in a part of town I'd never been in before. He was hard to keep up with, he walked fast and he had longer legs than me. Sometimes I'd think I'd lost him, but the suit over his arm always helped me pick him up again. I think without it I would have lost him sure.

Some of the streets had only about one light on them every two blocks, and between lights they were as black as the dickens. I didn't like the kind of people that seemed to live around here either. One time I passed a lady with yellow hair, with a cigarette in her mouth and swinging her purse around like a lasso. Another time I nearly bumped into a funny thin man hugging a doorway and wiping his hand under his nose like he had a cold.

I couldn't figure out why, if he lived this far away from Sammy's father's shop, the man with the suit had to come all this way over just to leave it to be cleaned. There must have been other tailors that were nearer. I guess he did it so he'd be sure the tailor wouldn't know who he was or where he lived. That looked like he had something to be careful about, didn't it?

Finally the lights got a little better again, and it was a good thing they did; by that time I was all winded, and my left shoe was starting to develop a bad squeak. I could tell ahead of time he was going to look back, by the way he slowed up a little and his shoulders started to turn around. I ducked down quick behind an ash can standing on the sidewalk. A grown-up couldn't have hidden behind it, but it hid me all over.

I counted ten and then I peeked around it. He was on his way again, so I stood up and kept going myself. He must have stopped and looked back like that because he was getting close to where he lived and he wanted to make sure no one was after him. But, just the same, I wasn't ready for him when he suddenly turned into a doorway and disappeared. I was nearly a block behind him, and I ran like anything to get down there on time, because I couldn't tell from where I'd been just which one of them it was, there were three or four of them that were alike.

The entrances had inside doors, and whichever one he'd just opened had finished closing already, and I couldn't sneak in the hall and listen to hear if the stairs were creaking under him or not. There were names under the letter boxes, but I didn't have any matches and there were no lights outside the doors, so I couldn't tell what they were.

Another thing, if he went that far out of his way to have a suit cleaned, he wouldn't give his right name on that little scrap of paper that was pinned to the sleeve.

Suddenly I got a bright idea. If he lived in the back of the house it wouldn't work, but maybe he had a room in the front. I backed up all the way across to the other side of the street and stood watching to see if any window would light up. Sure enough one did a minute or two later, a dinky one way up on the top floor of the middle house. I knew that must be his because no one else had gone in there just now.

Right while I was standing there he came to the window and looked down, and caught me staring square up at him with my head way back. This was one time I couldn't move quick enough to get out of sight. He stared down at me hard, without moving. I got the funniest creepy feeling, like I was looking at a snake or something and couldn't move. Finally I turned my head away as if I hadn't been doing anything, and stuck my hands in my pockets, and shuffled off whistling, as if I didn't know what to do with myself.

Then when I got a little further away, I walked faster and faster, until I'd turned the corner out of sight. I didn't dare look back, but something told me he'd stayed up there at that window the whole time looking at me.

It was pretty late, and this was miles from my own part of town, and I knew I'd better be getting back and put off anything else until tomorrow. At least I'd found out which house he lived in—305 Decatur St. I could come around tomorrow with Scanny.

I got back into my room from the outside without any trouble, but Ma sure had a hard time getting me up for school the next morning. She had to call me about six times, and I guess she thought studying hard didn't agree with me.

Scanlon and I got together the minute of three, and we left our books in our school lockers and started out right from there, without bothering to go home first. I told him what I'd found out. Then I said, "We'll find out this guy's name first, and then we'll find out if there's anyone living around there who has a glass eye, and who hasn't been seen lately."

"Who'll we ask?" he wanted to know.

"Who do you ask when you want to find out anything? The janitor."

"But suppose he don't want to tell us? Some people don't like to answer questions asked by kids."

I chopped my hand at his arm and said, "I just thought of a swell way! Wait'll we get there, I'll show you."

When we got there I took him across the street first and showed him the window. "That's it, up there on the top floor of the middle house." I swatted his hand down just in time. "Don't point, you dope. He might be up there watching behind the shade."

We went over and started looking under the letter boxes in the vestibule for his name. I don't think we would have found it so easy, it was hard to tell just which name went with which flat, only I happened to notice one that was a lot like the one he left his suit under at the tailor's: Petersen. "That must be it," I told Scanny. "He just changed the first part of it."

"What do we do now?" he said.

I pushed the bell that said Janitor. "Now watch," I said, "how I get it out of him."

He was a cranky old codger. "What you boys want?" he barked.

I said, "We been sent over with a message for somebody that lives in this house, but we forgot the name. He's got a glass eye."

He growled, "There's nobody here got a glass eye!"

"Maybe we got the wrong number. Is there anybody around here in the whole neighborhood got a glass eye?"

"Nobody! Now get out of here. I got vurk to do!"

We drifted back to the corner and hung around there feeling kind of disappointed. "It didn't get us nothing," I said. "If no one in his house has one, and if no one in the neighborhood has one, where'd he get it from?"

Scanlon was beginning to lose interest. "Aw, this ain't fun no more," he said. "Let's go back and dig up a game of—"

"This isn't any game," I told him severely. "I'm doing this to help my old man. You go back if you want to, I'm going to keep at it. He says what every good detective has to have is preservance."

"What's 'at, some kind of a jam?" he started to ask, but all of a sudden I saw something and jumped out of sight around the corner.

"Here's that guy now!" I whispered. "He just came out of the house. Duck!"

We got down in back of a stoop. There were plenty of people all around us, but nobody paid any attention to us, they thought we were just kids playing a game, I guess.

A minute later this Petersen got to the corner and stood there. I peeked up and got a good look at his face. It was just a face, it didn't look any different from anybody else's. I'd thought until now maybe a murderer ought to have a special kind of a face, but I'd never asked my old man about that, so I wasn't sure. Maybe they didn't, or maybe this guy wasn't a murderer after all, and I was just wasting a lot of good ball time prowling around after him.

He looked around a lot, like he wanted to make sure nobody was noticing him, and then he finally stepped down off the curb, crossed over, and kept going straight along Decatur Street.

"Let's follow him, see where he goes," I said. "I think he saw me last night from the window, and he might remember me, so here's how we better do it. You follow him, and then I'll follow you. I'll stay way back where he can't see me, and just keep you in sight."

We tried that for a while, but all of a sudden I saw Scanlon just standing there waiting for me ahead. "What'd you give up for?" I said when I got to him: "Now you lost him."

"No, I didn't. He just went in there to get somep'n to eat. You can see him sitting in there."

He was sitting in a place with a big glass front, and he was facing our way, so we had to get down low under it and just stick the top of our heads up. We waited a long time. Finally I said, "He oughta be through by now," and I took another look. He was still just sitting there, with that same one cup still in front of him. "He ain't eating," I told Scanlon, "he's just killing time."

"What do you suppose he's waiting for?"

"Maybe he's waiting for it to get dark." I looked around and it pretty nearly was already. "Maybe he's going some place that he don't want to go while it's still light, so no one can see him."

Scanlon started to scuff his feet around on the sidewalk like he was getting restless. "I gotta get back soon or I'll catch it," he said. "I'm in Dutch already for trying to sneak out last night."

"Yeah, and then when you do go back," I told him bitterly,

"you'll get kept in again like last night. You're a heck of a guy to have for a partner!"

"No, tonight I can make it," he promised. "It's Thursday, and Ma wants to try for a new set of dishes at the movies."

"All right, get back here fast as you can. And while you're there, here's what you do. Call up my house and tell my mother I'm staying for supper at your house. If she asks why, tell her we both got so much studying to do we decided to do it together. That way I won't have to leave here. This guy can't sit in there forever, and I want to find out where he goes when he does come out. If I'm not here when you come back, wait for me right here, where it says, 'Joe's Coffee Spot'."

He beat it for home fast and left me there alone. Just as I thought, he wasn't gone five minutes when the guy inside came out, so I was glad one of us had waited. I flattened myself into a doorway and watched him around the corner of it.

———◆———

It was good and dark now, like he wanted it to be, I guess, and he started up the street in the same direction he'd been going before—away from that room he lived in. I gave him a half a block start, and then I came out and trailed after him. We were pretty near the edge of town now, and big openings started to show between houses, then pretty soon there were more open places than houses, and finally there weren't any more houses at all, just lots, and then fields, and further ahead some trees.

The street still kept on, though, and once in a while a car would come whizzing by, coming from the country. He would turn his face the other way each time one did, I noticed, like he didn't want them to get a look at him.

That was one of the main things that kept me going after him. He hadn't been acting right ever since I first started following him the night before away from the tailor shop. He was too watchful and careful, and he was always looking around too much, like he was afraid of someone doing just what I was doing. People don't walk that way, unless they'd done something they shouldn't. I know, because that was the way I walked after my baseball busted the candy-store window and I wanted to pretend it wasn't me did it.

I couldn't stay up on the road out here, because there was no one else on it but him and me and he would have seen me easy. But there were a lot of weeds and things growing alongside of it, and I got off into them and kept going with my back bent even with the tops of them. When they weren't close together I had to make a quick dive from one clump to the next.

Just before he got to where the trees started in, he kind of slowed down, like he wasn't going very much further. I looked all around, but I couldn't see anything, only some kind of old frame house standing way back off the road. It didn't have any lights and didn't look like anyone lived in it. Gee, it was a spooky kind of a place if there ever was one, and I sure hoped he wasn't going anywhere near *there*.

But it looked like he was, only he didn't go straight for it. First he looked both ways, up and down the road, and saw there was no one around—or thought there wasn't. Then he twisted his head and listened, to make sure no car was coming just then. Then he took a quick jump that carried him off the road into the darkness. But I could still see him a little, because I knew where he'd gone in.

Then, when he'd gotten over to where this tumbledown house was, he went all around it first, very carefully, like he wanted to make sure there was no one hiding in it waiting to grab him. Luckily there were plenty of weeds and bushes growing all around, and it was easy to get up closer to him.

When he'd gotten back around to the front again, and decided there was no one in it—which I could have told him right from the start just by the looks of it—he finally got ready to go in. It had a crazy kind of a porch with a shed over it, sagging way down in the middle between the two posts that held it. He went in under that, and I could hardly see him any more, it was so dark. He was just a kind of black blot against the door.

I heard him fiddling around with something that sounded like a lock, and then the door wheezed, and scraped back. There was a white something on the porch and he picked it up and took it in with him.

He left the door open a crack behind him, like he was coming out again soon, so I knew enough not to sneak up on the porch and try to peep in. It would have squeaked under me, anyway. But I moved over a little further in the bushes, where I could get a better line on the door. A weak light came on, not a regular light, but a match that he must have lit there on the other side of the door. But I've got good eyes and it was enough to show me what he was doing. He was picking up a couple of letters that the postman must have shoved under the bottom of the door. He looked at them, and then he seemed to get sore. He rolled them up into a ball with one hand and pitched them way back inside the house. He hadn't even opened them, just looked at the outside.

His match burned out, but he lit another, only this time way back inside some place where I couldn't see him. Then that one went out too, and a minute later the door widened a little and he edged out again as quietly as he'd gone in. He put something down where he'd taken that white thing up from. Then he closed the door real careful after him, looked all around to make sure no one was in sight, and came down off the porch.

I was pretty far out in front of the door, further than I had been when he went in. But I had a big bush to cover me, and I tucked my head down between my knees and made a ball out of myself, to make myself as small as I could, and that was about the sixteenth time he'd missed seeing me. But I forgot about my hand, it was sticking out flat against the ground next to me, to help me balance myself.

He came by so close his pants leg almost brushed my cheek. Just then a car came by along the road, and he stepped quickly back so he wouldn't be seen. His whole heel came down on two of my fingers.

All I could remember was that if I yelled I would be a goner. I don't know how I kept from it. It felt like a butcher's cleaver had chopped them off. My eyes got all full of water, mixed with stars. He stayed on it maybe half a minute, but it seemed like an hour. Luckily the car was going fast, and he moved forward again. I managed to hold out without moving until he got out to the road, where there wasn't so much danger of him hearing me.

Then I rolled over on my face, buried it with both arms, and bawled good and hard, but without making any noise. By the time I got that out of my system, it didn't hurt so much any more. I guess they weren't busted, just skinned.

Then I sat up and thought things over, meanwhile blowing on my fingers to cool them. He'd gone back along the road toward the built-up part of town. I didn't know whether to keep on following him or not. If he was only going back where he came from, there didn't seem to be any sense to it, I knew where that was already. I knew he didn't live here in this house, people don't live in two places at once.

What did he want out here then? What had he come here for? He'd acted kind of sore, the way he looked over those letters and then balled them up and fired them down. Like they weren't what he wanted, like he'd had the trouble of coming all the way out here for nothing. He must be waiting for a letter, a letter that hadn't come yet. I decided to stick around and find out more about this house if I could.

———◆———

Well I waited until I couldn't hear him walking along the road any more, then I got up and sneaked up on the porch myself. That thing he had put down outside the door was only an empty milk bottle, like people leave for the milkman to take away with him when he brings the new milk. So that white thing he had picked up at first must have been the same bottle, but with the milk still in it. He must have just taken it in and emptied it out.

What did he want to do a thing like that for? He hadn't been in there long enough to drink it. He just threw it out, and then brought the empty bottle outside again. That showed two things. If the milkman left milk here, then there was supposed to be somebody living here. But if this guy emptied the bottle out, that showed there wasn't anyone living here any more, but he didn't want the milkman or the mailman or anyone else to find out about it yet.

My heart started to pick up speed, and I got all gooseflesh and I whispered to myself: "Maybe he murdered the guy that lives here, and nobody's found out about it yet! I bet that's what it is! I bet *this* is where that eye came from!" The only catch was, why did he keep coming back here afterwards, if he did? The only thing I could figure out was he must want some letter that he knew was going to show up here, but it hadn't come yet, and he kept coming back at nights to find out if it had been delivered. And maybe the whole time there was someone dead inside there. . . .

I kept saying to myself, "I'm going in there and see if there is. I can get in there easy, even if the door is locked." But for a long time I didn't move. Well, if you got to know the truth, I was good and scared.

Finally I said to myself like this: "It's only a house. What can a house do to you? Just shadows and emptiness can't hurt you. And even if there is somebody lying dead in there, dead people can't move any more. You're not a kid any more, you're twelve years and five months old, and besides your old man needs help. If you go in there you might find out something that'll help him." So I changed my belt over to the third slot, and whenever I do that I mean business.

I tried the door first, but like I'd thought, it was locked, so I couldn't get in that way. Then I walked slowly all around the outside of the house trying all the windows one after the other. They were up higher than my head, but the clap-boards stuck out in lots of places and it was easy to get a toe-hold on them and hoist myself up. That wouldn't work either. They were all latched or nailed down tight on the inside. I would have been willing to heave a rock and bust one of the panes so I could stick my arm in, but that wouldn't have been any good either, because they had cross-pieces in them that made little squares out of the pane, and they weren't big enough to squeeze through.

Finally I figured I might be able to open one of the top-floor windows, so I went around to the front again, spit on my hands, and shinnied up one of the porch posts. There were some old vine stalks twisted around them, so it was pie getting up. It was so old the whole thing shook bad, but I didn't weigh much, so nothing happened.

I started tugging at one of the windows that looked out over it. It was hard to get it started because it hadn't been opened in so long, but I kept at it, and finally it jarred up. The noise kind of scared me, but I swallowed hard and stuck my legs inside and slid into the room. The place smelled stuffy, and cobwebs tickled my face, but I just brushed them off. Who's afraid of a few spiders? I used to keep a collection of them when I was a kid of nine, until my mother threw them out.

I couldn't see much, just the gray where the walls were and the black where the door was. A grown-up would have had matches, but I had to use my hands out in front of me to tell where I was going.

I didn't bump into anything much, because I guess the upstairs rooms were all empty and there was nothing to bump into. But the floorboards cracked and grunted under me. I had a narrow escape from falling all the way down the stairs and maybe breaking my neck, because they came sooner than I thought they would. After that I went good and easy, tried out each one with my toe first to make sure it was there before I trusted my whole foot down on it. It took a long time getting down that way, but at least I got down in one piece. Then I started for where I thought the front door was. I wanted to get out.

I don't know what mixed me up, whether there was an extra turn in the stairs that I didn't notice in the dark, or I got my directions balled up by tripping a couple of times over empty boxes and picking myself up again. Anyway I kept groping in what I thought was a straight line out from the foot of the stairs, until I came up against a closed door. I thought it was the front door to the house, of course. I tried it, and it came right open. That should have told me it wasn't, because I'd seen him lock it behind him when he left.

The air was even worse on the other side of it than on my side, all damp and earthy like when you've been burrowing under the ground, and it was darker than ever in front of me, so I knew I wasn't looking out on the porch. Instead of backing up I took an extra step through it, just to make sure what it was, and this time I did fall— and, boy, how I fell! Over and over, all the way down a steep flight of brick steps that hurt like anything every time they hit me.

The only thing that saved me was that at the bottom I landed on something soft. Not real soft like a mattress, but kind of soft and at the same time stiff, if you know what I mean. At first I thought it was a bag or bolster of some kind filled with sawdust.

I was just starting to say to myself, "Gee, it's a good thing that was there!" when I put out my hand, to brace myself for getting up on my feet again, and all of a sudden I turned to ice all over.

My hand had landed right on top of another hand—like it was waiting there to meet it! It wasn't warm and soft like a hand, it felt more like a stiff leather glove that's been soaked in water, but I knew what it was all right. It went on up into a shoulder, and that went up into a neck, and that ended in a head.

I gave a yell, and jumped about a foot in the air and landed further over on another part of the floor. Then I started scrambling around on my hands and knees to get out of there fast. I don't think anyone was ever that scared in their life before.

⊰◈⊱

I couldn't get at the stairs again without stepping over it at the foot of them, and that kept me there a minute or two longer, until I had time to talk to myself. And I had to talk good and hard, believe me.

"He's murdered, because when dead people die regular they're buried, not left to lie at the bottom of cellar steps. So you see, that Petersen *did* murder someone, just like you been suspecting for two whole days. And instead of being scared to death, you ought to be glad you found him, because now you *can* help your old man just like you wanted to. Nobody knows about this yet, not even the milkman or the letterman, and he can have it all to himself."

That braced me up a lot. I wiped the wet off my forehead, and I pulled my belt over to the fourth notch, which was the last one there was on it. Then I got an idea how I could look at him, and make sure he was murdered. I didn't have any matches, but he was a grown-up, even if he was dead, and he just might have one, in—in his pocket.

I started to crawl straight back *toward* him, and when I got there, I clenched my teeth together real hard, and reached out one hand for about where his pocket ought to be. It shook so, it was no good by itself, but I steadied it by holding it with the other hand, and got it in. Then I had to go around to the other side of him and try that one. He had three of them in there, those long kind. My hand got caught getting it out, and I nearly went crazy for a minute, but I finally pulled the pocket off it with my other hand, and edged back further away from him.

Then I scraped one of them along the floor. His face was the first thing I saw. It was all wrinkled and dry-like and it had four black holes in it, one more than it should have. The mouth was a big wide hole, and the nostrils of the nose were two small ones, and then there was another under one eyelid, or at least a sort of a hollow place that was just like a hole. He'd worn a glass eye in that socket, and it was the very one I had in my pocket that very minute. I could see now how he'd come to lose it.

He'd been choked to death with an old web belt from behind when he wasn't looking. It was still around his neck, so tight and twisted you would have had to cut through it to get it off. It made his other eye, which was a real one, stand out all swollen like it was ready to pop out. And I guess that was what really did happen with the fake one. It got loose and dropped out while he was still struggling down on the floor between the murderer's spread-legs, and jumped into his trouser-cuff without him even seeing it. Then, when it was over, he either didn't notice it was missing from the dead man's face, or else thought it had rolled off into a corner and was lying there. Instead it was in the cuff of the suit he'd had cleaned to make sure it wouldn't have any suspicious dirt or stains on it.

The match was all the way down to my fingertips by now, so I had to blow it out. It had told me all it could. It didn't tell me who the dead old man was, or why that Petersen fellow had killed him. Or what he was after that made him come back again like that. I crept up the brick cellar steps in the dark, feeling like I could never again be as scared as I had been when I first felt that other hand under mine. I was wrong, wait'll you hear.

I found my way back to the front door without much trouble. The real front door, this time. Then I remembered the two letters I'd seen him crumple and throw away. They might tell me who the dead man was. I had to light one of the two matches I had left to look for them, but the door had no glass in it, just a crack under it, and Petersen must be all the way back in town by now, so I figured it was safe enough if I didn't keep it lit too long.

I found them right away, and just held the match long enough to smooth them out and read who they were sent to. The dead old man was Thomas Gregory, and that road out there must still be called Decatur Street even this far out, because they said: 1017 Decatur Street. They were just ads. One wanted to know if he wanted to buy a car, the other one wanted to know if he wanted to buy a set of books.

I blew the match out and stuck them up under the lining of my cap. I wanted to take thcm home and show them to my father, so he'd believe me when I told him I'd found someone murdered way out here. Otherwise he was liable to think I was just making it up.

I found out I couldn't get the door open after all, even from the inside. He'd locked it with Gregory's key and taken that with him. I found another door at the back, but that turned out to be even worse, it had a padlock on it. This Gregory must have been scared of people, or else kind of a crazy hermit, to live all locked up like that, with the windows nailed down and everything. I'd have to go all the way upstairs, climb out, catwalk over that dangerously wobbly porch, and skin down to the ground again.

I'd gotten back about as far as where the stairs started up, and I'd just put my foot on the bottom one, when I heard a scrunch outside. Then someone stepped on the porch! There was a slithering sound by the door, and a minute later a little whistle went *tweet!* I nearly jumped out of my skin. I don't know which of the three scared me most, I think it was that whispering sound under the door. The only reason I stayed where I was and didn't make a break up the stairs was, I could hear steps going away again outside.

I tiptoed to one of the front windows and rubbed a clean spot in the dust and squinted through it. I could see a man walking away from the house back toward the road again. He climbed on a bicycle and rode off. It was only a special delivery mailman.

I waited until he'd rode from sight, then I groped my way back toward the door, and I could see something white sticking through under it, even in the dark. I got down and pinched it between my thumb and finger, but it wouldn't come through, it seemed to have gotten caught. He hadn't shoved it all the way in, and first I thought maybe it was too thick or had gotten snagged on a splinter.

I opened my fingers for a minute to get a tighter grip, and right while I was looking at it, it started getting smaller and smaller, like it was slipping out the other way. I couldn't understand what was making it do that, there was no tilt to the sill. When there was only about an inch of it left, I grabbed at it quick and gave it a tug that brought all of it in again.

Then all of a sudden I let go of it, and stayed there like I was, without moving and with my heart starting to pound like anything. Without hearing a sound, something had told me all at once that there was someone out there on the other side of that door! I was afraid to touch the letter now, but the damage had already been done. That jerk I'd given it was enough to tell him there was someone in here.

<hr>

Plenty scared, I picked my way back to the window again, as

carefully as if I was walking on eggs, to try and see if I could get a side-look at the porch through it. Just as I got to it, one of those things like you see in the movies happened, only this time it wasn't funny. My face came right up against somebody else's. He was trying to look in, while I was trying to look out. Our two faces were right smack up against each other, with just a thin sheet of glass between.

We both jumped together, and he straightened up. He'd been bending down low to look in. Mine stayed down low where it was, and he could tell I was a kid. It was Petersen, I could recognize him even in the faint light out there by the shape of his hat and his pitcher-ears. He must have been waiting around near-by, and had seen the mailman's bike.

We both whisked from the window fast. He jumped for the door and started to stab a key at it. I jumped for the stairs and the only way out there was. Before I could get to them, I went headfirst over an empty packing case. Then I was on them and flashing up them. Just as I cleared the last one, I heard the door swing in below. I might be able to beat him out of the house through the window upstairs, but I didn't give much for my chances of beating him down the road in a straight run. My only hope was to be able to get into those weeds out there ahead of him and then lose myself, and I didn't know how I was going to do it with him right behind me.

I got to the upstairs window just as he got to the bottom step of the stairs. I didn't wait to look, but I think he'd stopped to strike a light so that he could make better time. I straddled the windowsill in a big hurry, tearing my pants on a nail as I did so. A minute later something much worse happened. Just as I got one foot down on the wooden shed over the porch, and was bringing the other one through the window after me, the two ends went up higher, the middle sank lower, and then the whole business slid to the ground between the two posts that had held it up. Luckily I was still holding onto the window frame with both arms. I pulled myself back just in time and got my leg up on the sill again.

If there'd been a clear space underneath, I would have chanced it and jumped from where I was, although it was a pretty high jump for a kid my size, but the way those jagged ends of splintered wood were sticking up all over, I knew one of them would stab through me sure as anything if I tried it. He'd run back to the door for a minute—I guess at first he thought the whole house was coming down on him—and when he saw that it was just the porch shed, he stuck his head out and around and looked up at me where I was, stranded up there on the window frame.

All he said was, "All right, kid, I've got you now," but he said it in such a calm, quiet way that it scared you more than if he'd cursed.

He went in and started up the stairs again. I ran all around the three sides of the room, looking for a way out, and on the third side I finally found a narrow brick fireplace. I jumped in through that and tried to climb up on the inside. I fell back again to the bottom just as he came into the room. He headed straight over to the fireplace and bent down, and his arm reached in for me and swept back and forth. It missed me the first time, but the second time it got me. There was nothing I could hang onto in there to keep from being pulled out. I came out kicking, and he straightened up and held me by the throat, out where I couldn't reach him with my feet.

He let me swing at his arm with both my fists until I got tired, and then he said in that same quiet, deadly way, "What're you doing around here, son?" Then he shook me a couple of times to bring it out faster.

"Just playin'," I said.

"Don't you think it's a funny place and a funny time of night for a kid your age to be playing?"

What was the use of answering that?

He said, "I've seen you before, son. I saw you standing on the street looking up at my window last night. You seem to be crossing my path a lot lately. What's the idea?" He shook me till my teeth darn near came out, then he asked me a second time, real slow: "What's the idear?" His actions were red-hot, his voice was ice-cold.

"Nothin'," I drooled. My head lolled all around on my shoulders, dizzy from the shaking.

"I think there is. Who's your father?"

"Frank Case."

"Who's Frank Case?"

I knew my only chance was not to tell him, I knew if I told him then he'd never let me get out of here alive. But I couldn't help telling him, it made me glad to tell him, proud to tell him; I didn't want any mercy from him. "The best damn dick in town!" I spit out at him.

"That's your finish," he said. "So you're a cop's son. Well, a cop's son is just a future cop. Squash them while they're little. Did your father teach you how to go out bravely, kid?"

Gee, I hated him! My own voice got nearly as husky as if it was changing already, and it wasn't yet. "My father don't have to teach me that. Just being his kid shows it to me."

He laughed. "Been down to the cellar yet, son?"

I didn't answer.

"Well, we're going down there now."

I hated him so, I didn't even remember to be scared much any more. You're only scared when there's a chance of not getting hurt, anyway. When there's no chance of not getting hurt, what's the use of being scared? "And I'm not coming up again any more, am I?" I said defiantly while he felt his way down the stairs with me.

"No, you're not coming up again any more. Glad you know it."

I said, "You can kill me like you did him, but I'm not afraid of you. My pop and every cop in the city'll get even on you, you dirty murderer, you. You stink!"

⪪◆⪫

We'd gotten down to the first floor by now. It was better than the basement, anyway. I twisted my head around and got my teeth into his arm, just below the elbow. I kept it up until they darn near came together, through his sleeve and skin and muscle. I couldn't even feel him hitting me, but I know he was, because all of a sudden I landed flat up against the wall all the way across the room, and my ears hummed like when you go through a tunnel.

I heard him say, "You copper-whelp! If you want it that quick, here it is!" The white of his shirt showed for a minute, like he'd pushed back his coat to take out something. Then a long tube of fire jumped at me, and there was a sound like thunder in the room, and some plaster off the wall got into my ear.

I'd never heard a gun go off before. It makes you kind of excited. It did me, anyway. I knew the wall was pale in back of me and that was bad because I was outlined against it. I dropped down flat on the floor, and started to shunt off sideways over it, keeping my face turned toward him. I knew another of those tubes of light was coming any second, this time pointed right, pointed low.

He heard the slithering sound my body was making across the floor. He must have thought I was hit but still able to move. He said, "You're hard to finish, ain't you, kid? Why ain't you whimpering? Don't it hurt you?" I just kept swimming sideways on the floor. I heard him say:

"Two shots don't make any more noise than one. I'll make sure this time." He took a step forward and one knee dipped a little. I saw his arm come out and point down at me.

I couldn't help shutting my eyes tight for a minute there on the floor. Then I remembered I was a detective's son and I opened them again right away. Not for any murderer was I going to close my eyes. I just stayed still. You can't get out of the way of a shot, anyway.

The tube of light came again, and the thunder, and a lot of splinters jumped up right in front of my face. One of them even caught in my lip and hurt like a needle. I couldn't keep quiet even if I wanted to; the way I hated him made me say, real quiet, like I was a grown-up talking to another grown-up, not a kid who knew he was going to die in another minute:

"Gee, you're lousy, mister, for a murderer!"

That was all there was time for. All of a sudden there was a sound like someone ploughing through that mass of wreckage outside the door, and the door swung in and hit back against the wall; he hadn't even locked it behind him in his hurry to get his hands on me. For a minute there was complete silence—me flat on the floor, him in the shadows, an outline holding its breath at the door, waiting for the first sound.

Then a low voice that I knew by heart whispered, "Don't shoot, fellows, he may have my kid in there with him."

You could make him out against the lighter sky outside, but he had to have light to see by, or I knew Petersen would get him sure. He was just holding his fire because he didn't want to give away where he was. I had one match left in my pocket from the dead man. But a match goes out if you try to throw it through the air. I got it out of my pocket, and I put its tip to the floor and held it there, ready. Then I drew my legs up under me, reared up on them, and ticked the match off as I straightened. I held it way out across the room toward Petersen, with my arm stretched as far as it could reach, as it flamed, and it showed him up in smoky orange from head to foot. "Straight ahead of you, Pop!" I yelled. "Straight ahead of you where I'm holding this out to!"

Petersen's gun started around toward me fast and angry, to put me and my match both out at once, but there's only one thing that can beat a bullet, and that's another bullet. The doorway thundered, and my pop's bullet hit him so hard in the side of the head that he kicked over sideways like a drunk trying to dance, and went nudging his shoulder all the way down the wall to the floor, still smoky orange from my match to the last.

I stood there holding it, like the Statue of Liberty, until they had a chance to get over to him and make sure he wouldn't still shoot from where he was lying.

But one of them came straight to me, without bothering about him, and I knew which one it was all right, dark or no dark. He said, "Frankie, are you all right? Are you all right, son?"

I said, "Sure, I'm all right, Pop."

And the funny part of it was, I still was while I was saying it; I was sure I could've gone on all night yet. But all of a sudden when I felt his hands reaching out for me, I felt like I was only twelve years old again and would have to wait a long time yet before I could be a regular detective, and I flopped up against him all loose and went to sleep standing up or something. . . .

When I woke up I was in a car with him and a couple of the others, riding back downtown again. I started to talk the minute my eyes were open, to make sure he hadn't missed any of it, because I wanted to get him re—you know that word.

I said, "Pop, he killed an old guy named Thomas Gregory, he's down—"

"Yeah, we found him, Frankie."

"And, Pop, there's a letter under the front door, which is why he killed him."

"We found that too, Frankie." He took it out of his pocket and showed it to me. It wasn't anything, just an old scrap of pale blue paper.

"It's a certified check for twelve thousand dollars, in payment for a claim he had against a construction company as a result of an industrial accident."

My father explained, almost like I was a grown-up instead of a kid, "He was hit in the eye by a steel particle, while he was walking past one of their buildings under construction. He had to have that eye taken out. That was five years ago. The suit dragged on ever since, while he turned sour and led a hand-to-mouth existence in that shack out there. They fought him to the last ditch, but the higher court made them pay damages in the end.

"The day the decision was handed down, some of the papers ran little squibs about it, space-fillers down at the bottom of the page like they do. One of these evidently caught Petersen's eye, and he mistakenly thought that meant the check had already come in and the old man had cashed it. He went out there, got himself admitted or forced his way in, probably tortured Gregory first, and when he couldn't get anything out of him, ended up by killing him.

"He was too quick about it. The check didn't come in until tonight, as you saw. He had to keep coming back, watching for it. Once the old man was gone and the check still uncashed, the only thing he could do was take a desperate chance on forging his name to it, and present it for payment, backed up by some credentials taken from Gregory. Probably with a black patch over one eye for good measure.

"He wasn't very bright or he would have known that he didn't have a chance in a thousand of getting away with anything like that. Banks don't honor checks for that amount, when the payee isn't known to them, without doing a little quiet investigating first. But he wanted *something* out of his murder. He'd killed the old man for nothing. . . . But how in the blazes did *you*—"

So then I took out the glass eye and showed it to him, and told him how I traced it back. I saw them give each other looks and shake their heads sort of surprised over it, and one of them said, "Not bad! Not bad at all!"

"Not bad?" snapped my father.

"How'd you know where I was?"

"In the first place," he said, "your mother caught right on that Scanny was lying when he said you were studying over at his house, because in your excitement you kids overlooked the fact that tomorrow's Thanksgiving and there's no school to study for. She sent me over there, I broke Scanny down, and he showed me where this room was you'd followed this man to earlier in the day.

"I broke in, looked it over, and found a couple of those newspaper items about this old man Gregory that he'd taken the trouble to mark off and clip out. I didn't like the looks of that to begin with, and your friend Scanny had already mentioned something about a glass eye. Luckily they gave the recluse's address—which was what had put Petersen onto him, too—and when eleven-thirty came and no sign of you, I rustled up a car and chased out there fast."

We stopped off at Headquarters first, so he could make out his report, and he had me meet some guy with white hair who was his boss, I guess. He clapped my shoulder right where it hurt most from all those falls I'd had, but I didn't let him see that. I saw my father wasn't going to say anything himself, so I piped up: "The whole case is my father's and nobody else's! Now is he going to get re-instituted?"

I saw them wink at each other, and then the man with white hair laughed and said, "I think I can promise that." Then he looked at me and added, "You think a lot of your father, don't you?"

I stood up straight as anything and stuck my chin out and said, "He's the best damn dick in town!"

AFTERWORD TO "THROUGH A DEAD MAN'S EYE"

In "Through a Dead Man's Eye" (*Black Mask*, December 1939) Woolrich reworked some of the elements from "If I Should Die Before I Wake" (1937), his first thriller with a boy as narrator and protagonist, and produced a tale just as vivid and suspenseful but more naturalistic and circumstantial, without the earlier story's fairy-tale overtones. The climax with 12-year-old Frankie being stalked by the man who takes long walks deep into the forest is an orgy of breathless terror that no one but Woolrich could have written so effectively.

THE FATAL FOOTLIGHTS

I

He saw Vilma first. She was the dark one. Then he saw Gilda. She was the golden one. He didn't see the man at all, that first night. He didn't know any of their names. He didn't want to. He'd just gone to a show on his night off.

He had an aisle seat, alongside the runway. He'd told the ticket seller he wanted to see more than just their baby-blue eyes. The ticket seller had said: "You will." He'd been right, as it turned out.

It was, of course, simply burlesque under a different name, to evade the licensing restrictions of the last few years. But at the moment Benson took his seat, there wasn't anything going on that a fourteen-year-old schoolgirl couldn't have watched with perfect propriety. A black-haired singer in a flowing, full-length dress was rendering *Mighty Lak a Rose*. And she was good, too. Benson noticed several onlookers, who certainly hadn't come in to be reminded of mother love, furtively sticking thumbs into the corners of their eyes.

But this was his night off and he felt kind of cheated. "Did I walk in on a funeral?" he asked himself. He shouldn't have asked that, maybe. The mocking little gods of circumstances were only too willing to arrange it for him.

The singer walked off, the orchestra gave out with an introductory flourish, and the proceedings snapped back into character. The curtains parted to reveal a "living statue" group—five or six nymphs enameled a chalky white and their torsos veiled by wisps of cheesecloth, presided over by a central "statue" poised on a pedestal in their midst. This was Gilda, the main attraction.

Gilda was without encumbering cheesecloth, as she stood up there, head thrown back, seemingly in the act of nibbling at a dangling cluster of grapes. Whether she was as innocent of vesture as she seemed was beside the point; her body was coated with a thick layer of scintillant golden paint which was certainly far more protective than any ordinary pair of tights would have been. But that didn't dampen the general enthusiasm any. It was just the principle of the thing that mattered. Good clean fun, so to speak. She got a tremendous hand without doing a thing, just for art's sake.

The curtains coyly came together again, veiling the tableau. There was a teasing pause, maintained just long enough to whet the audience's appetite for more, then they parted once more and the "statuary" had assumed a different position. Gilda was now shading her eyes with one hand, one leg poised behind her, and staring yearningly toward the horizon—or more strictly speaking, a fire door at the side of the auditorium.

Benson caught the spirit of the thing along with everyone else and whacked his hands. The curtains met, parted once more, and again the tableau had altered. This time Gilda was up on tiptoes on her pedestal, her body arched over as though she was looking at her own reflection in a pool.

<hr />

Just before the curtains obliterated her, Benson thought he saw her waver a little, as if having difficulty maintaining her balance. Or maybe it was simply faulty timing. She had prepared to change positions a little too soon, before the curtains entirely concealed her from view. That slight flaw didn't discourage the applause any. It had reached the pitch of a bombardment. The audience wasn't a critical one; it didn't care about complete muscular control as long as it got complete undress. Or the illusion of it, through gold-plating.

The pause was a little longer this time, as though there had been a slight hitch. Benson wondered where the dancing came in. They had billed her out front as "The Golden Dancer," he remembered, and he wanted his money's worth. He didn't have long to wait. The footlights along the runway, unused until now, gushed up, the curtains parted, and Gilda was down on the stage floor now, and in motion. The audience forgot it had homes and families.

She was coming out on the runway to dance over their heads. For this additional intimacy, she had provided herself with a protective mantle of gauzy black—just in case some of the Commissioner's men happened to be in the audience.

She wasn't any great shakes of a dancer, nobody expected her to be, nobody cared. It was mostly a matter of waving her arms, turning this way and that, and flourishing the mantle around her, a little bit like a bullfighter does his cape. She managed while continually promising revealing gaps in it, to keep it all around her at all times, in a sort of black haze, like smoke. It was simply the strip-tease in a newer variation.

But indifferent as her dancing ability was to begin with, a noticeable hesitation began to creep into its posturing after she had been on the runway a moment or two. She seemed to keep forgetting what to do next.

"They hardly have time to rehearse at all," Benson thought leniently.

Her motions had slowed down like a clock that needs winding. He saw her cast a look over her shoulders at the unoccupied main stage she had just come from, as if in search of help. The lesser nymphs hadn't come out with her this last time, were probably doing a quick change for the next number.

For a moment she stood up there perfectly still, no longer moving a muscle. The swirling black gauze deflated about her, fell limp. Benson's grin of approval dimmed and died while he craned his neck up at her. Suddenly she started to go off balance.

He had only had time to throw up his arms instinctively, half to ward her off, half to catch her and break her fall. Her looming body blurred the runway lights for an instant, and then she had landed across him, one foot still up there on the runway behind her. The black stuff of her mantle came down after her, like a parachute, and half-smothered him. He had to claw at it to free his head, get rid of it.

Those in the rows further back, who hadn't been close enough to notice the break in her performance that had come just before the fall, started to applaud and even laugh, like fools. They seemed to think it was still part of her routine, or else that she had actually missed her footing and tumbled down on him, and either way it struck them as the funniest thing they had ever seen.

Benson already knew better, by the inert way her head and shoulders lay across his knees. "Take it easy. I've got you," he whispered reassuringly, trying to hold her as she started to slide to the floor between the rows of seats.

Her eyes rolled unseeingly up at him, showing all whites, but some memory of where she was and what she had been doing still lingered in the darkness rolling over her.

"I'm so sorry. Did I hurt you, mister?" she breathed. The performer's courtesy to the spectator, so seldom returned. "Guess I've spoiled the show—" It ended with a long-drawn sigh—and she was still.

The laugher and handclapping was dying down, because her head didn't bob up again at the place where she had disappeared from view, and they were catching on that something was wrong. A hairy armed man in rolled blue shirtsleeves popped partly out of the wings, not caring if he was seen or not, and wigwagged frantically to the bandleader, then jumped back again where he'd come from. The droopy music they'd been playing for her broke off short and a rackety rumba took its place. A long line of chorus girls came spilling out on the stage, most of them out of step and desperately working to get their shoulder straps adjusted.

Benson was already struggling up the aisle with his inert golden burden by that time. A couple of ushers came hustling down to help him, but he elbowed them aside. "You quiet the house down. I can get her back there by myself."

A man with a cigar sticking flat out of his mouth like a tusk, met him at the back, threw open a door marked *Manager*. "Bring her in here to my office, until I can send out for a doctor—" Before closing it after the three of them, he stopped to scan the subsiding ripples of excitement in the audience. "How they taking it? All right, keep 'em down in their seats, usher. No refunds, understand?" He closed the door and came in.

Benson had to put her in the manager's swivel chair; there wasn't even a couch or sofa in the place. Even with the shaded desk light on, the place stayed dim and shadowy. Her body gleamed weirdly in the gloom, like some kind of a shiny mermaid.

"Thanks a lot, bud," the manager said to him crisply. "You don't have to wait; the doctor'll be here in a minute—"

"The tin says stick around." Benson reburied the badge in his pocket.

The manager widened his eyes. "That's a hot one. You're probably the only headquarters man out there tonight, and she keels over into your lap."

"That's the kind of luck I always have," Benson let him know, bending over the girl. "I can't even see a show once a year, without my job horning in."

The manager took another squint outside the door to see how his house was getting along. "Forgotten all about it already," he reported contentedly. He turned back. "How's she coming?"

"She's dead," Benson said muffledly, from below one arm, ear to the girl's gold brassiere.

The manager gave a sharp intake of breath, but his reaction was a purely professional one. "Gee, who'll I get to fill in for her on such short notice? What the hell happened to her? She was all right at the matinee!"

"What'd you expect her to do," Benson said short-temperedly. "Come and inform you she was going to die in the middle of her act tonight, so you'd have time to get a substitute?" He lifted one of the golden eyelids to try for optical reflex; there wasn't any.

———◆◆◆———

The hastily summoned doctor had paused outside the door, trying to take in as much of the show free as he could before he had to attend to business. He came in still looking fascinatedly behind him. "You're too late," the manager scowled. "This headquarters man says she's dead already."

Benson was on the desk phone by now with his back to the two of them. A big belly-laugh rolled in from outside before they could get the door closed, and drowned out what he was saying. He covered the mouthpiece until he could go ahead. "Forty-second

Street, just off Broadway. Okay." He hung up. "The examiner's office is sending a man over. We'll hear what he says."

The doctor smiled. "Well, he can't say any more than I can. She's dead and that's that."

"He can say why," Benson countered, dipping four fingers of each hand into his coat pockets and wiggling his thumbs.

The private doctor closed the door after him.

"Now he's going to stand and chisel the rest of the show free, just because he was called in," the manager predicted sourly.

"He can have my seat," Benson remarked. "I won't be using it any more tonight."

He brushed a fleck of gold paint off the front of his coat, then another off the cuff of his coatsleeve. "Let's get the arithmetic down." He took out a black notebook, poised a worn-down pencil stub over the topmost ruled line of a blank page. Those that had gone before—and many had gone before—were all closely scrawled over with names, addresses and other data. Then, one by one, wavy downward lines were scored through them. That meant: case closed.

He hadn't bothered to tear them out and throw them away. When the entire booklet itself was used up, he would probably throw that away, intact. But what a light it could have thrown on the vicissitudes of human existence in a large city, what a tale of theft, violence, accident, misfortune, crime!

The manager opened a drawer in his desk, took out a ledger, sought a pertinent page, traced a sausage-like thumb down a list of payroll names. "Here she is. Real name, Annie Willis. 'Gilda' was just her—"

Benson jotted. "I know."

He gave the address on West 135th. "There's a phone number to go with it, too."

Benson jotted. He looked up, said, "Oh, hello, Jacobson," as the man from the examiner's office came in, went back to his note-taking again.

———◆◆◆———

Outside, three-hundred-odd people sat watching a line-up of girls dance. Inside, the business of documenting a human death went on, with low-voiced diligence.

Benson repeated: "Nearest of kin, Frank Willis, husband—"

The examining assistant groused softly to himself: "I can't get anything out of it at all, especially through all this gilt. It mighta been a heart attack; it mighta been acute indigestion. All I can give you for sure, until we get downtown, is she's dead, good and dead—"

The manager was getting peevish at this protracted invasion of his privacy. "That makes three times she's been dead, already. I'm willing to believe it, if no one else is."

Benson murmured, "This is the part I hate worst," and began to dial with his pencil stub.

An usher sidled in, asked: "What'll we do about the marquee, boss? She's still up on it, and it's gotta be changed now for tomorrow's matinee."

"Just take down the 'G' from 'Gilda', see? Then stick in an 'H' instead, make it 'Hilda'. That saves the trouble of changing the whole—"

"But who's Hilda, boss?"

"I don't know myself! If the customers don't see anyone called Hilda, that'll teach them not to believe in signs!"

Benson was saying quietly: "Is this Frank Willis? Are you the husband of Annie Willis, working at the New Rotterdam Theater? . . . All right, now take it easy. She died during the performance this evening . . . Yeah, onstage about half an hour ago . . . No, you won't find her here by the time you get down. You'll be notified when the body's released by the medical examiner's office. They want to perform an autopsy . . . Now don't get frightened, that's just a matter of form, they always do that. It just means an examination . . . You can claim her at the city morgue when they're through with her."

He hung up, murmured under his breath: "Funny how a strange word they don't understand, like 'autopsy,' always throws a scare into them when they first hear it." He eyed the manager's swivel chair. It was empty now, except for a swath of gold-paint flecks down the middle of the back, like a sunset reflection. He grimaced discontentedly. "I shoulda stayed home tonight altogether. Then somebody else would have had to handle the blamed thing! Never saw it to fail yet. Every time I try to see a show—"

II

Next day at eleven a cop handed Benson a typewritten autopsy report.

Benson didn't place the name for minute. Then: "Oh yeah, that girl in the show last night—Gilda." He glanced down at his own form with rueful recollection. "It's going to cost me two bucks to have the front of that other suit dry-cleaned. Okay, thanks. I'll take it in to the lieutenant."

He scanned it cursorily himself first, before doing so. Then he stopped short, frowned, went back and read one or two of the passages more carefully.

". . . Death caused by sealing of the pores over nearly the entire body surface for a protracted period. This substance is deleterious when kept on for longer than an hour or two at the most. It is composed of infinitesimal particles of gold leaf which adhere to the pores, blocking them. This produces a form of bodily suffocation, as fatal in the end, if less immediate, than stoppage of the breathing passage would be. The symptoms are delayed, then strike with cumulative suddenness, resulting in weakness, dizziness, collapse and finally death. Otherwise the subject was perfectly sound organically in every way. There can be no doubt that this application of theatrical pigment and failure to remove it in time was the sole cause of mortality—"

He tapped a couple of nails on the desk undecidedly a minute or two. Finally he picked up the phone and got the manager of the New Rotterdam Theater. He hadn't come in yet, but they switched the call to his home. "This is Benson, headquarters man that was in your office last night. How long had this Gilda—Annie Willis, you know—been doing this gilt act?"

"Oh, quite some time—five or six months now."

"Then she wasn't green at it; she wasn't just breaking it in."

"No, no, she was an old hand at it."

He hung up, tapped his nails some more. "Funny she didn't know enough by this time to take it off before it had a chance to catch up with her," he murmured half under his breath. The report should have gone in to his lieutenant, and that should have ended it. Accidental death due to carelessness, that was all. She'd been too lazy or too rushed to remove the harmful substance between shows, and had paid the penalty.

But a good detective is five-sixths hard work and one-sixth blind, spontaneous "hunches." Benson wasn't a bad detective. And his one-sixth had come uppermost just then. He folded the examiner's report, put it in his pocket, and didn't take it in to his lieutenant. He went back to the New Rotterdam Theater on 42nd Street, instead.

It was open even this early, although the stage show didn't go on yet. A handful of sidewalk beachcombers were drifting in, to get in out of the sun. The manager had evidently thought better of his marquee short-change of the night before. The canopy still mis-leadingly proclaimed "Hilda, the Golden Dancer," but below it there was now affixed a small placard, so tiny it was invisible unless you got up on a ladder to scan it: "Next Week."

<hr />

The manager acted anything but glad to see him back so soon. "I knew that wasn't the end of it! With you fellows these things go on forever. Listen, she keeled over in front of everybody in the theater. People are dropping dead on the streets like that every minute of the day, here, there, everywhere. What's there to find out about? Something gave out inside. It was her time to go, and there you are."

Benson wasn't an argumentative sort of person. "Sure," he agreed unruffledly. "and now it's my time to come nosing around about it—and there *you* are. Who shared her dressing-room with her—or did she have one to herself?"

The manager shrugged disdainfully. "These aren't the days when the Ziegfeld Follies played this house. She split it with Vilma Lyons. That's the show's ballad-singer, you know, the only full-dressed girl in the company, and June McKee. She leads the chorus in a couple of numbers."

"Are her belongings still in it?"

"They must be. Nobody's called for them yet, as far as I know."

"Let's go back there," Benson suggested.

"Listen, the show's cooking to go on—"

"I won't get in its way," Benson assured him.

They came out of the office, went down a side aisle skirting the orchestra, with scattered spectators already lounging here and there. A seven-year-old talking picture, with Morse Code dots and dashes running up it all the time, was clouding the screen at the moment. They climbed onto the stage at the side, went in behind the screen, through the wings, and down a short, damp, feebly lighted passage, humming with feminine voices coming from behind doors that kept opening and closing as girls came in from the alley at the other end of the passage, in twos and threes.

The manager thumped one of the doors, turned the knob and opened it with one and the same gesture—and a perfect indifference to the consequences. "Put on something, kids. There's a detective coming in."

"What's the matter, isn't he over twenty-one?" one of them jeered.

The manager stood aside to let Benson pass, went back along the passageway toward his office with the warning: "Don't gum them up now. This show hits fast once it gets going."

There were two girls in there, working away at opposite ends of a three-paneled mirror. The middle space and chair were vacant. Benson's map appeared in all three of the mirrors at once, as he came in and closed the door after him. One girl clutched at a wrapper, flung it around her shoulders. The other calmly went ahead applying make-up, leaving her undraped backbone exposed to view down to her waist.

"You two have been sharing the same dressing-room with Annie Willis," he said. "Did she usually leave on this shiny junk between shows, or take it off each time?"

The chorus leader, the one the manager had called June McKee, answered, in high-pitched derogation at such denseness. "Whadd'ye think, she could go out and eat between shows with her face all gold like that? She woulda had a crowd following her along the street! Sure she took it off."

<hr/>

They looked at one another with a sudden flash of enlightened curiosity. The McKee girl, a strawberry blonde, turned around toward him on the make-up bench. "Sa-ay, is that what killed her, that gold stuff?" she asked in an awe-stricken, husky whisper.

Benson overrode that. "Did she take it off yesterday or did she leave it on?"

"She left it on." She turned to her bench mate, the brunette ballad singer, for corroboration. "Didn't she, Vilma? Remember?"

"Where is this gold stuff? I'd like to see it."

"It must be here with the rest of her stuff." The McKee girl reached over, pulled out the middle of the three table drawers, left it open for him to help himself. "Look in there."

It was in pulverized form, in a small jar. It had a greenish tinge to it that way. He read the label. It was put up by a reputable cosmetic manufacturing company. There were directions for application and removal, and then an explicit warning: "Do not allow to remain on any longer than necessary after each performance." She must have read that a dozen times in the course of using the substance. She couldn't have failed to see it.

"You say she left it on yesterday. Why? Have you any idea?"

Again it was the McKee girl who answered, spading her palms at him. "Because she mislaid the cleanser, the stuff that came with it to remove it. They both come together. You can't buy one without the other. It's a special preparation that sort of curls it up and *peels* it off clean and even. Nothing else works as well or as quick. You can't use cold cream, and even alcohol isn't much good. You can scrub your head off and it just makes a mess of your skin, gets it all red and fiery—"

"And yesterday it disappeared?"

"Right after the finale, she started to holler: 'Who took my paint remover? Anybody seen my paint remover?' Well, between the three of us, we turned the room inside out, and no sign of it. She emptied her whole drawer out. Everything else was there but that. She even went into a couple of the other dressing-rooms to find out if anybody had it in there. I told her nobody else would want it. She was the only one in the company who used that gilt junk. It wouldn't have been any good to anyone else. It never turned up."

"Finish telling me."

"Finally Vilma and me had to go out and eat. Time was getting short. Other nights, the three of us always ate together. We told her if she found it in time to hurry up after us. We'd keep a place for her at our table. She never showed up. When we got back for the night show, sure enough, she was still in her electroplating. She told us she'd had to send Jimmy, that's the colored handyman, out for something and had eaten right in the dressing-room."

Benson cocked his head slightly, as when one looks downward into a narrow space. "Are you sure this bottle of remover couldn't have been in the drawer and she missed seeing it?"

"That was the first place we cased. We had everything out—even two cockroaches that lived in a crack on the side. I remember holding it up in my hand empty and thumping the bottom of it just for luck!"

His wrist shot out of his cuff, hitched back into it again, like some sort of a hydraulic brake. "Then what's it doing in there now?" He was holding a small bottle, mate to the first, except that its contents were liquid and there was a small sponge attached to its neck.

It got quiet in the dressing-room, deathly quiet. So quiet you could even hear the sound track from the screen out front: "This is Ed Torgerson bringing you latest camera highlights from the sport news of the day."

They both had such frightened looks on their faces, the super-stitious fright of two giddy, thoughtless creatures who have suddenly come face to face with nameless evil.

The McKee girl's lower lip was trembling with awe. "It was put back—*after!* Somebody *wanted* her to die like that! With us right here in the same room with her!" She took a deep breath, threw open her own drawer, and with a defiant look at Benson, as if to say, "Try and stop me," tilted a small, flat gin bottle to her mouth.

The ballad singer, Vilma Lyons, suddenly dropped her head into her folded arms on the littered dressing table and began to sob.

The stage manager bopped a fist on the door and called in: "The customers are waiting to see your operations. If that dick ain't through questioning you in there, tell him to put on a girdle and follow you out on the runway!"

III

"Yes, sir, boss, I'm Jimmy, the handyman." He put down his bucket, followed Benson out into the alley, where they wouldn't be in the way of the girls hustling in and out on quick changes. "Yes, sir, Miss

Gilda done send me out last night between shows to try to git her another bottle of that there stuff which took off the gold paint."

"Why didn't you get it?"

"I couldn't! I went to the big theat'cal drugstore on Eighth where she tole me. It's the only place aroun' here where you can git it and even there they don't keep much on hand, never git much call for it. The drugstore man tole me somebody else just beat me to it. He tole me he just got through selling the last bottle he had in stock, before I got there."

"Keep on," Benson said curtly.

"That's about all. The drugstore man promise to order another bottle for her right away from his company's warehouse or the wholesaler what puts it up, see that it's in by the first thing in the morning. So I go back and tell her. Then she send me across the street to Bickford's to bring her in a sanwitch. When I come back the second time, she already sitting there acting kind of low, holding her haid. She say: 'Jimmy, I'm sorry I ordered that bite, after all. I don't feel well. I hope nothing happens to me from leaving this stuff on too long.' "

All Benson said was: "You come along and point out that druggist to me."

<hr/>

"Come in, Benson."

"Lieutenant, I've got a problem. I've got a report here from Jacobson that I haven't turned in to you yet. I've been keeping it until I know what to do about it."

"What's the hitch?"

"Lieutenant, is there such a thing as a *negative* murder? By that I mean, when not a finger is lifted against the victim, not a hair of her head is actually touched. But the murder is accomplished by *withholding* something, so that death is caused by its absence or lack."

The lieutenant was quick on the trigger. "Certainly! If a man locks another man up in a room, and withholds food from him until the guy has starved to death, you'd call that murder, wouldn't you? Even though the guy that caused his death never touched him with a ten-foot pole, never stepped in past the locked door at all."

Benson plucked doubtfully at the cord of skin between his throat and chin. "But what do you do when you have no proof of *intention?* I mean, when you've got evidence that the act of withholding or removal was committed, but no proof that the intention was murderous. And how you gonna get proof of intention, anyway? It's something inside the mind, isn't it?"

The lieutenant glowered, said, "What do you do? I'll tell you what you do? You bring your bird in and you beat the living tar out of him until you get the intention *out* of his mind and down in typewriting! That's what you do!"

⬥

The man was alone when he started down the three flights of stairs in the shoddy walk-up apartment on West 135th. He was still alone when he got down to the bottom of them. And then somehow, between the foot of the stairs and the street door, he wasn't alone any more. Benson was walking along beside him, as soundlessly as though his own shadow had crept forward and overtaken him along the poorly lit passage.

He shied sideways and came to a dead stop against the wall, the apparition was so unexpected. He was gaping.

Benson said quietly: "Come on, what're you stopping for? You were leaving the house, weren't you, Willis? Well, you're still leaving the house, what's the difference?"

They walked on as far as the street entrance. Benson just kept one fingertip touching the other's elbow, in a sort of mockery of guidance. Willis said: "What am I pinched for?"

"Who said you were pinched? Do *you* know of anything you should be pinched for?"

"No, I don't."

"Then you're not pinched. Simple enough, isn't it?"

Willis didn't say another word after that. Benson only said two things more himself, one to his charge, the other to a cab driver. He remarked: "Come on, we'll ride it. I'm no piker." And when a cab had sidled up to his signal, he named a precinct police station. They rode the whole way in stony silence from then on, Willis starting straight ahead in morbid reverie; Benson with his eyes toward the cab window—but on the shadowy reflection of Willis' face given back by the glass, not the street outside.

They got out and Benson took him in and left him waiting in a room at the back for a few minutes, while he went off to attend to something else. This wasn't accidental; it was the psychological buildup—or rather, breakdown—preceding the grill. It had been known to work wonders.

It didn't this time.

Benson wiped off his smirched belt buckle on a piece of waste, ran the strap of it through the loops of his trousers, refastened it. "Take him out," he said to the subordinate who had been lending him a hand—or rather a fist.

Willis went out on his own feet, waveringly, leaning lopsided against his escort, but on his own feet. A sense of innocence can sometimes lend one moral support. But so can a sense of having outwitted justice.

"The guy must be innocent," the other dick remarked when he had come back.

"He knows we can't get him. There's nothing further in his actions to be uncovered, don't you see? We've got everything there is to get on him, and it isn't enough. And we can't get at his intentions. They got to come out through his own mouth. All he has to do is hold out. And he'll hold out until we kill him first, if he has to. It's easy to keep a single, simple idea like that in your mind, even when your head is bouncing back from the four walls like a punching bag.

"What breaks down most of them is the uncertainty of something they did wrong, something they didn't cover up right, cropping up and tripping them—an exploded alibi, a surprise identification by a material witness. He had none of that uncertainty to buck. All he had to do was sit tight inside his own skin." He held his knuckles under the filter-tap in the corner, let a little water trickle over the abrasions.

⋙—◆—⋘

To his lieutenant, the next day, he said: "I'm morally certain he killed her. What are the three things that count in every crime? Motive, opportunity and method. He rings the bell on each count. Motive? Well, the oldest one in the world between men and women. He was sick of her; he'd lost his head about some one else, and didn't know how else to get rid of her. She was in the way in more than just the one sense. She was a deterrent, because of the other woman's sense of loyalty, as long as she remained alive. It wouldn't have done any good if he walked out on her or divorced her; the other woman wouldn't have had him at her friend's expense and he knew it.

"It so happens that the other woman was a lifelong friend of the wife; the kind of friendship that is more often met with between men than women, a real thick-and-thin partnership. She even lived with them, up at the 135th Street place, for awhile after they were first married. Then she got out, maybe 'cause she realized three's a crowd and a set-up like that was only asking for trouble."

"Have you found out who this other woman is?"

"Certainly. Vilma Lyons, the ballad singer in the same show with the wife. I went up to the theater yesterday afternoon. I questioned the two girls who shared Annie Willis' dressing-room with her. One of them talked a blue streak. The other one didn't open her mouth; I don't recall her making a single remark during the entire interview. She was too busy *thinking back*. She knew; her intuition must have already told her who had done it. At the end, she suddenly buried her face in her arms and cried. Don't think I didn't take notice. I let her think it over. I knew she'd come to me of her own accord sooner or later. She did, after curtain time last evening, down here at the station house. Weren't we going to *get* the person that had done that to her friend, she wanted to know? Weren't they going to be punished for it. Were they going to get away with it scot-free?"

"Did she accuse him?"

"She had nothing to accuse him on. He hadn't said anything to her. He hadn't even shown her by the look on his face. And then little by little I caught on, by reading between the lines of what she said, that he'd liked her a little too well."

He shrugged. "She can't help us, she admitted it herself. Because he started giving her these long, haunting looks when he thought she wasn't noticing, and falling into reveries, and acting discontented and restless, that isn't evidence he killed his wife. But she *knows*, in her own mind, just as I *know* in mine, who hid that remover from Annie Willis, and with what object, and why. She hates him like poison now. I could read it on her face. He's taken her friend from her. They'd chummed together since they were both in pigtails, at the same orphanage."

"All right. What about Opportunity, your second factor?"

"He rings the bell there, too. And again it doesn't do us any good. Sure, he admits he was sitting out front at the matinee day before yesterday. But so was he a dozen times before. Sure, he admits he went backstage to her dressing-room, after she'd gone back to it alone and while the other two were still onstage. But so had he a dozen times before. He claims it was already missing then. She told him so, and asked him to go out to get her another bottle. But who's to prove that? She's not alive, and neither of the two other girls had come off the stage yet."

"Well, what happened to the second bottle that would have saved her life?"

"He paid for it. The clerk wrapped it for him. He started out holding it in his hand the way one does any circular package. And at the drugstore entrance, he collided with some one coming in. It was jarred out of his grasp, and it shattered on the floor!"

And as if he could sense what the lieutenant was going to say, he hurriedly added: "There were witnesses galore to the incident; the clerk himself, the soda jerk, the cashier. I questioned every one of them. Not one could say for sure that it wasn't a genuine accident. Not one could swear that he'd seen Willis actually relax his hand and let it fall, or deliberately get in this other party's way."

"Then why didn't he go back and tell her? Why did he leave her there like that with this stuff insidiously injuring her system, so that she had to send this Jimmy out to see if he could get hold of any for her?"

"We can't get anything on him for that, either. He did the natural thing; he went scouting around for it in other places—the way a man would, who was ashamed to come back empty-handed and tell her he'd just smashed the one bottle they had left in stock, afraid she'd bawl him out maybe." And through thinned lips he added acidly: "Everything he did was so natural. That's why we can't get him!"

The lieutenant said: "There's an important little point lurking in that smashed-bottle angle. Did he know it was the last bottle on hand *before* he dropped it, or did he only find out after he stepped back to the counter and tried to get another?"

Benson nodded. "I bore down heavy on that with the drug clerk. Unless Willis was deaf, dumb and blind, he knew that that was the last bottle in the store before he started away from the counter with it. The clerk not only had a hard time finding it, but when he finally located it, he remarked: 'This is the last one we've got left.' "

"Then that accident was no accident."

"Can *you* prove it?" was all Benson said.

The lieutenant answered that by discarding it. "Go ahead," he said sourly.

———◆———

"I checked with every one of the other places he told me he'd been to after leaving there, and he *had* asked for it in each one. They corroborated him on that. He wasn't in much danger of coming across it anywhere else and he knew it! The drug clerk had not only forewarned him that he didn't think he'd find it anywhere else, but his wife must have told him the same thing before she sent him out." And screwing his mouth up, he said: "But it looked good for the record, and it kept him away from the theater—while she was dying by inches from cellular asphyxiation, without knowing it!"

"Didn't he go back at all? Did he stay out from then on?"

"No one saw him come back, not a soul. I made sure of that before I put it up to him." Benson smiled bleakly. "I know what you're thinking there, and I thought of that, too. If he didn't go back at all, then he wasn't responsible for making the remover disappear in the first place. Because it was back in the drawer before the next matinee, I found it there myself. Now get the point involved.

"He had a choice between the natural thing and the completely exonerating thing. But an exonerating thing that would have meant behaving a little oddly. The natural thing for a man sent out on an errand by his wife is to return eventually, even if it's an hour later, even if it's only to report that he was unsuccessful. The exonerating thing, in this case, was for him to stay out for good. All he had to do was claim he never went back, and he was absolutely in the clear, absolutely eliminated."

"Well?" The lieutenant could hardly wait for the answer.

"He played it straight all the way through. He admitted, of his own accord and without having been seen by anybody, that he stopped back for a minute to tell her he hadn't been able to get it, after chasing all over the Forties for the stuff. And that, of course, is when the mysteriously missing bottle got back into the drawer."

The lieutenant was almost goggle-eyed. "Well I'll be—! She was still alive, the murder hadn't even been completed yet, and he was already removing the traces of it by replacing the bottle where he'd taken it from!"

"The timing of her act guaranteed that she was already as good as dead, even with the bottle back within her reach. She couldn't take the gilt off now for another three hours. Using it continuously had already lowered her resistance. That brief breathing spell she would have had between shows spelled the difference between life and death.

"In other words, Lieutenant, he left her alive, with fifty people around her who talked to her, rubbed shoulders with her in the wings, after he'd gone. And later she even danced onstage before a couple hundred more. But he'd already murdered her."

"But you say he didn't have to admit he stopped back at the theater, and yet he did."

"Sure, but to me that doesn't prove his innocence, that only proves his guilt and infernal cleverness. By avoiding the slightest lie, the slightest deviation in his account of his actual movements, he's much safer than by grasping at a chance of automatic, complete vindication. Somebody just *might* have seen him come back, he couldn't be sure."

———⟨⋄⟩———

He took a deep breath. "There it all is, Lieutenant: motive, opportunity and method. And it don't do us much good, does it? There isn't any more evidence to be had. There never will be. I've been beating him all night, but there's nothing more to uncover— because it all *is* uncovered already. We couldn't get him on a disorderly conduct charge on all of it put together, much less for murder. What do I do with him now?"

The lieutenant took a long time answering, as though he hated to have to. Finally he did. "We'll have to turn him loose; we can't hold him indefinitely."

"Gee, I hate to see him walk out of here free," Benson said.

"There's no use busting your brains about it. It's a freak that only happens maybe once in a thousand times—but it happened this time."

Later that same morning Benson walked out to the entrance of the precinct house with Willis, after the formalities of release had been gone through. Willis had a lot of court-plaster here and there, but he was free again. That was what mattered. Court-plaster wears off after awhile; several thousand volts of electricity does not.

"Well, I guess you think you're pretty mart," Benson said taciturnly.

Willis said: "That's the word for people that have held out something, getting away with it. I got a beating for something I didn't do. Unlucky is the word for me, not smart."

Benson stopped short at the top of the entrance steps, marking the end of his authority. He smiled. "Well, if we couldn't get anything out of you in there last night, I didn't expect to get anything out of you out here right now." His mouth thinned. "Here's the street. Beat it."

Willis went down the steps, walked on a short distance alone and unhindered. Then he decided to cross over to the opposite side of the street. When he had reached it, he stopped a minute and looked back.

Benson was still standing there on the police-station steps, looking after him. Their stares met. Benson couldn't read his look, whether it conveyed mockery or relief or just casual indifference. But for that matter, Willis couldn't read Benson's either; whether it conveyed regret or philosophic acceptance of defeat or held a vague promise that things between them weren't over yet. And it wasn't because of the sizable distance that separated them, either; it was because the thoughts of both of them were locked up in their minds.

There was a brittle quality of long-smoldering rancor about her, even when she first opened the door, even before she'd had time to see who was standing there. She must have just got home from the show. She still had her coat and hat on. But she was already holding a little jigger glass of colorless liquid between two of her fingers, as if trying to cauterize inner resentment that was continually gnawing at her. Her eyes traveled over his form from head to foot and back again.

"Been letting any more killers go since I saw you last?" she said sultrily.

"You've taken that pretty much to heart, haven't you?" Benson answered levelly.

"Why wouldn't I? Her ghost powders its nose on the bench next to me twice a day! A couple performances ago I caught myself turning around and saying: 'Did you get paid this week, An—' before I stopped to think." She emptied the jigger, backfired slightly. "And do you know what keeps the soreness from healing? Because that person that did it is still around, untouched, unpunished. Because he got away with it. You know who I mean or do I have to break out with a name?"

"You can't prove it, any more than we could, so why bring up a name?"

"Prove it! *Prove* it! You make me sick." She went back and refilled the jigger. Her face was livid. "You're the police! Why weren't you able to get him?"

"You talk like a fool," he said patiently. "You talk like we let him go purposely. D'you think I enjoyed watching him walk out scot-free under my nose? And that ain't all. I've been passed over on the promotion list, on account of it. They didn't *say* it was that; they didn't say it was anything. They didn't have to. I can figure it out for myself. It's the first blank I've drawn in six years. It's eating at my insides, too, like yours."

She relented at the signs of nursed bitterness that matched her own. "Misery likes company, I guess. Come on in, as long as you're here, detective-by-courtesy. Have a stab," she said grudgingly, and pushed the gin slightly toward him.

They sat in brooding silence for several minutes, two frustrated people. Finally she spoke again, a cruller of white hate outlining her mouth. "He had the nerve to put *his* flowers on her grave! Imagine, flowers from the killer to the one he killed! I found them there when I went up myself, before the matinee today, to leave some roses of my own. The caretaker told me whose they were. I tore them in a thousand pieces when he wasn't looking."

"I know," he said vindictively. "He goes up twice a week, leaves fresh flowers each time. I've been casing him night and day. The hypocritical rat! All the way through from the beginning, he's done the natural thing. He does it whether he thinks anyone's watching or not, and that's the safe way to do it."

He refilled his own jigger without asking her permission. He laughed harshly. "But he's already found a refill, just the same. He's not pining away. I cased his flat while he was out of it today, and I found enough evidence to show there's some blonde been hanging around to console him. Gilt hairpins on the kitchen floor, a double set of dirty dishes—two of everything—in the sink. He's probably just waiting for the temperature to go down enough, before he hooks up with her."

<hr />

She lidded her eyes, touched a hand to her own jet-black hair. "I'm not surprised," she said huskily. "That would be about his speed." She got up suddenly. "These jiggers are too small." She came back with a tumbler, a third full. "Maybe you can still get something on him through her," she suggested balefully.

He shook his head. "He can go around with ten blondes if he feels like it. He's within his rights. We can't hold him just for that alone—"

"What's the matter with the laws these days?" she said almost savagely. "Here we are, you and I, sitting here in this room. We both know he killed Annie Willis. You're drawing pay from the police department, and he's moving around immune and fancy-free only a few blocks away from us at this very minute!"

He nodded as though he agreed with her. "They fail you every once in awhile," he admitted gloomily, "the statutes as they are written down on the books. They slip a cog and let someone fall through—" Then he went on: "But there's an older law than the statutes we work under. I don't know if you ever heard of it or not. It's called the Mosaic Law. 'An eye for an eye, and a tooth for a tooth.'

And when the modern set-up goes back on you, that one never does. It's short and sweet, got no amendments, dodges or habeas corpuses to clutter it up. 'An eye for an eye, and a tooth for a tooth.' "

"I like the way that sounds better," she said.

"You're getting a little lit. I shouldn't be talking like this."

"I'm not getting lit. I understand every word you say. But more important still, *I hear the words you're not saying.*"

He just looked at her, and she looked at him. They were like two fencers, warily circling around each other to find an opening. She got up, moved over to the window, stared grimly out toward the traffic intersection at the corner ahead. "Green light," she reported. Then she turned toward him with a bitter, puckered smile. "Green light. That means go ahead—doesn't it?"

"Green light," he murmured. "That means go ahead—if you care to." The gin was making him talk a little more freely, although that was the only sign of it he showed. "The man that throws the switch in the deathhouse at Sing Sing, what makes him a legal executioner and not a murderer? The modern statutes. The Mosaic Code can have its legal executioners, too, who are not just murderers."

She had come over close to him again.

"But never," he went on, looking straight up at her, "exceed or distort its short, simple tenet. Never repay the gun with the knife, or the knife with the club. Then that's murder, not the Mosaic Code any more. In the same way, if the State executioner shot the condemned man on his way to the chair, or poisoned him in his cell, then he wouldn't be a legal executioner any more, he'd be just a murderer himself." And he repeated it again for her slowly. " 'An eye for an eye, a tooth for a tooth.' Annie Willis met her death by having something withheld from her that her safety required. No weapon was used on Annie Willis, remember."

———◆———

"Yes," she said with flaming dreaminess. "And I know where there's a trunk that belongs to me, down in a basement storage room, seldom entered, seldom used. One of these big, thick theatrical trunks, roomy enough to carry around the props for a whole act. I left it behind when I moved out. I was going to send for it but—" She didn't finish it.

He looked down at his empty jigger, as if he was listening intently to her, but without looking at her.

"And if I came to you, for instance, and said: 'What's been bothering you and me both has been taken care of,' how would you receive me—as a criminal under the modern law or a legal executioner under the old one?"

He looked straight up at her with piercing directness. "The modern law failed you and me, didn't it? Then what right would I have to judge you by it?"

She murmured half audibly, as if endeavoring to try him out: "Then why not you? Why me?"

"The injury was done to you, not me. A friend is a personal belonging, a professional disappointment isn't. Nothing was done to me personally. Under the Mosaic Law, a frustrated job can only be repaid by another frustrated job, by making the person who injured you suffer a like disappointment in *his* work."

She laughed dangerously. "I can do better than that," she said softly.

She kept shaking her head, looking at him from time to time as if she still found the situation almost past belief. "The strangest things never get down on the record books! They wouldn't be believed if they did! Here you are, sitting in my room, a man drawing pay from the police department, with a shield in your pocket at this very minute—" She didn't finish it.

"I'm a little bit tight on your gin," he said, getting up, "and we haven't been talking."

She held the door open for him. "No," she smiled, "we haven't been talking. You weren't here tonight, and nothing was said. But perfect understanding doesn't need words. I'll probably see you again to let you know how—what we haven't been talking about is coming along."

The door closed and First Grade Detective Benson went down the stairs with an impassive face.

——◆——

What followed was even more incredible yet. Or, at least, the surroundings it occurred in were. A cop came in to him, at the precinct house three nights later, said: "There's a lady out there asking for you, Benson. Won't state her business."

Benson said: "I think I know who you mean. Look, Corrigan, you know that little end room on the left, at the back of the hall? Is there anyone in there right now?"

The cop said: "Naw, there's never anyone in there."

"Take her back there, will you? I'll be back there."

He got there first. She stood outlined in the open doorway first, watching the cop return along the hall to where he'd come from, before she'd come in.

He didn't pretend to be preoccupied going over papers or anything like that, possibly because there were none to be found in there. It was one of those blind spots that even the most bustling, overcrowded buildings occasionally develop, unused, avoided the greater part of the time by the personnel. He acted slightly frightened. Perhaps startled, taken aback by her unexpected effrontery, would be a better word. He kept pacing nervously back and forth, waiting for her to come in.

When she finally turned away from seeing the cop off, she came in and closed the door after her. He said: "Couldn't you have waited until I dropped over to see you?"

"How did I know when you'd be around again? I felt like I couldn't wait another half hour to get it off my chest." There was something almost gloating in the way she looked around her. "Is it safe to talk here?"

"Sure, if you keep your voice down." He went over to the door, opened it, looked along the passageway outside, closed it again. "It's all right."

She said, half-mockingly, with that intimacy of one conspirator for another: "No dictaphones around?"

He was too on edge to share her bantering mood. "Don't be stupid," he snapped. "How did I know you were going to pull a raw stunt like this? This is the last place I ever expected you to—"

She lit a cigarette, preened herself. "You think you're looking at a cheap ballad singer on a burlesque circuit, don't you?"

"What am I looking at, then?"

"You're looking at a legal executioner, under the Mosaic Code. I have a case of Biblical justice to report. I had a friend I valued very highly, and she was caused to die by having the skin of her body deprived of air. Now the man who did that to her is going to die sometime during the night, if he hasn't already, by having the skin of *his* body—and his lungs and his heart—deprived of air in the same way."

He lit a cigarette to match hers. His hands were so steady—too steady, rigid almost—that you could tell they weren't really. He was forcing them to be that way. His color was paler than it had been when he first came in.

"What have you got to say to that?" She clasped her own sides in a parody of macabre delight.

"I'll tell you in a minute." He went over to the door, opened it and looked out again, as if to make sure there was no one out there to overhear. He'd dropped his cigarette on the way over to it.

She misunderstood. "Don't be so jittery—" she began scornfully.

He'd raised his voice suddenly, before she knew what to expect. It went booming down the desolate hallway. "Corrigan! C'mere a minute!" A blue-suited figure had joined his in the opening before she knew what was happening. He pointed in toward her.

"*Arrest this woman for murder!* Hold her here in this room until I get back! I'm making you personally responsible for her!"

A bleat of smothered fury ripped from her. "Why, you dirty, doublecrossing— The guy ain't even dead yet—"

"I'm not arresting you for the murder of Frank Willis. I'm arresting you for the murder of his wife, Annie Willis, over a month and a half ago at the New Rotterdam Theater!"

The greater part of it came winging back from the far end of the hallway, along which he was moving fast on his way to try to save a man's life.

⟫◆⟪

They came trooping down single file, fast, into the gloom. White poker chips of light glanced off the damp, cemented brick walls from their torches. The janitor was in the lead. He poked at a switch by his sense of memory alone, and a feeble parody of electricity illuminated part of the ceiling and the floor immediately under it, nothing else.

"I ain't seen him since yesterday at noon," he told them in a frightened voice. "I seen him going out then. That was the last I seen of him. Here it is over here, gents. This door."

They fanned out around it in a half-circle. All the separate poker chips of torchlight came to a head in one big wagon wheel on it. It was fireproof; nail-studded iron, rusty but stout. But it was fastened simply by a padlock clasping two thick staples.

"I remember now, my wife said something about his asking her for the key to here, earlier in the evening while I was out," the janitor said. "So he was still all right then."

"Yes, he was still all right *then*," Benson agreed shortly. "Get that thing. Hurry up!" A crowbar was inserted behind the padlock chain; two of the men with him got on one end of it and started to pry. Something snapped. The unopened lock bounced up, and they swung the storage-space door out with a grating sound.

The torch-beams converged inside and lit it up. It was small and cramped. The air was already musty and unfit to breathe—even the unconfined air at large between its four sides—and it was lifeless. All the discarded paraphernalia of forgotten tenants over the years choked it. Cartons, empty packing cases, a dismantled iron bed frame, even a kid's sled with one runner missing. But there was a clear space left between the entrance and the one large trunk that loomed up in it, like a towering headstone on a tomb.

It stood there silent, inscrutable. On the floor before it lay, in eloquent meaning, a single large lump of coal brought from the outside part of the basement and discarded after it had served its purpose. Two smaller fragments had chipped off it, lay close by.

"A blow on the head with that would daze anyone long enough to—" Benson scuffed it out of the way with his foot. "Hurry up, fellows. She'd only just left here when she looked me up. It's not a full hour yet. The seams may be warped with age, there's still a slim chance—"

They pushed the scared, white-lipped janitor back out of their way. Axe blades began to slash around the rusted snaplock. "Not too deep," Benson warned. "Give it flat strokes from the side, or you're liable to cut in and—Got that pulmotor ready?"

The axes held off at his signal and he pulled the dangling lock off the splintered seams with his bare hands. They all jumped in,

began pulling in opposite directions. The trunk split open verti-
cally. A face stared sightlessly into the focused torchbeams, a contorted mask of strangulation and unconsciousness that had been
pressed despairingly up against the seam as close as it could go, to
drink in the last precious molecule or two of air.

—❦—

Willis' body, looking shrunken, tumbled out into their arms. They
carried him out into the more open part of the basement, one hand
that ended in mangled nails trailing inertly after him. An oxygen
tank was hooked up, and a silent, grim struggle for life began in the
eerie light of the shadowy basement.

Twice, they wanted to quit, and Benson wouldn't let them. "If
he goes, that makes a murderer out of me! And I won't be made a
murderer out of! We're going to bring him back, if we stay here
until tomorrow night!"

And then in the middle of the interminable silence, a simple,
quiet announcement from the man in charge of the squad: "He's
back, Benson. He's going again!"

Somebody let out a long, whistling breath of relief. It was a
detective who had just escaped being made into a murderer.

At the hospital later, in the early hours of the morning, when he
was able to talk again, Willis told him the little there was to tell.

"She showed up and said she wanted to get something out of
that trunk she'd left behind here in our care, when she'd moved
away. I got the key to the storage room from the janitor's wife. I
should have tumbled she had something up her sleeve when she
asked me not to mention who it was for. Let them think I wanted
it for myself. Then she got me to go down there with her by pretending there were some things of Annie's in the trunk, from their
days in show business together, that she wanted to give back to me.

"I didn't open my mouth to her, didn't say a word. I was afraid
to trust myself, afraid if I came out with what was on my mind, I'd
beat her half-senseless and only get in more trouble with you
police guys. I couldn't wait to get rid of her, to see the last of her—

"I even helped her to open the trunk, because it was pretty
heavy to handle. Then she asked me to bend down and see if I

could reach something that was all the way down at the bottom of one of the two halves, and I stepped between them like a fool.

"Something that felt like a big rock hit the back of my head, and before my senses had a chance to clear, the two sides had swung closed on me like a—" He shuddered. "Like a coffin when you're still alive." He swung one finger-bandaged paw in front of his eyes to shut out the recollection. "The rest was pretty awful."

—————◈—————

The lieutenant came in, holding the confession in his hands. Benson followed.

"She put away?"

"Yes, sir."

The lieutenant went ahead, reading the confession. Benson waited in silence until he'd finished. The lieutenant looked up finally. "This'll do. It's strong enough to hold her on, anyway. You got results, but I don't get the technique. What was this business of her coming here and confiding in you that she'd made an attempt on Willis' life tonight, and how does that tie in with the murder of Annie Willis? You hit the nail on the head. This confession proves that, but I don't follow your line of reasoning. I miss the connecting links."

Benson said: "Here was the original equation. A wife in the middle, a man and a woman on the ends. She was in the way, but of which one of them? Vilma Lyons claimed it was Willis who had a pash on her. Willis didn't claim anything; the man as a rule won't.

"I watched them to see which would approach the other. Neither one did. The innocent party, because he had never cared in the first place; the guilty, because he or she had a guilty conscience, was not only afraid they were being watched by us, but also that the other might catch on in some way, connect the wife's death with him or her, if they made a move too soon after.

"But still I couldn't tell which was which—although my money was still on Willis, up to the very end.

"Here was the technique. When I saw neither of them was going to tip a hand, I tipped it, instead. There's nothing like a shot of good, scalding jealousy in the arm for tipping the hand. I went to *both* of them alike, gave them the same buildup treatment. I was bitter and sore, because I'd muffed the job. It was a mark against me on my record, and so on. In Willis' case, because we'd already held him for it once. I had to vary it a little, make him think I'd changed my mind, now thought it was Vilma, but couldn't get her for it.

"In other words, I gave them both the same unofficial all-clear to go ahead and exact retribution personally. And I lit the same spark to both their fuses. I told Willis that Vilma had taken up with some other guy; I told her he had taken up with some other girl.

"One fuse fizzled out. The other flared and exploded. One of them didn't give a damn, because he never had. The other, having already committed murder to gain the object of her affections, saw red, would have rather seen him dead than have somebody else get him.

"You see, Lieutenant, murder always comes easier the second time than the first. Given equal provocation, whichever one of those two had committed the murder the first time, I felt wouldn't hesitate to commit it a second time. The one that hadn't, probably couldn't be incited to contemplate it, no matter what the circumstances. Willis had loved his wife. He smoldered with hate when I told him we had evidence Vilma had killed her, but he didn't act on the hints I gave him. It never occurred to him to.

"Only one took advantage of the leeway I seemed to be giving them, and went ahead. That one was the real murderer. Having murdered once, she didn't stop at murder a second time.

"It's true," he conceded, "that that's not evidence that would have done us very much good by itself, in trying to prove the other case. But what it did manage to do was make a dent in the murderer's armor. All we had to do was keep hacking away and she finally crumbled. Being caught in the act the second time weakened her self-confidence in her immunity for what she'd done the first time, gave us a psychological upper-hand over her, and she finally came through." He indicated the confession.

"Well," pondered the lieutenant, stroking his chin, "it's not a technique that I'd care to have you men make a habit of using very frequently. In fact, it's a damn dangerous one to monkey around with, but it got results this time, and that's the proof of any pudding."

AFTERWORD TO "THE FATAL FOOTLIGHTS"

"The Fatal Footlights" (*Detective Fiction Weekly*, June 14, 1941) seems to have been intended for Woolrich's New York Landmarks series, and for a recluse he captures remarkably well the tawdry glitter of a cheap 42nd Street burlesque house. The early scenes set the stage and lead up to the discovery of the means of Gilda's death, which is as bizarre as anything in the Woolrich canon of weird murder methods; but then the homicide detective Benson morphs into a psychotic sadist and the story into one of the most chilling of Woolrich's Noir Cop thrillers. The murder-by-gilding gimmick seems somehow to have come to the attention of Ian Fleming, who used it almost twenty years later in his classic James Bond novel *Goldfinger* (1959).

3 Kills for 1

CHAPTER ONE

Come Along With Me

That night, like all the other nights before it, around a quarter to twelve Gary Severn took his hat off the hook nearest the door, turned and said to his pretty, docile little wife in the room behind him: "Guess I'll go down to the corner, bring in the midnight edition."

"All right, dear," she nodded, just as she had on all the other nights that had come before.

He opened the door, then stood there undecidedly on the threshold. "I feel kind of tired," he yawned, backing a hand to his mouth. "Maybe I ought to skip it. It wouldn't kill me to do without it one night. I usually fall asleep before I can turn to page two, anyway."

"Then don't bother getting it, dear. Let it go if you feel that way," she acquiesced. "Why put yourself out? After all, it's not that important."

"No, it isn't, is it?" he admitted. For a moment he seemed about to step inside again and close the door after him. Then he shrugged. "Oh well," he said, "I may as well go now that I've got my hat on. I'll be back in a couple of minutes." He closed the door from the outside.

Who knows what is important, what isn't important? Who is to recognize the turning-point that turns out to be a trifle, the trifle that becomes a turning-point?

A pause at the door, a yawn, a three-cent midnight paper that he wouldn't have remained awake long enough to finish anyway.

He came out on the street. Just a man on his way to the corner for a newspaper, and then back again. It was the 181st day of the year, and on 180 other nights before this one he had come out at this same hour, for this same thing. No, one night there'd been a blizzard and he hadn't. 179 nights, then.

He walked down to the corner, and turned it, and went one block over the long way, to where the concession was located. It was just a wooden trestle set up on the sidewalk, with the papers stacked on it. The tabs were always the first ones out, and they were on it already. But his was a standard-size, and it came out the last of all of them, possibly due to the complexities of make-up.

The man who kept the stand knew him by his paper, although he didn't know his name or anything else about him. "Not up yet," he greeted him. "Any minute now."

Why is it, when a man has read one particular paper for any length of time, he will refuse to buy another in place of it, even though the same news is in both? Another trifle?

Gary Severn said: "I'll take a turn around the block. It'll probably be here by the time I get back."

The delivery trucks left the plant downtown at 11:30, but the paper never hit the stands this far up much before twelve, due to a number of variables such as traffic-lights and weather which were never the same twice. It had often been a little delayed, just as it was tonight.

He went up the next street, the one behind his own, rounded the upper corner of that, then over, and back into his own again. He swung one hand, kept his other pocketed. He whistled a few inaccurate bars of *Elmer's Tune*. Then a few even more inaccurate bars of *Rose O'Day*. Then he quit whistling. It had just been an expression of the untroubled vacancy of his mind, anyway. His thoughts went something like this: "Swell night. Wonder what star that is up there, that one just hitting the roof? Never did know much about them. That Colonna sure was funny on the air tonight." With a grin of reminiscent appreciation. "Gee I'm sleepy. Wish I hadn't come out just now." Things like that.

He'd arrived back at his own doorway from the opposite direction by now. He slackened a little, hesitated, on the point of going in and letting the paper go hang. Then he went on anyway. "I'm out now. It'll just take a minute longer. There and back." Trifle.

———◆———

The delivery truck had just arrived. He saw the bale being pitched off the back to the asphalt, for the dealer to pick up, as he rounded the corner once more. By the time he'd arrived at the stand the dealer had hauled it onto the sidewalk, cut the binding, and stacked the papers for sale on his board. A handful of other customers who had been waiting around closed in. The dealer was kept busy handing them out and making change.

Gary Severn wormed his way in through the little cluster of customers, reached for a copy from the pile, and found that somebody else had taken hold of it at the same time. The slight tug from two different directions brought their eyes around toward one another. Probably neither would have seen the other, that is to look at squarely, if it hadn't been for that.

It was nothing. Gary Severn said pleasantly, "Go ahead, help yourself," and relinquished that particular copy for the next one below it.

"Must think he knows me," passed through his inattentive mind. The other's glance had come back a second time, whereas his own hadn't. He paid no further heed. He handed the dealer his nickel, got back two cents, turned and went off, reading the headlines as he went by the aid of the fairly adequate shop-lights there were along there.

He was dimly aware, as he did so, of numbers of other footsteps coming along the same way he was. People who had just now bought their papers as he had, and had this same direction to follow. He turned the corner and diverged up into his own street. All but one pair of footsteps went on off the long way, along the avenue, died out. One pair turned off and came up his way, as he had, but he took no notice.

He couldn't read en route any more, because he'd left the lights behind. The paper turned blue and blurred. He folded it and postponed the rest until he should get inside.

The other footfalls were still coming along, a few yards back. He didn't look around. Why should he? The streets were free to everyone. Others lived along this street as well as he. Footsteps behind him had no connection with him.

He reached his own doorway. As he turned aside he started to drag up his key. The other footsteps would go on past now, naturally. Not that his mind was occupied with them. Simply the membranes of his ears. He'd pulled out the building street-door, had one foot already through to the other side. The footsteps had come abreast—

A hand came down on his shoulder.

"Just a minute."

He turned. The man who had been buying a paper, the one who had reached for the same one he had. Was he going to pick a quarrel about such a petty—

"Identify yourself."

"Why?"

"I said identify yourself." He did something with his free hand, almost too quick for Gary Severn to take in its significance. Some sort of a high-sign backed with metal.

"What's that for?"

"That's so you'll identify yourself."

"I'm Gary Severn. I live in here."

"All right. You'd better come with me." The hand on his shoulder had shifted further down his arm now, tightened.

Severn answered with a sort of peaceable doggedness: "Oh no, I won't go with you unless you tell me what you want with me. You can't come up to me like this outside my house and—"

"You're not resisting arrest, are you?" the other man suggested.

"I wouldn't."

"Arrest?" Severn said blankly. "Is this arrest? Arrest for what?"

A note of laughter sounded from the other, without his grim lips curving in accompaniment to it. "I don't have to tell you that, do I? Arrest for murder. For the worst kind of murder there is. Murder of a police officer. In the course of an armed robbery. On Farragut Street." He spaced each clipped phrase. "Now do you remember?"

Arrest for murder.

He said it over to himself. It didn't even frighten him. It had no meaning. It was like being mistaken for Dutch Schultz or— Some sort of a freak mixup. The thing was, he wouldn't get to bed until all hours now probably, and that might make him late in the morning. And just when he was so tired, too.

All he could find to say was a very foolish little thing. "Can I go inside first and leave my paper? My wife's waiting in there, and I'd like to let her know I may be gone for half an hour or so—"

The man nodded permission, said: "Sure, I'll go inside with you a minute, while you tell your wife and leave your paper."

A life ends, and the note it ends on is: "Can I go inside first and leave my paper?"

⬤

On the wall was a typical optician's sight-chart, beginning with a big beetling jumbo capital at the top and tapering down to a line of fingernail-size type at the bottom. The detectives had been occupied in trying themselves out on it while they were waiting. Most, from a distance of across the room, had had to stop at the fourth line below the bottom. Normal eyesight. One man had been able to get down as far as the third, but he'd missed two of the ten letters in that one. No one had been able to get down below that.

The door on the opposite side opened and the Novak woman was brought in. She'd brought her knitting.

"Sit down there. We'd like to try you out on this chart first."

Mrs. Novak tipped her shoulders. "Glasses you're giving out?"

"How far down can you read?"

"All the way."

"Can you read the bottom line?"

Again Mrs. Novak tipped her shoulders. "Who couldn't?"

"Nine out of ten people couldn't," one of the detectives murmured to the man next to him.

She rattled it off like someone reading a scare-head. "p,t,b,k,j,h,i,y,q,a."

Somebody whistled. "Far-sighted."

She dropped her eyes complacently to her needles again. "This I don't know about. I only hope you gentlemen'll going to be through soon. While you got me coming in and out of here, my business ain't getting my whole attention."

The door opened and Gary Severn had come in. Flanked. His whole life was flanked now.

The rest of it went quick. The way death does.

She looked up, held it, nodded. "That's him. That's the man I saw running away right after the shots."

Gary Severn didn't say anything.

One of the detectives present—his name was Eric Rogers—didn't say anything either. He was just there, a witness to it.

The other chief witness' name was Storm. He was a certified accountant, he dealt in figures. He was, as witnesses go, a man of good will. He made the second line from the bottom on the chart, better than any of the detectives had, even if not as good as Mrs. Novak. But then he was wearing glasses. But then—once more—he'd also been wearing them at the time the fleeing murderer had bowled him over on the sidewalk, only a few doors away from the actual crime, and snapped a shot at him which miraculously missed. He'd promptly lain inert and feigned death, to avoid a possible second and better-aimed shot.

"You realize how important this is?"

"I realize. That's why I'm holding back. That's why I don't like to say I'm a hundred per cent sure. I'd say I'm seventy-five per cent sure that it's him."

"What you'd like to say," he was cautioned, "has nothing to do with it. Either you are sure or you aren't. Sureness has no percentages. Either it's one hundred or it's zero. Keep emotion out of this. Forget that it's a man. You're an accountant. It's a column of figures to you. There's only one right answer. Give us that answer. Now we're going to try you again."

Gary Severn came in again.

Storm moved his figures up. "Ninety per cent sure," he said privately to the lieutenant standing behind him. "I still got ten per cent doubt left."

"*Yes or no!*"

"I can't say no, when I got ninety percent on the yes-side and only—"

"YES or NO!"

It came slow, but it came. It came low, but it came. "Yes."

Gary Severn didn't make a sound. He'd stopped saying anything long ago. Just the sound of one's own voice, unheard, unanswered, what good is that?

The detective named Rogers, he was there in the background again. He just took it in like the rest. There was nothing he felt called on to say.

———◈◆◈———

The news-dealer, his name was Mike Mosconi, sat in jackknife position in the chair and moved his hat uneasily around in his hands while he told them: "No, I don't know his name and I'm not even sure which house he lives in, but I know him by sight as good as you can know anybody, and he's telling the truth about that. He hasn't missed buying a paper off me, I don't think more than once or twice in the whole year."

"But he did stay away once or twice," the lieutenant said. "And what about this twenty-second of June, is that one of those once or twices he stayed away?"

The news-dealer said unhappily: "I'm out there on the street every night in the year, gents. It's hard for me to pick out a certain night by the date and say for sure that that was the one out of all of 'em—but if you can get me the weather for that night, I can do better for you."

"Get him the weather for that night," the lieutenant consented.

The weather came back. "It was clear and bright on the twenty-second of June."

"Then he bought his paper from me that night," Mike Mosconi said inflexibly. "It's the God's honest truth. I'm sure of it and you can be too. The only one or two times he didn't show up was when—"

"How long did it take him to buy his paper each time?" the lieutenant continued remorselessly.

Mike Mosconi looked down reluctantly. "How long does it take to buy a paper? You drop three cents, you pick it up, you walk away—"

"But there's something else you haven't told us. At what time each night did he do this quick little buying of the paper? Was it the same time always, or did it vary, or what time was it?"

Mike Mosconi looked up in innocent surprise. "It was the same time always. It never varied. How could it? He always gets the midnight edition of the *Herald-Times*. It never hits my stand until quarter to twelve—he never came out until then. He knew it wouldn't be there if he did—"

"The twenty-second of June . . . ?"

"Any night, I don't care which it was. If he came at all, he came between quarter of and twelve o'clock."

"You can go, Mosconi."

Mosconi went. The lieutenant turned to Severn.

"The murder was at ten o'clock. What kind of an alibi was that?"

Severn said in quiet resignation: "The only one I had."

CHAPTER TWO

DEATH CELL

Gates didn't look like a criminal. But then there is no typical criminal look, the public at large only thinks there is. He was a big husky black-haired man, who gave a misleading impression of slow-moving genial good-nature totally unwarranted by the known facts of his career. He also had an air of calm self-assurance, that most likely came more from a lack of imagination than anything else.

He said: "So what do you expect me to say? If I say no, this ain't the guy, that means *I* was there but with someone else. If I say yes, it is him, that means the same thing. Don't worry—Mr. Strassburger, my counsel, wised me up about the kind of trick questions you guys like to ask. Like when they want to know, 'Have you quit beating your wife?' "

He looked them over self-possessedly. "All I'm saying is, I wasn't there myself. So if I wasn't there myself, how can there be a right guy or a wrong guy that was there with me? *I'm* the wrong guy, more than anybody else." He tapped himself on the breastbone with emphatic conviction. "Get the right guy in my place first, and then he'll give you the right second guy."

He smiled a little at them. Very little. "All I'm saying, now and at any other time, is—I never saw this guy before in my life. If you want it that way, you can have it."

The lieutenant smiled back at him. Also very little. "And you

weren't on Farragut Street that night? And you didn't take part in
the murder of Sergeant O'Neill?"

"That," said Gates with steely confidence, "goes with it."

———◆◆———

Gates got up, but not fast or jerkily, with the same slowness that
had always characterized him. He wiped the sweat off his palms by
running them lightly down his sides. As though he were going to
shake hands with somebody.

He was. He was going to shake hands with death.

He wasn't particularly frightened. Not that he was particularly
brave. It was just that he didn't have very much imagination.
Rationalizing, he knew that he wasn't going to be alive any more
ten minutes from now. Yet he wasn't used to casting his imagination ten minutes ahead of him, he'd always kept it by him in the
present. He couldn't visualize it. So he wasn't as unnerved by it as
the average man would have been.

Yet he was troubled by something else. The ridges in his forehead showed that.

"Are you ready, my son?"

"I'm ready."

"Lean on me."

"I don't have to, Father. My legs'll hold up. It ain't far." It was
made as a simple statement of fact, without sarcasm or rebuke
intended.

They left the death cell.

"Listen, that Severn kid," Gates said in a quiet voice, looking
straight ahead. "He's following me in in five minutes. I admit I
did it. I held out until now, to see if I'd get a reprieve or not. I
didn't get the reprieve, so it don't matter now any more. All right,
I killed O'Neill, I admit it. But the other guy, the guy with me
that helped me kill him, it wasn't Severn. Are you listening? Can
you hear me? It was a guy named Donny Blake. I never saw
Severn before in my life until they arrested him. For God's sake,
tell them that, Father! All right, I'm sorry for swearing at such a
time. But tell them that, Father! You've got to tell them that!
There's only five minutes left."

"Why did you wait so long, my son?"

"I told you, the reprieve—I been telling the warden since last night. I think he believes me, but I don't think he can get them to do anything about it, the others, over him— Listen, *you* tell him, Father! You believe me, don't you? The dead don't lie!"

His voice rose, echoed hollowly in the short passage. "Tell them not to touch that kid! He's not the guy that was with me—"

And he said probably the strangest thing that was ever said by a condemned man on the way to execution. "Father, don't walk any further with me! Leave me now, don't waste time. Go to the warden, tell him!"

"Pray, my son. Pray for yourself. You are my charge—"

"But I don't need you, Father. Can't you take this off my mind? Don't let them bring that kid in here after me!"

"Yes, my son." No need to tell the doomed man that Gary Severn had already preceded him into death.

Something cold touched the crown of his head. The priest's arm slowly drew away, receded into life.

"Don't forget what you promised me, Father. Don't let them—" And then, in a tired voice: "Helen, I love you. I—"

The hood, falling over his face, cut the rest of it short.

The current waned, then waxed, then waned again . . . .

———⊰⬦⊱———

They didn't have the chart on the wall any more. It had done them poor service. The door opened and Mrs. Novak was ushered in. She had her knitting with her again. Only she was making a different article, of a different color, this time. She nodded restrainedly to several of them, as one does to distant acquaintances encountered before.

She sat down, bent her head, the needles began to flicker busily.

Somebody came in, or went out. She didn't bother looking.

The toecaps of a pair of shoes came to a halt just within the radius of vision of her downcast eyes. They remained motionless there on the floor, as though silently importuning her attention. There wasn't a sound in the room.

Mrs. Novak became aware of the shoes at last. She raised her eyes indifferently, dropped them. Then they shot up again. The knitting sidled from her lap as the lap itself dissolved into a straight line. The ball of yarn rolled across the floor unnoticed. She was clutching at her own throat with both hands.

There wasn't a sound in the room.

She pointed with one trembling finger. It was a question, a plea that she be mistaken, but more than anything else a terrified statement of fact.

"It's him—the man that ran past by my store—from where the police officer . . . !"

"But the last time you said—"

She rolled her eyes, struck her own forehead. "I know," she said brokenly. "He looked *like* him. But only he looked *like* him, you understand? This one, it *is* him!" Her voice railed out at them accusingly. "Why you haf to bring me here that other time? If you don't I don't make such a mistake!"

"There were others made the same mistake," the lieutenant tried to soothe her. "You were only one of five or six witnesses. Every one of them—"

She wouldn't listen. Her face crinkled into an ugly mask. Suddenly, with no further ado, tears were working their way down its seams. Somebody took her by the arm to help her out. One of the detectives had to pick up the fallen knitting, hand it back to her, otherwise she would have left without it. And anything that could make her do that—

"I killed him," she mourned.

"It wasn't you alone," the lieutenant acknowledged bitterly as she was led from the room. "We all did."

They seated Donny Blake in a chair, after she had gone, and one of them stood directly behind it like a mentor. They handed this man a newspaper and he opened it and held it spread out before Blake's face, as though he were holding it up for him to read.

The door opened and closed, and Storm, the chartered accountant, was sitting there across the room, in the exact place the Novak woman had been just now.

He looked around at them questioningly, still unsure of just why he had been summoned here. All he saw was a group of detectives, one of them buried behind a newspaper.

"Keep looking where that newspaper is," the lieutenant instructed quietly.

Storm looked puzzled, but he did so.

The detective behind the chair slowly began to raise it, like a curtain. Blake's chin peered below first. Then his mouth. Then nose, eyes, forehead. At last his whole face was revealed.

Storm's own face whitened. His reaction was quieter than the woman's had been, but just as dramatic. He began to tremble as he sat there in the chair. They could see it by his hands mostly. "Oh my God," he mouthed in a sickened undertone.

"Have you anything to say?" the lieutenant urged. "Don't be afraid to say it."

He stroked his mouth as though the words tasted rotten even before they'd come out. "That's—that's the face of the man I collided with—on Farragut Street."

"You're sure?"

His figures came back to him, but you could tell they gave him no comfort any longer. "One hundred per cent!" he said dismally, leaning way over his own lap as though he had a cramp.

"They're not altogether to blame," the lieutenant commented to a couple of his men after the room had been cleared. "It's very hard, when a guy looks a good deal like another, not to bridge the remaining gap with your own imagination and supply the rest. Another thing, the mere fact that we were already holding Severn in custody would unconsciously influence them in identifying him. We thought he was the guy, and we ought to know, so if we thought he was, he probably was. I don't mean they consciously thought of it in that way, but without their realizing it, that would be the effect it would have on their minds."

A cop looked in, said: "They've got Blake ready for you, Lieutenant."

"And I'm ready for him," the lieutenant answered grimly, turning and leading the way out.

———⬥———

The doctor came forward, tipped up one of Blake's eyelids. Sightless white showed. He took out a stethoscope and applied it to the region of the heart.

In the silence their panting breaths reverberated hollowly against the basement walls.

The doctor straightened up, removed the stethoscope. "Not very much more," he warned in a guarded undertone. "Still O. K., but he's wearing down. This is just a faint. Want him back?"

"Yeah," one of the men said. "We wouldn't mind."

The doctor extracted a small vial from his kit, extended it toward the outsize, discolored mass that was Blake's nose. He passed it back and forth in a straight line a couple of times.

Blake's eyelids flickered up. Then he twitched his head away uncomfortably.

There was a concerted forward shift on the part of all of them, like a pack of dogs closing in on a bone.

"Wait'll the doc gets out of the room," the lieutenant checked them. "This is our own business."

Donny Blake began to weep. "No, I can't stand any more. Doc," he called out frantically, "Doc! Don't leave me in here with 'em! They're killing me!"

The doctor had scant sympathy for him. "Then why don't you tell 'em what they want to know?" he grunted. "Why waste everyone's time?" He closed the door after him.

Maybe because the suggestion came from an outsider, at least someone distinct from his tormentors. Or maybe because this really was the time for it anyway.

Suddenly he said: "Yeah, it was me. I did it. I was with Gates and the two of us killed this guy O'Neill. He horned in on us in the middle of this uncut diamond job we were pulling. He didn't see me. I came up behind him while he was holding Gates at the point of his gun. I pinned him to the wall there in the entrance and we took his gun away from him. Then Gates said, 'He's seen us now,' and he'd shot him down before I could stop him. I said, 'He's still alive, he'll tell anyway,' and I finished him off with one into the head."

He covered his face with palsied hands. "Now I've given it to you. Don't hurt me any more. Lemme alone."

"See who that is," the lieutenant said.

A cop was on the other side of the door when it was opened. "The D.A.'s office is on the phone for you, Lieutenant. Upstairs in your own office."

"Get the stenographer," the lieutenant said, "I'll be right back."

He was gone a considerable time, but he must have used up most of it in the slow, lifeless way he came back. Dawdling along. He came in with a funny look on his face, as though he didn't see any of them any more. Or rather, did, but hated to have to look at them now.

"Take him out," he said curtly.

No one said anything until the prisoner was gone. Then they all looked at the lieutenant curiously, waiting for him to speak. He didn't.

"Aren't you going to have it taken down, Lieutenant, while it's still flowing free and easy?"

"No," the lieutenant said, tight-lipped.

"But he'll seal up again, if we give him time to rest—"

"We're not going to have a chance to use it, so there's no need getting it out of him." He sank deflatedly onto the chair the prisoner had just been propped in. "He's not going to be brought to trial. Those are the orders I just got. The D. A.'s office says to turn him loose."

He let the commotion eddy unheard above his head for a while.

Finally someone asked bitterly; "What is it, politics?"

"No. Not altogether, anyway. It's true it's an election year, and they may play a part, but there's a lot more involved than just that. Here's how they lined it up to me. Severn has been executed for that crime. There's no way of bringing him back again. The mistake's been made, and it's irretrievable. To bring this guy to trial now will unleash a scandal that will affect not only the D.A's office, but the whole police department. It's not only their own skins, or ours, they're thinking of. It's the confidence of the public. It'll get a shock that it won't recover from for years to come. I guess they feel they would rather have one guilty criminal walk out scot-free than bring about a condition where, for the next few years, every time the law tries to execute a criminal in this State, there'll be a hue and cry raised that it's another miscarriage of justice like the Severn case. They won't be able to get any convictions in our courts. All a smart defense lawyer will have to do is mention the name of Severn, and the jury will automatically acquit the defendant, rather than take a chance. It's a case of letting one criminal go now, or losing dozens of others in the future." He got up with a sigh. "I've got to go up now and get him to sign a waiver."

The handful of men stood around for a minute or two longer. Each one reacted to it according to his own individual temperament. One, of a practical turn of mind, shrugged it off, said: "Well, it's not up to us—only I wish they'd told us before we put in all that hard work on him. Coming, Joe?"

Another, of a legalistic turn of mind, began to point out just why the D. A's office had all the wrong dope. Another, of a clannish turn of mind, admitted openly: "I wouldn't have felt so sore, if only it hadn't happened to be a police sergeant."

One by one they drifted out. Until there was just one left behind. The detective named Rogers. He stayed on down there alone after all the rest had gone. Hands cupped in pockets, staring down at the floor, while he stood motionless.

His turn of mind? That of a zealot who has just seen his cause betrayed. That of a true believer who has just seen his scripture made a mockery of.

———◆———

They met in the main corridor at headquarters a few hours later, the detective and the murderer who was already a free man, immune, on his way back to the outer world.

Rogers just stood there against the wall as he went by. His head slowly turned, pacing the other's passage as their paths crossed. Not a word was exchanged between them. Blake had a strip of plaster alongside his nose, another dab of it under his lip. But Gary Severn was dead in the ground. And so was Police Sergeant O'Neill.

And the little things about him hurt even worse. The untrammeled swing of his arms! The fastidious pinch he was giving his necktie-knot. He was back in life again, full-blast.

He met the detective's eyes arrogantly, turning his own head to maintain the stare between them unbroken. Then he gave a derisive chuckle deep in his throat. It was more eloquent, more insulting than any number of words could have been. "Hagh!" it said. "The police—hagh! Their laws and regulations—hagh! Murder—hagh!"

It was like a blow in the face. It smarted. It stung. It hurt
Rogers where his beliefs lay. His sense of right and wrong. His
sense of justice. All those things that people—some of them
anyway—have, and don't like to let on they have.

Rogers' face got white. Not all over. Just around the mouth and
chin. The other man went on. Along the short remainder of the corridor, and out through the glass doors, and down the steps out of
sight. Rogers stood there without moving, and his eyes followed
him to the bitter end, until he was gone, and there was nothing
more to look at.

He'd never be back here again. He'd never be brought back for
that one particular crime, anyway.

Rogers turned and went swiftly down the other way. He came to
a door, his lieutenant's door, and he pushed it open without
knocking and went in. He put his hand down flat on the desk, then
he took it away again.

The lieutenant looked down at the badge left lying there, then
up at him.

"My written resignation will follow later. I'm quitting the
Force." He turned and went back to the door again.

"Rogers, come back here. Now wait a minute—you must be crazy."

"Maybe I am a little, at that," Rogers admitted.

"Come back here, will you? Where you going?"

"Wherever Blake is, that's where I'll be from now on. Wherever
he goes, that's where you'll find me." The door closed softly, and he
was gone.

"Which way'd he go?" Rogers said to a cop standing on the front
steps.

"He walked down a ways, and then he got in a cab, down there
by the corner. There it is, you can still see it up ahead there,
waiting for that light to change—"

Rogers summoned another cab.

"Where to, chief?"

"See that cab, crossing the intersection up there ahead? Just go
whichever way that goes, from now on."

CHAPTER THREE

WHITHER THOU GOEST—

Blake left the blonde at the desk and came slowly and purposefully across the lobby toward the overstuffed chair into which Rogers had just sunk down. He stopped squarely in front of him, legs slightly astraddle. "Why don't you get wise to yourself? Was the show good? Was the rest'runt good? Maybe you think I don't know your face from that rat-incubator downtown. Maybe you think I haven't seen you all night long, everyplace where I was."

Rogers answered quietly, looking up at him: "What makes you think I've been trying for you not to see me?"

Blake was at a loss for a minute. He opened his mouth, closed it again, swallowed. "You can't get me on that O'Neill thing. You guys wouldn't have let me go in the first place, if you could have held me on it, and you know it! It's finished, water under the bridge."

Rogers said as quietly, as readily as ever: "I know I can't. I agree with you there. What makes you think I'm trying to?"

Again Blake opened and closed his mouth abortively. The best answer he could find was: "I don't know what you're up to, but you won't get anywhere."

"What makes you think I'm trying to get anywhere?"

Blake blinked and looked more at a loss than ever. After an awkward moment, having been balked of the opposition he'd expected to meet, he turned on his heel and went back to the desk.

He conferred with the blonde for a few minutes. She began to draw away from him. Finally she shrugged off the importuning hand he tried to lay on her arm. Her voice rose. "Not if you're being shadowed—count me out! I ain't going to get mixed up with you. You should have told me sooner. You better find somebody else to go around with!" She flounced indignantly out.

Blake gave Rogers the venomous look of a beady-eyed cobra. Then he strode ragingly off in the opposite direction, entered the waiting elevator.

Rogers motioned languidly to the operator to wait for him, straightened up from his chair, ambled leisurely over, and stepped in in turn. The car started up with the two of them in it. Blake's face was livid with rage. A pulse at his temple kept beating a tattoo.

"Keep it up," he said in a strangled undertone behind the operator's back.

"Keep what up?" answered Rogers impassively.

The car stopped at the sixth and Blake flung himself off. The door closed behind him. He made a turn of the carpeted corridor, stopped, put his key into a door. Then he whirled savagely as a second padded tread came down the corridor in the wake of his own.

"Where d'ya think you're going," he shrilled exasperatedly, "right inside my room with me?"

"No," Rogers said evenly, putting a key to the door directly opposite, "into my own."

The two doors closed one after the other.

That was at midnight, on the sixth floor of the Congress Hotel. When Blake came out again, at ten the next morning, all freshly combed and shaven, to go down to breakfast, it was from a room on the tenth floor of the Hotel Colton. He'd changed abodes in the middle of the night. As he came out he was smiling to himself behind the hand he traced lightly over the lower part of his face to test the efficacy of his recent shave.

He closed the door and moved down the corridor toward the elevator.

The second door down from his own, on the same side, opened a moment or two after he'd gone by, before he'd quite reached the turn of the hall. Something made him glance back. Some lack of completion, maybe the fact that it hadn't immediately closed again on the occupant's departure as it should have.

Rogers was standing sidewise in it, back to door-frame, looking out after him while he unhurriedly completed hitching on his coat.

"Hold the car for me a sec, will you?" he said matter-of-factly. "I'm on my way down to breakfast myself."

On the third try he managed to bring the cup up to its highest level yet, within an inch of his lips, but he still couldn't seem to manage that remaining inch. The cup started to vibrate with the uncontrollable vibration of the wrist that supported it, slosh over at the sides. Finally it sank heavily down again, with a crack that nearly broke the saucer under it, as though it were too heavy for him to hold. Its contents splashed up.

Rogers, sitting facing him, two tables away but in a straight line, went ahead enjoyably and calmly mangling a large dish of bacon and eggs. He grinned through a full mouth, while his jaw continued inexorably to rotate with a sort of traction movement.

Blake's wrists continued to tremble, even without the cup to support. "I can't stand it," he muttered, shading his eyes for a minute. "Does he have to—" Then he checked the remark.

The waiter, mopping up the place before him, let his eye travel around the room without understanding. "Is there something here that bothers you, sir?"

"Yes," Blake said in a choked voice, "there is."

"Would you care to sit this way, sir?"

Blake got up and moved around to the opposite side of the table, with his back to Rogers. The waiter refilled his cup.

He started to lift it again, using both hands this time to make sure of keeping it steady.

He couldn't see him any more, but he could still hear him. The peculiar crackling, grating sound caused by a person chomping on dry toast reached him from the direction in which he had last seen Rogers. It continued incessantly after that, without a pause, as though the consumer had no sooner completed one mouthful of the highly audible stuff than he filled up another and went to work on that.

The cup sank down heavily, as if it weighed too much to support even in his double grasp. This time it overturned, a tan puddle overspread the table. Blake leaped to his feet, flung his napkin down, elbowed the solicitous waiter roughly aside.

"Lemme out of here," he panted. "I can still feel him, every move I make, watching me, watching me from behind!"

The waiter looked around, perplexed. To his eyes there was no one in sight but a quiet, inoffensive man a couple of tables off, minding his own business, strictly attending to what was on the plate before him, not doing anything to disturb anyone.

"Gee, you better see a doctor, mister," he suggested worriedly. "You haven't been able to sit through a meal in days now."

Blake floundered out of the dining-room, across the lobby, and into the drugstore on the opposite side. He drew up short at the fountain, leaned helplessly against it with a haggard look on his face.

"Gimme an aspirin!" His voice frayed. "Two of them, three of them!"

<hr />

"Century Limited, 'Ca-a-awgo, Track Twenty-five!" boomed dismally through the vaulted rotunda. It filtered in, thinned a little, through the crack in the telephone-booth panel that Blake was holding fractionally ajar, both for purposes of ventilation and to be able to hear the dispatch when it came.

Even now that it had come, he stayed in the booth and the phone stayed on the hook. He'd picked the booth for its strategic location. It not only commanded the clock out there, more important still it commanded the wicket leading down to that particular track that he was to use, and above all, the prospective passengers who filed through it.

He was going to be the last one on that train—the last possible one—and he was going to know just who had preceded him aboard, before he committed himself to it.

It was impossible, with all the precautions he had taken, that the devil in human form should sense the distance he was about to put between them once and for all, come after him this time. If he did, then he was a mind-reader, pure and simple. There would be no other way to explain it.

It had been troublesome and expensive, but if it succeeded, it would be worth it. The several unsuccessful attempts he had made to change hotels had shown him the futility of that type of disappearance. This time he hadn't made the mistake of asking for his final bill, packing his belongings, or anything like that. His clothes, such as they were, were still in the closet. His baggage was still empty. He'd paid his bill for a week in advance, and this was only the second day of that week. He'd given no notice of departure. Then he'd strolled casually forth as on any other day, sauntered into a movie, left immediately by another entrance, come over here, picked up the reservation they'd been holding for him under another name, and closed himself up in this phone-booth. He'd been in it for the past three-quarters of an hour now.

And his nemesis, meanwhile, was either loitering around outside that theater waiting for him to come out again, or sitting back there at the hotel waiting for him to return.

He scanned them as they filed through in driblets—now one, now two or three at once, now one more again, now a brief let-up.

The minute-hand was beginning to hit train-time. The guard was getting ready to close the gate again. Nobody else was passing through any more now.

He opened the booth-flap, took a tight tug on his hat-brim, and poised himself for a sudden dash across the marble floor.

He waited until the latticed gate was stretched all the way across, ready to be latched onto the opposite side of the gateway. Then he flashed from the booth and streaked over toward it. "Hold it!" he barked, and the guard widened it again just enough for him to squeeze through sidewise.

He showed him his ticket on the inside, after it was already made fast. He looked watchfully out and around through it, in the minute or two this took, and there was no sign of anyone starting up from any hidden position around the waiting-rooms or any place nearby and starting after him.

He wasn't here. He'd lost him, given him the slip.

"Better make it fast, mister," the guard suggested.

He didn't have to tell him that. The train didn't exist that could get away from him now, even if he had to run halfway through the tunnel after it.

He went tearing down the ramp, wigwagging a line of returning redcaps out of his way.

He got on only by virtue of a conductor's outstretched arm, a door left aslant to receive him, and a last-minute flourish of tricky footwork. He got on, and that was the only thing that mattered.

"That's it," he heaved gratifiedly. "Now close it up and throw the key away! There's nobody else, after me."

"They'd have to be homing pigeons riding a tail-wind, if there was," the conductor admitted.

❦

He'd taken a compartment, to make sure of remaining unseen during the trip. It was two cars up, and after he'd reached it and checked it with the conductor, he locked himself in and pulled down the shade to the bottom, even though they were still in the tunnel under the city.

Then he sank back on the upholstered seat with a long sigh. Finally! A complete break at last. "He'll never catch up with me again now as long as I live," he murmured bitterly. "I'll see to that."

Time and trackage ticked off.

They stopped for a minute at the uptown station. There was very little hazard attached to that, he felt. If he'd guessed his intentions at all, he would have been right at his heels down at the main station, he wouldn't take the risk of boarding the train later up here. There wouldn't be time enough to investigate thoroughly, and he might get on the wrong train and be carried all the way to the Mid-west without his quarry.

Still, there was nothing like being sure, so after they were well under way again, he rang for the conductor, opened the door a half-inch, and asked him through it: "I'm expecting to meet somebody. Did anyone get on just now, uptown?"

"Just a lady and a little boy, that who . . . ?"

"No," said Blake, smiling serenely, "that wasn't who." And he locked the door again. All set now.

Sure, he'd come out there after him maybe, but all he, Blake, needed was this momentary headstart. He'd never be able to close in on him again, he'd keep it between them from now on, stay always a step ahead.

They stopped again at Harmon, to change to a coal-powered engine. That didn't bother him, that wasn't a passenger-stop.

There was a knock on the compartment door, opposite West Point, and dread came back again for a moment. He leaped over and put his ear to it, and when it came again, called out tensely, making a shell of his two hands to alter his voice: "Who is it?"

A stewardess' voice came back. "Care for a pillow, sir?"

He opened it narrowly, let her hand it in to him more to get rid of her than because he wanted one. Then he locked up again, relaxed.

He wasn't disturbed any more after that. At Albany they turned west. Somewhere in Pennsylvania, or maybe it was already Ohio, he rang for a tray and had it put down outside the locked door. Then he took it in himself and locked up again. When he was through he put it down outside again, and locked up once more. That was so he wouldn't have to go out to the buffet-car. But these were just fancy trimmings, little extra added precautions, that he himself knew to be no longer necessary. The train was obviously empty of danger. It had been from the moment of departure.

Toward midnight, way out in Indiana, he had to let the porter in to make up the two seats into a bed for him. He couldn't do that for himself.

"I guess you the las' one up on the whole train," the man said cheerfully.

"They all turned in?"

"Hours ago. Ain't nobody stirrin' no mo', from front to back."

That decided him. He figured he might as well step outside for a minute and stretch his legs, while the man was busy in there. There wasn't room enough for two of them at once. He made his way back through sleeping aisles of green berth-hangings. Even the observation-car was empty and unlighted now, with just one small dim lamp standing guard in the corner.

The whole living cargo of humanity was fast asleep.

He opened the door and went out on the observation platform to get a breath of air. He stretched himself there by the rail and drank it in. "Gee," he thought, "it feels good to be free!" It was the first real taste of freedom he'd had since he'd walked out of police headquarters—

A voice in one of the gloom-obscured basket-shaped chairs offside to him said mildly: "That you, Blake? Been wondering when you'd show up. How can you stand it, cooped up for hours in that stuffy two-by-four?" And a cigar-butt, which was all that could be seen of the speaker, glowed red with comfortable tranquillity.

Blake had to hang onto the rail as he whirled, to keep from going over. "When did you get on?" he wailed against the wind.

"I was the first one on," Rogers' voice said from the dark. "I got myself admitted before the gates were even opened, while they were still making the train up." He chuckled appreciatively. "I thought sure *you* were going to miss it."

CHAPTER FOUR

The Test of a Killer

He knew what this was that was coming next. It had been bound to come sooner or later, and this was about the time for it now. Any number of things were there to tell him—minor variations in the pattern of his adversary's behavior. Not for nothing had he been a detective for years. He knew human nature. He was already familiar with Blake's pattern of behavior. The danger-signals studding it tonight were, to his practiced eye, as plainly to be read as lighted buoys flashing out above dark, treacherous waters.

Blake hadn't sought one of his usual tinseled, boisterous resorts tonight. He'd found his way instead to a dingy out-of-the-way rat-hole over on the South Side, where the very atmosphere had a furtive cast to it. The detective could scent "trap" a mile away as he pushed inside after him. Blake was sitting alone, not expansively lording it over a cluster of girls as was his wont. He even discouraged the one or two that attempted to attach themselves to him. And finally, the very way in which he drank told the detective there was something coming up. He wasn't drinking to get happy, or to forget. He was drinking to get nerve. The detective could read what was on his mind by the very hoists of his arm. They were too jerky and unevenly spaced, they vibrated with nervous tension.

He himself sat there across the room, fooling around with a beer, not taking any chances on letting it past his gums, in case it had been drugged. He had a gun on him, but that was only because he always carried one. He had absolutely no intention of using it, not even in self-defense. Because what was coming up now was a test, and it had to be met, to keep the dominance of the situation on his side. If he flinched from it, the dominance of the situation shifted over to Blake's side. And mastery didn't lie in any use of a gun, either, because that was a mastery that lasted only as long as your finger rested on the trigger. What he was after was a long-term mastery.

Blake was primed now. The liquor had done all it could for him, embalmed his nerves like novocaine. Rogers saw him get up slowly from the table. He braced himself at it a moment, then started on his way out. The very way he walked, the stiff-legged, interlocking gait, showed that this was the come-on, that if he followed him now, there was death at the end of it.

And he knew by the silence that hung over the place, the sudden lull that descended, in which no one moved, no one spoke, yet no one looked at either of the two principals, that everyone there was in on it to a greater or a lesser extent.

He kept himself relaxed. That was important, that was half the battle—otherwise it wouldn't work. He let him get as far as the door, and then he slowly got to his feet in turn. In his technique there was no attempt to dissimulate, to give the impression he was *not* following Blake, patterning his movements on the other's. He threw down money for his beer and he put out his cigar with painstaking thoroughness.

The door had closed behind the other. Now he moved toward it in turn. No one in the place was looking at him, yet he knew that in the becalmed silence everyone was listening to his slow, measured tread across the floor. From busboy to tawdry hostess, from waiter to dubious patron, no one stirred. The place was bewitched with the approach of murder. And they were all on Donny Blake's side.

The man at the piano sat with his fingers resting lightly on the keyboard, careful not to bear down yet, ready for the signal to begin the death-music. The man at the percussion-instrument held his drumstick poised, the trumpeter had his lips to the mouthpiece of his instrument, waiting like the Angel Gabriel. It was going to happen right outside somewhere, close by.

He came out, and Blake had remained in sight, to continue the come-on. As soon as he saw Rogers, and above all was sure Rogers had marked him, he drifted down an alley there at that end of the building that led back to the garage. That was where it was going to happen. And then into a sack, and into one of the cars, and into Lake Michigan.

Rogers turned without a moment's hesitation and went down that way and turned the corner.

———

Blake had lit the garage up, to show him the way. They'd gotten rid of the attendant for him. He went deeper inside, but he remained visible down the lane of cars. He stopped there, near the back wall, and turned to face him, and stood and waited.

Rogers came on down the alley, toward the garage-entrance. If he was going to get him from a distance, then Rogers knew he would probably have to die. But if he let him come in close—

He made no move, so he wasn't going to try to get him from a distance. Probably afraid of missing him.

The time-limit that must have been arranged expired as he crossed the threshold into the garage. There was suddenly a blare of the three-piece band, from within the main building, so loud it seemed to split the seams of the place. That was the cover-up.

Rogers pulled the corrugated tin slide-door across after him, closing the two of them up. "That how you want it, Blake?" he said. Then he came away from the entrance, still deeper into the garage, to where Blake was standing waiting for him.

Blake had the gun out by now. Above it was a face that could only have been worn by a man who has been hounded unendurably for weeks on end. It was past hatred. It was maniacal.

Rogers came on until he was three or four yards from him. Then he stopped, empty-handed. "Well?" he said. He rested one hand on the fender of a car.

A flux of uncertainty wavered over Blake, was gone again.

Rogers said: "Go ahead, you fool. This is as good a way as any other, as far as we're concerned. As long as it hands you over to us, I'm willing. This is just what we've been looking for all along, what's the difference if it's me or somebody else?"

"You won't know about it," Blake said in a hoarse voice. "They'll never find you."

"They don't have to. All they've got to do is find you without me." He heeled his palms toward him. "Well, what're you waiting for? I'm empty-handed."

The flux of uncertainty came back again, it rinsed all the starch out of him, softened him all up. It bent the gun down uselessly floorward in his very grasp. He backed and filled helplessly. "So you're a plant—so they want me to do this to you—I mighta known you was too open about it—"

For a moment or two he was in awful shape. He backed his hand to his forehead and stood there bandy-legged against the wall, his mind fuming like a Seidlitz powder.

He'd found out long ago he couldn't escape from his tormentor. And now he was finding out he couldn't even kill him. He had to live with him.

Rogers rested his elbow in his other hand, and stroked the lower part of his face, contemplating him thoughtfully. He'd met the test and licked it. Dominance still rested with him.

The two men faced each other, the hunter and the hunted. Blake was breathing hard, all unmanned by the recent close shave. Rogers was as calm as though nothing had happened.

⎯⎯◆⎯⎯

Rogers sat there on the edge of his bed, in the dark, in his room. He was in trousers, undershirt, and with his shoes off. He was sitting the night through like that, keeping the death-watch. This was the same night as the spiked show-down in the garage, or what there was left of it. It was still dark, but it wouldn't be dark much longer.

He'd left his room door open two inches, and he was sitting in a line with it, patiently watching and waiting. The pattern of human behavior, immutable, told him what to be on the look-out for next.

The door-opening let a slender bar of yellow in from the hall. First it lay flat across the floor, then it climbed up the bed he was on, then it slanted off across his upper arm, just like a chevron. He felt he was entitled to a chevron by now.

He sat there, looking patiently out through the door-slit, waiting. For the inevitable next step, the step that was bound to come. He'd been sitting there like that watching ever since he'd first come in. He was willing to sit up all night, he was so sure it was coming.

He'd seen the bellboy go in the first time, with the first pint and the cracked ice, stay a minute or two, come out again tossing up a quarter.

Now suddenly here he was back again, with a second pint and more cracked ice. The green of his uniform showed in the door-slit. He stood there with his back to Rogers and knocked lightly on the door across the way.

Two pints, about, would do it. Rogers didn't move, though.

The door opened and the boy went in. He came out again in a moment, closed it after him.

Then Rogers did move. He left the bed in his stocking feet, widened his own door, went "Psst!" and the boy turned and came over to him.

"How much did he give you this time?"

The boy's eyes shone. "The whole change that was left! He cleaned himself out!"

Rogers nodded, as if in confirmation of something or other to himself. "How drunk is he?"

"He's having a hard time getting there, but he's getting there," the boy said.

Rogers nodded again, for his own private benefit. "Lemme have your passkey," he said.

The boy hesitated.

"It's all right, I have the house-dick's authorization. You can check on it with him, if you want. Only, hand it over—I'm going to need it, and there won't be much time."

The boy tendered it to him, then showed an inclination to hang around and watch.

"You don't need to wait, I'll take care of everything."

He didn't go back into his own room again. He stayed there outside that other door, just as he was, in undershirt and stocking-feet, in a position of half-crouched intentness, passkey ready at hand.

The transom was imperfectly closed, and he could hear him moving around in there, occasionally striking against some piece of furniture. He could hear it every time the bottle told off against the rim of the glass. Almost he was able to detect the constantly-ascending angle at which it was tilted, as its contents became less.

Pretty soon now. And in between, footsteps faltering back and forth, weaving aimlessly around—like those of someone trying to find his way out of a trap.

Suddenly the bottle hit the carpet with a discarded thud. No more in it.

Any minute now.

A rambling, disconnected phrase or two became audible, as the tempo of the trapped footsteps accelerated, this way and that, and all around, in blundering search of a way out. "I'll fool him! I'll show him! There's one place he can't—come after me—"

There was the sound of a window going up.

Now!

Rogers plunged the passkey in, swept the door aside, and dove across the room.

———◆◆◆———

He had both feet up on the window-sill already, ready to go out and over and down. All the way down to the bottom. The only thing still keeping him there was he had to lower his head and shoulders first, to get them clear of the upper pane. That gave Rogers time enough to get across to him.

His arms scissored open for him, closed again, like a pair of pliers. He caught him around the waist, pulled him back, and the two of them fell to the floor together in a mingled heap.

He extricated himself and regained his feet before the other had. He went over, closed and securely latched-down the window, drew the shade. Then he went back to where the other still lay soddenly inert, stood over him.

"Get up!" he ordered roughly.

Blake had his downward-turned face buried in the crook of one arm. Rogers gave him a nudge with his foot that was just short of a kick.

Blake drew himself slowly together, crawled back to his feet by ascending stages, using the seat of a chair, then the top of a table next to it, until finally he was erect.

They faced one another.

"You won't let me live, and you won't even let me die!" Blake's voice rose almost to a full-pitched scream. "Then whaddya *after?* Whaddya *want?*"

"Nothing." Rogers' low-keyed response was almost inaudible coming after the other's strident hysteria. "I told you that many times, didn't I? Is there any harm in going around where you go, being around where you are? There's plenty of room for two, isn't there?"

Rogers pushed him back on the bed, and Blake lay there sprawled full-length, without attempting to rise again. Rogers took a towel and drenched it in cold water, then wound it around itself into a rope.

He laced it across Blake's face a couple of times, with a heavy, sluggish swing of the arm, trailing a fine curtain of spray through the air after it. Then he flung it down.

When he spoke again his voice had slowed still further, to a sluggard drawl. "Take it easy. What's there to get all steamed-up about? Here, look this over."

He reached into his rear trouser-pocket, took out a billfold, extracted a worn letter and spread it open, holding it reversed for the other to see. It was old, he'd been carying it around with him for months. It was an acknowledgment, on a police department letterhead, of his resignation. He held it a long time, to let it sink in. Then he finally put it away again.

Blake quit sniveling after a while, and was carried off on the tide of the alcohol in him into oblivion.

Rogers made no move to leave the room.

He gave the latched window a glance. Then he scuffed over a chair and sat down beside the bed. He lit a cigarette, and just sat there watching him. Like a male nurse on duty at the bedside of a patient.

He wanted him alive and he wanted him in his right mind.

CHAPTER FIVE

THE TRAP FALLS SHUT

Hatred cannot remain at white heat indefinitely. Neither can fear. The human system would not be able to support them at that pitch, without burning itself out. But nature is great at providing safety-valves. What happens next is one of two things: either the conditions creating that hatred or fear are removed, thus doing away with them automatically. Or else custom, familiarity, creeps in, by unnoticeable degrees, tempering them, blurring them. Pretty soon the hatred is just a dull red glow. Then it is gone entirely. The subject has become *used* to the object that once aroused hatred or fear—

And that happened to Donny Blake. He became so accustomed to Rogers that he forgot to be afraid of him—even took to boasting, among his friends, about Rogers' trailing him.

One night, at a hotel back in New York, there was a knock at the door of Rogers' room. He opened it and Blake was standing there.

They stood looking at one another a minute.

A tentative grin flickered around the edges of Blake's mouth. Rogers answered it in kind.

"You doing anything, Rodge?" They were Donny and Rodge to each other now.

"No, come on in," Rogers answered, stepping back.

Donny Blake nonchalantly leaned in at an angle, from the waist up. "Fellow I used to know, guy named Bill Harkness, just dropped in to the room. Haven't seen him in years. We been chewing the rag and now we're fresh out of gab. Thought maybe you'd like to come on over and join us in a little three-handed game, what d'ya say?"

"Only for half an hour or so," Rogers answered. "I'm turning in early tonight."

Blake withdrew, leaving the door ajar to speed Rogers on his way in to them. He left his own that way too, opposite it.

Rogers put out his light and got ready to go over to them. Then he stopped there on the threshold, half in, half out, yawned undecidedly, like someone else once had, one night a long time ago, on his way out to get a midnight edition of a newspaper.

He didn't have to be right at his elbow every night, did he? He could let it ride for one night, couldn't he, out of so many hundreds of them? He'd be right across the hall from them, he could leave his door slightly ajar. He was tired, and that bed looked awfully good. He was a human being, not a machine. He had his moments of letdown, and this was one of them. Nothing was ever going to happen. All he'd managed to accomplish was play the parole-officer to Blake, keep him straight. And that wasn't what he'd been after.

He was about to change his mind, go back inside again.

But they'd seen him from where they were, and Blake waved him on. "Coming, Rodge? What're you standing there thinking about?"

That swung the balance. He closed his own door, crossed over, and went in there with them.

They were sitting there at the table waiting for him to join them. This Harkness struck him as being engaged in some shady line of business. But then that was an easy guess. Anyone on Blake's acquaintance list was bound to be from the other side of the fence anyway.

"Pleased to meet you."

"Likewise."

He shook hands with him without demur. That was a thing he'd learned to do since he'd been around Blake, shake hands with all manner of crooks.

Blake, to put them at their ease together, trotted out that same worn theme he was so fond of harping on, "Harkness don't wanna believe you used to be a dick. Tell him yourself." He told it to everyone he knew, at every opportunity. He seemed to take a perverse pride in it, as though it reflected a sort of distinction on him. A detective had once been after him, and he'd tamed him into harmlessness.

"Don't you ever get tired of that?" was all Rogers grunted, disgustedly. He took up his cards, shot a covert glance at Blake's friend. "No folding money, only nickels and dimes."

Blake took it in good part. "Ain't that some guy for you?"

The game wore on desultorily. The night wore on along with it. Just three people at a table, killing time.

Harkness seemed to have a fidgety habit of continually worrying at the cuff of his coatsleeve.

"I thought they quit hiding them up there years ago," Blake finally remarked with a grin. "We're not playing for stakes, anyway."

"No, you don't get it, there's a busted button on my sleeve, and it keeps hooking onto everything every time I reach my arm out."

Only half of it was left, adhering to the thread, sharp-pointed and annoying as only such trivial things are apt to be. He tried to wrench it off bodily and it defeated him because there wasn't enough of it left to get a good grip on. All he succeeded in doing was lacerating the edges of his fingers. He swore softly and licked at them.

"Why don't you take the blame coat off altogether? You don't need it," Blake suggested, without envincing any real interest.

Harkness did, and draped it over the back of his chair.

⸺⬥⸺

The game wore on again. The night wore on. Rogers' original half-hour was gone long ago. It had quadrupled itself by now. Finally the game wore out, seemed to quit of its own momentum.

They sat there, half-comatose, around the table a moment or two longer. Rogers' head was actually beginning to nod. Harkness was the first one to speak. "Look at it, one o'clock. Guess I'll shove off." He stood up and got back into his coat. Then he felt at the mangled thatch the game had left in its wake. "Got a comb I can borry before I go?"

Blake, mechanically continuing to shuffle cards without dealing them any more, said, "In that top drawer over there," without looking around. "And wipe it off after you use it, I'm particular."

The drawer slid out. There was a moment of silence, then they heard Harkness remark: "Old Faithful."

Rogers opened his heavy-lidded eyes and Blake turned his head. He'd found Blake's gun in the drawer, had taken it out and was looking it over. "Ain't you afraid of him knowing you've got this?" he grinned at Blake.

"Aw, he's known I've had it for years. He knows I'm licensed for it, too." Then he added sharply: "Quit monkeying with it, Harkness. Put it back where it belongs."

"O.K., O.K.," Harkness consented casually.

He laid the gun down on the bureau-scarf, reached for the comb instead.

Blake turned back again to his repetitious card-shuffling. Rogers, who was facing that way, suddenly split his eyes back to full-size at something he saw. The blurred sleepiness suddenly left his voice.

"Hey, that busted button of yours is tangled in the fringe of the scarf, I can see it from here, and the gun's right on the edge. Move it over, you're going to—"

The warning had precisely a reverse effect. It brought on what he'd been trying to avoid instead of averting it. Harkness jerked up his forearm, to look and see for himself—anyone's instinctive reflex in the same situation. The scarf gave a hitch along its entire length, and the gun slid off into space.

Harkness made a quick stabbing dive for it, to try to catch it before it hit the floor. He made it. His mind was quick enough, and so was his muscular coordination. He got it on the drop, in mid-air, in the relatively short distance between bureau-top and floor. But he got it the wrong way, caught at it in the wrong place.

A spark jumped out of his hand and there was a heavy-throated boom.

Then for a minute more nothing happened. None of them moved, not even he. He remained bent over like that, frozen just as he'd grabbed for it. Rogers remained seated at the table, staring across it. Blake continued to clutch the cards he'd been shuffling, while his head slowly came around. Rogers, at least, had been a witness to what had happened.

Donny Blake had even missed seeing that much.

Harkness was moving again. He folded slowly over, until his face was resting on the floor, while he remained arched upward in the middle like a croquet-wicket. Then he flattened out along there too, and made just a straight line, and lay quiet, as though he was tired.

Rogers jumped up and over to him, got down by him, turned him over. "Help me carry him over onto the bed," he said. "It must have hit him—" Then he stopped again.

Blake was still stupidly clutching the deck of cards.

"He's gone," Rogers said, in an oddly blank voice. "It must have got him instantly." He straightened up, still puzzled by the suddenness with which the thing had occurred. "I never saw such a freaky—" Then he saw the gun. He stooped for it. "What did you leave it lying around like that for?" he demanded irritably. "Here, take it!" He thrust it at its owner, and the latter's hand closed around it almost unconsciously.

———◆———

Blake was finally starting to get it. "A fine mess!" he lamented. He went over to the door, listened. Then he even opened it cautiously, looked out into the hall. The shot apparently hadn't been heard through the thick walls and doors of the building. He closed the door, came back again. He was starting to perspire profusely. Then, as another thought struck him belatedly, he took out a handkerchief and began to mop at himself with something akin to relief. "Hey, it's a good thing you were right in here with the two of us, saw it for yourself. Otherwise you might have thought—"

Rogers kept staring down at the still figure. He couldn't seem to come out of his preoccupation.

Blake came over and touched him in anxious supplication on the arm, to attract his attention. "Hey, Rodge, maybe you better be the one to report it. It'll look better coming from you, you used to be on the Force yourself—"

"All right, I'll handle it," Rogers said with sudden new-found incisiveness. "Let's have the gun." He lined his hand with a folded handkerchief before closing it on it.

Blake relinquished it only too willingly, went ahead mopping his face, like someone who had just had the narrowest of narrow escapes.

Rogers had asked for his old precinct number. "Give me Lieutenant Colton." There was a moment's wait. He balanced the instrument on one shoulder, delved into his pockets, rid himself of all the paper currently he had on him. He discarded this by flinging it at the table, for some reason best known to himself.

In the moment's wait, Blake said again, mostly for his own benefit: "Boy, it's the luckiest thing I ever did to ask you in here with us to—"

Rogers straightened slightly and spoke into the phone. "Eric Rogers reporting back, Lieutenant, after an extended leave of absence without pay. I'm in room seven-ten at the Hotel Lancaster, here in the city. I've just been a witness to a murder. Donny Blake has shot to death, with his own gun, a man named William Harkness. Under my own eyes, that's right. Orders, Lieutenant? Very well, I'll hold him until you get here, sir."

He hung up.

Blake's face was a white bubble. It swelled and swelled with dismay, until it had exploded into all the abysmal fright there is in the world. "I wasn't near him! I wasn't touching it! I wasn't even *looking!* I was turned the other way, with my back to— You know that! Rogers, you know it!"

Rogers kept holding his own gun on him, with the handkerchief around it. "Sure, I know it," he agreed readily. "I know it and you know it. We both know it. You hear me say it to you now, freely, for the last time, while we're still alone here together. And after this once, neither God nor man will ever hear me say it again. I've waited a long time for this. Now it's here. You found a loophole once. Now I've found a loophole this time. Your loophole was to get out. My loophole is to get you back in again.

"Listen to me, so you'll understand what I'm doing, Blake.

You're going to be arrested in a few more minutes for murder. You're going to be tried for murder. You're going to be—if there's any virtue left in the laws of this State—executed for murder. They're going to call that murder by the name of this man, Harkness. That's the only name that'll be mentioned throughout the proceedings. But the murder you're really about to be arrested, tried, and electrocuted for will be that of a man whose name won't appear in it once, from first to last, from beginning to end—Police Sergeant O'Neill. *That's* the murder you're going to die for now!"

AFTERWORD TO "THREE KILLS FOR ONE"

"Three Kills for One" (*Black Mask,* July 1942) is the most shattering of all Woolrich's Noir Cop stories. Its opening scenes, portraying the last quiet moments in the life of a man marked for destruction, are strikingly similar in mood to the first half-hour of Alfred Hitchcock's haunting *The Wrong Man* (1956). When Rogers resigns from the force and devotes three years of his life to shadowing and hounding Blake, carrying on the quest without money or visible means of support as if his rage for "justice" were all the food and drink he needed, we are reminded both of the psychotic Julie in *The Bride Wore Black* and of Javert's sadistic stalking of the hapless Jean Valjean in Victor Hugo's *Les Miserables.* Anyone who thinks we're meant to agree with Rogers, or to see him as a hero, has wandered off into a Dirty Harry world radically at odds with the world of Woolrich where, with very few exceptions, these monsters with licenses to torture and kill are the vicars of the unseen malevolent powers that rule our lives.

THE DEATH ROSE

She found him in a place that the men in his division called "The Greek's," a lunch-counter just around the corner from the precinct house to which he was attached. He was at the far end of the counter, sitting slumped over a mug of coffee. She sidled up alongside him without his seeing her and sat down next to him.

"I guess you forgot what time our date was for."

"No," he said glumly. "No, I didn't. But what's the use? I guess you better quit seeing me. I'm just a dick on the Homicide Squad. That's all I'll ever be, I guess. And you're . . ."

"I'm what?"

"You're a rich girl, a debutante—that kind of thing. We don't belong together, Ginny. If I hadn't stopped your horse from running away with you that day in the park, we would never even have met. And maybe it would have been better for both of us."

She smiled understandingly, as though this wasn't the first time she'd heard him talk that way. "What is it this time, Terry?" she asked. "What went wrong?"

"They call him The Rose Killer," he said moodily. "And he's got to be stopped. There's a general demotion coming on if he isn't—all along the line from top to bottom. We were told that just now. And it was no kidding. That's all I need yet—to go back into uniform. I'd look great then, going around with a girl like you, wouldn't I?"

"I'm not complaining," she said softly. "I've got your handcuffs on, and the key was thrown away a long time ago. What are you going to do with your prisoner?"

"Turn her loose."

"She refuses to be freed." She waited a moment, finally put her hand on his sleeve. "Then why don't you get him, Terry, if that would make it easier for the two of us?"

He gave her a look. "Nice work if you can get it," he said caustically.

"What's he like?"

"That's the stumble. He could be anybody. Nobody's seen him—only the dead—and they don't talk about it afterward. He just slips out of the shadows, kills, and then slips back again. We're no further than we were in the beginning."

She gulped a sip of coffee, as if to warm herself. "How many times?" she asked fearfully.

He held up four fingers. "And he's not through yet. It's going to be one of these chain things, if he's allowed to keep on."

"Are you sure it was always him? Couldn't it have been somebody else one of those times?"

He shook his head. "That part of it we're sure of. There's the same touch every time. You know what that is, don't you?"

"You explained it to me once. What is it this time?"

"I shouldn't be telling you stuff like this. You should be dancing at some party—not listening to things like this."

"Anything that concerns you concerns me. I want to know."

"It's always the same—a rose. A white rosebud. A death rose. He puts it into each one's hand before he leaves her lying there. We've found each one like that."

"Her?" she breathed.

"It's always a woman. A young woman of a certain age. Between nineteen and twenty-three. Never any younger, never any older."

"What is it? What makes him . . . ?"

"I've been reading up in a book of abnormal psychology. It was part of the instructions we were given—not that it's helped much in tracking him down. But it has helped to clear the fog away from the motive. This is just deduction, pure and simple, but here's what I get out of it. You know what the rose is, don't you, speaking symbolically? The flower of love. It's always stood for that. So there's a shell-shocked love involved. Now the *white* rose—the bud—has an additional meaning of its own—purity, loyalty, devotion—and especially it stands for a young girl—for youth. So the factor involved here is a doublecross, committed against him by someone young, whom he worshipped, and who betrayed his faith in her.

"Now, the second point is this: It has always happened either during or immediately after a blackout. We all mistakenly thought at first that the great opportunity offered by the darkness and the emptiness of the streets had something to do with it. Now we've decided that it hasn't. At least one of those crimes occurred a *full hour* after the lights had gone on again and everything had returned to normal. The victim had been seen alive and had been spoken to by numerous people well after the all-clear had sounded. It wasn't until more than sixty-five minutes later that he struck."

"Then?"

"I'm frightening you."

"This is *our* problem—not yours."

"Here, have a detective's cheap brand of cigarette to steady you."

She took an impatient puff. "Then it isn't the darkness of the blackout?"

"No, it isn't the darkness of the blackout itself. Here's how it stacks up now. The original act of betrayal occurred during a blackout. Now, we haven't had many of them over here yet, so that probably means London. They were continuous there—night after night—and the tension was terrific. Everyone's nerves stretched to the breaking point. All that anybody, who already had any latent mental instability, needed was an extra push to go off the deep end altogether. One night some one man in London did, and that's the same man that's over here now, doing this.

"Maybe he came home stunned one night, from a bomb-concussion, or with his equilibrium teetering after being dug out from being buried alive. Maybe he came home to someone he adored, someone whom he thought was loyal and true to him, and caught her double-crossing him—getting ready to run off with someone else, under the impression that he'd never turn up alive again. Maybe he even discovered some plot under way, engineered by her, to kill him if he should come back, and then collect his insurance. The result is the thing—what it did to him. It gave him that final push over into the darkness. It was a shock on top of a shock. One shock too many.

"Whether there was an original crime, at that time, has never come to light. We don't know. Probably there was, but if so, that's on the doorstep of Scotland Yard. All that we're concerned with is that he's shown up over here. And four times, during our own blackouts, the original crime has repeated itself."

"But if, in London, he once. . ."

"The mind remembers. Now every time the sirens wail and the lights go down, he lives that first time over again. The shock occurs again. His sanity overbalances again. He finds her, somewhere, somehow, and he kills her all over again. And then he puts a white rose in her hand. But the body *we* find is that of some innocent girl who was a total stranger to him—who never knew him—who never did him any harm—who only had the misfortune of looking a little like that first one, over in London."

She hunched her shoulders a little. Her teeth were lightly tapping together, like typewriter keys, but she was careful not to let him notice. "And how does he—is it always the same?"

"Always. Strangulation between the hands, with a thumb into the windpipe to keep them from crying out. They die in swift and sudden silence. And it must have been that way the first time too."

"Isn't there anything about him you know? At least, you do know he's English?"

"No," he said, "not even that. Hundreds of Americans have been living in London all during the war. Or for that matter, he could be any other nationality. It's just that it was probably there that it happened."

He ran his fingers through his hair, dislodging his hat a little.

"And here's what's so hopeless about it—what's so dangerous about him. He's insane, of course, but there's only this one phase to his insanity. You probably think of him as some twisted, snarling, hunched-over thing, someone out of a Boris Karloff picture, prowling along glary-eyed, with his hands curved, so that you can spot him coming from a block away. He isn't—or we would have caught him long ago. He's probably perfectly normal in appearance and behavior. Maybe even clean-cut and rather likable looking. You could pass him on the street and never know. You could be around him for days at a time and never be any the wiser, never catch on that there was anything the matter with him. I bet many a time he's brushed elbows with our own fellows, coming and going, and they never gave him a second look. But when the sirens hoot and the corner lamp-posts go out, the scene comes back to him. Then he sees someone vaguely like her in the dimness around him—or right afterward when the lights go on again. And that one defective wire in him is jangled and—pfft!—a short circuit!"

"Don't the flowers tell you? They don't grow wild on the city streets. He must get them from somewhere. Isn't there some way of checking on who buys white roses, just before or during a blackout?"

"We've worked on that. No one buys flowers during a blackout. And he doesn't buy them ahead, because he doesn't know himself that it's going to happen to him. We don't know where he gets them. May as well admit it. He might never buy them the same way twice. Or he may always use the same method of getting them. He may steal them from some bush in some hot-house or conservatory that he knows of. Maybe he steps into a flower shop and buys some other kind of flower, and at the same time steals one of the white death-buds without being detected. Or he may have simply snatched one up from some street peddler, who sells so many of them one at a time all day long that he couldn't be expected to remember. Or he may have done all these things alternately, one time one, next time another."

"Terry, if you were the one to get him?"

"It would mean a citation and a promotion."

"And all the things that stand between us—that you insist stand between us—would disappear?"

"Well, they'd become a lot slimmer." He flung his cigarette down disgustedly. "But what chance have I? There isn't one of us who hasn't tried. We've all been working our heads off for weeks. And there isn't one of us who hasn't failed."

"Maybe you've all tried in the wrong way. You've tried as the police, out to catch a criminal," she said vaguely.

"What other way is there?"

She didn't answer that. She was saying to herself: *You haven't tried as one of the girls whom he stalks and kills.*

"Terry," she said, "what were they like? You know—the ones he killed? What was it they all had that was the same. Give me kind of a composite picture of them, can you?"

He took out a little pocket notebook and turned the pages. "I told you about the age. They were all between nineteen and twenty-three. Their average height was pretty much the same, too. They were all tall girls, around five-six or seven." He glanced at her. "About your height, maybe an inch taller. They were all dark-haired."

"How did they wear their hair?"

"I haven't got that down here. The death struggle disarranged it, of course, but I saw photographs of a couple of them. From what I can remember, they wore it sort of curly and loose, down their backs."

He closed the notebook.

"That's about as close as you get to a common denominator among them. I suppose each had a superficial resemblance, in the dim light or shadowy darkness where he came upon them, to that long-dead love of his own."

"Where—where did it happen?"

"One took place a few blocks from a dance hall. He must have followed her away from there. Another worked late at night, in the business office of a taxi-company garage. He must have looked in through the window as he was passing and saw her alone in there. One was a girl from a small town upstate who came here looking for work. She was last seen at an employment agency where she registered to apply for a job. She was sent out to an address, and before she could get there a blackout occurred. She never reached the address. She was found halfway between the agency and her destination, where the blackout—and he—must have overtaken her.

"The last one worked in a department store. We think in that case he must have taken refuge in the store when the alert sounded outside. He evidently saw her there behind the counter and trailed her home at closing time. She was found right outside her own door, with her latchkey in one hand, ready to insert into the lock—and the white rose in the other.

"And that's how the record stands as of tonight. We're all waiting for it to happen again. We're like a bunch of helpless amateurs."

She didn't say anything for a long time. Finally he turned and looked at her curiously. "Why are you sitting like that—so quiet? I guess I've frightened you by telling you all this."

"Take me home," she said absently, staring down at the counter before her.

He got up, threw down a coin, and escorted her toward the entrance.

"I shouldn't have told you all that stuff. I've given you the creeps."

She didn't tell him so, but he hadn't given her the creeps. He'd given her an idea.

<hr/>

The hollow-cheeked, gaunt-eyed Trowbridge butler, whose face bore a startling death-like look, stepped softly up behind Virginia Trowbridge's chair, halfway through the dinner party. He whispered, "There's a gentleman asking for you on the phone, Miss Ginny. He says he's calling from some headquarters or other. I couldn't quite get the name."

She jumped up, nearly upsetting the chair in her hurry, and ran out of the room as if her life depended on it.

"This is Tom," a man's voice said when she had reached the phone. "I'm keeping my word to you, letting you know ahead . . ."

"Is there—is there going to be one tonight?" she asked in an excited undertone.

"I'm not supposed to tell you this. It's a serious matter. But you know, Ginny, I can't refuse you anything. And you promised me you wouldn't let it go any further, if I did give you advance warning on each blackout."

"I swear I won't tell anyone else, Tom. I give you my word I won't pass it on to another living soul. This is just for my own information. It's—well, it's hard to explain. It's just a whim of mine."

"I know I can depend on you to keep it to yourself. Well, the order's just gone out. There's going to be a complete city-wide blackout tonight."

"How much time have I—" She quickly corrected herself. "I mean, how soon is it coming—what time is it set for?"

"It's going to be at exactly nine thirty."

She looked around her. "It's twenty-five to nine now. That means in less than, an hour—in fifty-five minutes . . ."

She hung up and ran for the stairs. On the bottom step she stopped short. There was a shadow cast on the wall, the shadow of a figure arched in the dining-room doorway.

"Burton, is that you?" she called sharply.

The shadow moved and the butler came around the turn of the hall, holding a small tray in his hands.

"You weren't listening to my conversation, were you?"

"No, miss. I was waiting for it to end."

"Put that down a minute and have Edwards bring the car around to the door. Hurry! I have to be out of here in ten minutes!"

He looked at her in gloomy deprecation. "Beg pardon, miss, I believe I overheard Mrs. Trowbridge say she intended using the car herself to take her friends to the opera."

She was halfway up the stairs by now. "He can come back for Mother and her friends afterward, as soon as he's taken me where I want to go. And don't say anything about it to anyone until after I've gone. I haven't time to go back in there and start apologizing."

She flung the door of her room shut and began to prepare herself. She dressed faster than she ever had before. She had a date with death— in the oncoming pall of the blackout.

She thrust her feet into a pair of newly purchased shoes, with almost stilt-like heels. Five-six or seven, he'd said; about an inch taller than you. She took a fastening or two out of her hair and let it tumble down about her shoulders. She ran a comb through it and left it that way. Worn curly and loose, down the back, he'd said, and dark-haired. Her own had been a medium brown, but three visits to a hairdresser inside of three days had darkened it progressively to a brown that was now almost black. In the dark, or in uncertain light, it could not be told from black.

She gave a couple of half turns before the glass, studying herself. Would Death know her, when he saw her? "The mind remembers," Terry's voice came back to her again. She shivered slightly, then hastily opened a drawer and ferreted out a small scrap of paper which had lain there in readiness with a name and address penciled on it. She hurried from the room.

She ran down the stairs, flashing past the dining room. The quick hum of conversation made her hasty departure unnoticed. A moment later she was in the car and Edwards, the chauffeur, had taken his place in the driver's seat.

As they glided into motion she reached over his shoulder and handed him the penciled scrap of paper she'd brought with her.

He looked at it, and touched his cap without saying anything.

It was only later, when they were waiting for a light, that he looked up and sought her eyes questioningly in his rear-sight mirror. "Are you sure you want to go there unescorted, miss? It's one of the cheapest dance halls in the whole city."

"I'm not only sure I want to go there," she answered firmly, "but I want to be inside the place by nine at the latest. Please be sure to get me there in time!"

⪼•◆•⪻

Her chair at the dinner-table had remained vacant, with her unfinished glass of wine still standing before it.

The butler stepped forward and leaned over confidentially at the older Mrs. Trowbridge's belated inquiry. "She's gone out, madam," he reported, "without saying where." Then he withdrew from the room.

"Why do you keep that man?" one of the guests asked, glancing curiously after him. "I should think you would find him depressing."

"He is quite cadaverous, isn't he?" Mrs. Trowbridge agreed cheerfully. "They're very hard to obtain now. Besides, we've grown rather used to him so that we don't mind any more. It's his night off, later on tonight, and he always looks particularly gruesome on his night off."

She laughed a little and idly fingered one of the tightly furled white rosebuds she had ordered for the dinner-table decorations.

⪼•◆•⪻

"Are you here with anyone?"

The figure standing alongside her had edged up by imperceptible degrees, pretending to watch the dancers with a sort of evasive vacancy. Every few bars of music he was closer than he had been before, and yet she could never catch him actually moving.

She shook her ahead. Something caught in her throat and prevented her from answering more fully.

"I didn't figure you were. I've been watching you the whole time you were standing here like this."

She'd been watching him too, but she didn't say so.

His face was weatherbeaten and shrewd. He was of medium height and stocky build. He wasn't actually ominous-looking, but neither was he the type to inspire confidence. She didn't like his hands. Whatever purpose had brought him up here, she was certain it was more than just the sheer love of dancing. He didn't have the limberness of the typical dancing fanatic, nor the nattiness of dress that so often accompanies that quality.

"I haven't seen you dance with anybody yet," he offered.

"I don't know anyone here."

He hitched up his head. "How about me, then?"

She could feel a curious, numbing little shock run through her body as her fingers touched the coarse cloth of his sleeve. "Terry would kill me for this, if he knew," she shivered.

They moved around the glistening floor in silence, very slowly.

"How am I going to know? What way is there?" she kept thinking. "I should have been prepared . . ."

"Do you come here often?" she asked.

"I never go to the same place twice."

Why not, she wondered—is he afraid?

They came back to the spot from where they'd started. The music stopped, and his hand dropped from hers. Nothing had happened. She glanced over at the large, circular wall clock above the entrance. Nine more minutes.

Others kept applauding. The music started once more. His hand came up again, this time without asking. Again in stony silence they went through the motions of their strange death dance. Occasionally a green spotlight from above would flicker across their faces, giving them the appearance of ghouls.

Suddenly he spoke. "You know, you kind of remind me of someone I once knew. I'm trying to think who."

She missed a step, got back in time again. "I do?"

She waited, but he said nothing more.

Again they were coming back toward their starting place. It took about two minutes to go all the way around. In six minutes, now.

"I like the dance halls here better than over in London, don't you?" she blurted out. She hadn't known she was going to say it herself. She would have been afraid to, if she had.

This time he lost a step. "How did you know I'd been to London?"

She had to think quickly. "I can tell by your shoes. Only the English make those heavy, thick, hand-sewn brogues."

He looked down at them, but he didn't contradict her. It was a shot in the dark, but it must have hit the mark.

Five minutes now. It was an eerie feeling, to be the only one in all that crowd who knew that at a given moment all this brightness would be blotted out.

He'd caught her that time. She was becoming careless, giving herself away. "Why do you keep looking at the clock?" he asked.

"I only—I want to see what time it is, that's all."

"Are you expecting anyone?"

Death, she thought, but she didn't tell him.

It was twenty-six minutes past nine. Four more minutes.

The blaring music stopped and an odd silence hung over the place. This time the applause couldn't get the musicians to begin again. They wanted to rest. The dancers separated, drifting off the center of the floor toward the sidelines, trailing their inverted reflections along its shiny surface like ghosts.

They stayed together, walking around the floor. They came around to the rear of the bandstand, where there was a lane and a counter where they sold soft drinks. And on the other . . .

"Look, they sell flowers here, too," she said, her voice steady.

"Yeah, not a bad idea."

She couldn't see the clock from here. The lights were burning brighter—as if they knew that in three more minutes they were going to die, and were having a last fling. All the others were fanning themselves, but her hands felt cold.

"Can I get you some kind of refreshment?"

"I'd rather have a flower. Just one."

"Sure. What kind would you like?" He turned aside and led her to the counter.

"You pick it out," she said and hoped he didn't notice the tremor in her voice.

He put his hand out. Then he stopped and looked at her face several times, and back at the flowers again. "There's something kind of innocent and young about you, different from most of the girls who come up here. I think this kind would go good on you."

He was holding a white rosebud in his hand.

Terry's phrase for it sounded in her mind like a warning bell. The death rose! Her eyes brew bigger and her breath came faster. She tried to hide her excitement—and her fear.

"You dropped it," he said. He picked it up and put it back in her hand a second time. Then he added, "Why is your hand shaking like that? You can hardly hold it."

"The stem is a little wet. I'm doing that to dry it."

They came back in sight of the clock again. Two minutes.

The music began, and they went out on the floor. She said to herself. "It'll happen while this one is going on. Before we come all the way around again."

She'd pinned the flower to her dress. She looked at the clock again, slyly so that he wouldn't notice. The minute hand was straightening itself out. Darkness was on its way.

For a minute everything hung suspended. Only she knew what was coming. The music crashed and pounded. The circling figures swam around. The lights blazed down.

Then suddenly a different noise crept into the music. A trumpet or a horn was getting too loud and going off-key. First, the music submerged it, but it kept coming to the surface again. Then it climbed above and, in turn, submerged the music. It was like a foghorn now, deep and steady. The music stopped. The long-drawn eerie hoot went on and on, surging through the night outside.

A group of lights went out, leaving a circle of darkness on the floor below where they'd been. Then another circuit went out, leaving still another circle of shadows. The dancers scattered in all directions, not knowing which way to go.

A hollow voice kept trumpeting, "Lights out! Lights out!"

"Come on over against the wall," he said, "while we can still see how to get there." He took her by the arm and started to pull her after him.

The last circuit of light overhead died just as they reached the wall, but there were still two solitary bulbs burning, one at each end, over the exits.

She watched his face tensely, while she still could, in the feeble glimmer that was left. She didn't like the way he looked. His eyes kept opening and closing, as though he were suffering.

He hadn't let go of her hand. She tried to withdraw it, but he held onto it tightly.

"Stand here by me," he whispered, "so I won't lose you. Here, perfectly still against the wall."

The light at the upper end had gone out now. There was only one left in the entire place, an automatic night-light that they couldn't disconnect in time. Somebody was climbing a chair to it. She couldn't see his face any more, just his eyes, shining like little wet pebbles in the dark.

He was shaking. She could feel it through his hand.

"You don't hear the bombs," she heard him say in a smothered undertone, as if he'd forgotten where he was.

"What was that?" she caught him up.

That brought him back for a minute. "I've been through this before. Not here—some place else—where it was real."

"And then you went home and killed someone," she said to herself, unheard.

Suddenly, in the final instant before the last light went out, she saw something. Her free hand went to her throat, in an instinctive protective gesture. Why was he looking at her neck like that?

The last stubborn light went out and the darkness became complete. Almost smothering, it was so dense. The blackout was in full swing.

She was limp against the wall. She might have toppled over if it hadn't been for his taut grip on her hand.

She was helpless now, caught in the very trap she'd tried to arrange for him. She should have gone to the telephone while she still had the chance. There was a pay booth in the rear. She had seen it while they were dancing, but it was too late now.

She could hear his breathing beside her. He was breathing hard. The siren had stopped now and there was that awful, hushed, waiting silence that was even worse. It was oppressive, like a sense of doom. An occasional foot scraped restlessly, or some girl gave a nervous giggle, but for the most part they could have been alone in a vast empty cave.

He couldn't do it right here. Or could he? She wondered. Then she thought, "Yes, he could, if he covered my mouth quickly enough." What was that Terry had said? They died in sudden, swift silence.

She started violently away from the wall and choked back a scream. "What was that? I felt something touch the side of my neck."

"It was just my hand. I put it up against the wall, to lean against it."

She shuddered and tried to relax again. Then he spoke again.

"Let's go downstairs, shall we? I can hardly breathe up here."

This was it, coming now.

"We're not supposed to go out while the blackout is on."

"Just down to the street door. We can stand there till it's over. We're right near the stairs. I saw where they were before the lights went out."

He began to pull her again. If there wasn't any actual violence in the pull, there was a sort of undulating pressure that she couldn't hold out against. Her feet couldn't get a grip on the glossy floor and she tottered unwillingly after him.

They passed a few other couples standing silently against the wall and she wanted to reach out and grasp at them—call out to them to help her.

"I wanted to find out," she thought ruefully. "Now I'm going to find out!"

There was a swish as he pushed aside a swinging glass door and then they were outside at the head of the stairs. There were a few couples out there, too, sitting on the steps, so it was postponed another minute or two. He picked his way down through them, still holding her hand. "Hold onto the rail," he whispered, "so you don't miss a step going down."

She kept trying to pull back, away from him, but he seemed not to notice or else he purposely disregarded it.

He pushed aside a second glass door, and they were in the open street-doorway now, cut off from all the others inside.

It was deathly still all around them. In the distance a warden's voice could be heard, shouting a warning to some householder, but it had a far-off sound, blocks away.

She was starting to lose her head. "Wait a minute, I want to go in again. Let me go in again—just for a minute . . ."

He kept her there by flattening the hinged door against its frame with one hand, so that she couldn't swing it open.

His voice was treacherously reassuring. "Don't be frightened. I know it's scary, but isn't it better down here in the fresh air? Let's just walk down a little way, and back. Close up against the building. Nobody'll see us."

He urged her forward. She took a step or two after him, off-balance. The doorway slipped behind them, already swallowed up in the dark.

She didn't see the little alley in time, until it had already opened up beside them. He must have known it was there all along or he couldn't have recognized it so immediately in the darkness.

Suddenly his lethargy of movement was gone and he was all quick, remorseless action. The careless hand on her shoulder put on pressure, twirled her aside, thrust her headlong into the gap. He came in after her, sealing up her escape, for the alley was so narrow the buildings pressed against her.

The hand that had been on her wrist all along let go at last, clamped itself to her mouth instead, stifling the scream that was just beginning to form. The other hand reached for her neck, around toward the back.

Something snapped back there with a violent wrench, hurting her as it did—and the necklace of gold, which she'd forgotten she was wearing, was ripped away and disappeared into his pocket.

"Gee, I had to work hard for that!" he grunted resentfully, and gave her a violent fling of release that sent her sprawling to the ground.

And that was all. It was over. He gave a quick turn on his heel and darted away, just as the all-clear sounded and the lights began to pepper on again.

She picked herself up dazedly. She wanted to laugh and cry at the same time. "Just a cheap thief," she thought wryly. "Only after a necklace, worth maybe twenty-five dollars. All that terror for that!"

The lights were coming on more and more fully every minute. The windows of the dance hall overhead flared up suddenly in a rosy-orange glow, some of it spilling down the walls into the narrow alley where he'd flung her, lighting up its recesses by reflection.

As she turned to look behind her, to see if she had dropped anything to the ground, she stifled a scream and flattened against the wall.

Directly behind her, so close that if she moved another step or two she would have trodden on it, lay a hunched form. A dead girl, dark hair streaming over her face. One outstretched hand extended limply along the ground, as if in search of help. In its nerveless grasp was a white rosebud . . .

———✦———

He was sitting there brooding into his empty cup again. Her hand came to rest gently on his coat sleeve, to show him she was there. She didn't say anything about a date this time. He had no time for dates now. She had none either.

"Last night again," he said tersely. "I told you how it would be."

"Any luck so far?"

"Not a sign. He might just as well float through the air, for all the trace he leaves."

"He must have bought the flower upstairs in the dance hall. He must have been up there earlier and has been saving it since."

He shook his head. "Only one white rose was sold up there all night and to a man who had a different girl with him; we had the concessionaire look at the—" She saw him stop and gaze at her. "How did you know that? I didn't tell you they sold flowers up there."

"I—I must have read about it, somewhere."

"You couldn't have. It hasn't been in any of the papers. We've kept as much of it out of the papers as we could. Just let them print a bald statement that an unidentified body was found."

"I—I just imagined that they'd sell them in a place like that."

"I'm glad *you* don't go near places like that. I'm glad it couldn't happen to *you*," he said fervently.

He didn't know how close it had come to happening to her.

———✦———

A white armband, seeming to float detachedly through the darkness like some sort of ghostly apparition, without any visible arm to support it, came to a halt in front of the doorway. A pocket-light winked on and threw a cartwheel of light against the doorway. The figure of a girl was revealed, pressed against one side of the wall. About five-feet six or seven, black hair cascading down her back, a cheap little coat belted around her. She put her hand to her face to ward off the light.

The air raid warden grunted, "That's not a very good place, but stay where you are until you hear the all-clear. It's due in another minute."

The light clicked off and the detached armband floated away on the darkness.

In two or three minutes the light had winked on again, this time far down the street. Pointed at somebody else, in another doorway. This time the cartwheel was no bigger than a poker chip, from where the girl peered out around the edge of her own sheltering-place. Who or what it fell on could not be seen. Then it snuffed out, and receded still farther into the night-blind distance.

The short blasts of the all-clear began to sound in the distance, coming nearer all the time as they were relayed from one siren to the next.

Ginny Trowbridge's foot made a soft little *tick* as it descended from the doorstep and she resumed her interrupted way along the street. A scanty light returned to the desolate scene, but somehow only made it more desolate. A car that had been parked two or three blocks away meshed gears and whined off into the distance, the sound carrying clearly in the new stillness that had followed the all-clear. A row of widely-separated street lights went on in unison and struggled in vain against the darkness. Hooded as they were, they only shone downward in a straight line, each one making a little pale puddle beneath itself.

Her shoes struck a clean-cut, brisk little tap along the echoing street. It was the only sound in the silence around her. It was as though she was the only thing moving in the whole spellbound city.

She passed the doorway where the warden's torch had given its second flicker of investigation. Its occupant, if there had been one, must already have left. It was an impenetrable mass of obscurity now. Yet she had a curious sense of someone's eyes being on her as she walked past it. She tried to shake it off but the dim feeling persisted.

She even turned her head to look back. At that very minute the glow from the nearest street light glanced over her, revealing her as in a snapshot. Then the tap of her footfalls went on into the darkness on the other side.

Suddenly it was no longer alone in the brooding stillness. Another tread had joined in, was subtly underscoring it, somewhere behind her. It was impossible to tell just when the accompaniment had set in. At the first moment of awareness it was already there, in full progress, blending in with the sharper rhythm of her own steps.

It was a quiet tread, unhurried and deliberate. At first it held no alarm for her. Somebody had left a second doorway, that was all. It might be that one she had passed just now, or it might be some other one.

It was easily recognizable as a man's tread. But it wasn't conspicuous. In fact, it was sometimes hard to catch at all. Then each time she thought it had died out, it would come back again.

It would diverge soon, go off in a direction of its own, she told herself. No two people were ever likely to maintain the same course for more than two or three blocks.

The two or three blocks passed and still it came on.

She put it to a test. She crossed over to the other side of the street. It would stay over on the first side now. It didn't. It crossed over after her. She could tell by the change in resonance when it stepped down and stepped up again on this side.

It was following her.

She came to a corner and turned down the side street. That would tell. That would be the final test.

It dwindled for a minute, then it rang out clear again. It had come around the corner after her.

It wasn't hurrying. It didn't seem to want to overtake her so much as to keep pace with her. It was patient. It was biding its time.

She quickened her steps. It quickened in turn. Then, though her impulse was to run, she forced herself to slacken, to come almost to a halt. The tempo of steps behind her slowed up. It did whatever she did. It was stalking her. She was its quarry.

She could have escaped. Not on foot, perhaps. But there was the subway into which it would probably not follow her. There were taxis. But she didn't want to escape. She wasn't trying to save her own skin. If she had wanted to, she wouldn't have been out alone on the streets.

She purposely tried to maneuver it into revealing itself, this anonymous tread that had no body. The dim-out regulations, even now that the lights were on again, didn't give her many opportunities. But she tried to use the few that existed. Store windows, which would have suited her purpose best of all, were all rigidly dark now that it was late. There remained only the street lights and an occasional building entrance. It skirted both types alike with satanic dexterity—sidled around the dark outside of the lights whenever she hoped to see it pass directly under them. The most she could ever see was an anonymous black outline gliding by just beyond the range of the light.

He—if it were he—was smart. While she was still alive, she wouldn't see him. Only when she was about to die would she see him. Then it would be too late. Terry had said, "Only the dead see him, and they can't tell about it afterward."

She had the courage to keep moving slowly ahead of him, but not enough courage to stand still, waiting for him to come up to her. She had to keep on walking—hoping that he would try soon.

He might be uncertain yet that she was the fever-image he took her to be. That might be the reason for the long delay in striking. She tried to egg him on, to convince him. When she came to a place where there was slightly better light, she stopped and held herself under it, almost posing, turning this way and that as if uncertain of her direction. Even from a distance her height, her black hair and all the other details must have stood out conspicuously.

The death-tread had stopped when she did, waiting for her to go on. He was watching. Her skin crept, remembering those others. She glanced up at the street sign for a touch of security. Then she went on again. Certainly he would strike now that he had seen her under the light and had noticed how much she looked like that first one.

She saw that she'd been right. Almost at once the tread was faster. It was closing in now. Closing in for the kill. Her heart started to pound. It was hard to make her feet maintain their former pace, to keep from running. She pressed her fingers through the soft leather of her handbag to feel the reassuring shape of the small gun. That had a steadying effect.

He was trying to catch up quietly now. His feet were a whisper on the pavement. He was coming closer every minute.

She'd better get the gun out, or at least have it ready.

Aboout twenty yards now. Maybe even less. There was a dark stretch immediately behind her that she'd just passed through. If she turned now, close as he was, she still wouldn't be able to recognize him. There was another light coming, up ahead. If he only waited until she could reach that.

Without any warning there was a slurring sound directly beside her and the white top of a police patrol car swam up to the curb.

One of the men in it called out, "Are you in trouble, miss? You seem to be walking kind of funny."

There was no sound of retreat from back there. The footsteps had simply melted away into nothingness, vanishing from the face of the earth as if they had never existed. He was gone already beyond recall. It was no good telling them, they'd never get him. And even if they got someone, they could only hold him as a suspicious character. They could never prove what he'd been about to do. You can't convict on intention alone.

"Why don't you mind your own business?" she flared. "If I wanted police protection, I would have called for it!"

There was a shocked pause. Then the car glided on without another word from its occupants.

After a while she turned and started back along the way she had just come.

She wasn't in any danger now, she knew. She wouldn't meet him again even if she walked the rest of the night looking for him. He was too smart.

She came back to the preceding light—the one before which it had so nearly happened. She stopped short. There was something under her foot. She moved back a step and looked down. A white flower lay where it had been dropped a moment before.

———◈———

This time it was she who had the doleful face when she walked into the Greek's. She slumped down beside him without saying hello. She held her head pillowed against her hand as she handed him the newspaper she'd been carrying tucked under her arm. It was folded carefully.

"What's the matter? More about the Rose Killer?" he asked.

"Not this time. Read the gossip column."

The third item down said: "What daughter of a socially prominent family is that way about a detective and waits for him outside the station house in her limousine every might, private chauffeur and all? Mama says no, not until he gets his man."

She laughed bitterly. "When did I ever wait for you outside the station house with a limousine or without it?"

"This is just around the corner. I suppose that's what he means." He smiled bleakly.

"They held a big family war-council over me just now. Feathered headdresses and everything. I was asked to give my word I wouldn't see you any more. I refused, of course. So I'm to be exiled. Our summer place out on Long Island, all by myself, with just an old-lady caretaker who lives out there."

"Maybe they're right. Why don't you listen to them?" he suggested.

"Are you on their side too?" she asked scornfully.

"No, I'm on ours," he said quietly. "When are you leaving?"

"Right away. Edwards is driving me out in the car. I just slipped out to let you know." She handed him a slip of paper. "This is where I'll be, in. case you want to reach me. Here's the address and the phone number. Don't lose it. But I'll be in again. They can't stop me. There are trains and buses. I'll meet you here in the Greek's every time it's your night off, just as we've been doing right along. Look for me."

"That's a date," he said. "I'll be waiting."

"I've got to get back now, before they miss me and get my scalp." The last thing she said was, "We'll get the Rose Killer, Terry, and you'll have your promotion. Then I'm marrying you whether they like it or not, and they can whistle."

He thought that "we" was just a slip of the tongue. She'd meant to say "you," of course

He sat there looking after her. She was a great girl, he thought.

———◆◆◆———

She kept watching him through the glass while she dialed the numbers with one finger. Sitting at the little table, his back was to her. He couldn't watch her phoning.

This time she was sure of it. This time there would be no mistake as in the first time, and no slip-up as in the second. While the slots of the dial whirred around, she recapitulated the results of a whole evening of research.

He was English, and freely admitted it. That was nothing in

itself. But he'd incautiously given her the date of his arrival, and that *was* something. May fifteenth last. The first of the white rose killings had taken place on the seventh of June. She had the exact date from Terry. In other words, those killings had begun exactly three weeks after the time of his arrival. But there was something even more incriminating than that. From Tom she'd obtained a calendar of past blackouts, giving the dates on which they'd occurred throughout the year. The one on the seventh of June, which was the one coinciding with the first murder, was also the *first one* to have occurred following his arrival. His arrival and the murders and the blackouts were all in perfect synchronization.

Terry might call all this circumstantial, but there was more to it than that. She'd been followed the other night by the actual Rose Killer. She was positive of that.

She'd tested him just now on their way to this place. It hadn't been easy to manage, but she'd accomplished it. She'd pretended to stop and look into a shop window. Then she had sent him down to the corner ahead of her, on the excuse of looking to see whether a bus was coming or not. Then she beckoned him to come back, as if she wanted to point out something in the window to him. He'd rejoined her at an easy strolling gait, about the same as the other night. She'd strained her ears.

Just as no two people have the same fingerprints, no two people have exactly the same footfall. She had a good ear for music and she knew her ears weren't playing her false. The pace, the weight of the body, the bulk of shoe, were all the same.

It was incredible that she should have met him a second time like this. She'd had a stroke of luck. She'd met him at a flower show, an annual exhibit. Seen him hovering around the white roses there. Others just admired them and passed on. But even when he'd finally moved along to other displays, he still kept looking over at them.

She'd questioned the supervisor in charge of that particular display. That same man had been in every day since the show had first opened. These white roses seemed to exert an irresistible attraction to him. They innocently supposed he was some amateur fancier who specialized in them. She didn't.

Now he was with her—waiting at the table for her. There wasn't any blackout scheduled for tonight, or Tom would have let her know. But this time she wouldn't wait for him to make the first move. Terry could break him down. They had ways. If it took weeks or months, they'd keep at it once they got their hands on him. And that was her job right now, to put him into those hands.

Some stupid desk-sergeant got on.

"Get Terry for me, hurry! I haven't very much time. Please!"

He seemed to take forever. Finally he spoke up again. "He's not here right now. Off duty tonight. If this is police business, you better tell me what it is and I can get you someone else."

It was Terry she wanted to have the promotion. She had to get him. The Greek's! Of course—she should have remembered that sooner. It was Tuesday and he would be there, waiting for her. Her finger started toward the dial once more.

He'd got up and was coming over. No, he was going toward the door. He was walking out on her.

She came out fast and caught up with him just as he reached the entrance.

"Do you always go into a telephone booth when you want to powder your nose?"

She thought he hadn't been watching! His back had been toward her the whole time. Maybe he'd used a cigarette case as a mirror.

"I'm afraid I'll have to leave you now. I have an appointment," he said.

Something had made him uneasy. She'd overplayed her hand in some way. Maybe by asking him one question too many. Or maybe that acoustic test out on the sidewalk before.

She had to string along with him at any cost, until she had a chance to put in another call to Terry at the Greek's." No matter how she worked it, she mustn't lose sight of him until then.

"Well, wait, let me come along with you just as far as—"

He felt her sudden start as they came out onto the sidewalk. "What's the matter?" he asked, turning to look at her.

It was the car. She would have known it anywhere. It had just driven up. Complete to the monogram on the door. For a minute she had a vision of her mother and the other members of the family stepping out and confronting her in all their majesty. But there was only Edwards in it.

"Hurry up, let's get away from here fast!" She began to tug at her suspect's sleeve. "There's someone who knows me in that car."

They took a few quick steps together away from the entrance, trying to escape into the darkness. The hunter and hunted were both in the same boat now. Edwards had already seen her. His hail came after her. "Miss Trowbridge!"

The car-door slapped open, there was a throb of overtaking foot-steps behind them, and she found herself separated from her companion and at bay against the wall.

"I'm sorry, miss, but I must speak to you a minute." Edwards touched his cap to her respectfully, but he was still blocking her way.

She tried to thrust him aside. "That man! Where'd that man I was just with go?"

He'd vanished as completely as if he'd been whisked out of sight on a wire. Gone again, just when she thought she had him. Well, now she knew what he looked like, but all that painstaking work had been a waste.

She whirled on Edwards in a fury. "What do you want? What do you mean by doing such a thing?

"You'd better come with me at once, miss. I've been looking everywhere for you. Your mother's been taken seriously ill."

"Where is she, here in town?"

"No, miss, she's out at the country place. I drove her out myself shortly before dinner. She wanted to pay you a surprise visit. I imagine the shock of not finding you there had a great deal to do with it."

"Is she quite bad?"

"She had the doctor with her when I left. I imagine it will help some as soon as she sees you."

She didn't wait to hear any more; she stepped into the car in a hurry. "You'd better drive fast, Edwards."

"I'll do my best, miss."

———◆———

There were only two or three dim lights to be seen behind the windows when they finally turned in the driveway. One of them was in the room habitually occupied by her mother whenever she stayed at the country place.

She jumped out of the car, ran up the steps, and used her own key on the door without waiting to be admitted. "Thank you, Edwards. I'll leave the door open for you while you're putting the car away. I'll go right up and see how she is!"

She ran up the inside staircase, stopping before her mother's door. She knocked firmly. "Mother. Mother, are you all right? Is the doctor in there with you?"

There was no answer.

She grasped the knob and opened the door.

The room was empty. The bed was undisturbed. It was just as it had been left on her mother's last visit. She stood there stunned.

Then the implication slowly percolated through her. She knew what it was. She turned—terrified—to look toward the stairs. The front door. She could still keep him out, if she got down to it before he. . . .

She ran back to the head of the stairs, then stopped with a sickening jolt. He was standing inside the door and it was already closed. He'd just finished locking it and drawing the bolt.

He reached into his pocket and she saw him take out a knife. He opened the blade with quick thumb-pressure. She didn't understand in time, thinking it was meant to be a weapon of attack. He squatted down on his heels, close up against the wall, and sawed away at something just over the baseboard. Two ends of wire sprang out. The telephone. He'd cut it. Then he calmly put the knife away again.

He looked up and saw her standing there, frozen. He was very natural about everything. His whole attitude was calm and rational. No frenzied mania, no popping eyes, no foaming mouth. You wouldn't have known what was on his mind.

"So you've been trying to get the Rose Killer," he said. "I could have told you that you'd never get him. Because I'm the Rose Killer myself. Driving you and your whole family around day after day. Sitting there right in front of you the whole time."

She saw him unfastening a cuff link, to give his arm a better swing. In that cold, trivial action there was more undiluted horror than in ten berserk rages.

The real thing at last, but what good did it do her to know that now? Right under the same roof with her the whole time, while she went out night after night hunting for him all over town! But, as Terry had said, you could be around him for weeks at a time and never guess.

"But he said you were mad—that you didn't know any better! You *know* I'm not that girl in England. Look at me. You *know* I'm Ginny Trowbridge."

"I'm not mad. Not this time." He started coming up the stairs.

She fled back along the upper hall. "Mrs. Crosby!" she shrieked at the top of her lungs.

"I don't think she'll hear you" she heard him say. The way he said it sounded twice as quiet after the shattering way she'd just screamed. She got to the caretaker's room, flung the door wide, jabbed at the light switch. "Mrs. Crosby, help me!"

Mrs. Crosby didn't move. She'd gone to bed, and the bed wasn't disturbed much. You could hardly tell. Only, the pillow was *over* her face instead of under it. There was a hollow in it, punched by someone's knee that had pressed down hard.

She didn't scream this time. She smothered it in her hands.

He was coming up slowly. He was so sure of her that he was taking his time.

She fled from room to room, looking for something, anything, with which to defend herself. There wasn't even a gun in the place. The one she owned had been left behind her in the city. She found a hammer in a linen closet at the back of the hall. It wasn't a large one, but it was the only thing there was. She might be able to stun him long enough to get the door-key out of his pocket or to break one of the lower-floor windows and get out that way.

She went back into her own room and got into position behind the door, leaving it half ajar. She knew she was only going to have a chance for one blow. It had to count. She gripped the hammer with both hands and held it poised.

She could hear him coming up slowly, a step at a time, with the deliberation of a machine. She nearly went a little mad herself, waiting for him to get to her room.

He stopped just outside the door. She went up on her toes. He started to push the door slowly inward. It swung around and left his head exposed, sidewise to her, making a perfect target. She swung with all her strength.

She could feel the sudden loss of weight as she swept it forward. She knew what had happened even before she heard it bounce off the wall behind her. The hammer-head had flown off. Just the stick part fell harmlessly across his skull, not heavy enough to do anything but sting him a little.

He swung around and wrenched it from her hands. She scuttled back along the wall, like a mouse looking for a hole. He caught up with her on the other side of the room, over by the window. The chase stopped.

Her flailing hand went down into something soft. Earth— around a potted plant standing on the inside window-ledge. It went over with a shattering crash, but not before she'd got a handful of it. She waited until his eyes were so close to her face she couldn't miss. She didn't.

He was blinded for a minute, pawing helplessly at his eyes. She ducked under his arm, streaked across to the door and out. She knew she'd never get downstairs in time, so she went up instead, heading for the roof. He was quicker than she'd thought he'd be. He tore out after her, nearly at her heels. There was a lightweight rattan settee just short of the roof staircase. She threw that over, blocking him. He went sprawling over it. She got up to the top, opened the trap door, and climbed out into the open.

The roof was gabled and covered with treacherous slates. She skidded down them as far as a squat brick chimney. She got below it and held on with both arms. She couldn't go any lower than that. It sloped down to a leaded rain-gutter and then dropped off into space.

She heard him coming after her. He must have seen her arms looped around the chimney. Some of the slates detached themselves at his unseen approach and went slithering past where she crouched.

Suddenly a hand touched her arm. It was ice-cold—like the fingers of death. She screamed and tore her arms away—or tried to. One swung out free, but he'd caught the other by the wrist. Braced on the other side of the chimney, he held her in an iron grip. She dangled there, legs threshing helplessly against the slates.

A light suddenly slashed up at them from below, blinding her. It was the adjustable spotlight of a car. She heard a voice cry out hoarsely, "Good heavens, look at the two of them!" There were figures moving around down there on the lawn, but they were too late. They might as well not have come.

Terry's voice reached her from far away, as in a dream. Crooning in reassurance, and yet half wild with smothered terror. "Ginny girl, edge over, edge over, pull more of his arm out!"

She braced herself against the unstable slates, then hitched violently away from the chimney, almost leaning flat against the roof. His hand came around the corner of the chimney, still welded to hers. His wrist came, then a little of his forearm. But he was strong. She couldn't pull him any farther.

Something went *bang!* and chips of brick flew off. Something went *bang!* again, and the hand jarred open. She was prone against the roof. She just skidded a little farther down and stayed there, hanging on by a hair's-breath.

Something came tumbling down around the other side of the chimney and over into the night, clawing at nothing as it went.

The light went out, in order not to blind her and make her lose her precarious hold. She was all by herself now. She knew that all she had to do was just hang on a little while longer. Then Terry climbed out against the night-sky over her, with a rope around him. He came scaling down to where she was and his reassuring arms went around her.

———◈———

In the car, on the way back to the city, they talked about it.

"They'll give you your promotion now," she said.

"I'm not sure that you shouldn't have it instead."

"How did you get out there when you did?"

"Nothing very brilliant. It was my night off and you'd promised to meet me at the Greek's. You never break your word. If you couldn't come I knew you would have called me there or sent some message. That brought on a hunch that something was wrong. It was just a hunch, but I couldn't fight it down. So finally I gave in to it. Then when I couldn't reach the place by telephone, I remembered that you'd said this caretaker was out here at all times, and that did the rest."

"There's only one thing I don't understand. That man I was with earlier tonight . . . He seemed to fit the specifications so perfectly."

He laughed. "I heard about that. He told us about it afterwards. You were a little wide of the mark that time. Know who that was? A Scotland Yard man, sent over here to work on the case. He's been in for several conferences with us."

"But he *followed* me the other night! The tread was the same!"

"I wouldn't be surprised. He might have had some idea of using you as live bait. The cat following the cheese in hopes of seeing the rat go for it."

"I'm afraid I wasn't very good as your deputy—confusing detectives with criminals."

"You got him, didn't you? And neither Scotland Yard nor Center Street did. Pretty good for one little girl on her own."

"There's just one thing more. There was no blackout tonight. Why did he go for me like that? I thought it was only during . . ."

"He must have recognized the man he saw you with as a Yard operative. Maybe he'd already seen him during some previous investigation over there. When he saw the two of you together like that, he was afraid you were beginning to suspect him, thought you might be on the point of divulging his identity and where-abouts, if you hadn't already. That was enough to bring on the so-called shock without the aid of any blackout. Only it was a very sane, level-headed 'shock' in this case. He knew what he was doing. Well, the fall to the ground did what the hangman's rope was waiting to do, and a lot more cheaply—broke his neck."

She pressed her face against his coat. "I'm glad it's over."

"Sure. It's all over and done with now. In a little while you'll forget all about it."

"All but one thing. I'll never be able to look at a white rose again as long as I live."

AFTERWORD TO "THE DEATH ROSE"

In "The Death Rose" (*Baffling Detective Stories*, March 1943) Woolrich recycled the storyline of his classic "Dime a Dance" (1938): a young woman stakes herself out as bait to trap a psychotic serial killer of women. This time she's a wealthy debutante rather than a taxi dancer, the tale takes place during Manhattan's World War II practice blackouts rather than in peacetime and the narration is in third rather than first person. As so often in Woolrich the suspense depends on wild coincidence—how likely is it that every man Ginny meets would match the killer's psychological profile so closely?—but while his emotional roller-coaster is spinning, flaws like this are all but unnoticeable. The radio version of the story, broadcast on the CBS series *Suspense* (July 6, 1943) and starring Maureen O'Hara as Ginny, captured the *noir* mood so miraculously well that I'm half convinced Woolrich wrote the script himself.

New York Blues

It's six o'clock; my drink is at the three-quarter mark—three-quarters down, not three-quarters up—and the night begins.

Across the way from me sits a little transistor radio, up on end, simmering away like a teakettle on a stove. It's been going steadily ever since I first came in here, two days, three nights ago; it chisels away the stony silence, takes the edge off the being alone. It came with the room, not with me.

Now there's a punctuation of three lush chords, and it goes into a traffic report. "Good evening. The New York Municipal Communications Service presents the 6:00 P.M. Traffic Advisory. Traffic through the Holland and Lincoln tunnels and over the George Washington Bridge, heavy westbound, light eastbound. Traffic on the crosscut between the George Washington and Queens-Whitestone bridges, heavy in both directions. Traffic through the Battery Tunnel, heavy outbound, very light inbound. Traffic on the West Side Highway, bumper to bumper all the way. Radar units in operation there. Traffic over the Long Island Expressway is beginning to build, due to tonight's game at Shea Stadium. West 70th Street between Amsterdam and West End avenues is closed due to a water-main break. A power failure on the East Side I.R.T. line between Grand Central and 125th Street is causing delays of up to forty-five minutes. Otherwise all subways and buses, the Staten Island Ferry, the Jersey Central, the Delaware and Lackawanna, and the Pennsylvania railroads, and all other commuter services, are operating normally. At the three airports, planes are arriving and departing on time. The next regularly scheduled traffic advisory will be given one-half hour from now—"

The big weekend rush is on. The big city emptying itself out at once. Just a skeleton crew left to keep it going until Monday morning. Everybody getting out—everybody but me, everybody but those who are coming here for me tonight. We're going to have the whole damned town to ourselves.

I go over to the window and open up a crevice between two of the tightly flattened slats in one of the blinds, and a little parallelogram of a New York street scene, Murray Hill section, six-o'clock-evening hour, springs into view. Up in the sky the upper-echelon light tiers of the Pan Am Building are undulating and rippling in the humidity and carbon monoxide ("Air pollution index: normal, twelve percent; emergency level, fifty percent").

Down below, on the sidewalk, the glowing green blob of a street light, swollen to pumpkin size by foreshortened perspective, thrusts upward toward my window. And along the little slot that the parted slats make, lights keep passing along, like strung-up, shining, red and white beads. All going just one way, right to left, because 37th Street is westbound, and all going by twos, always by twos, headlights and tails, heads and tails, in a welter of slowed-down traffic and a paroxysm of vituperative horns. And directly under me I hear a taxi driver and would-be fares having an argument, the voices clearly audible, the participants unseen.

"But it's only to Fifty-ninth Street—"

"I don't *ca-a-are*, lady. Look, I already tolje. I'm not goin' up that way. Can'tje get it into your head?"

"Don't let's argue with him. Get inside. He can't put you out."

"No, but I can refuse to move. Lady, if your husband gets in here, he's gonna sit still in one place, 'cause I ain't budgin'."

New York. The world's most dramatic city. Like a permanent short circuit, sputtering and sparking up into the night sky all night long. No place like it for living. And probably no place like it for dying.

I take away the little tire jack my fingers have made, and the slats snap together again.

The first sign that the meal I phoned down for is approaching is the minor-key creak from a sharply swerved castor as the room-service waiter rounds a turn outside my door. I'm posted behind a high-backed wing chair, with my wrists crossed over the top of it and my hands dangling like loose claws, staring a little tensely at the door. Then there's the waiter's characteristically deferential knock. But I say "Who is it?" anyway, before I go over to open it.

He's an elderly man. He's been up here twice before, and by now I know the way he sounds.

"Room service," comes through in that high-pitched voice his old age has given him.

I release the double lock, then I turn the knob and open the door.

He wheels the little white-clothed dinner cart forward into the room, and as the hall perspective clears behind him I get a blurred glimpse of a figure in motion, just passing from view, then gone, too quickly to be brought into focus.

I stand there a moment, holding the door to a narrow slit, watching the hall. But it's empty now.

There's an innocuous explanation for everything. Everything is a coin that has two sides to it, and one side is innocuous but the other can be ominous. The hall makes a right-angle turn opposite my door, and to get to the elevators, those whose rooms are back of this turn have to pass the little setback that leads to my door.

On the other hand, if someone wanted to pinpoint me, to verify which room I was in, by sighting my face as I opened the door for the waiter, he would do just that: stand there an instant, then quickly step aside out of my line of vision. The optical snapshot I'd had was not of a figure in continuous motion going past my point of view, but of a figure that had first been static and then had flitted from sight.

And if it's that, now they know which room I'm in. Which room on which floor in which hotel.

"Did you notice anyone out there in the hall just now when you came along?" I ask. I try to sound casual, which only makes me not sound casual.

He answers with a question of his own. "*Was* there somebody out in the hall, sir?"

"That's what I asked you, did you see anyone?"

He explains that years of experience in trundling these food-laden carts across the halls have taught him never to look up, never to take his eyes off them, because an unexpected bump on the floor under the carpet might splash ice water out of the glass and wet the tablecloth or spill consommé into its saucer.

It sounds plausible enough. And whether it is or not, I know it's all I'm going to get.

I sign the check for the meal, add the tip, and tell him to put it on the bill. Then just as he turns to leave I remember something I want to do.

"Just a second; that reminds me." I shoot one of my cuffs forward and twist something out of it. Then the other one. And I hold out my hand to him with the two star-sapphire cuff links he admired so much last night. (Innocently, I'm sure, with no venal intent.)

He says I'm not serious, I must be joking. He says he can't take anything like that. He says all the things he's expected to say, and I override them. Then, when he can't come up with anything else, he comes up with, half-hopefully (hopeful for a yes answer): "You tired of them?"

"No," I say quite simply, "no—they're tired of me."

He thanks me over and thanks me under and thanks me over again, and then he's gone, and I'm glad he's gone.

Poor old man, wasting his life bringing people their meals up to their rooms for thirty-five, forty-odd years. He'll die in peace, though. Not in terror and in throes of resistance. I almost envy him.

I turn my head a little. The radio's caroling "Tonight," velvety smooth and young and filled with plaintive desire. Maria's song from *West Side Story*. I remember one beautiful night long ago at the Winter Garden, with a beautiful someone beside me. I tilt my nose and breathe in, and I can still smell her perfume, the ghost of her perfume from long ago. But where is she now, where did she go, and what did I *do* with her?

Our paths ran along so close together they were almost like one, the one they were eventually going to be. Then fear came along, fear entered into it somehow, and split them wide apart.

Fear bred anxiety to justify. Anxiety to justify bred anger. The phone calls that wouldn't be answered, the door rings that wouldn't be opened. Anger bred sudden calamity.

Now there aren't two paths anymore; there's only one, only mine. Running downhill into the ground, running downhill into its doom.

—◆—

Tonight, tonight—there will be no morning star—Right, kid, there won't. Not for me, anyway.

There's a tap at the door, made with the tip of a key, not the tip of a finger. The voice doesn't wait, but comes right through before the signal has a chance to freeze me stiff. A woman's voice, soft-spoken, reassuring. "Night maid."

I wait a second to let a little of the white drain from my face before she sees me, and then I go over and let her in.

Her name is Ginny. She told me last night. I asked her, that's why she told me. I wanted to hear the sound of somebody's name, that's why I asked her. I was frightened and lonely, that's why I wanted to hear the sound of somebody's name.

On her face the beauty of two races blends, each contributing its individual hallmark. The golden-warm skin, the deep glowing eyes, the narrow-tipped nose, the economical underlip.

While she's turning back the bedcovers in a neat triangle over one corner, I remark, "I notice you go around the outside of the room to get to the bed, instead of cutting across the middle, which would be much shorter. Why do you?"

She answers plausibly, "People are often watching their television sets at this time, when I come in, and I don't want to block them off."

I point out, "But mine isn't on, Ginny."

I see how the pupils of her eyes try to flee, to get as far away from looking at me as possible, all the way over into their outside corners. And that gives it away. She's afraid of me. The rumors have already reached her. A hotel is like a beehive when it comes to gossip. *He never leaves his room, has all his meals sent up to him, and keeps his door locked all the time.*

"I want to give you something," I say to her. "For that little girl of yours you were telling me about."

I take a hundred-dollar bill out of the wallet on my hip. I fold the bill a few times so that the corner numerals disappear, then thrust it between two of her fingers.

She sees the "1" first as the bill slowly uncoils. Her face is politely appreciative.

She sees the first zero next—that makes it a ten. Her face is delighted, more than grateful.

She sees the last zero. Suddenly her face is fearful, stunned into stone; in her eyes I can see steel filings of mistrust glittering. Her wrist flexes to shove the bill back to me, but I ward it off with my hand upended.

I catch the swift side glance she darts at the fifth of rye on the side table.

"No, it didn't come out of that. It's just an impulse—came out of my heart, I suppose you could say. Either take it or don't take it, but don't spoil it."

"But why? What for?"

"Does there have to be a reason for everything? Sometimes there isn't."

"I'll buy her a new coat," she says huskily. "A new pink coat like little girls all seem to want. With a little baby muff of lamb's wool to go with it. And I'll say a prayer for you when I take her to church with me next Sunday."

It won't work, but— "Make it a good one."

The last part is all she hears.

Something occurs to me. "You won't have to do any explaining to her father, will you?"

"She has no father," she says quite simply. "She's never had. There's only me and her, sir."

Somehow I can tell by the quick chip-chop of her feet away from my door that it's not lost time she's trying to make up; it's the tears starting in her eyes that she wants to hide.

I slosh a little rye into a glass—a fresh glass, not the one before; they get rancid from your downbreaths that cling like a stale mist around the inner rim. But it's no help; I know that by now, and I've been dousing myself in it for three days. It just doesn't take hold. I think fear neutralizes alcohol, weakens its anesthetic power. It's good for small fears; your boss, your wife, your bills, your dentist; all right then to take a drink. But for big ones it doesn't do any good. Like water on blazing gasoline, it will only quicken and compound it. It takes sand, in the literal and the slang sense, to smother the bonfire that is fear. And if you're out of sand, then you must burn up.

I have it out now, paying it off between my fingers like a rosary of murder. Those same fingers that did it to her. For three days now I've taken it out at intervals, looked at it, then hidden it away again. Each time wondering if it really happened, hoping that it didn't, dreading that it did.

It's a woman's scarf; that much I know about it. And that's about all. But whose? Hers? And how did I come by it? How did it get into the side pocket of my jacket, dangling on the outside, when I came in here early Wednesday morning in some sort of traumatic daze, looking for room walls to hide inside of as if they were a folding screen. (I didn't even know I had it there; the bellboy who was checking me in spotted it on the way up in the elevator, grinned, and said something about a "heavy date.")

It's flimsy stuff, but it has a great tensile strength when pulled against its grain. The strength of the garotte. It's tinted in pastel colors that blend, graduate, into one another, all except one. It goes from a flamingo pink to a peach tone and then to a still paler flesh tint—and then suddenly an angry, jagged splash of blood color comes in, not even like the others. Not smooth, not artificed by some loom or by some dye vat. Like a star, like the scattered petals of a flower. Speaking of—I don't know how to say it— speaking of violence, of struggle, of life spilled out.

The blood isn't red anymore. It's rusty brown now. But it's still blood, all the same. Ten years from now, twenty, it'll still be blood; faded out, vanished, the pollen of, the dust of, blood. What was once warm and moving. And made blushes and rushed with anger and paled with fear. Like that night—

I can still see her eyes. They still come before me, wide and white and glistening with fright, out of the amnesiac darkness of our sudden, unpremeditated meeting.

They were like two pools of fear. She saw something that I couldn't see. And fear kindled in them. I feared and I mistrusted but I couldn't bear to see my fear reflected in her eyes. From her I wanted reassurance, consolation; only wanted to draw her close to me and hold her to me, to lean my head against her and rest and draw new belief in myself. Instead she met my fear with her fear.

Eyes that should have been tender were glowing with unscreaming fear.

It wasn't an attack. We'd been together too many times before, made love together too many times before, for it to be that. It was just that fear had suddenly entered, and made us dangerous strangers.

She turned and tried to run. I caught the scarf from behind. Only in supplication, in pleading; trying to hold on to the only one who could save me. And the closer I tried to draw her to me, the less she was alive. Until finally I got her all the way back to me, where I wanted her to be, and she was dead.

I hadn't wanted that. It was only love, turned inside out. It was only loneliness, outgoing.

And now I'm alone, without any love.

And the radio, almost as if it were taking my pulse count, electrographing my heartbeats, echoes them back to me: *For, like caressing an empty glove, Is night without some love, The night was made for—*

The hotel room ashtrays are thick glass cubes, built to withstand cracking under heat of almost any degree. I touch my lighter to it, to the scarf compressed inside the cube. The flame points upward like a sawtoothed orange knife. There goes love. After a while it stops burning. It looks like a black cabbage, each leaf tipped by thin red lines that waver and creep back and forth like tiny red worms. Then one by one they go out.

I dump it into the bathroom bowl and flip the lever down. What a hell of a place for your love to wind up. Like something disemboweled.

I go back and pour out a little more. It's the seatbelt against the imminent smash-up, the antidote for terror, the prescription against panic. Only it doesn't work. I sit there dejectedly, wrists looping down between my legs. I'm confused; I can't think it out. Something inside my mind keeps fogging over, like mist on a windshield. I use the back of my hand for a windshield wiper and draw it slowly across my forehead a couple times, and it clears up again for a little while.

"Remember," the little radio prattles. "Simple headache, take aspirin. Nervous tension, take—"

All I can say to myself is: there *is* no fix for the fix you're in now.

Suddenly the phone peals, sharp and shattering as the smashing of glass sealing up a vacuum. I never knew a sound could be so frightening, never knew a sound could be so dire. It's like a short circuit in my nervous system. Like springing a cork in my heart with a lopsided opener. Like a shot of sodium pentathol up my arm knocking out my will power.

All I keep thinking is: this is it. Here it is. It's not a hotel-service call, it can't be, not at this hour anymore. The waiter's been and gone, the night maid's been and gone. It can't be an outside call, because nobody on the outside knows I'm here in the hotel. Not even where I work, where I used to work, they don't know. This is it; it's got to be.

How will they put it? A polite summons. "Would you mind coming down for a minute, sir?" And then if I do, a sudden preventive twisting of my arm behind my back as I step out of the elevator, an unnoticeable flurry tactfully covered up behind the backs of the bellboys—then quickly out and away.

Why don't they come right up here to my door and get me? Is it because this is a high-class hotel on a high-class street? Maybe they don't want any commotion in the hall, for the sake of the other guests. Maybe this is the way they always do it.

Meanwhile it keeps ringing and ringing and ringing.

The damp zigzag path my spilled drink made, from where I was to where I am now, is slowly soaking into the carpet and darkening it. The empty glass, dropped on the carpet, has finished rocking on its side by now and lies still. And I've fallen motionless into the grotesque posture of a badly frightened kid. Almost prone along the floor, legs sprawled out in back of me in scissors formation, just the backs of my two hands grasping the edge of the low stand the phone sits on, and the rim of it cutting across the bridge of my nose so that just two big staring, straining eyes show up over the top.

And it rings on and on and on.

Then all at once an alternative occurs to me. Maybe it's a wrong-number call, meant for somebody else. Somebody in another room, or somebody in this room who was in it before I came. Hotel switchboards are overworked places: slip-ups like that can happen now and then.

I bet I haven't said a prayer since I finished my grammar-school final-exam paper in trigonometry (and flunked it; maybe that's why I haven't said a prayer since), and that was more a crossed-fingers thing held behind my back than a genuine prayer. I say one now. What a funny thing to pray for. I bet nobody ever prayed for a wrong number before, not since telephones first began. Or since prayers first began, either.

Please, make it a mistake and not for me. Make it a mistake.

Suddenly there's open space between the cradle and the receiver, and I've done it. I've picked it up. It's just as easy as pulling out one of your own teeth by the roots.

The prayer gets scratched. The call is for me, it's not a wrong number. For me, all right, every inch of the way. I can tell from the opening words. Only—it's not the one I feared; it's friendly, a friendly call no different from what other people get.

A voice from another world, almost. Yet I know it so well. Always like this, never a cloud on it; always jovial, always noisy. When a thing should be said softly, it says it loudly; when a thing should be said loudly, it says it louder still. He never identifies himself, never has to. Once you've heard his voice, you'll always know him.

That's Johnny for you—the pal of a hundred parties. The bar-kick of scores of binges. The captain of the second-string team in how many foursome one-night stands? Every man has had a Johnny in his life sometime or other.

He says he's been calling my apartment since Wednesday and no answer: what happened to me?

I play it by ear. "Water started to pour down through the ceiling, so I had to clear out till they get it repaired. . . . No, I'm not on a tear. . . . No, there's nobody with me, I'm by myself. . . . Do I? Sound sort of peculiar? No, I'm all right there's nothing the matter, not a thing."

I pass my free hand across the moist glisten on my forehead. It's tough enough to be in a jam, but it's tougher still to be in one and not be able to say you are.

"How did you know I was here? How did you track me to this place? . . . You went down the yellow pages, hotel by hotel, alphabetically. Since three o'clock yesterday afternoon? . . . Something to tell me?"

His new job had come through. He starts on Monday. With a direct line, and two, count 'em, two secretaries, not just one. And the old bunch is giving him a farewell party. A farewell party to end all farewell parties. Sardi's, on 44th. Then they'll move on later to some other place. But they'll wait here at Sardi's for me to catch up. Barb keeps asking, Why isn't your best-man-to-be here with us?

The noise of the party filters through into my ear. Ice clicking like dice in a fast-rolling game. Mixing sticks sounding like tiny tin flutes as they beat against glass. The laughter of girls, the laughter of men. Life is for the living, not the already dead.

"Sure, I'll be there. Sure."

If I say I won't be—and I won't, because I can't—he'll never quit pestering and calling me the rest of the night. So I say that I will, to get off the hook. But how can I go there, drag my trouble before his party, before his friends, before his girl? And if I go, it'll just happen there instead of here. Who wants a grandstand for his downfall? Who wants bleachers for his disgrace?

Johnny's gone now, and the night goes on.

Now the evening's at its noon, its meridian. The outgoing tide has simmered down, and there's a lull—like the calm in the eye of a hurricane—before the reverse tide starts to set in.

The last acts of the three-act plays are now on, and the after-theater eating places are beginning to fill up with early comers; Danny's and Lindy's—yes, and Horn & Hardart too. Everybody has got where they wanted to go—and that was out somewhere. Now everybody will want to get back where they came from—and that's home somewhere. Or as the coffee-grinder radio, always on the beam, put it at about this point: *New York, New York, it's a helluva town, The Bronx is up, the Battery's down, And the people ride around in a hole in the ground—*

Now the incoming tide rolls in; the hours abruptly switch back to single digits again, and it's a little like the time you put your watch back on entering a different time zone. Now the buses knock off and the subway expresses turn into locals and the locals space themselves far apart; and as Johnny Carson's face hits millions of screens all at one and the same time, the incoming tide reaches its crest and pounds against the shore. There's a sudden splurge, a slew of taxis arriving at the hotel entrance one by one as regularly as though they were on a conveyor belt, emptying out and then going away again.

Then this too dies down, and a deep still sets in. It's an around-the-clock town, but this is the stretch; from now until the garbage-grinding trucks come along and tear the dawn to shreds, it gets as quiet as it's ever going to get.

This is the deep of the night, the dregs, the sediment at the bottom of the coffee cup. The blue hours; when guys' nerves get tauter and women's fears get greater. Now guys and girls make love, or kill each other or sometimes both. And as the windows on the "Late Show" title silhouette light up one by one, the real ones all around go dark. And from now on the silence is broken only by the occasional forlorn hoot of a bogged-down drunk or the gutted-cat squeal of a too sharply swerved axle coming around a turn. Or as Billy Daniels sang it in *Golden Boy: While the city sleeps, And the streets are clear, There's a life that's happening here—*

In the pin-drop silence a taxi comes up with an unaccompanied girl in it. I can tell it's a taxi, I can tell it's a girl, and I can tell she's unaccompanied; I can tell all three just by her introductory remark.

"Benny," she says. "Will you come over and pay this for me?"

Benny is the hotel night-service man. I know his name; he brought drinks up to the room last night.

As the taxi drives away paid, Benny reminds her with aloof dignity, "You didn't give me my cut last week." Nothing personal, strictly business, you understand.

"I had a virus week before last," she explains. "And it took me all last week to pay off on my doctor bills. I'll square it with you tonight." Then she adds apprehensively, "I'm afraid he'll hurt me." Not her doctor, obviously.

"Na, he won't hurt you," Benny reassures.

"How would you know?" she asks, not unreasonably.

Benny culls from his store of call-girl-sponsorship experience. "These big guys never hurt you. They're meek as mice. It's the little shrimps got the sting."

She goes ahead in. A chore is a chore, she figures.

This of course is what is known in hotel-operational jargon as a "personal call." In the earthier slang of the night bellmen and deskmen it is simply a "fix" or a "fix-up." The taxi fare, of course, will go down on the guest's bill, as "Misc." or "Sundries." Which actually is what it is. From my second-floor window I can figure it all out almost without any sound track to go with it.

So much for the recreational side of night life in the upper-bracket-income hotels of Manhattan. And in its root-origins the very word itself is implicit with implication: re-create. Analyze it and you'll see it also means to reproduce. But clever, ingenious Man has managed to sidetrack it into making life more livable.

The wafer of ice riding the surface of my drink has melted freakishly in its middle and not around its edges and now looks like an onion ring. Off in the distance an ambulance starts bansheeing with that new broken-blast siren they use, scalp-crimping as the cries of pain of a partly dismembered hog. Somebody dead in the night? Somebody sick and going to be dead soon? Or maybe somebody going to be alive soon—did she wait too long to start for the hospital?

All of a sudden, with the last sound there's been all night, I can tell they're here. Don't ask me how, I only know they're here. It's beginning at last. No way out, no way aside and no way back.

Being silent is their business, and they know their business well. They make less sound than the dinner cart crunching along the carpeted hall, than Ginny's stifled sob when I gave her that hundred-dollar bill, than the contestants bickering over the taxi. Or that girl who was down there just a little while ago on her errand of fighting loneliness for a fee.

How can I tell that they're here? By the absence of sound more than by its presence. Or I should say by the absence of a complementary sound—the sound that belongs with another sound and yet fails to accompany it.

Like:

There's no sound of arrival, but suddenly two cars are in place down there along the hotel front. They must have come up on the glide, as noiselessly as a sailboat skimming over still water. No sound of tires, no sound of brakes. But there's one sound they couldn't quite obliterate—the cushioned thump of two doors closing after them in quick succession, staccato succession, as they spilled out and siphoned into the building. You can always tell a car door, no other door sounds quite like it.

There's only one other sound, a lesser one, a sort of follow-up: the scratch of a single sole against the abrasive sidewalk as they go hustling in. He either put it down off-balance or swiveled it too acutely in treading at the heels of those in front of him. Which is a good average, just one to sound off, considering that six or eight pairs of them must have been all going in at the same time and moving fast.

I've sprung to my feet from the very first, and I'm standing there now like an upright slab of ice carved in the outline of a man—burning-cold and slippery-wet and glassy with congealment. I've put out all the lights—they all work on one switch over by the door as you come in. They've probably already seen the lights though if they've marked the window from outside, and anyway, what difference does it make? Lighted up or dark, I'm still here inside the room. It's just some instinct as old as fear: you seek the dark when you hide, you seek the light when the need to hide is gone. All the animals have it too.

Now they're in, and it will take just a few minutes more while they make their arrangements. That's all I have left, a few minutes more. Out of a time allotment that once stretched so far and limitlessly ahead of me. Who short-changed me, I feel like crying out in protest, but I know that nobody did; I short-changed myself.

"It," the heartless little radio jeers, "takes the worry out of being close."

Why is it taking them such a long time? What do they have to do, improvise as they go along? What for? They already knew what they had to do when they set out to come here.

I'm sitting down again now, momentarily; knees too rocky for standing long. Those are the only two positions I have left; no more walking, no more running, no more anything else now. Only stand up and wait or sit down and wait. I need a cigarette terribly bad. It may be a funny time to need one, but I do. I dip my head down between my outspread legs and bring the lighter up from below, so its shine won't glow through the blind-crevices. As I said, it doesn't make sense, because they know I'm here. But I don't want to do anything to quicken them. Even two minutes of grace is better than one. Even one minute is better than none.

Then suddenly my head comes up again, alerted. I drop the cigarette, still unlit. First I think the little radio has suddenly jumped in tone, started to come on louder and more resonant, as if it were spooked. Until it almost sounds like a car radio out in the open. Then I turn my head toward the window. It is a car radio. It's coming from outside into the room.

And even before I get up and go over to take a look, I think there's something familiar about it, I've heard it before, just like this, just the way it is now. This sounding-board effect, this walloping of the night like a drum, this ricochet of blast and din from side to side of the street, bouncing off the house fronts like a musical handball game.

Then it cuts off short, the after-silence swells up like a balloon ready to pop, and as I squint out, it's standing still down there, the little white car, and Johnny is already out of it and standing alongside.

He's come to take me to the party.

He's parked on the opposite side. He starts to cross over to the hotel. Someone posted in some doorway whistles to attract his attention. I hear it up at the window. Johnny stops, turns to look around, doesn't see anyone.

He's frozen in the position in which the whistle caught him. Head and shoulders turned inquiringly half around, hips and legs still pointed forward. Then a man, some anonymous man, glides up beside him from the street.

I told you he talks loud; on the phone, in a bar, on a street late at night. Every word he says I hear; not a word the other man says.

First, "Who is? What kind of trouble?"

Then, "You must mean somebody else."

Next, "Room 207. Yeah, that's right, 207."

That's my room number.

"How'd you know I was coming here?"

Finally, "You bugged the call I made to him before!"

Then the anonymous man goes back into the shadows, leaving Johnny in mid-street, taking it for granted he'll follow him as he was briefed to do, commanded to do.

But Johnny stands out there, alone and undecided, feet still one way, head and shoulders still the other. And I watch him from the window crevice. And the stakeout watches him from his invisible doorway.

Now a crisis arises. Not in my life, because that's nearly over; but in my illusions.

Will he go to his friend and try to stand by him, or will he let his friend go by?

He can't make it, sure I know that, he can never get in here past them; but he *can* make the try, there's just enough slack for him to do that. There's still half the width of the street ahead of him clear and untrammeled, for him to try to bolt across, before they spring after him and rough him up and fling him back. It's the token of the thing that would count, not the completion.

But it doesn't happen that way, I keep telling myself knowingly and sadly. Only in our fraternity pledges and masonic inductions, our cowboy movies and magazine stories, not in our real-life lives. For, the seventeenth-century humanist to the contrary, each man *is* an island complete unto himself, and as he sinks, the moving feet go on around him, from nowhere to nowhere and with no time to lose. The world is long past the Boy Scout stage of its development; now each man dies as he was meant to die, and as he was born, and as he lived: alone, all alone. Without any God, without any hope, without any record to show for his life.

My throat feels stiff, and I want to swallow but I can't. Watching and waiting to see what my friend will do.

He doesn't move, doesn't make up his mind, for half a minute, and that half a minute seems like an hour. He's doped by what he's been told, I guess. And I keep asking myself while the seconds are ticking off: What would *I* do? If there were me down there, and he were up here: What would *I* do? And I keep trying not to look the answer in the face, though it's staring at me the whole time.

You haven't any right to expect your friends to be larger than yourself, larger than life. Just take them as they are, cut down to average size, and be glad you have them. To drink with, laugh with, borrow money from, lend money to, stay away from their special girls as you want them to stay away from yours, and above all, never break your word to, once it's been given.

And that is all the obligation you have, all you have the right to expect.

The half-minute is up, and Johnny turns, slowly and reluctantly, but he turns, and he goes back to the opposite side of the street. The side opposite to me.

And I knew all along that's what he would do, because I knew all along that's what I would have done too.

I think I hear a voice say slurredly somewhere in the shadows, "That's the smart thing to do," but I'm not sure. Maybe I don't, maybe it's me I hear.

He gets back in the car, shoulders sagging, and keys it on. And as he glides from sight the music seems to start up almost by itself; it's such second nature for him to have it on by now. It fades around the corner building, and then a wisp of it comes back just once more, carried by some cross-current of the wind: *Fools rush in, Where wise men never dare to go*—and then it dies away for good.

I bang my crushed-up fist against the center of my forehead, bring it away, then bang it again. Slow but hard. It hurts to lose a long-term friend, almost like losing an arm. But I never lost an arm, so I really wouldn't know.

Now I can swallow, but it doesn't feel good anymore.

I hear a marginal noise outside in the hall, and I swing around in instant alert. It's easy enough to decipher it. A woman is being taken from her room nearby—in case the going gets too rough around here in my immediate vicinity, I suppose.

I hear them tap, and then she comes out and accompanies them to safety. I hear the slap-slap of her bedroom slippers, like the soft little hands of children applauding in a kindergarten, as she goes hurrying by with someone. Several someones. You can't hear them, only her, but I know they're with her. I even hear the soft *sch sch* of her silk wrapper or kimono as it rustles past. A noticeable whiff of sachet drifts in through the door seam. She must have taken a bath and powdered herself liberally just moments ago.

Probably a nice sort of woman, unused to violence or emergencies of this sort, unsure of what to bring along or how to comport herself.

"I left my handbag in there," I hear her remark plaintively as she goes by. "Do you think it'll be all right to leave it there?"

Somebody's wife, come to meet him in the city and waiting for him to join her. Long ago I used to like that kind of woman. Objectively, of course, not close-up.

After she's gone, another brief lull sets in. This one is probably the last. But what good is a lull? It's only a breathing spell in which to get more frightened. Because anticipatory fear is always twice as strong as present fear. Anticipatory fear has both fears in it at once—the anticipatory one and the one that comes simultaneously with the dread happening itself. Present fear only has the one, because by that time anticipation is over.

I switch on the light for a moment, to see my way to a drink. The one I had is gone—just what used to be ice is sloshing colorlessly in the bottom of the glass. Then when I put the recharged glass down again, empty, it seems to pull me after it, as if it weighed so much I couldn't let go of it from an upright position. Don't ask me why this is, I don't know. Probably simple loss of equilibrium for a second, due to the massive infusion of alcohol.

Then with no more warning, no more waiting, with no more of anything, it begins. It gets under way at last.

There is a mild-mannered knuckle rapping at the door. They use my name. A voice, mild-mannered also, says in a conciliatory way, "Come out, please. We want to talk to you." "Punctilious," I guess, would be a better word for it. The etiquette of the forcible entry, of the break-in. They're so considerate, so deferential, so attentive to all the niceties. Hold your head steady, please, we don't want to nick your chin while we're cutting your throat.

I don't answer.

I don't think they expected me to. If I had answered, it would have astonished them, thrown them off their timing for a moment.

The mild-voiced man leaves the door and somebody else takes his place. I can sense the shifting over more by intuition than by actual hearing.

A wooden toolbox or carryall of some sort settles down noisily on the floor outside the door. I can tell it's wooden, not by its floor impact but by the "settling" sound that accompanies it, as if a considerable number of loose and rolling objects in it are chinking against its insides. Nails and bolts and awls and screwdrivers and the like. That tells me that it's a kit commonly used by carpenters and locksmiths and their kind.

They're going to take the lock off bodily from the outside.

A cold surge goes through me that I can't describe. It isn't blood. It's too numbing and heavy and cold for that. And it breaks through the skin surface, which blood doesn't ordinarily do without a wound, and emerges into innumerable sting pin pricks all over me. An ice-sweat.

I can see him (not literally, but just as surely as if I could), down on one knee, and scared, probably as scared as I am myself, pressing as far back to the side out of the direct line of the door as he can, while the others, bunched together farther back, stand ready to cover him, to pile on me and bring me down if I should suddenly break out and rush him.

And the radio tells me sarcastically to "Light up, you've got a good thing going."

I start backing away, with a sleepwalker's fixity, staring at the door as I retreat, or staring at where I last saw it, for I can't see it in the dark. What good would it do to stay close to it, for I can't hold it back, I can't stop it from opening. And as I go back step after step, my tongue keeps tracking the outside outline of my lips, as if I wondered what they were and what they were there for.

A very small sound begins. I don't know how to put it. Like someone twisting a small metal cap to open a small medicine bottle, but continuously, without ever getting it off. He's started already. He's started coming in.

It's terrible to hear that little thing move. As if it were animate, had a life of its own. Terrible to hear it move and to know that a hostile agency, a hostile presence, just a few feet away from me, is what is making it move. Such a little thing, there is almost nothing smaller, only the size of a pinhead perhaps, and yet to create such terror and to be capable of bringing about such a shattering end-result: entry, capture, final loss of reason, and the darkness that is worse than death. All from a little thing like that, turning slowly, secretively, but avidly, in the lockplate on the door, on the door into my room.

I have to get out of here. Out. I have to push these walls apart, these foursquare tightly seamed walls, and make space wide enough to run in, and keep running through it, running and running through it, running and running through it, and never stopping. Until I drop. And then still running on and on, inside my head. Like a watch with its case smashed open and lying on the ground, but with the works still going inside it. Or like a cockroach when you knock it over on its back so that it can't ambulate anymore, but its legs still go spiraling around in the air.

The window. They're at the door, but the window—that way out is still open. I remember when I checked in here the small hours of Wednesday, I didn't ask to be given a room on the second floor, they just happened to give me one. Then when I saw it later that day in the light, I realized the drop to the ground from one of the little semicircular stone ledges outside the windows wouldn't be dangerous, especially if you held a pillow in front of you, and remembered to keep your chin tilted upward as you went over. Just a sprawling shake-up fall maybe, that's all.

I pull at the blind cords with both hands, and it spasms upward with a sound like a lot of little twigs being stepped on and broken. I push up the window sash and assume a sitting position on the sill, then swing my legs across and I'm out in the clear, out in the open night.

The little stone apron has this spiked iron rail guard around it, with no space left on the outer side of it to plant your feet before you go over. You have to straddle it, which makes for tricky going. Still, necessity can make you dexterous, terror can make you agile. I won't go back inside for the pillow, there isn't time. I'll take the leap neat.

The two cars that brought them here are below, and for a moment, only for a moment, they look empty, dark and still and empty, standing bumper to bumper against the curb. Someone gives a warning whistle—a lip whistle, I mean, not a metal one. I don't know who, I don't know where, somewhere around. Then an angry, ugly, smoldering, car-bound orange moon starts up, lightens to yellow, then brightens to the dazzling white of a laundry-detergent commercial. The operator guiding it slants it too high at first, and it lands over my head. Like a halo. *Some* halo and *some time* for a halo. Then he brings it down and it hits me as if someone had belted me full across the face with a talcum-powder puff. You can't see through it, you can't see around it.

Shoe leather comes padding from around the corner—maybe the guy that warded off Johnny—and stops directly under me. I sense somehow he's afraid, just as I am. That won't keep him from doing what he has to do, because he's got the backing on his side. But he doesn't like this. I shield my eyes from the light on one side, and I can see his anxious face peering up at me. All guys are scared of each other, didn't you know that? I'm not the only one. We're all born afraid.

I can't shake the light off. It's like ghostly flypaper. It's like slapstick-thrown yoghurt. It clings to me whichever way I turn.

I hear his voice talking to me from below. Very near and clear. As if we were off together by ourselves somewhere, just chatting, the two of us.

"Go back into your room. We don't want you to get hurt." And then a second time: "Go back in. You'll only get hurt if you stand out here like this."

I'm thinking, detached, as in a dream: I didn't know they were this considerate. Are they always this considerate? When I was a kid back in the forties, I used to go to those tough-guy movies a lot. Humphrey Bogart, Jimmy Cagney. And when they had a guy penned in, they used to be tough about it, snarling: "Come on out of there, yuh rat, we've got yuh covered!" I wonder what has changed them? Maybe it's just that time has moved on. This is the sixties now.

What's the good of jumping now? Where is there to run to now? And the light teases my eyes. I see all sorts of interlocked and colored soap bubbles that aren't there.

It's more awkward getting back inside than it was getting out. And with the light on me, and them watching me, there's a self-consciousness that was missing in my uninhibited outward surge. I have to straighten out one leg first and dip it into the room toes forward, the way you test the water in a pool before you jump in. Then the other leg, and then I'm in. The roundness of the light beam is broken into long thin tatters as the blind rolls down over it, but it still stays on out there.

There are only two points of light in the whole room—I mean, in addition to the indirect reflection through the blind. Which gives off a sort of phosphorescent haziness—two points so small that if you didn't know they were there and looked for them, you wouldn't see them. And small as both are, one is even smaller than the other. One is the tiny light in the radio, which, because the lens shielding the dial is convex, glows like a miniature orange scimitar. I go over to it to turn it off. It can't keep the darkness away anymore; the darkness is here.

"Here's to the losers," the radio is saying. "Here's to them all—"

The other point of light is over by the door. It's in the door itself. I go over there close to it, peering with my head bowed, as if I were mourning inconsolably. And I am. One of the four tiny screwheads set into the corners of the oblong plate that holds the lock is gone, is out now, and if you squint at an acute angle you can see a speck of orange light shining through it from the hall. Then, while I'm standing there, something falls soundlessly, glances off the top of my shoe with no more weight than a grain of gravel, and there's a second speck of orange light at the opposite upper corner of the plate. Two more to go now. Two and a half minutes of deft work left, maybe not even that much.

What careful planning, what painstaking attention to detail, goes into extinguishing a man's life! Far more than the hit-or-miss, haphazard circumstances of igniting it.

I can't get out the window, I can't go out the door. But there *is* a way out, a third way. I can escape inward. If I can't get away from them on the outside, I can get away from them on the inside.

You're not supposed to have those things. But when you have money you can get anything, in New York. They were on a prescription, but that was where the money came in—getting the prescription. I remember now. Some doctor gave it to me—sold it to me—long ago. I don't remember why or when. Maybe when fear first came between the two of us and I couldn't reach her anymore.

I came across it in my wallet on Wednesday, after I first came in here, and I sent it out to have it filled, knowing that this night would come. I remember the bellboy bringing it to the door afterward in a small bright-green paper wrapping that some pharmacists use. But where is it now?

I start a treasure hunt of terror, around the inside of the room in the dark. First into the clothes closet, wheeling and twirling among the couple of things I have hanging in there like a hopped-up discothèque dancer, dipping in and out of pockets, patting some of them between my hands to see if they're flat or hold a bulk. As if I were calling a little pet dog to me by clapping my hands to it. A little dog who is hiding away from me in there, a little dog called death.

Not in there. Then the drawers of the dresser, spading them in and out, fast as a card shuffle. A telephone directory, a complimentary shaving kit (if you're a man), a complimentary manicure kit (if you're a girl).

They must be down to the last screwhead by now.

Then around and into the bathroom, while the remorseless dismantling at the door keeps on. It's all white in there, white as my face must be. It's dark, but you can still see that it's white against the dark. Twilight-colored tiles. I don't put on the light to help me find them, because there isn't enough time left; the lights in here are fluorescent and take a few moments to come on, and by that time they'll be in here.

There's a catch phrase that you all must have heard at one time or another. You walk into a room or go over toward a group.

Someone turns and says with huge emphasis: "*There* he is." As though you were the most important one of all. (And you're not.) As though you were the one they were just talking about. (And they weren't.) As though you were the only one that mattered. (And you're not.) It's a nice little tribute, and it don't cost anyone a cent.

And so I say this to them now, as I find them on the top glass slab of the shallow medicine cabinet: *There* you are. Glad to see you—you're important in my scheme of things.

As I bend for some running water, the shower curtain twines around me in descending spiral folds—don't ask me how, it must have been ballooning out. I sidestep like a drunken Roman staggering around his toga, pulling half the curtain down behind me while the pins holding it to the rod about tinkle like little finger cymbals, dragging part of it with me over one shoulder, while I bend over the basin to drink.

No time to rummage for a tumbler. It's not there anyway—I'd been using it for the rye. So I use the hollow of one hand for a scoop, pumping it up and down to my open mouth and alternating with one of the nuggets from the little plastic container I'm holding uncapped in my other hand. I've been called a fast drinker at times. Johnny used to say—never mind that now.

I only miss one—that falls down in the gap between me and the basin to the floor. That's a damned good average. There were twelve of them in there, and I remember the label read: *Not more than three to be taken during any twenty-four-hour period.* In other words, I've just killed myself three times, with a down payment on a fourth time for good measure.

I grab the sides of the basin suddenly and bend over it, on the point of getting them all out of me again in rebellious upheaval. *I* don't want to, but they do. I fold both arms around my middle, hugging myself, squeezing myself, to hold them down. They stay put. They've caught on, taken hold. Only a pump can get them out now. And after a certain point of no return (I don't know how long that is), once they start being assimilated into the bloodstream, not even a pump can get them out.

Only a little brine taste shows up in my mouth, and gagging a little, still holding my middle, I go back into the other room. Then I sit down to wait. To see which of them gets to me first.

It goes fast now, like a drumbeat quickening to a climax. An upended foot kicks at the door, and it suddenly spanks inward with a firecracker sound. The light comes fizzing through the empty oblong like gushing carbonation, too sudden against the dark to ray clearly at first.

They rush in like the splash of a wave that suddenly has splattered itself all around the room. Then the lights are on, and they're on all four sides of me, and they're holding me hard and fast, quicker than one eyelid can touch the other in a blink.

My arms go behind me into the cuffless convolutions of a strait jacket. Then as though unconvinced that this is enough precaution, someone standing back there has looped the curve of his arm around my throat and the back of the chair, and holds it there in tight restraint. Not choking-tight as in a mugging, but ready to pin me back if I should try to heave out of the chair.

Although the room is blazing-bright, several of them are holding flashlights, all lit and centered inward on my face from the perimeter around me, like the spokes of a blinding wheel. Probably to disable me still further by their dazzle. One beam, more skeptical than the others, travels slowly up and down my length, seeking out any bulges that might possibly spell a concealed offensive weapon. My only weapon is already used, and it was a defensive one.

I roll my eyes toward the ceiling to try and get away from the lights, and one by one they blink and go out.

There they stand. The assignment is over, completed. To me it's my life, to them just another incident. I don't know how many there are. The man in the coffin doesn't count the number who have come to the funeral. But as I look at them, as my eyes go from face to face, on each one I read the key to what the man is thinking.

One face, soft with compunction: Poor guy, I might have been him, he might have been me.

One, hard with contempt: Just another of those creeps something went wrong with along the way.

Another, flexing with hate: I wish he'd shown some fight; I'd like an excuse to—

Still another, rueful with impatience: I'd like to get this over so I could call her unexpectedly and catch her in a lie; I bet she never stayed home tonight like she told me she would.

And yet another, blank with indifference, its thoughts a thousand miles away: And what's a guy like Yastrzemski got, plenty of others guy haven't got too? It's just the breaks, that's all—

And I say to my own thoughts dejectedly: Why weren't you that clear, that all-seeing, the other night, that terrible other night. It might have done you more good then.

There they stand. And there I am, seemingly in their hands but slowly slipping away from them.

They don't say anything. I'm not aware of any of them saying anything. They're waiting for someone to give them further orders. Or maybe waiting for something to come and take me away.

One of them hasn't got a uniform on or plainsclothes either like the rest. He has on the white coat that is my nightmare and my horror. And in the crotch of one arm he is upending two long poles intertwined with canvas.

The long-drawn-out death within life. The burial-alive of the mind, covering it over with fresh graveyard earth each time it tries to struggle through to the light. In this kind of death you never finish dying.

In back of them, over by the door, I see the top of someone's head appear, then come forward, slowly, fearfully forward. Different from their short-clipped, starkly outlined heads, soft and rippling in contour, and gentle. And as she comes forward into full-face view, I see who she is.

She comes up close to me, stops, and looks at me.

"Then it wasn't—you?" I whisper.

She shakes her head slightly with a mournful trace of smile. "It wasn't me," she whispers back, without taking them into it, just between the two of us, as in the days before. "I didn't go there to meet you. I didn't like the way you sounded."

But someone was there, I came across someone there. Someone whose face became hers in my waking dream. The scarf, the blood on the scarf. It's not my blood, it's not my scarf. It must belong to someone else. Someone they haven't even found yet, don't know even about yet.

The preventive has come too late.

She moves a step closer and bends toward me.

"Careful—watch it," a voice warns her.

"He won't hurt me," she answers understandingly without taking her eyes from mine. "We used to be in love."

Used to? Then that's why I'm dying. Because I still am. And you aren't anymore.

She bends and kisses me, on the forehead, between the eyes. Like a sort of last rite.

And in that last moment, as I'm straining upward to find her lips, as the light is leaving my eyes, the whole night passes before my mind, the way they say your past life does when you're drowning: the waiter, the night maid, the taxi argument, the call girl, Johnny—it all meshes into start-to-finish continuity. Just like in a story. An organized, step-by-step, timetabled story.

This story.

Afterword to "New York Blues"

"New York Blues" (*Ellery Queen's Mystery Magazine*, December 1970) is the last, best, and bleakest of the original stories *EQMM* founding editor Frederic Dannay bought from Woolrich during their long association. Within its minimalist storyline we find virtually every motif, belief, device that had pervaded Woolrich's fiction for generations: flashes of word magic, touches of evocative song lyrics, love and loneliness, madness and death, paranoia, partial amnesia, total despair. If this was the last story Woolrich completed, he couldn't have ended his career more fittingly.